FANTASTIC STORIES PRESENTS THE

FANTASTIC UNIVERSE
SUPER PACK #3

Positronic Publishing
PO Box 632
Floyd VA 24091

ISBN 13: 978-1-5154-1062-1

First Positronic Publishing Edition
10 9 8 7 6 5 4 3 2 1

FANTASTIC STORIES PRESENTS THE
FANTASTIC UNIVERSE
SUPER PACK #3

THE SUPER PACK EBOOK SERIES

If you enjoyed this Super Pack you may wish to find the other books in this series. We endeavor to provide you with a quality product. But since many of these stories have been scanned typos do occasionally creep in. If you spot one please share it with us at positronicpress@yahoo.com so that we can fix it. We occasionally add additional stories to some of our Super Packs so make sure that you download fresh copies of your Super Packs from time to time to get the latest edition.

Science Fiction Super Pack #1: ISBN 978-1-63384-240-3
Science Fiction Super Pack #2: ISBN 978-1-51540-477-4
Science Fiction Super Pack #3: (Forthcoming)
Fantasy Super Pack #1: ISBN 978-1-63384-282-3
Fantasy Super Pack #2: (Forthcoming)
Conan the Barbarian Super Pack: ISBN 978-1-63384-292-2
Lord Dunsany Super Pack: ISBN 978-1-63384-725-5
Philip K. Dick Super Pack: ISBN 978-1-63384-799-6
The Pirate Super Pack # 1: ISBN 978-1-51540-193-3
The Pirate Super Pack # 2: ISBN 978-1-51540-196-4
Harry Harrison Super Pack: ISBN 978-1-51540-217-6
Andre Norton Super Pack: ISBN 978-1-51540-262-6
Marion Zimmer Bradley Super Pack: ISBN 978-1-51540-287-9
Frederik Pohl Super Pack: ISBN 978-1-51540-289-3
King Arthur Super Pack: ISBN 978-1-51540-306-7
Alan E. Nourse Super Pack: ISBN 978-1-51540-393-7
Space Science Fiction Super Pack: ISBN 978-1-51540-440-8
Wonder Stories Super Pack: ISBN 978-1-51540-454-5
Galaxy Science Fiction Super Pack #1:ISBN 978-1-51540-524-5
Galaxy Science Fiction Super Pack #2: 978-1-5154-0577-1
Science Fiction Novel Super Pack #1: ISBN 978-1-51540-363-0
Science Fiction Novel Super Pack #2: (Forthcoming)
Dragon Super Pack #1: Forthcoming
Weird Tales Super Pack #1: ISBN 978-1-5154-0548-1
Weird Tales Super Pack #2: (Forthcoming)
Poul Anderson Super Pack: ISBN 978-1-5154-0609-9
Fantastic Universe Super Pack #1: ISBN 978-1-5154-0981-6
Fantastic Universe Super Pack #1: ISBN (Forthcoming)

ACKNOWLEDGMENTS

"Gods of the North by Robert E. Howard originally appeared in *Fantastic Universe*, December 1956.

"The Hohokam Dig" by Theodore Pratt originally appeared in *Fantastic Universe*, November 1956.

"Operation Earthworm" by Joe Archibald" originally appeared in *Fantastic Universe*, September 1955.

"G-r-r-r . . . !" by Roger Arcot originally appeared in *Fantastic Universe*, January 1957.

"The Hoofer" by Walter M. Miller, Jr. originally appeared in *Fantastic Universe*, September 1955.

"Conquest over Time" by Michael Shaara originally appeared in *Fantastic Universe*, November 1956.

"Rescue Squad" by Thomas J. O'Hara originally appeared in *Fantastic Universe*, September 1955.

"The Shining Cow" by Alex James originally appeared in *Fantastic Universe*, September 1957.

"Of Time and Texas" by William F. Nolan originally appeared in *Fantastic Universe*, November 1956.

"The Helpful Robots" by Robert J. Shea originally appeared in *Fantastic Universe*, September 1957.

"The Flying Cuspidors" by V. R. Francis originally appeared in *Fantastic Universe*, August 1958.

"The Psilent Partner" by Edward S. Staub and John Victor Peterson originally appeared in *Fantastic Universe*, March 1954.

"Happy Ending" by Mack Reynolds and Fredric Brown originally appeared in *Fantastic Universe*, September 1957.

"It's a Small Solar System" by Allan Howard originally appeared in *Fantastic Universe*, September 1957.

"The Very Black" by Dean Evans originally appeared in *Fantastic Universe*, Aug-Sept 1953.

"The Second Voice" by Mann Rubin originally appeared in *Fantastic Universe*, arch 1954.

"Rastignac the Devil" by Philip José Farmer originally appeared in *Fantastic Universe*, May 1954.

"Texas Week" by Albert Hernhuter originally appeared in *Fantastic Universe*, January 1954.

"The House from Nowhere" by Arthur G. Stangland originally appeared in *Fantastic Universe*, Aug-Sept 1953.

"A World Apart" by Sam Merwin, Jr. originally appeared in *Fantastic Universe*, May 1954.

"Bear Trap" by Alan E. Nourse originally appeared in *Fantastic Universe*, December 1957.

"Now We Are Three" by Joe L. Hensley originally appeared in *Fantastic Universe*, August 1957.

"One out of Ten" by J. Anthony Ferlaine originally appeared in *Fantastic Universe*, November 1956.

"The Calm Man" by Frank Belknap Long originally appeared in *Fantastic Universe*, May 1954.

"Foundling on Venus" by John & Dorothy de Courcy originally appeared in *Fantastic Universe*, March 1954.

"The Doorway" by Evelyn E. Smith originally appeared in *Fantastic Universe*, September 1955.

"Second Sight" by Basil Wells originally appeared in *Fantastic Universe*, September 1957.

"Lighter than You Think" by Nelson Bond originally appeared in *Fantastic Universe*, August 1957.

"The Long Voyage by Carl Jacobi originally appeared in *Fantastic Universe*, September 1955.

"Year of the Big Thaw" by Marion Zimmer Bradley originally appeared in *Fantastic Universe*, May 1954.

TABLE OF CONTENTS

GODS OF THE NORTH

by Robert E. Howard

Publisher's Note: *The publication of this strange story by Robert E. Howard, author of the Conan stories, so much a part of the Living Library of Fantasy, represents a departure for this magazine. Without abandoning our policy of bringing you, month after month, the best in NEW Science Fiction and Fantasy, we will, from time to time, publish material such as this, hitherto known to only a few students of the field!*

*

She drew away from him, dwindling in the witch-fire of the skies, until she was a figure no bigger than a child.

The clangor of the swords had died away, the shouting of the slaughter was hushed; silence lay on the red-stained snow. The pale bleak sun that glittered so blindingly from the ice-fields and the snow-covered plains struck sheens of silver from rent corselet and broken blade, where the dead lay in heaps. The nerveless hand yet gripped the broken hilt: helmeted heads, back-drawn in the death throes, tilted red beards and golden beards grimly upward, as if in last invocation to Ymir the frost-giant.

Across the red drifts and mail-clad forms, two figures approached one another. In that utter desolation only they moved. The frosty sky was over them, the white illimitable plain around them, the dead men at their feet. Slowly through the corpses they came, as ghosts might come to a tryst through the shambles of a world.

Their shields were gone, their corselets dinted. Blood smeared their mail; their swords were red. Their horned helmets showed the marks of fierce strokes.

One spoke, he whose locks and beard were red as the blood on the sunlit snow.

"Man of the raven locks," said he, "tell me your name, so that my brothers in Vanaheim may know who was the last of Wulfhere's band to fall before the sword of Heimdul."

"This is my answer," replied the black-haired warrior: "Not in Vanaheim, but in Valhalla will you tell your brothers the name of Amra of Akbitana."

Heimdul roared and sprang, and his sword swung in a mighty arc. Amra staggered and his vision was filled with red sparks as the blade shivered into bits of blue fire on his helmet. But as he reeled he thrust with all the power of his great shoulders. The sharp point drove through brass scales and bones and heart, and the red-haired warrior died at Amra's feet.

Amra stood swaying, trailing his sword, a sudden sick weariness assailing him. The glare of the sun on the snow cut his eyes like a knife and the sky seemed shrunken and strangely far. He turned away from the trampled expanse where yellow-bearded warriors lay locked with red-haired slayers in the embrace of death. A few steps he took, and the glare of the snow fields was suddenly dimmed. A rushing wave of blindness engulfed him, and he sank down into the snow, supporting himself on one mailed arm, seeking to shake the blindness out of his eyes as a lion might shake his mane.

A silvery laugh cut through his dizziness, and his sight cleared slowly. There was a strangeness about all the landscape that he could not place or define—an unfamiliar tinge to earth and sky. But he did not think long of this. Before him, swaying like a sapling in the wind, stood a woman. Her body was like ivory, and save for a veil of gossamer, she was naked as the day. Her slender bare feet were whiter than the snow they spurned. She laughed, and her laughter was sweeter than the rippling of silvery fountains, and poisonous with cruel mockery.

"Who are you?" demanded the warrior.

"What matter?" Her voice was more musical than a silver-stringed harp, but it was edged with cruelty.

"Call up your men," he growled, grasping his sword. "Though my strength fail me, yet they shall not take me alive. I see that you are of the Vanir."

"Have I said so?"

He looked again at her unruly locks, which he had thought to be red. Now he saw that they were neither red nor yellow, but a glorious compound of both colors. He gazed spell-bound. Her hair was like elfin-gold, striking which, the sun dazzled him. Her eyes were neither wholly blue nor wholly grey, but of shifting colors and dancing lights and clouds of colors he could not recognize. Her full red lips smiled, and from her slim feet to the blinding crown of her billowy hair, her ivory body was as perfect as the dream of a god. Amra's pulse hammered in his temples.

"I can not tell," said he, "whether you are of Vanaheim and mine enemy, or of Asgard and my friend. Far have I wandered, from Zingara to the Sea of Vilayet, in Stygia and Kush, and the country of the Hyrkanians; but a woman like you I have never seen. Your locks blind me with their brightness. Not even among the fairest daughters of the Aesir have I seen such hair, by Ymir!"

"Who are you to swear by Ymir?" she mocked. "What know you of the gods of ice and snow, you who have come up from the south to adventure among strangers?"

"By the dark gods of my own race!" he cried in anger. "Have I been backward in the sword-play, stranger or no? This day I have seen four score warriors fall, and I alone survive the field where Mulfhere's reavers met the men of Bragi. Tell me, woman, have you caught the flash of mail across the snow-plains, or seen armed men moving upon the ice?"

"I have seen the hoar-frost glittering in the sun," she answered. "I have heard the wind whispering across the everlasting snows."

He shook his head.

"Niord should have come up with us before the battle joined. I fear he and his warriors have been ambushed. Wulfhere lies dead with all his weapon-men.

"I had thought there was no village within many leagues of this spot, for the war carried us far, but you can have come no great distance over these snows, naked as you are. Lead me to your tribe, if you are of Asgard, for I am faint with the weariness of strife."

"My dwelling place is further than you can walk, Amra of Akbitana!" she laughed. Spreading wide her arms she swayed before him, her golden head lolling wantonly, her scintillant eyes shadowed beneath long silken lashes. "Am I not beautiful, man?"

"Like Dawn running naked on the snows," he muttered, his eyes burning like those of a wolf.

"Then why do you not rise and follow me? Who is the strong warrior who falls down before me?" she chanted in maddening mockery. "Lie down and die in the snow with the other fools, Amra of the black hair. You can not follow where I would lead."

With an oath the man heaved himself upon his feet, his blue eyes blazing his dark scarred face convulsed. Rage shook his soul, but desire for the taunting figure before him hammered at his temples and drove his wild blood riotously through his veins. Passion fierce as physical agony flooded his whole being so that earth and sky swam red to his dizzy gaze, and weariness and faintness were swept from him in madness.

He spoke no word as he drove at her fingers hooked like talons. With a shriek of laughter she leaped back and ran, laughing at him over her white shoulder. With a low growl Amra followed. He had forgotten the fight, forgotten the mailed warriors who lay in their blood, forgotten Niord's belated reavers. He had thought only for the slender white shape which seemed to float rather than run before him.

Out across the white blinding plain she led him. The trampled red field fell out of sight behind him, but still Amra kept on with the silent tenacity of his race. His mailed feet broke through the frozen crust; he sank deep in the drifts and forged through them by sheer strength. But the girl danced across the snow as light as a feather floating across a pool; her naked feet scarcely left their imprint on the hoar-frost. In spite of the fire in his veins, the cold bit through the warrior's mail and furs; but the girl in her gossamer veil ran as lightly and as gaily as if she danced through the palms and rose gardens of Poitain.

Black curses drooled through the warrior's parched lips. The great veins swelled and throbbed in his temples, and his teeth gnashed spasmodically.

"You can not escape me!" he roared. "Lead me into a trap and I'll pile the heads of your kinsmen at your feet. Hide from me and I'll tear apart the mountains to find you! I'll follow you to hell and beyond hell!"

Her maddening laughter floated back to him, and foam flew from the warrior's lips. Further and further into the wastes she led him, till he saw the wide plains give way to low hills, marching upward in broken ranges. Far to the north he caught a glimpse of towering mountains, blue with the distance, or white with the eternal snows. Above these mountains shone the flaring rays of the borealis. They spread fan-wise into the sky, frosty blades of cold flaming light, changing in color, growing and brightening.

Above him the skies glowed and crackled with strange lights and gleams. The snow shone weirdly, now frosty blue, now icy crimson, now cold silver. Through a shimmering icy realm of enchantment Amra plunged doggedly onward, in a crystaline maze where the only reality was the white body dancing across the glittering snow beyond his reach—ever beyond his reach.

Yet he did not wonder at the necromantic strangeness of it all, not even when two gigantic figures rose up to bar his way. The scales of their mail were white with hoar-frost; their helmets and their axes were sheathed in ice. Snow sprinkled their locks; in their beards were spikes of icicles; their eyes were cold as the lights that streamed above them.

"Brothers!" cried the girl, dancing between them. "Look who follows! I have brought you a man for the feasting! Take his heart that we may lay it smoking on our father's board!"

The giants answered with roars like the grinding of ice-bergs on a frozen shore, and heaved up their shining axes as the maddened Akbitanan hurled himself upon them. A frosty blade flashed before his eyes, blinding him with its brightness, and he gave back a terrible stroke that sheared through his foe's thigh. With a groan the victim fell, and at the instant Amra was dashed into the snow, his left shoulder numb from the blow of the survivor, from which the warrior's mail had barely saved his life. Amra saw the remaining giant looming above him like a colossus carved of ice, etched against the glowing sky. The axe fell, to sink through the snow and deep into the frozen earth as Amra hurled himself aside and leaped to his feet. The giant roared and wrenched the axe-head free, but even as he did so, Amra's sword sang down. The giant's knees bent and he sank slowly into the snow which turned crimson with the blood that gushed from his half-severed neck.

Amra wheeled, to see the girl standing a short distance away, staring in wide-eyed horror, all mockery gone from her face. He cried out fiercely and the blood-drops flew from his sword as his hand shook in the intensity of his passion.

"Call the rest of your brothers!" he roared. "Call the dogs! I'll give their hearts to the wolves!"

With a cry of fright she turned and fled. She did not laugh now, nor mock him over her shoulder. She ran as for her life, and though he strained every nerve and thew, until his temples were like to burst and the snow swam red to his gaze, she drew away from him, dwindling in the witch-fire of the skies, until she was a figure no bigger than a child, then a dancing white flame on the snow, then a dim blur in the distance. But grinding his teeth until the blood started from his gums, he reeled on, and he saw the blur grow to a dancing white flame, and then she was running less than a hundred paces ahead of him, and slowly the space narrowed, foot by foot.

She was running with effort now, her golden locks blowing free; he heard the quick panting of her breath, and saw a flash of fear in the look she cast over her alabaster shoulder. The grim endurance of the warrior had served him well. The speed ebbed from her flashing white legs; she reeled in her gait. In his untamed soul flamed up the fires of hell she had fanned so well. With an inhuman roar he closed in on her, just as she wheeled with a haunting cry and flung out her arms to fend him off.

His sword fell into the snow as he crushed her to him. Her supple body bent backward as she fought with desperate frenzy in his iron arms. Her golden hair blew about his face, blinding him with its sheen; the feel of her slender figure twisting in his mailed arms drove him to blinder madness. His strong fingers sank deep into her smooth flesh, and that flesh was cold as ice. It was as if he embraced not a woman of human flesh and blood, but a woman of flaming ice. She writhed her golden head aside, striving to avoid the savage kisses that bruised her red lips.

"You are cold as the snows," he mumbled dazedly. "I will warm you with the fire in my own blood—"

With a desperate wrench she twisted from his arms, leaving her single gossamer garment in his grasp. She sprang back and faced him, her golden locks in wild disarray, her white bosom heaving, her beautiful eyes blazing with terror. For an instant he stood frozen, awed by her terrible beauty as she posed naked against the snows.

And in that instant she flung her arms toward the lights that glowed in the skies above her and cried out in a voice that rang in Amra's ears for ever after:

"Ymir! Oh, my father, save me!"

Amra was leaping forward, arms spread to seize her, when with a crack like the breaking of an ice mountain, the whole skies leaped into icy fire. The girl's ivory body was suddenly enveloped in a cold blue flame so blinding that the warrior threw up his hands to shield his eyes. A fleeting instant, skies and snowy hills were bathed in crackling white flames, blue darts of icy light, and frozen crimson fires. Then Amra staggered and cried out. The girl was gone. The glowing snow lay empty and bare; high above him the witch-lights flashed and played in a frosty sky gone mad and among the distant blue mountains there sounded a rolling thunder as of a gigantic war-chariot rushing behind steeds whose frantic hoofs struck lightning from the snows and echoes from the skies.

Then suddenly the borealis, the snowy hills and the blazing heavens reeled drunkenly to Amra's sight; thousands of fireballs burst with showers of sparks, and the sky itself became a titanic wheel which rained stars as it spun. Under his feet the snowy hills heaved up like a wave, and the Akbitanan crumpled into the snows to lie motionless.

*

In a cold dark universe, whose sun was extinguished eons ago, Amra felt the movement of life, alien and un-guessed. An earthquake had him in its grip and was shaking him to and fro, at the same time chafing his hands and feet until he yelled in pain and fury and groped for his sword.

"He's coming to, Horsa," grunted a voice. "Haste—we must rub the frost out of his limbs, if he's ever to wield sword again."

"He won't open his left hand," growled another, his voice indicating muscular strain. "He's clutching something—"

Amra opened his eyes and stared into the bearded faces that bent over him. He was surrounded by tall golden-haired warriors in mail and furs.

"Amra! You live!"

"By Crom, Niord," gasped he, "am I alive, or are we all dead and in Valhalla?"

"We live," grunted the Aesir, busy over Amra's half-frozen feet. "We had to fight our way through an ambush, else we had come up with you before the battle was joined. The corpses were scarce cold when we came upon the field. We did not find you among the dead, so we followed your spoor. In Ymir's name, Amra, why did you wander off into the wastes of the north? We have followed your tracks in the snow for hours. Had a blizzard come up and hidden them, we had never found you, by Ymir!"

"Swear not so often by Ymir," muttered a warrior, glancing at the distant mountains. "This is his land and the god bides among yonder mountains, the legends say."

"I followed a woman," Amra answered hazily. "We met Bragi's men in the plains. I know not how long we fought. I alone lived. I was dizzy and faint. The land lay like a dream before me. Only now do all things seem natural and familiar. The woman came and taunted me. She was beautiful as a frozen flame from hell. When I looked at her I was as one mad, and forgot all else in the world. I followed her. Did you not find her tracks. Or the giants in icy mail I slew?"

Niord shook his head.

"We found only your tracks in the snow, Amra."

"Then it may be I was mad," said Amra dazedly. "Yet you yourself are no more real to me than was the golden haired witch who fled naked across the snows before me. Yet from my very hands she vanished in icy flame."

"He is delirious," whispered a warrior.

"Not so!" cried an older man, whose eyes were wild and weird. "It was Atali, the daughter of Ymir, the frost-giant! To fields of the dead she comes, and shows herself to the dying! Myself when a boy I saw her, when I lay half-slain on the bloody field of Wolraven. I saw her walk among the dead in the snows, her naked body gleaming like ivory and her golden hair like a blinding flame in the moonlight. I lay and howled like a dying dog because I could not crawl after her. She lures men from stricken fields into the wastelands to be slain by her brothers, the ice-giants, who lay men's red hearts smoking on Ymir's board. Amra has seen Atali, the frost-giant's daughter!"

"Bah!" grunted Horsa. "Old Gorm's mind was turned in his youth by a sword cut on the head. Amra was delirious with the fury of battle. Look how his helmet is dinted. Any of those blows might have addled his brain. It was an hallucination he followed into the wastes. He is from the south; what does he know of Atali?"

"You speak truth, perhaps," muttered Amra. "It was all strange and weird—by Crom!"

THE HOHOKAM DIG

by Theodore Pratt

From where had these attacking Indians come? Out of a long forgotten and dim past? Had their medicine man seen the one supreme vision?

At first they thought the attack was a joke. And then they realized the truth!

AT FIRST the two scientists thought the Indian attack on them was a joke perpetrated by some of their friends. After all, modern Indians did not attack white men any more.

Except that these did.

George Arthbut and Sidney Hunt were both out of New York, on the staff of the Natural History Museum. George was an ethnologist who specialized in what could be reconstructed about the prehistoric Indians of North America, with emphasis on those of the Southwest. He was a tall, lean, gracious bald man in his early sixties.

Sidney was an archeologist who was fascinated by the ruins of the same kind of ancient Indians. Medium-sized, with black hair that belied his sixty-five years, he and George made an excellent team, being the leaders in their field.

They had come west on a particular bit of business this spring, trying to solve the largest question that remained about the old cliff dwellers and the prehistoric desert Indians, both of whom had deserted their villages and gone elsewhere for reasons that remained a mystery.

One theory was that drought had driven them both away. Another theory ran to the effect that enemies wiped them out or made off with them as captives. Still another supposition, at least for the Hohokam desert people, the builders of Casa Grande whose impressive ruins still stood near Coolidge, had to do with their land giving out so they could no longer grow crops, forcing them to go elsewhere to find better soil.

No one really knew. It was all pure guesswork.

*

The two scientists meant to spend the entire summer trying to solve this riddle for all time, concentrating on it to the exclusion of everything else. They drove west in a station wagon stuffed with equipment and tracking a U-Haul-It packed with more.

George drove, on a road that was only two sand tracks across the wild empty desert between Casa Grande Monument and Tonto National Monument where cliff dwellers had lived. It was here, not far ahead, in new ruins that were being excavated, that they hoped to solve the secret of the exodus of the prehistoric Indians. The place was known as the Hohokam Dig.

16

They topped a rise of ground and came to the site of the dig. Here the sand tracks ended right in the middle of long trenches dug out to reveal thick adobe walls. In the partially bared ruins the outline of a small village could be seen; the detailed excavation would be done this summer by workmen who would arrive from Phoenix and Tucson.

George stopped their caravan and the two men got out, stretching their legs. They looked about, both more interested in the dig, now they were back at it, than setting up camp. They walked around, examining various parts of it, and the excitement of the promise of things to be discovered in the earth came to them. "This summer we'll learn the answer," Sidney predicted.

With skeptical hope George replied, "Maybe."

It was early afternoon when they set up camp, getting out their tent from the U-Haul-It. They took out most of their gear, even setting up a portable TV set run on batteries brought along. They worked efficiently and rapidly, having done this many times before and having their equipment well organized from long experience. By the middle of the afternoon all was ready and they rested, sitting on folding chairs at a small table just outside the opening of their tent.

Looking around at the dig Sidney remarked, "Wouldn't it be easy if we could talk to some of the people who once lived here?"

"There's a few questions I'd like to ask them," said George. "I certainly wish we had some to talk with."

He had no more than uttered this casual wish than there sounded, from all sides of where they sat, screeching whoops. The naked brown men who suddenly appeared seemed to materialize from right out of the excavations. As they yelled they raised their weapons. The air was filled, for an instant, with what looked like long arrows. Most of them whistled harmlessly past the two scientists, but one hit the side of the station wagon, making a resounding thump and leaving a deep dent, while two buried themselves in the wood of the U-Haul-It and remained there, quivering.

George and Sidney, after the shock of their first surprise at this attack, leaped to their feet.

"The car!" cried Sidney. "Let's get out of here!"

They both started to move. Then George stopped and grabbed Sidney's arm. "Wait!"

"Wait?" Sidney demanded. "They'll kill us!"

"Look," advised George, indicating the red men who surrounded them; they now made no further move of attack.

George gazed about. "Oh," he said, "you think somebody's playing a joke on us?"

"Could be," said George. He ran one hand over his bald head.

17

"Some dear friends," Sidney went on, resenting the scare that had been thrown into them, "hired some Indians to pretend to attack us?"

"Maybe Pimas," said George. He peered at the Indians, who now were jabbering among themselves and making lamenting sounds as they glanced about at the ruins of the ancient village. There were eighteen of them. They were clad in nothing more than a curious cloth of some kind run between their legs and up and over a cord about their waists, to form a short apron, front and back.

"Or Zunis," said Sidney.

"Maybe Maricopas," said George.

"Except," Sidney observed, "none of them look like those kind of Indians. And those arrows they shot." He stared at the two sticking in the U-Haul-It. "Those aren't arrows, George—they're atlatl lances!"

"Yes," said George.

Sidney breathed, "They aren't holding bows—they've got atlatls!"

"No modern Indian of any kind," said George, "uses an atlatl."

"Most of them wouldn't even know what it was," Sidney agreed. "They haven't been used for hundreds of years; the only place you see them is in museums."

An atlatl was the weapon which had replaced the stone axe in the stone age. It was a throwing stick consisting of two parts. One was the lance, a feathered shaft up to four feet long, tipped with a stone point. The two-foot flat stick that went with this had a slot in one end and two rawhide finger loops. The lance end was fitted in the slot to be thrown. The stick was an extension of the human arm to give the lance greater force. Some atlatls had small charm stones attached to them to give them extra weight and magic.

Charm stones could be seen fastened to a few of the atlatls being held by the Indians now standing like bronze statues regarding them.

George whispered, "What do you make of it?"

"It isn't any joke," replied Sidney. He gazed tensely at the Indians. "That's all I'm sure of."

"Have you noticed their breechclouts?"

Sidney stared again. "They aren't modern clouts. George, they're right out of Hohokam culture!"

"They aren't made of cloth, either. That's plaited yucca fibre."

"Just like we've dug up many times. Only here . . . " George faltered. "It's being worn by—by I don't know what."

"Look at their ornaments."

Necklaces, made of pierced colored stones, hung about many of the brown necks. Shell bracelets were to be seen, and here and there a carved piece of turquoise appeared.

"Look at the Indian over there," George urged.

Sidney looked to the side where George indicated, and croaked, "It's a girl!"

It was a girl indeed. She stood straight and magnificent in body completely bare except for the brief apron at her loins. Between her beautiful full copper breasts there hung a gleaming piece of turquoise carved in the shape of a coyote.

At her side stood a tall young Indian with a handsome face set with great pride. On her other side was a wizened little old fellow with a wrinkled face and ribs corrugated like a saguaro.

Sidney turned back and demanded, "What do you make of this? Are we seeing things?" Hopefully, he suggested, "A mirage or sort of a mutual hallucination?"

In a considered, gauging tone George replied, "They're real."

"Real?" cried Sidney. "What do you mean, real?"

"Real in a way. I mean, Sidney, these—I sound crazy to myself saying it—but I think these are—well, Sid, maybe they're actual prehistoric Indians."

"Huh?"

"Well, let's put it this way: We asked for them and we got them."

Sidney stared, shocked at George's statement. "You're crazy, all right," he said. "Hohokams in the middle of the Twentieth Century?"

"I didn't say they're Hohokams, though they probably are, of the village here."

"You said they're prehistoric," Sidney accused. He quavered, "Just how could they be?"

"Sid, you remember in our Indian studies, again and again, we meet the medicine man who has visions. Even modern ones have done things that are pretty impossible to explain. I believe they have spiritual powers beyond the capability of the white man. The prehistoric medicine men may have developed this power even more. I think the old man there is their medicine man."

"So?" Sidney invited.

"I'm just supposing now, mind you," George went on. He rubbed his bald pate again as though afraid of what thoughts were taking place under it. "Maybe way back—a good many hundreds of years ago—this medicine man decided to have a vision of the future. And it worked. And here he is now with some of his people."

"Wait a minute," Sidney objected. "So he had this vision and transported these people to this moment in time. But if it was hundreds of years ago they're already dead, been dead for a long time, so how could they—"

"Don't you see, Sid? They can be dead, but their appearance in the future—for them—couldn't occur until now because it's happened with us and we weren't living and didn't come along here at the right time until this minute."

Sidney swallowed. "Maybe," he muttered, "maybe."

"Another thing," George said. "If we can talk with them we can learn everything we've tried to know in all our work and solve in a minute what we're ready to spend the whole summer, even years, digging for."

Sidney brightened. "That's what we wanted to do."

George studied the Indians again. "I think they're just as surprised as we are. When they discovered themselves here and saw us—and you must remember we're the first white men they've ever seen—their immediate instinct was to attack. Now that we don't fight back they're waiting for us to make a move."

"What do we do?"

"Take it easy," advised George. "Don't look scared and don't look belligerent. Look friendly and hope some of the modern Indian dialects we know can make connection with them."

*

The two scientists began, at a gradual pace, to make their way toward the old man, the young man, and the girl. As they approached, the girl drew back slightly. The young man reached over his shoulder and from the furred quiver slung on his back drew an atlatl lance and fitted it to his throwing stick, holding it ready. The other warriors, all about, followed suit.

The medicine man alone stepped forward. He held up a short colored stick to which bright feathers were attached and shook it at the two white men. They stopped.

"That's his aspergill," observed Sidney. "I'd like to have that one."

The medicine man spoke. At first the scientists were puzzled, then George told Sidney, "That's Pima, or pretty close to it, just pronounced differently. It probably shows we were right in thinking the Pimas descended from these people. He wants to know who we are."

George gave their names. The medicine man replied, "The man who has white skin instead of red speaks our language in a strange way. I am Huk." He turned to the young man at his side and said, "This is Good Fox, our young chief." He indicated the girl. "That is Moon Water, his wife."

George explained what he and the other white man with him were doing here. Huk, along with all the other Indians, including Good Fox and Moon Water, listened intently; they seemed greatly excited and disturbed.

When George was finished Good Fox turned to Huk and said, "You have succeeded, wise one, in bringing us forward, far in the future to the time of these men with white skins."

"This is the truth," said the wrinkled Huk; he did not boast but rather seemed awed.

Moon Water spoke in a frightened tone. She looked about at the partially excavated ruins and asked, "But what has happened to our village?" She faltered, "Is this the way it will look in the future?"

"It is the way," Good Fox informed her sorrowfully.

"I weep for our people," she said. "I do not want to see it." She hung her pretty face over her bare body, then, in a moment, raised it resolutely.

Good Fox shook the long scraggly black hair away from his eyes and told the white men, "We did not mean to harm you. We did not know what else to do upon finding you here and our village buried."

Ignoring that in his excited interest, Sidney asked, "What year are you?"

"Year?" asked Good Fox. "What is this word?"

Both Sidney and George tried to get over to him what year meant in regard to a date in history, but Good Fox, Huk, and Moon Water, and none of the others could understand.

"We do not know what you mean," Huk said. "We know only that we live here in this village—not as you see it now—but one well built and alive with our people. As the medicine man I am known to have extra power and magic in visions. Often I have wondered what life would be like in the far future. With this group I conjured up a vision of it, carrying them and myself to what is now here before us."

George and Sidney glanced at each other. George's lips twitched and those of Sidney trembled. George said softly to the Indians, "Let us be friends." He explained to them what they were doing here. "We are trying to find out what you were—are—like. Especially what made you desert people leave your villages."

They looked blank. Huk said, "But we have not left—except in this vision."

In an aside to George, Sidney said, "That means we've caught them before they went south or wherever they went." He turned back to Huk. "Have the cliff people yet deserted their dwellings?"

Huk nodded solemnly. "They have gone. Some of them have joined us here, and more have gone to other villages."

"We have read that into the remains of your people, especially at Casa Grande," Sidney told him. With rising excitement in his voice he asked, "Can you tell us why they left?"

Huk nodded. "This I can do."

Now the glance of Sidney and George at each other was quick, their eyes lighting. "I'll take it down on the typewriter," Sidney said. "Think of it! Now we'll know."

He led Huk to the table set in front of the tent, where he brought out a portable typewriter and opened and set it up. He sat on one chair, and Huk, gingerly holding his aspergill before him as though to protect himself, sat on the other.

Good Fox, Moon Water and the other Indians crowded about, curious to see the machine that came alive under Sidney's fingers as Huk began to relate his story. Soon their interest wandered in favor of other things about the two men with white skin. They wanted to know about the machine with four legs.

George opened up the hood of the station wagon and showed them the engine. He sat in the car and started the motor. At the noise the Indians jumped back, alarmed, and reaching for their atlatls. Moon Water approached the rear end of the car. Her pretty nose wrinkled at the fumes coming from it and she choked, drawing back in disgust. "It is trying to kill me," she said.

Clearly, she did not approve of an automobile.

George cut off its engine.

Over Good Fox's shoulder hung a small clay water jug hung in a plaited yucca net. George asked for a drink from it and when he tasted it and found it fresh it was wondrous to him that its water was hundreds of years old. He brought out a thermos, showing the Indians the modern version of carrying water. They tasted of its contents and exclaimed at its coolness. Good Fox held the thermos, admiring it.

"Would you like to have it?" asked George.

"You would give it to me?" the handsome young Indian asked.

"It's yours."

"Then I give you mine." He gave George his clay water jug and could not know how much more valuable it was than the thermos.

George then took them to the portable television set and turned it on. When faces, music, and words appeared the Indians jerked back, then jabbered and gathered closer to watch. A girl singer, clad in a gown that came up to her neck, caused Moon Water to inquire, "Why does she hide herself? Is she ashamed?"

The standards of modesty, George reflected as he glanced at the lovely nude form of the prehistoric Indian girl, change with the ages.

Of the people and noises on the TV screen Good Fox wanted to know quite solemnly, "Are these crazy people? Is it the way you treat your people who go crazy?"

George laughed. "You might say it's something like that."

A shout came from Sidney at the card table near the tent where he was taking down Huk's story. "George! He's just told me why the cliff people left! And why the desert people will have to leave in time. It's a reason we never thought of! It's because—"

Just then a big multi-engined plane came over, drowning out his words. The Indians stared skyward, now in great alarm. They looked about for a place to run and hide, but there was none. They held their hands over their ears and glanced fearfully at the TV which now spluttered, its picture and sound thrown off by the plane. Awesomely, they waited until the plane went over.

"We fly now in machines with wings," George explained.

"To make such a noise in the air," Moon Water said, "is wicked, destroying all peace."

"I'll agree with you there," said George.

"You have this," Good Fox observed, indicating the TV, which was now back to normal, "and you send the other through the sky to make it crazier than before." He shook his head, not comprehending.

George shut off the TV. He took up a camera of the kind that automatically finishes a picture in a minute's time. Grouping Good Fox, Moon Water and the other warriors, he took their picture, waited, then pulled it out and showed it to them.

They cried out, one man shouting in fear, "It is great magic!"

George took a number of photographs, including several of Huk as he sat talking with Sidney. No matter what happened he would have this record as Sidney would have that he was taking down on the typewriter.

Next he showed them a pair of binoculars, teaching them how to look through them. They exclaimed and Good Fox said, "With this we could see our enemies before they see us."

"You have enemies?" George asked.

"The Apache," Good Fox said fiercely.

George handed him the binoculars. "It is yours to use against the Apache."

Solemnly the young chief answered, "The man with white skin is thanked. The red man gives in return his atlatl and lances." He held out his throwing stick and unslung his quiver of lances. George accepted them with thanks; they would be museum pieces.

Finally George showed them a rifle. He looked about for game and after some searching saw a rabbit sitting on a mound in the excavations. As he took aim Good Fox asked, "You would hunt it with your stick?"

George nodded.

"This cannot be done from here," stated one warrior.

George squeezed the trigger. Instantaneously with the explosion of the shell the rabbit jumped high and then came down, limp and dead. The Indians yelled with fright and ran off in all directions. Huk jumped up from the table. Then all stopped and cautiously returned. One went to the rabbit and picked it up, bringing it back. All, including Huk who left the table, stared with fright at it and at the rifle.

Moon Water expressed their opinion of it. "The thunder of the killing stick is evil."

"Moon Water speaks the truth," said Huk.

"It would make hunting easy," said Good Fox, "but we do not want it even if given to us."

He drew back from the rifle, and the others edged away from it.

George put it down.

Sidney held up a sheaf of papers. "I've got it all, George," he said exultantly in English, "right here! I asked Huk if they can stay with us in our time, at least for a while. We can study them more, maybe even take them back to show the world."

"What did he say?"

"He didn't have a chance to reply when you shot the rifle."

George put it formally to the Indians, addressing Huk, Good Fox, Moon Water and the rest. "You have seen something of the modern world. We would like you to stay in it if it is your wish. I don't know how long you could stay in Huk's vision, but if you can remain here permanently and not go back to your time and—well, not being alive there any more—we hope you will consider this."

Huk replied, "It is possible that we could stay in your time, at least as long as my vision lasts, which might be for as long as I lived." He glanced at Good Fox.

The young chief in turn looked at Moon Water. Her gaze went to the station wagon, to the TV, then up at the sky where the plane had appeared, at the rifle, the camera, the thermos, and all else of the white man. She seemed to weigh their values and disadvantages, looking dubious and doubtful.

Good Fox announced, "We will hold a council about it. As is our custom, all have words to say about such a thing."

Abruptly he led his people away, into the excavations and over a slight rise of ground, behind which they disappeared.

Sidney murmured, "I don't like that so much."

"They must do as they want." George led the way to the card table and they sat there. On it rested Huk's aspergill.

"He gave it to me," Sidney explained.

George placed Good Fox's netted clay water jug and his atlatl and furred quiver of lances on the table, together with the pictures he had taken of the ancient Indians. They waited.

Sidney, glancing at the low hill behind which the Indians had gone, said, "What they're doing is choosing between living in modern civilization and remaining dead. What do you think they'll do?"

"I don't know," said George. "They didn't think so much of us."

"But they couldn't choose death and complete oblivion!"

"We'll see."

They waited some more.

"At least," said Sidney, indicating the articles on the table, "we'll have these for evidence." He held up the sheaf of papers containing Huk's story. "And this, giving the real reason the cliff dwellers left. I haven't told you what it was, George. It's so simple that—"

He didn't complete his sentence, for just then Huk, Good Fox, Moon Water, and the other warriors made their choice. It was announced dramatically.

The water jug, the aspergill, and the atlatl and quiver of lances disappeared from the table. In their places, suddenly, there were the thermos and the binoculars.

Sidney stared stupidly at them.

George said quietly, "They've gone back."

"But they can't do this!" George protested.

"They have."

Sidney's hand shook as he picked up the sheaf of papers holding Huk's story. Indicating it and the photographs, he said, "Well, they haven't taken these away."

"Haven't they?" asked George. He picked up some of the pictures. "Look."

Sidney looked and saw that the pictures were now blank. His glance went quickly to the typewritten sheets of paper in his hands. He cried out and then shuffled them frantically.

They, too, were blank.

Sidney jumped up. "I don't care!" he exclaimed. "He told me and I've got it here!" He pointed to his head. "I can remember it, anyway."

"Can you?" asked George.

"Why, certainly I can," Sidney asserted confidently. "The reason the cliff dwellers left, George, was that they . . . " Sidney stopped.

"What's the matter, Sid?"

"Well, I—it—I guess it just slipped my mind for a second." His brow puckered. He looked acutely upset and mystified. "Huk told me," he faltered. "Just a minute ago I was thinking of it when I started to tell you. Now . . . I can't remember."

"That's gone, too."

"I'll get it!" Sidney declared. "I've just forgotten it for a minute. I'll remember!"

"No," said George, "you won't."

Sidney looked around. "There must be something left." He thought. "The atlatl lances they shot at us!" He looked at the U-Haul-It. The lances no longer stuck in its side. Nor were those that had fallen to the ground to be seen.

Sidney sat down again, heavily. "We had it all," he moaned. "Everything we'd been working for. And now . . . "

"Now we'll have to dig for it again," said George. "Do it the hard way. We'll start tomorrow when the workmen come."

Sidney looked up. "There's one thing!" he cried. "The dent in the car made by the lance! It's still there, George! However everything else worked, that was forgotten. It's still there!"

George glanced at the dent in the side panel of the station wagon. "It's still there," he agreed. "But only to tell us this wasn't a dream. No one else would believe it wasn't caused by a rock."

George groaned. He stared at the rise of ground behind which the Indians had disappeared. "Huk," he pleaded. "Good Fox. Moon Water. The others. Come back, come back . . . "

No one appeared over the rise of ground as the cool desert night began to close in.

OPERATION EARTHWORM

by Joe Archibald

Here he is again, the irrepressible Septimus Spink, in a tale as rollicking as an elder giant juggling the stars and the planets in his great, golden hands and laughing mirthfully as one tiny world—our own—goes spinning away from him into caverns measureless to man. With specifications drawn to scale, Joe Archibald, whose versatility with the quill never ceases to amaze us, has managed with slangy insouciance to achieve a rare triumph over space and time, and to aureole Spink in a resplendent sunburst of imperishable renown.

Septimus Spink didn't need to read Jules Verne's "Journey to the Center of the Earth." He had more amazing ideas of his own.

Interplanetary Press, Circa 2022—Septimus Spink, the first Earthman to reach and return from New Mu in a flying saucer, threw a hydroactive bombshell into the meeting of the leading cosmogonists at the University of Cincinnatus today. The amazing Spink, uninvited, crashed this august body of scientists and laughed at a statement made by Professor Apsox Zalpha as to the origin of Earth and other planets.

"That theory is older than the discovery of the antiquated zipper," Spink orated. "Ha, you big plexidomes still believe the Earth was condensed from a filament, and was ejected by the sun under the gravitational attraction of a big star passing close to the Earth's surface. First it was a liquid drop and cooling solidified it after a period of a few million years. You citizens still think it has a liquid core. Some of you think it is pretty hot inside like they had atomic furnaces all fired up. Ha, the exterior ain't so hot either what with taxes we have to pay after seven wars."

Professor Yzylch Mgogylvy, of the University of Juno, took violent exception to Septimus Spink's derisive attitude and stoutly defended the theory of adiabatic expansion. It was at this juncture that Spink practically disintegrated the meeting.

"For the last seventy years," he orated, "all we have thought about was outer space. All that we have been hepped up about is what is up in the attic and have forgot the cellar. What proof has any knucklehelmet got that nobody lives far under the coal mines and the oil pockets? Something lives everywhere! Adam never believed anythin' lived in water until he was bit by a crab. Gentlemen, I am announcin' for the benefit of the press and everybody from here to Mars and Jupiter and back that I intend to explore inner space! I have already got the project underway."

A near panic ensued as representatives of the press made for the audio-viso stellartypes. "You think volcanoes are caused by heat generated far down inside the earth. They are only boils or carbuncles. Awright, where do earthquakes come from?" Here Spink laughed once more. "They are elastic waves sent out through the body of the Earth, huh? Their observed times of transmission give a means of finding their velocities of propagation at great depths.

I read that in a book that should be in the Terra-firmament Institute along with the Spirit of St. Louis."

Septimus Spink walked out at this point, surrounded by Interplanetary scribes, one of whom was Exmud R. Zmorro. Spink informed the Fourteenth Estate that he would let them have a gander at the model of his inner space machine in due time. He inferred that one of his financial backers in the fabulous enterprise was Aquintax Djupont, and that the fact that Djupont had recently been brain-washed at the Neuropsychiatorium in Metropolita had no bearing on the case whatsoever.

*

I AM seeing and listening to that news item right now which has been repeated a dozen times the last twenty-four hours as if nobody could believe it. I am Septimus Spink, and descended from a long line of Spinks that began somewhere back at the time they put up the pyramids.

All my ancestors was never satisfied with what progress they saw during when they lived, and they are the reasons we have got where we are today. And if there was no Spinks today the scientists would get away with saying that the Earth was only a drop from the sun that got a crust on it after millions of years. And they want to send me back to get fitted for a duronylon strait jacket again.

An hour after I shut off the viso-screen, and while I am taking my calves' liver and onion capsules, my friend and space-lanceman, D'Ambrosia Zahooli comes in. He just qualifies as a spaceman as he takes up very little and is not much easier to look at than a Nougatine. Once D'Ambrosia applied for a plasticectomy but the surgeons at the Muzayo clinic just laughed and told him there was a limit to science even in the year 2022. But the citizen was at home when they divided the brains. Of course that is only my opinion. He is to fly with me into inner space.

"Greetin's and salutations, and as the Martians say, 'max nabiscum,' Sep," Zahooli says. "I have been figuring that we won't have to go deeper than about four thousand kilometers. All that is worryin' me is gettin' back up. I still do not fully believe that we won't melt. Supposin' Professor Zalpha is right and that we will dive down into a core of live iron ore. You have seen them pour it out of the big dippers in the mills, Sep."

"Columbus started off like us," I says. "Who knew what he would find or where he ended up? Chris expected to fall right off the edge of the world, but did that scare him? No!"

"Of course you can count on me," Zahooli says. "When do we start building this mechanical mole?"

"In just two days," I says. "Our backers have purchased an extinct spaceship factory not far from Commonwealth Seven. Yeah, we will call our project 'Operation Earthworm,' pal."

D'Ambrosia sits down and starts looking chicken. "We wouldn't get no astrogator in his right mind to go with us, Sep. How many times the thrust will we need over what we would use if we was just cutting space? We start out in about a foot of topsoil, then some hard rock and then more hard rock. Can we harness enough energy to last through the diggin'? Do you mind if I change my mind for a very good reason which is that I'm an awful coward?"

"Of course not," I says. "It would be a coincidence if you quit though, my dear old friend, and right after Coordinator One found out who was sipping Jovian drambuie on a certain space bistro last Monday with his Venutian wife."

"You have sold me," Zahooli says. "I wouldn't miss this trip for one of those four-legged turkey farms up in Maine. It is kind of frustratin' though, don't you think, Septimus? We are still not thirty and could live another hundred years what with the new arteries they are making out of Nucrolon and the new tickers they are replacing for the old ones."

"Let us look over the model again," I says. "You are just moody today, D'Ambrosia."

It still looks like it would work to me. It is just a rocket ship pointed toward terra firma instead of the other way, and has an auger fixed in place at the nose. It is about twenty feet long and four feet wide and made out of the strongest metal known to modern science, cryptoplutonite. It won't heat up or break off and it will start spinning around as soon as we cut loose with the tail blasts.

"How much time do we need and how much energy for only four thousand kilometers?" I asks Zahooli. "We got enough stored up to go seventy million miles into space? We'll cross that bridge when we get to the river."

"You mean the Styx?"

"That is one thing I will not believe," I sniff. "We will never find Attila the Hun or Hitler down there. Or Beelzebub."

All at once we hear a big rumbling noise and the plexidomed house we are in shakes and rattles and we are knocked out of our chairs and deposited on the seats of our corylon rompers. The viso-screen blacks out, I get to all fours and ask, "You think the Nougatines have gone to war again, D'Ambrosia?"

"It was not mice," Zahooli gulps. "It is either a hydroradium plant backfired or a good old-fashioned earthquake."

After a while we have the viso-screen working. The face of Coordinator Five appears. He says the worst earthquake in five centuries has happened. There is a crack in the real estate of Department X6 near the Rockies that makes the Grand Canyon look like a kid just scraped a stick through some mud. Infra-Red Cross units, he says, are rocketing to the area.

"There might be somethin' goin' on inside this earth," I says. "If you don't poke a hole in a baked potato its busts right open from heat generated inside. Our project, D'Ambrosia, seems even more expedient than ever."

"That is a new word for 'insane' I must look up," Zahooli says.

Professor Apsox Zalpha comes out with a statement the next morning. He says the quake confirms his theory that the inside of the Earth is as hot as a Venutian calypso number, and that gases are being generated by the heat and that we haven't volcanoes enough on the surface to allow them to escape.

Exmud R. Zmorro comes and asks me if I have an opinion.

"Ha," I laugh. "I have many on file in the Neuropsychiatorium. Just go and take your pick. However, I will give you one ad lib and sub rosa. There is more downstairs than Professor Zalpha dreams about. Who is he to say there is no civilization in inner space as well as outer? How do we know that there is not a globe inside a globe with some kind of space or atmosphere in between?"

Exmud R. Zmorro says thanks and leaves in quite a hurry. I snap off the gadget and head for my rocket jeep, and fifteen seconds later I am walking into the factory where a hundred citizens are already at work on the inner spaceship. It is listing a little to port from the quake but the head mech says it will be all straightened out in a few hours. It is just a skeleton ship at the moment with the auger already in place and the point about three feet into the ground.

D'Ambrosia Zahooli comes in and says he has been to see Commander Bizmuth Aquinox. "He will give just enough of the atom pile for seventy million miles," he says. "And only enough superhydrogenerated radium to push us twenty million miles, Sep. I think we should write to Number One. I explained to the space brass that we have got to come up again after going down and have to reverse the blast tubes. It is radium we have to have to make the return trip. I says a half a pound would do it. You know what I think? I bet they don't believe we'll ever git back. And was their laughs dirty!"

"Skeptics have lived since the beginnin' of time," I scoff. "They laughed at Leonardo da Vinci, Columbus, Edison, a guy named Durante. Even the guy who first sat down at a pianer. We will take what we can git, pal, and then come back and laugh at them."

"I wish you was more convincin'," D'Ambrosia says. "I have claustrophobia and would hate to git stuck in an over-sized fountain pen halfway to the middle of this earth."

"Hand me those plans," I says sharply. "And stop scarin' me."

Three months later we have it made. Technicians come from four planets to look at the Magnificent Mole. The area is alive with members of the Interplanetary Press, the Cosmic News Bureau, and the Universe Feature Service. Two perspiring citizens arrive and tear up two insurance policies right in front of my eyes. An old buddy of mine in the war against the Nougatines says he wants to go with me. His name is Axitope Wurpz. He has been flying cargo between Earth and Parsnipia and says he is quite unable to explain certain expense items in his book. A Parsnipian D.A. is trying to serve him a subpoena.

"You are in, Axie," I says. "A crew of three is enough as that is about all the oxygen we can store up. Meet D'Ambrosia Zahooli."

"Why is he wearing a mask?" Wurpz quips.

"You are as funny as a plutonium crutch," Zahooli says.

"No hard feelin's," Wurpz says, and takes a small flask out of his pocket. "We will drink to Operation Earthworm."

As might have been expected, we run into some snags. The Euthanasia Society serve us with papers as they maintain nobody can commit suicide in the year 2022 without permission from the Board. Gulflex and other oil companies protest to Number One as they say we might open up a hole that will spill all the petroleum out of the earth all at once, so fast they couldn't refine it. A spark could ignite it and set the globe on fire like it was a brandied Christmas pudding. But then another earthquake shakes Earth from the rice fields of China to the llamas in Peru just when it looks as if we were about to be tossed into an outer space pokey.

The seismologists get together and agree that they can't possibly figure out the depth of the focus and state that the long waves have to pass through the epicenter or some such spot underground. Anyway, all the brass agrees that something is going on in inner space not according to Hoyle or Euclid or anybody else and that we three characters might just hit on something of scientific value.

The Magnificent Mole is built mostly of titanium, a metal which is only about half as heavy as steel and twice as rugged. It is not quite as big in diameter as the auger, for if it was any Martian moron knows we would scrape our sides away before we got down three miles. We store concentrated chow to last six months and get the acceleration couches ready. We are to blast down at eighteen point oh-four hours, Friday, May

26th, 2022. Today is Wednesday. The big space brass, the fourteenth estate haunt the spot marked X.

We get it both barrels from the jokers carrying press cards. They call it Operation Upside Down. At last three characters were really going to dig a hole and pull it in after them. Three hours before Dig-day, Exmud R. Zmorro interviews us. We are televised around the orbit.

"Laying all joking aside, Spink," the news analyst says dolefully, "you don't expect this to work."

"Of courst!" I says emphatically. "You forget the first man to reach New Mu was a Spink. A Spink helped Columbus wade ashore in the West Indies. The first man to invent a road-map all citizens could unfold and understand was a Spink."

Zmorro turns to Zahooli and Wurpz. "Don't ask us anythin'!" they yelp in unison. "You would only git a silly answer."

"A world inside of a world you said once, Spink. Ha—"

"Is that impossible? You have seen those ancient sailing ships built inside of a bottle, Mr. Zmorro," I says.

He paws at his dome and takes a hyperbenzadrine tablet. "Well, thank you, Septimus Spink. And have a good trip."

It is Friday. We climb up the ladder and into the Magnificent Mole. "Check everything," I says to Wurpz. "You are the sub-strata astrogator."

"Rogeria. I hope this worm can turn," Wurpz says.

*

Zahooli checks the instruments. We don't put on space suits, but have a pressure chamber built in to insure against the bends. I wave good-bye to the citizens outside and close the door.

"I have got to git out," D'Ambrosia Zahooli says and heads for the door. "I forgot somethin'."

"Huh?"

"I forgot to resign," he says, and I pull a disintegrator Betsy on him and tell him to hop back to the controls.

"Awright, we have computed the masses of fuel we need. Stand by for the takeoff—er, takedown. Eight seconds. Seven—Six—Five—Four—"

"I know now my mother raised one idiot," Zahooli says.

"Three seconds—two seconds—one second!" I go on. "Awright, unload the pile in one and three tubes! Then when we have gone about five hundred miles, give us the radium push."

Whir-r-r-r-r-r-r-r-r-o-o-om! The Mole shudders like a citizen looking at his income tax bite and then starts boring. There is a big bright light all around us, changing color every second, then there is a sound like all the pneumatomic drills in all the universe is biting through a thousand four-inch layers of titanium plate. And with it is a rumble of thunder from all the electric storms since the snake bit Cleopatra. In less than five seconds we turn on the oxygen just in case, and I jump to the instrument panel and look at the arrow on a dial.

"Hey," I yell, "we are makin' a thousand miles per hour through the ground!"

"Don't look through the ports," Wurpz says. "In passin' I saw an angleworm three times the size of a firehose, and a beetle big enough to saddle."

"Git into the compression chamber quick," I says to him. "You are gettin' hallucinations."

I turn on the air conditioning as it gets as humid in the Mole as in the Amazon jungle during the dog days. The boring inner spaceship starts screeching like a banshee.

I look at the instrument panel again and see we are close to being seven thousand miles down, and all at once the gauges show we are out of energy. I look out the port and see a fish staring in at me, and a crab with eyes like two poached eggs swimming in ketchup.

Then we are going through dirt again and all of a sudden we come out of it and I see a city below us all lit up and the buildings are made of stuff that looks like jade run through with streaks of black.

The Mole drops down about a thousand more feet and then hits the floor of the subterranean city and we land like a fountain pen with its point slammed into the top of a lump of clay. Bo-o-o-o-i-ing! We twang like a plucked harp string for nearly five minutes and I hit my noggin against the pilot's seat.

When I pick up my marbles I look around for either an Elysium field or a slag heap but instead a creep is staring down at me. He looks part human and part beetle and has a face the color of the meat of an avocado. His head is shaped like a pear standing on its stem and has two eyes spaced about six inches apart and they are as friendly as those of a spitting cobra irked by hives. He is about four feet tall and has two pairs of arms. I guess I am still a little delirious or I would not have told the thing he would make a swell paper hanger.

The subterranean creep throws a fit and belts me with four fists. "Dummkopf!" it says, and then I really get scared as he has got a lop of hair falling down over one eye and has a black mustache the size of a Venutian four centra stamp over his mouth which is like that of a pouting goldfish.

I get to my feet and grab for a railing, and I see Wurpz and Zahooli held by two other monsters that look more like beetles than the one standing beside me.

"Zo!" the creep with the mustache says. "It is a surprise I talk Universa? We have radar and telepathometers that give us everything that is said in the upper world."

I think back and try not to. In the hermetically sealed cylinder back upstairs among my Americana Spink I have some photographs, Circa 1945. One is of a citizen of old Nazi Germany who was supposed to have cremated himself in a bunker. Papers there record that my forebear, Cyril Spink, had his doubts at the time.

"I am the Neofeuhrer, Earthman," this creep says. "I will conquer the universe."

"Look," I says, pawing beads of sweat as big as the creep's eyes from my brow, "have you been testin' atom bombs and worse down here?"

"Jar."

"There, I knew Professor Zalpha was off the beam," I yelp at Wurpz. "This is what is causin' the earthquakes."

"Come, schwine," the creep says. "I will show you something. The tomb of my ancestor. Then to the museum to show you how he arrived in Subterro in the year 1945. This is the city of Adolfus. Mach schnell! Heil Hitler. I am Agrodyte Hitler, grandson of the Liberator."

The short hairs on the back of my neck start crawling down my spine. We leave the Mole and walk along a big square paved with a mineral we never saw upstairs. Thousands of inhabitants of Subterro hiss at us and click their long black fingers. We walk up a long flight of steps and come to a cadaver memorial and on the front there are big letters and numerals in what looks like bloodstone that says: ADOLPH HITLER. 1981.

"Jar, Earthmen, mortal enemies of Subterro's hero, you thought he did not escape, hah? Come, we go to the museum."

We do. In a glass case is an antique U-boat. "I can't believe it," I says to Zahooli.

"Neither do I. We never took off. They have us locked up in the booby hatch in Metropolita. We went nuts."

"He escaped in a submarine, bringing three of Nazi Germany's smartest scientists with him. He brought plans showing us he could split the atom. He brought working models." The creep laughs mockingly. "We have certain elements down here also. Puranium, better than your uranium. And pitchblende Plus Nine. It will power our fleet of submarines that will conquer Earth. It is nearly der tag! We will leave through the underground river that our benefactor found three miles below the surface of the ocean near Brazil. It spirals down through this earth and empties into Lake Schicklegruber eighty miles from here."

"And Hitler took one of those Subterro dames as a mate, huh," I says. "It figures. He was not human himself."

I get another cuffing around but I am too punchy already to feel anything. The next thing I know I am in the Subterro clink with Wurpz and Zahooli. D'Ambrosia says maybe we will get released from the strait jackets soon and get shock treatments and find ourselves back in Metropolita in our favorite night spot.

"We have to be dreamin' this," I keep telling myself. The guard looks in at us and he has little slanting eyes.

"How did Jap beetles get here?" I ask Wurpz. I shiver. I think of all the Subterro subs pouring out of a hole under Brazil and sinking all Earthian merchant marines, and shooting guided missiles that will land all over the U.S. They could have rays that would reach up over a million miles and wash up space traffic.

Then we get another jolt. They bring us our chow and say it is angleworm and hellgrammite porridge as that is what the Subterro denizens live on mostly. There is a salad made out of what looks like skunk cabbage leaves. We found out later that Hitler's brain trust had made an artificial sun for the Subterrors and they had been given greens for the first time and increased in size over a hundred per cent.

"We have got to escape," I says to my pals.

"That is easy," Zahooli sniffs. "First we have to break through the walls here, get to the Mole which can't never move again, and then fight off maybe six million creeps. We would git reduced to cinders by ray Betsys the minute we hit the street."

I sigh deeply and reach into my knapsack. I find some lamb stew and tapioca pudding capsules and split them with Zahooli and Wurpz. Then I come up with a little box and glance at the label. It says, URGOXA'S INSECT POWDER—Contains Radiatol.

I get up nonchalantly and call the guard to the barred window. Beetlehead sticks his face in close and asks what I want. I empty some of the powder into the palm of my hand and then blow it into his face. The Subterro sentry's eyes cross. His face turns as pale as milk and he collapses like a camp stool.

"Eureka!" I yelp. "We are in business, pals."

I hide the box of bug powder when I hear two other creeps come running. They start yakking in Universa and in bug language both. Agrodyte Hitler appears and looks in at us.

"What happened, Great One?" I ask very politely.

"We will perform an autopsy," Hitler's grandson says, and turns to another beetlehead. "Open the door," he says. "I am showing my guests something before we exterminate them. Too bad about Voklogoo. Most likely a coronary entomothrombosis. Achtung! Raus mitt!"

"It means get the lead out in old Germanic literature," I says to Wurpz and Zahooli.

"It is curtains," D'Ambrosia gulps. "In about five minutes we will be residue."

The Neofeuhrer is like all egomaniacs before him. He wants to brag. We get into a Subterro Jetjeep and drive about twenty miles through the underground countryside to the entrance to a cave guarded by some extra tall Subterrors. Hitler the Third leads us into the spelunker's nightmare and we finally come to a big metal door about eighty feet long and twenty feet high.

Agrodyte pushes a button and the steel door lifts. Then we walk up a flight of steps to the top of a dam and take a gander at a fleet of submarines that makes Earthian pigboats look like they belonged in antique shops.

"We will take you for a ride in one," the dictator of Subterro says. "After that I will turn you over to the executioner."

"We need lawyers," Wurpz says.

We cross a thin gangplank and enter the sub. The lights in it are indirect and are purplish green. Hitler Number Three shows us the telepathic machine, the radar, and the viso-screen that pictures everything going on upstairs on Earth, and on Mars, Jupiter and all other planets. There are four other beetleheads on the sub and they carry disintegrators.

"These Subterro U-boats," our genial host brags, "can go as fast in reverse as full speed ahead, as the situation warrants. They are alive with guided missiles no larger than this flashlight I have here, but one would blow up your Metropolita and leave hardly an ash."

He looks at me, and then goes on: "We will proceed to the lock that will raise us to the underground river and cruise along its course for a few hundred miles. It is the treat I should accord such distinguished visitors from the outside of Earth, nein?"

The skipper of the Subterro sub pulls a switch and there is a noise like three contented cats purring. The metal fish slides along the surface of the underground lake and comes to a hole in a big rock ledge.

We see all this through a monitor which registers the scenery outside the sub within a radius of three miles. The sub slides into the side of the rock, and then is lifted up to the underground river that winds and winds upward like a corkscrew to the outlet under Brazil. Every once in a while a blast of air that smells like a dentist's office goes through the sub from bow to stern and I ask why.

"There is such terrific potency to the power we use from our puranium," Hitler Number Three says, "that we purify the air every few seconds with formula XYB and Three-fifth. The basis of the gas is galena."

I nudge Wurpz and Zahooli as the Neofeuhrer goes over to converse with his crew. "It is our big chance," I whisper. "You watch how they run this tub for the next few minutes. Then when I cough three times you be ready. I do not know how much powder it will take to knock off the big bug as he is half human. Once I blow this insect powder at the same time as the purifying blast is to take place, you two be ready to jump Agrodyte. I noticed that a small purple light flashes on over the monitor just before that stuff turns loose. It is a warning so the beetleheads can take deep breaths."

"Sep," D'Ambrosia Zahooli says. "I take back all the insults of the past five hours. Shake."

"I am doin' that already," I says. "We have to work fast while we are in the underground river."

We wait. The Neofeuhrer comes walking back to where we are sitting. The purple light flashes on, and I count to three. Just as the blast of air loaded with XYB plus cuts loose I throw all the bug powder left in the box into the current. Hitler Number Three breathes in a big gob of it and buckles a little at the knees.

"Grab him!" I screech. "Don't let him yank that disintegrator loose. Hit him with anything you see, pals!"

I see the other beetleheads collapse like they had been hit with bulldozers and I know now that insecticide is more dangerous in Subterro than all the radioactivity harnessed up on six planets.

Agrodyte Hitler, however, has some moxey left in him as he has two of his hands around Wurpz's throat, the third around Zahooli's leg and is reaching for a ray Betsy with his fourth. He grabs the disintegrator just as I belt him over his ugly noggin with a wrench about two feet long and which was certainly not made of aluminum or balsa wood.

"Himmel!" the Neofeuhrer gulps. "Ach du lebensraum!" He has to be hit once more which is enough and we tie him up with rope that looks like it was made out of plutonium filaments.

"Well," I says. "We have a sub from Subterro. Wurpz, you just sit there at the controls and make sure that needle on the big dial don't move as I am sure this creep has it on robot so that this tub will automatically follow the course of the river."

"We are sure takin' a powder," D'Ambrosia yelps. "Look at the monitor!"

We see fish gaping at us from the screen that even Earth citizens with delirium tremens never saw, and I look quite anxiously at the instrument panel.

"A thousand miles per and we are climbin'," I says. "I am glad this Hitler used old Germanic on his subs, and that I majored in it once. I—er—I am gettin' arthritis all at once! The bends! Uh—er—look, peel them suits off the other creeps and fast, Zahooli, as I bet they can be inflated and made into compression chambers. They have got connections that plug into something."

We pull on the suits which were too big for the beetleheads and for a good reason. More bends than there are in the Ohio River are with us before we plug into the right socket. The suits bulge out until our feet almost leave the floor. I grin through my helmet at Wurpz.

The sub keeps purring and purring. The altimeter registers four thousand feet. It is a caution, an altimeter in a sub. Two hours later we shoot out through a hole deep under the coast of Brazil and I know we are in the ocean as the monitor shows some old wrecked ships about three miles from us. We disconnect the Subterro anti-bends kimonos and peel them off. Agrodyte Hitler is moving two of his arms when we climb toward the surface.

"Hah, we will make a sucker out of history," I says to Wurpz. "And wait until we show this creep to Professor Zalpha and Exmud R. Zmorro."

We come to the surface and contact an Earthian Franco-Austro atomic luxury liner. The skipper's pan registers on the viso-screen. "This is Septimus Spink," I says. "Commander of Inner Spaceship Magnificent Mole. I have come from the center of Earth with a captured Subterro submarine and Agrodyte Hitler, the Neofeuhrer. Over and out."

The universe goes into a cosmic dither when we slide into a berth in Hampton Rhodus. Thousands of citizens hail us as we ride to Metropolita in a Supercaddijet. Behind us in a truck trailer made mostly of transparent duralucite is our captive, the descendant of Adolph Hitler and three dead Subterro beetle people.

"Well, you won't give up so easy on a Spink from now on," I says to Zahooli. "We are heroes and will get medals. First thing we have to do, though," I says to Coordinator One sitting in the jet sedan with us, "is to take care of the hole Earth has in its head. All we have to do is drop that new bomb down the tunnel we made and it will wash up all those subs that are left and most likely cause a flood that will inundate Subterro. What do you think?"

The brass is still tongue-tied. "One thing I must do and that is see that a certain insecticide manufacturer gets a plug on Interplanetary TV," I continue. "Ha, we took the bugs out of this planet. It should work quite smooth from now on."

"I still believe in reincarnation," D'Ambrosia Zahooli says. "I have the darndest feeling I've been through almost as big nightmares with you before, Sep."

*

Interplanetary Press, Circa 2022, Junius XXIV—Professor Apsox Zalpha, eminent professor of cosmogony, and Exmud R. Zmorro, leading news analyst of seven worlds, have entered the Metropolita Neuropsychiatorium for a routine checkup. They emphatically denied that it was connected in any way with a lecture given recently by Septimus Spink, first man to explore inner space, at the Celestial Cow Palace in San Francisco. Both men expect to remain for two weeks. "Of course there is nothing wrong with either of us," Professor Zalpha told your correspondent. "But if you see a beetle, please do not step on it. It could be somebody's mother."

He broke off, glaring at the object that still dangled from his clenched left fist; the others gaped silently at the veil he held up—a wisp of gossamer that was never spun by human distaff.

Ḃ-R-R-R . . . !

by Roger Arcot

Roger Arcot explores the fringes of a really never forgotten world, the introduction to which is an aged manuscript *De Necromantiae, and the wish, not too repressed, to pledge your soul to the Devil! There are many strange memories and unhappy frustrated souls in this Fantastic Universe of ours—strange and sinister memories and stranger urges, frightening urges that refuse to die in the heart of Brother Ambrose.*

He had borne the thousand and one injuries with humility and charity. But the insults! These were more than he could suffer . . . .

GR-R-R! There he goes again! Brother Ambrose could scarce restrain the hatred that seethed and churned in his breast, as his smallish eyes followed Brother Lorenzo headed once more for his beloved geraniums, the inevitable watering-pot gripped in both hands, the inevitable devotions rising in a whispered stream from his saintly lips. The very fact the man lived was a mockery to human justice: God's blood, but if thoughts could only kill.

Ave, Virgo!

The thousand and one injuries of Fray Lorenzo he had borne as a Christian monk should, with humility and charity. But the insults, aye, the insults to faith and reason! They were more than a generous Father could expect His most adoring servant to suffer, weren't they? To have to sit next to the man, for instance, at evening meal and hear his silly prattle of the weather. Next year's crop of cork: we can scarcely expect oak-galls, he says. Isn't *petroselinum* the name for parsley? (No, it's Greek, you swine. And what's the Greek name for Swine's Snout? I could hurl it at you, like the Pope hurling anathema.) *Salve tibi!* It sticks in one's craw to bless him with the rest. Would God our cloister numbered thirty-and-nine instead of forty.

For days now, for weeks, Brother Ambrose had witnessed and endured the false piety of the man. How he'd ever got admitted to the order in the first place beat all supposition. It must have been his sanctimonious apple-cheeks or (Heaven forbid such simony), some rich relative greased the palm of the Prior. *Saint, forsooth!*

Brother Ambrose recalled just a week previous; they had been outside the walls, a round dozen of the brothers, gathering the first few bushels of grapes to make the good Benedictine wine. And all men tended to their duty in the vineyard—save who? Save lecherous Lorenzo, whose job was to attend the press. Picked the assignment himself, most likely, so he could ogle the brown thighs and browner ankles of Dolores squatting on the Convent bank, *gitana* slut with her flashing eyes and hint of sweet delight in those cherry-red lips and coquettish tossing shoulders. A man could see she was child of the devil, flesh to tempt to eternal hellfire.

But how skillful Brother Lorenzo had been in keeping the glow in his dead eye from being seen by the others! Only Ambrose had known it was there. Invisible to even the world, perhaps; but lurking just the same in Lorenzo's feverishly disguised brain. *Si*, there and lusting beyond a doubt. By one's faith, the blue-black hair of Dolores would make any weak man itch; and the stories that had floated on the breeze that day, livelily exchanged between her and that roguish Sanchicha, the *lavandera*; Lorenzo must surely have lapped them all up like a hungry spaniel, though he cleverly turned his head away so you would not guess. After all, Ambrose, scarcely a step closer, could recall clearly every word of the bawdy tales!

Back to the table again; and Brother Ambrose once more noticed how Fray Lorenzo never let his fork and knife lie crosswise, an obvious tribute he, himself, always made in Our Senor's praise. Nor did Lorenzo honor the Trinity by drinking his orange-pulp in three quiet sips; rather (the Arian heretic) he drained it at a gulp. Now, he was out trimming his myrtle-bush. And touching up his roses.

Gr-r-r, again! Watching his enemy putter away in the deepening twilight that followed the decline of the Andalusian sun, Brother Ambrose recalled the other traps he had lain to trip the hypocrite. Traps set and failed; but, oh, so delicious anyhow, these attempts to send him flying off to Hell where he belonged: a Cathar or a Manichee. That last one, involving the pornographic French novel so scrofulous and wicked. How could it failed to have snared its prey? Especially, when Fray Ambrose had spent such sleepless nights, working out his plot in great detail?

Brother Ambrose allowed himself an inward chortle, as he paced along the portico, recollecting how close to success the scheme had come. The book had had to be read first (or re-read, rather) by Ambrose to determine just which chapter would be most apt to damn a soul with concupiscent suggestion. Gray paper with blunt type, the whole book had been easy enough to grasp for that matter—what with the words so badly spelled out. The cuckoldry tales of Boccaccio and that gay old archpriest, Juan Ruiz de Hita, what dry reading they seemed by comparison—almost like decretals.

As if by misadventure, Brother Ambrose had left the book in Lorenzo's cell, the pages doubled down at the woeful sixteenth print. Ah, there had been a passage! Simply glancing at it, you groveled hand and foot in Belial's grip.

But, that twice-cursed Lorenzo must have had the devil's luck that day. A breeze sprang up to flip the volume closed; and the monk, not knowing the book's owner and espying only its name, had handed it over to the Prior who had promptly turned the monastery upside down in search of further such adulterous contraband!

Worse fortune followed. The next day, Brother Lorenzo had come down with a temporary stroke of blindness—it lasted only a week; but even so, for seven days Ambrose had been forced to labor in his stead in the drafty library, copying boresome scrolls in a light scarcely less dim than moonlight. Worse still, the Prior had found mistakes: letters dropped, transposed (Latin was so bothersomely regular; compared to the vulgar tongue). For what he called such "inexcusable slovenliness," the Prior had imposed a penance of bread and water and extra toil.

Slovenliness! Why didn't the Prior—was he blind, too?—notice the deadly sins that were each day so neatly practised by Brother Lorenzo? They went unpunished. Probably, God's Angel would even be found to have been asleep when Judgment Day came around and Lorenzo would slip into Heaven by a wink, as one might say.

Obviously, there was no justice, except such as man would make himself, Brother Ambrose had at last decided.

Ave Maria, plena gratia.

Now at last, he was alone in his cell, free finally from the unendurable (sometimes it seemed everlasting) torment of Brother Lorenzo's presence. Twenty-nine distinct damnations listed in Galatians, if you cared to look up the text; and not one of them could the enemy be made to trip on, a-dying.

In fact, of late, so bad had the situation grown that Brother Ambrose had even once considered pledging his soul to Satan. Oh, not for keeps! No enmity was worth that dread sacrifice. But as a trick, sort of—with a flaw in the indenture that proud Lucifer would miss until it was too late to wriggle out of the bargain.

But that had been two days ago.

Now, a better scheme presented itself to Brother Ambrose, engendered by that forced labor within the dreary precincts of the convent library. For that was where (and when) he had made his delightful discovery, the one that would now redeem him from all his irritations and travail. The discovery that would rid him of Brother Lorenzo for always!

It had happened like this.

Inasmuch as the monastery was over eight hundred years old, many ancient books and moldy scrolls lay forgotten in the cobwebby corners of the great library, especially where the light was gloomy. One afternoon during his week of enforced toil, Brother Ambrose had sought the shelter of one of these ill-lighted and seldom-visited nooks of the building to recover certain lost hours of sleep, hours that had gone astray the night before as he sat up in his lonely cell and brooded over his wrongs. But before his drowsy head could nod off into dreams completely, his eye had chanced to notice a faded scroll that jutted forth from its fellows on the shelves. Starting to push the offender back in place, Ambrose's fingers had hesitated when he noticed the title: *De Necromantiae.*

Surely, thought the monk, such a book belonged on the Index. Then, it occurred to him that possibly the copy in front of him was the only one of its kind in the world, in which case not even the Holy Father could be expected to know it existed. Then, how could it be on the Index or be forbidden?

Taking advantage of this personal achievement in casuistry, Brother Ambrose promptly untied the scroll and began reading.

What he discovered there interested him very much. We do not intend to describe all of the marvels unfolded for him in that venerable mildewed manuscript, for some of the more gruesome mysteries of the supernatural world are better left unrevealed; but let it be said at least, that one chapter intrigued Brother Ambrose immensely. So much so, that he shamelessly whipped out his scissors and, nipping that section, stuck it inside his rough wool robes so he might peruse it at greater leisure within the privacy of his cell.

The chapter that evoked such delight and interest within Brother Ambrose's complicated brain was one that had been penned in the early ages of the Church by a lay-brother who had concerned himself with pagan magic. In it, he had described the fiendish habits and activities of werewolves and had actually even presented a formula. *Ut Fiat Homo Lupinus* it was entitled, which purported to give the secret words and ritual necessary to achieve the transformation from man to beast.

At last, the opportunity had arrived Ambrose's way to achieve his long-desired revenge on Brother Lorenzo!

Twenty-four hours had passed since the momentous discovery. The moment was at hand. Night again had settled upon the Spanish cloisters, the last bell had tolled; and all the good and hardy men were supposed to be at sound sleep on their rough iron cots. But in Brother Ambrose's chilly cell, a small candle burned—casting sickly light that produced huge flickering shadows against the whitewashed walls.

Brother Ambrose held the treasured piece of manuscript between his hands. It was difficult to make out the faded Latin; the writing was cramped and crude, and Ambrose was no scholar to boot. But like all persons of his times, he was quite well-aware of the existence of werewolves, werefoxes, and other such monsters; and he held no doubt but what the spell would work.

It was the scheming brother's plan to creep in the stealth of night down the corridor to the barred oak door of Lorenzo's own simple cell. There, he would knock; lightly enough to disturb no other sleepers, yet loud enough that the rapping would summon

Brother Lorenzo from whatever wicked dreams might be festering in his own sleeping mind.

As Fray Lorenzo's naked footsteps were heard pattering across the bare floor, Ambrose would drink the bat's blood he had collected, sniff the wolfbane he had ground to ash, and pronounce the obscure Celtic words that would alter the very atoms of his flesh, transforming them into an obscene travesty of life. Brother Lorenzo, when he opened the door, would be met not by a fellow human being, but by a snarling fanged wolf that would hurl its hairy bulk at the drowsy monk's own throat.

The next day, the entire monastery would be awakened, of course, by shouts of the news that foul murder had been discovered. But no amount of detection would ever manifest the bestial murderer. Brother Ambrose would hug to his soul the secret of his crime until the day of his shriving.

At length, the hour had grown so late that it was certain even the Prior himself must have long since retired.

Brother Ambrose made ready to carry out his deed. He rose from his cot, removed the coarse brown robe that normally he wore to bed as well as in his daily rounds so that his long-unwashed body stood naked. There must be no chance for tell-tale blood to stain his clothes, when his fierce talons and wolfish teeth tore and rended at human flesh.

Carrying his precious piece of scroll, he departed from his cell and groped his way down the stone corridor until the light improved enough for him to see his way. Luckily, a patch of moonlight illuminated the very space in front of the accursed Brother Lorenzo's door. What fortune!

Brother Ambrose halted and stared at the door as though his eyes could see through it, at the sleeping form within. He sucked in a deep breath. His palms were sweaty; his heartbeat rapid. For a moment, he was almost ready to back out.

Then suddenly, the memory of all the hundreds of grudges he bore against Lorenzo surged through him. Hatred built up a massive reservoir, that broke out over his crumbling conscience and flooded his body with anger and wild resentment. His teeth gritted. What had he been thinking of—to retreat now, with revenge so nearly at hand!

He rapped. A moment later, he heard a creaking sound like Brother Lorenzo slipping out of bed.

Trembling, he lifted the phial of bat's blood, drank it down. It tasted salty. He chewed on the wolfbane powder until it mixed with the saliva of his mouth, then he swallowed. Holding the ancient scroll-segment before him, he began to repeat the badly-written incantation: *Ut fiat homo lupinus, pulvis arnicae facenda est et dum . . . .*

A thousand jolts assailed his body, as if he had been struck by all the lightnings in heaven. Then, came a rushing paralysis, a distortion of time and space, a dread feeling of disintegration and death . . .

The door to Brother Lorenzo's cell began to recede, swelling in volume as it did. The ceiling of the corridor likewise retreated at ever-increasing pace. Staring down at his own dwindling frame, Ambrose saw that the slug-white flesh was now covered with thick fur, even as the limbs were gnarling—

Then, suddenly the door opened. Brother Lorenzo stepped out, his kindly pious face wrinkled with sleep but otherwise showing no irritation or displeasure at being summoned from his rest. At first, the monk seemed not to have noticed Ambrose's form, for he gazed above him and away.

Ambrose kept on shrinking.

Finally, Brother Lorenzo's gaze chanced to glance downward. But still, his features mirrored no recognition or alarm; only puzzlement.

Now, thought Ambrose, *now is the time for me to snarl.*

But no snarl, nor semblance of a snarl, emerged from his lips. Rather, his lips had elongated into long sucking proboscises, while already a third pair of limbs had commenced growing from his furred-over abdomen.

This was not a wolf-like form, he was assuming, Ambrose suddenly realized in terror. But if it was not lupine, what was it? Had he misread the incantation? Had he mispronounced a simple word?

The weird crawling form into which he had metamorphosed was now hardly an inch higher than the surface of the floor. But Ambrose's eyes had bulged into great many-faceted orbs capable of seeing objects with greater clarity than ever. Inches away from him, he made out the segment of scroll he had discarded after reading aloud from it. Crawling over to it, he perused the beginning words of the spell.

And it suddenly dawned on him (while what passed for a heart and ventricles within his pulpy form began simulating horror) that the ancient monk of centuries ago who had first copied the incantation must have been as careless of spelling as he. For the charm obviously did not convert its user into a werewolf, but rather some other animal . . .

Dredging up all the miserable Latin he knew, Ambrose fished for some word similar to *lupinus*.

And suddenly he had it!

Pulicus! That was the word the sloppy copyist of yesteryear had wrongly transcribed. From the word *pulex*, meaning "flea."

45

Not how to become a wolf-like man, but a flea-like man—that was what the formula had described.

Ambrose, the flea, braced himself. Gathering his powerful legs under him, he leaped in soaring flight to land upon the object of hatred—the giant Brother Lorenzo, who towered so high above him.

But the gentle and considerate Brother Lorenzo, who probably would not have hurt hair nor hide of any other creature on Earth—even he knew full well that there is only one thing you can do to discourage a flea.

Swat!

THE HOOFER

by Walter M. Miller, Jr.

A wayfarer's return from a far country to his wife and family may be a shining experience, a kind of second honeymoon. Or it may be so shadowed by Time's relentless tyranny that the changes which have occurred in his absence can lead only to tragedy and despair. This rarely discerning, warmly human story by a brilliant newcomer to the science fantasy field is told with no pulling of punches, and its adroit unfolding will astound you.

A space rover has no business with a family. But what can a man in the full vigor of youth do—if his heart cries out for a home?

THEY ALL knew he was a spacer because of the white goggle marks on his sun-scorched face, and so they tolerated him and helped him. They even made allowances for him when he staggered and fell in the aisle of the bus while pursuing the harassed little housewife from seat to seat and cajoling her to sit and talk with him.

Having fallen, he decided to sleep in the aisle. Two men helped him to the back of the bus, dumped him on the rear seat, and tucked his gin bottle safely out of sight. After all, he had not seen Earth for nine months, and judging by the crusted matter about his eyelids, he couldn't have seen it too well now, even if he had been sober. Glare-blindness, gravity-legs, and agoraphobia were excuses for a lot of things, when a man was just back from Big Bottomless. And who could blame a man for acting strangely?

Minutes later, he was back up the aisle and swaying giddily over the little housewife. "How!" he said. "Me Chief Broken Wing. You wanta Indian wrestle?"

The girl, who sat nervously staring at him, smiled wanly, and shook her head.

"Quiet li'l pigeon, aren'tcha?" he burbled affectionately, crashing into the seat beside her.

The two men slid out of their seats, and a hand clamped his shoulder. "Come on, Broken Wing, let's go back to bed."

"My name's Hogey," he said. "Big Hogey Parker. I was just kidding about being a Indian."

"Yeah. Come on, let's go have a drink." They got him on his feet, and led him stumbling back down the aisle.

"My ma was half Cherokee, see? That's how come I said it. You wanta hear a war whoop? Real stuff."

"Never mind."

He cupped his hands to his mouth and favored them with a blood-curdling proof of his ancestry, while the female passengers stirred restlessly and hunched in their seats.

The driver stopped the bus and went back to warn him against any further display. The driver flashed a deputy's badge and threatened to turn him over to a constable.

"I gotta get home," Big Hogey told him. "I got me a son now, that's why. You know? A little baby pigeon of a son. Haven't seen him yet."

"Will you just sit still and be quiet then, eh?"

Big Hogey nodded emphatically. "Shorry, officer, I didn't mean to make any trouble."

When the bus started again, he fell on his side and lay still. He made retching sounds for a time, then rested, snoring softly. The bus driver woke him again at Caine's junction, retrieved his gin bottle from behind the seat, and helped him down the aisle and out of the bus.

Big Hogey stumbled about for a moment, then sat down hard in the gravel at the shoulder of the road. The driver paused with one foot on the step, looking around. There was not even a store at the road junction, but only a freight building next to the railroad track, a couple of farmhouses at the edge of a side-road, and, just across the way, a deserted filling station with a sagging roof. The land was Great Plains country, treeless, barren, and rolling.

Big Hogey got up and staggered around in front of the bus, clutching at it for support, losing his duffle bag.

"Hey, watch the traffic!" The driver warned. With a surge of unwelcome compassion he trotted around after his troublesome passenger, taking his arm as he sagged again. "You crossing?"

"Yah," Hogey muttered. "Lemme alone, I'm okay."

The driver started across the highway with him. The traffic was sparse, but fast and dangerous in the central ninety-mile lane.

"I'm okay," Hogey kept protesting. "I'm a tumbler, ya know? Gravity's got me. Damn gravity. I'm not used to gravity, ya know? I used to be a tumbler—*huk!*—only now I gotta be a hoofer. 'Count of li'l Hogey. You know about li'l Hogey?"

"Yeah. Your son. Come on."

"Say, you gotta son? I bet you gotta son."

"Two kids," said the driver, catching Hogey's bag as it slipped from his shoulder. "Both girls."

"Say, you oughta be home with them kids. Man oughta stick with his family. You oughta get another job." Hogey eyed him owlishly, waggled a moralistic finger, skidded on the gravel as they stepped onto the opposite shoulder, and sprawled again.

The driver blew a weary breath, looked down at him, and shook his head. Maybe it'd be kinder to find a constable after all. This guy could get himself killed, wandering around loose.

"Somebody supposed to meet you?" he asked, squinting around at the dusty hills.

"*Huk!*—who, me?" Hogey giggled, belched, and shook his head. "Nope. Nobody knows I'm coming. S'prise. I'm supposed to be here a week ago." He looked up at the driver with a pained expression. "Week late, ya know? Marie's gonna be sore—woo-hoo!—is she gonna be sore!" He waggled his head severely at the ground.

"Which way are you going?" the driver grunted impatiently.

Hogey pointed down the side-road that led back into the hills. "Marie's pop's place. You know where? 'Bout three miles from here. Gotta walk, I guess."

"Don't," the driver warned. "You sit there by the culvert till you get a ride. Okay?"

Hogey nodded forlornly.

"Now stay out of the road," the driver warned, then hurried back across the highway. Moments later, the atomic battery-driven motors droned mournfully, and the bus pulled away.

Big Hogey blinked after it, rubbing the back of his neck. "Nice people," he said. "Nice buncha people. All hoofers."

With a grunt and a lurch, he got to his feet, but his legs wouldn't work right. With his tumbler's reflexes, he fought to right himself with frantic arm motions, but gravity claimed him, and he went stumbling into the ditch.

"Damn legs, damn crazy legs!" he cried.

The bottom of the ditch was wet, and he crawled up the embankment with mud-soaked knees, and sat on the shoulder again. The gin bottle was still intact. He had himself a long fiery drink, and it warmed him deep down. He blinked around at the gaunt and treeless land.

The sun was almost down, forge-red on a dusty horizon. The blood-streaked sky faded into sulphurous yellow toward the zenith, and the very air that hung over the land seemed full of yellow smoke, the omnipresent dust of the plains.

A farm truck turned onto the side-road and moaned away, its driver hardly glancing at the dark young man who sat swaying on his duffle bag near the culvert. Hogey scarcely noticed the vehicle. He just kept staring at the crazy sun.

He shook his head. It wasn't really the sun. The sun, the real sun, was a hateful eye-sizzling horror in the dead black pit. It painted everything with pure white pain, and you saw things by the reflected pain-light. The fat red sun was strictly a phoney, and it didn't fool him any. He hated it for what he knew it was behind the gory mask, and for what it had done to his eyes.

*

With a grunt, he got to his feet, managed to shoulder the duffle bag, and started off down the middle of the farm road, lurching from side to side, and keeping his eyes on the rolling distances. Another car turned onto the side-road, honking angrily.

Hogey tried to turn around to look at it, but he forgot to shift his footing. He staggered and went down on the pavement. The car's tires screeched on the hot asphalt. Hogey lay there for a moment, groaning. That one had hurt his hip. A car door slammed and a big man with a florid face got out and stalked toward him, looking angry.

"What the hell's the matter with you, fella?" he drawled. "You soused? Man, you've really got a load."

Hogey got up doggedly, shaking his head to clear it. "Space legs," he prevaricated. "Got space legs. Can't stand the gravity."

The burly farmer retrieved his gin bottle for him, still miraculously unbroken. "Here's your gravity," he grunted. "Listen, fella, you better get home pronto."

"Pronto? Hey, I'm no Mex. Honest, I'm just space burned. You know?"

"Yeah. Say, who are you, anyway? Do you live around here?"

It was obvious that the big man had taken him for a hobo or a tramp. Hogey pulled himself together. "Goin' to the Hauptman's place. Marie. You know Marie?"

The farmer's eyebrows went up. "Marie Hauptman? Sure I know her. Only she's Marie Parker now. Has been, nigh on six years. Say—" He paused, then gaped. "You ain't her husband by any chance?"

"Hogey, that's me. Big Hogey Parker."

"Well, I'll be—! Get in the car. I'm going right past John Hauptman's place. Boy, you're in no shape to walk it."

He grinned wryly, waggled his head, and helped Hogey and his bag into the back seat. A woman with a sun-wrinkled neck sat rigidly beside the farmer in the front, and she neither greeted the passenger nor looked around.

"They don't make cars like this anymore," the farmer called over the growl of the ancient gasoline engine and the grind of gears. "You can have them new atomics with their loads of hot isotopes under the seat. Ain't safe, I say—eh, Martha?"

The woman with the sun-baked neck quivered her head slightly. "A car like this was good enough for Pa, an' I reckon it's good enough for us," she drawled mournfully.

Five minutes later the car drew in to the side of the road. "Reckon you can walk it from here," the farmer said. "That's Hauptman's road just up ahead."

He helped Hogey out of the car and drove away without looking back to see if Hogey stayed on his feet. The woman with the sun-baked neck was suddenly talking garrulously in his direction.

It was twilight. The sun had set, and the yellow sky was turning gray. Hogey was too tired to go on, and his legs would no longer hold him. He blinked around at the land, got his eyes focused, and found what looked like Hauptman's place on a distant hillside. It was a big frame house surrounded by a wheatfield, and a few scrawny trees. Having located it, he stretched out in the tall grass beyond the ditch to take a little rest.

Somewhere dogs were barking, and a cricket sang creaking monotony in the grass. Once there was the distant thunder of a rocket blast from the launching station six miles to the west, but it faded quickly. An A-motored convertible whined past on the road, but Hogey went unseen.

When he awoke, it was night, and he was shivering. His stomach was screeching, and his nerves dancing with high voltages. He sat up and groped for his watch, then remembered he had pawned it after the poker game. Remembering the game and the results of the game made him wince and bite his lip and grope for the bottle again.

He sat breathing heavily for a moment after the stiff drink. Equating time to position had become second nature with him, but he had to think for a moment because his defective vision prevented him from seeing the Earth-crescent.

Vega was almost straight above him in the late August sky, so he knew it wasn't much after sundown—probably about eight o'clock. He braced himself with another swallow of gin, picked himself up and got back to the road, feeling a little sobered after the nap.

He limped on up the pavement and turned left at the narrow drive that led between barbed-wire fences toward the Hauptman farmhouse, five hundred yards or so from the farm road. The fields on his left belonged to Marie's father, he knew. He was getting close—close to home and woman and child.

He dropped the bag suddenly and leaned against a fence post, rolling his head on his forearms and choking in spasms of air. He was shaking all over, and his belly writhed. He wanted to turn and run. He wanted to crawl out in the grass and hide.

What were they going to say? And Marie, Marie most of all. How was he going to tell her about the money?

Six hitches in space, and every time the promise had been the same: *One more tour, baby, and we'll have enough dough, and then I'll quit for good. One more time, and we'll have our stake—enough to open a little business, or buy a house with a mortgage and get a job.*

And she had waited, but the money had never been quite enough until this time. This time the tour had lasted nine months, and he had signed on for every run from station to moon-base to pick up the bonuses. And this time he'd made it. Two weeks ago, there had been forty-eight hundred in the bank. And now . . .

"*Why?*" he groaned, striking his forehead against his forearms. His arm slipped, and his head hit the top of the fencepost, and the pain blinded him for a moment. He staggered back into the road with a low roar, wiped blood from his forehead, and savagely kicked his bag.

It rolled a couple of yards up the road. He leaped after it and kicked it again. When he had finished with it, he stood panting and angry, but feeling better. He shouldered the bag and hiked on toward the farmhouse.

They're hoofers, that's all—just an Earth-chained bunch of hoofers, even Marie. And I'm a tumbler. A born tumbler. Know what that means? It means—God, what does it mean? It means out in Big Bottomless, where Earth's like a fat moon with fuzzy mold growing on it. Mold, that's all you are, just mold.

A dog barked, and he wondered if he had been muttering aloud. He came to a fence-gap and paused in the darkness. The road wound around and came up the hill in front of the house. Maybe they were sitting on the porch. Maybe they'd already heard him coming. Maybe . . .

He was trembling again. He fished the fifth of gin out of his coat pocket and sloshed it. Still over half a pint. He decided to kill it. It wouldn't do to go home with a bottle sticking out of his pocket. He stood there in the night wind, sipping at it, and watching the reddish moon come up in the east. The moon looked as phoney as the setting sun.

He straightened in sudden determination. It had to be sometime. Get it over with, get it over with now. He opened the fence-gap, slipped through, and closed it firmly behind him. He retrieved his bag, and waded quietly through the tall grass until he reached the hedge which divided an area of sickly peach trees from the field. He got over the hedge somehow, and started through the trees toward the house. He stumbled over some old boards, and they clattered.

"*Shhh!*" he hissed, and moved on.

The dogs were barking angrily, and he heard a screen door slam. He stopped.

"Ho there!" a male voice called experimentally from the house.

One of Marie's brothers. Hogey stood frozen in the shadow of a peach tree, waiting. "Anybody out there?" the man called again.

Hogey waited, then heard the man muttering, "Sic 'im, boy, sic 'im."

The hound's bark became eager. The animal came chasing down the slope, and stopped ten feet away to crouch and bark frantically at the shadow in the gloom. He knew the dog.

"Hooky!" he whispered. "Hooky boy—here!"

The dog stopped barking, sniffed, trotted closer, and went "*Rrrooff!*" Then he started sniffing suspiciously again.

"Easy, Hooky, here boy!" he whispered.

The dog came forward silently, sniffed his hand, and whined in recognition. Then he trotted around Hogey, panting doggy affection and dancing an invitation to romp. The man whistled from the porch. The dog froze, then trotted quickly back up the slope.

"Nothing, eh, Hooky?" the man on the porch said. "Chasin' armadillos again, eh?"

The screen door slammed again, and the porch light went out. Hogey stood there staring, unable to think. Somewhere beyond the window lights were—his woman, his son.

What the hell was a tumbler doing with a woman and a son?

After perhaps a minute, he stepped forward again. He tripped over a shovel, and his foot plunged into something that went*squelch* and swallowed the foot past the ankle. He fell forward into a heap of sand, and his foot went deeper into the sloppy wetness. He lay there with his stinging forehead on his arms, cursing softly and crying. Finally he rolled over, pulled his foot out of the mess, and took off his shoes. They were full of mud—sticky sandy mud.

The dark world was reeling about him, and the wind was dragging at his breath. He fell back against the sand pile and let his feet sink in the mud hole and wriggled his toes. He was laughing soundlessly, and his face was wet in the wind. He couldn't think. He couldn't remember where he was and why, and he stopped caring, and after a while he felt better.

The stars were swimming over him, dancing crazily, and the mud cooled his feet, and the sand was soft behind him. He saw a rocket go up on a tail of flame from the station, and waited for the sound of its blast, but he was already asleep when it came.

It was far past midnight when he became conscious of the dog licking wetly at his ear and cheek. He pushed the animal away with a low curse and mopped at the side of his face. He stirred, and groaned. His feet were burning up! He tried to pull them toward him, but they wouldn't budge. There was something wrong with his legs.

For an instant he stared wildly around in the night. Then he remembered where he was, closed his eyes and shuddered. When he opened them again, the moon had emerged from behind a cloud, and he could see clearly the cruel trap into which he had accidentally stumbled. A pile of old boards, a careful stack of new lumber, a pick and shovel, a sand-pile, heaps of fresh-turned earth, and a concrete mixer—well, it added up.

He gripped his ankles and pulled, but his feet wouldn't budge. In sudden terror, he tried to stand up, but his ankles were clutched by the concrete too, and he fell back in the sand with a low moan. He lay still for several minutes, considering carefully.

He pulled at his left foot. It was locked in a vise. He tugged even more desperately at his right foot. It was equally immovable.

He sat up with a whimper and clawed at the rough concrete until his nails tore and his fingertips bled. The surface still felt damp, but it had hardened while he slept.

He sat there stunned until Hooky began licking at his scuffed fingers. He shouldered the dog away, and dug his hands into the sand-pile to stop the bleeding. Hooky licked at his face, panting love.

"Get away!" he croaked savagely.

The dog whined softly, trotted a short distance away, circled, and came back to crouch down in the sand directly before Hogey, inching forward experimentally.

Hogey gripped fistfuls of the dry sand and cursed between his teeth, while his eyes wandered over the sky. They came to rest on the sliver of light—the space station—rising in the west, floating out in Big Bottomless where the gang was—Nichols and Guerrera and Lavrenti and Fats. And he wasn't forgetting Keesey, the rookie who'd replaced him.

Keesey would have a rough time for a while—rough as a cob. The pit was no playground. The first time you went out of the station in a suit, the pit got you. Everything was falling, and you fell, with it. Everything. The skeletons of steel, the tire-shaped station, the spheres and docks and nightmare shapes—all tied together by umbilical cables and flexible tubes. Like some crazy sea-thing they seemed, floating in a black ocean with its tentacles bound together by drifting strands in the dark tide that bore it.

*

Everything was pain-bright or dead black, and it wheeled around you, and you went nuts trying to figure which way was down. In fact, it took you months to teach your body that *all* ways were down and that the pit was bottomless.

He became conscious of a plaintive sound in the wind, and froze to listen.

It was a baby crying.

It was nearly a minute before he got the significance of it. It hit him where he lived, and he began jerking frantically at his encased feet and sobbing low in his throat. They'd hear him if he kept that up. He stopped and covered his ears to close out the cry of his firstborn. A light went on in the house, and when it went off again, the infant's cry had ceased.

Another rocket went up from the station, and he cursed it. Space was a disease, and he had it.

"Help!" he cried out suddenly. "I'm stuck! Help me, help me!"

He knew he was yelling hysterically at the sky and fighting the relentless concrete that clutched his feet, and after a moment he stopped.

The light was on in the house again, and he heard faint sounds. The stirring-about woke the baby again, and once more the infant's wail came on the breeze.

Make the kid shut up, make the kid shut up . . .

But that was no good. It wasn't the kid's fault. It wasn't Marie's fault. No fathers allowed in space, they said, but it wasn't their fault either. They were right, and he had only himself to blame. The kid was an accident, but that didn't change anything. Not a thing in the world. It remained a tragedy.

A tumbler had no business with a family, but what was a man going to do? Take a skinning knife, boy, and make yourself a eunuch. But that was no good either. They needed bulls out there in the pit, not steers. And when a man came down from a year's hitch, what was he going to do? Live in a lonely shack and read books for kicks? Because you were a man, you sought out a woman. And because she was a woman, she got a kid, and that was the end of it. It was nobody's fault, nobody's at all.

He stared at the red eye of Mars low in the southwest. They were running out there now, and next year he would have been on the long long run . . .

But there was no use thinking about it. Next year and the years after belonged to *little* Hogey.

He sat there with his feet locked in the solid concrete of the footing, staring out into Big Bottomless while his son's cry came from the house and the Hauptman menfolk came wading through the tall grass in search of someone who had cried out. His feet were stuck tight, and he wouldn't ever get them out. He was sobbing softly when they found him.

CONQUEST OVER TIME

by Michael Shaara

"Now this here planet," he said cautiously, "is whacky in a lot of ways. First of all they call it Mert. Just plain Mert. And they live in houses strictly from Dickens, all carriages, no sewers, narrow streets, stuff like that." But that wasn't all . . . . Travis, in reaching Diomed III before any others, found himself waging a one-man fight against more than this; he was bucking the strangest way of life you have ever heard of!

What was the startling secret of Diomed III that almost caused Travis to lose his life? And who was Lappy?...

*

When the radiogram came in it was 10:28 ship's time and old 29 was exactly 3.4 light years away from Diomed III. Travis threw her wide open and hoped for the best. By 4:10 that same afternoon, minus three burned out generators and fronting a warped ion screen, old 29 touched the atmosphere and began homing down. It was a very tense moment. Somewhere down in that great blue disc below a Mapping Command ship sat in an open field, sending up the beam which was guiding them down. But it was not the Mapping Command that was important. The Mapping Command was always first. What mattered now was to come in second, any kind of second, close or wide, mile or eyelash, but second come hell or high water.

The clouds peeled away. Travis staring anxiously down could see nothing but mist and heavy cloud. He could not help sniffing the air and groaning inwardly. There is no smell quite as expensive as that of burned generators. He could hear the Old Man repeating over and over again—as if Allspace was not one of the richest companies in existence—"burned generators, boy, is burned *money*, and don't you forget it!" Fat chance me forgetting it, Travis thought gloomily, twitching his nostrils. But a moment later he did.

For Diomed III was below him.

And Diomed III was an Open Planet.

It happened less often, nowadays, that the Mapping Command ran across intelligent life, and it was even less often that the intelligent life was humanoid. But when it happened it was an event to remember. For space travel had brought with it two great problems. The first was Contact, the second was Trade. For many years Man had prohibited contact with intelligent humanoids who did not yet have space travel, on the grounds of the much-discussed Maturity Theory. As time went by, however, and humanoid races were discovered which were biologically identical with Man, and as great swarms of completely alien, often hostile races were also discovered, the Maturity Theory went into discard. A human being, ran the new slogan, is a Human Being, and so came the first great Contact Law, which stated that any humanoid race, regardless of its place on the evolutionary scale, was to be contacted. To be accepted, "yea, welcomed," as the phrase went, into the human community. And following this, of course, there came Trade. For it was the businessmen who had started the whole thing in the first place.

Hence the day of the Open Planet. A humanoid race was discovered by the Mapping Command, the M.C. made its investigation, and then sent out the Word. And every company in the Galaxy, be it monstrous huge or piddling small, made a mad rush to be first on the scene. The Government was very strict about the whole business, the idea being that planets should make their contracts with companies rather than the government itself, so that if any shady business arose the company at fault could be kicked out, and there would be no chance of a general war. Also, went the reasoning, under this system there would be no favorites. Whichever company, no matter its resources, had a ship closest at the time of the call, was the one to get first bargaining rights. Under this setup it was very difficult for any one company to grow too large, or to freeze any of the others out, and quite often a single contract on a single planet was enough to transform a fly-by-night outfit into a major concern.

So that was the basis of the Open Planet, but there the real story has only begun. Winning the race did not always mean winning the contract. It was what you found when you got down that made the job of a Contact Man one of the most hazardous occupations in history. Each new planet was wholly and completely new, there were no rules, and what you learned on all the rest meant nothing. You went from a matriarchy which refused absolutely to deal with men (the tenth ship to arrive had a lady doctor and therefore got the contract) to a planet where the earth was sacred and you couldn't dig a hole in it so mining was out, to a planet which considered your visit the end of the world and promptly committed mass suicide. The result of this was that a successful Contact Man had to be a remarkable man to begin with: a combined speed demon, sociologist, financier, diplomat and geologist, all in one. It was a job in which successful men not only made fortunes, they made legends. It was that way with Pat Travis.

Sitting at the viewscreen, watching the clouds whip by and the first dark clots of towns beginning to shape below, Travis thought about the legend. He was a tall, frail, remarkably undernourished looking man with large soft brown eyes. He did not look like a legend and he knew it, and, being a man of great pride, it bothered him. More and more, as the years went by, his competitors blamed his success on luck. It was not Pat Travis that was the legend, it was the luck of Pat Travis. Over the years he had learned not to argue about it, and it was only during these past few months, when his luck had begun to slip, that he mentioned it at all.

Luck no more makes a legend, he knew, than raw courage makes a fighter. But legends die quick in deep space, and his own had been a-dying for a good long while now, while other lesser men, the luck all theirs, plucked planet after planet from under his nose. Now at the viewscreen he glanced dolefully across the room at his crew: the curly-headed young Dahlinger and the profound Mr. Trippe. In contrast to his own weary relaxation, both of the young men were tensed and anxious, peering into the screen. They had come to learn under the great Pat Travis, but in the last few months what they seemed to have learned most was Luck: if you happened to be close you were lucky and if you weren't you weren't. But if they were to get anywhere in this business, Travis knew, they had to learn that luck, more often than not, follows the man who burns his generators . . . .

*

He stopped thinking abruptly as a long yellow field came into view. He saw silver flashing in the sun, and his heart jumped into his throat. Old 29 settled fast. One ship or two? In the distance he could see the gray jumbled shapes of a low-lying city. The sun was shining warmly, it was spring on Diomed III, and across the field a blue river sparkled, but Travis paid no attention. There was only one silver gleam. Still he waited, not thinking. But when they were close enough he saw that he was right. The Mapping Command ship was alone. Old 29, burned generators and all, had won the race.

"My boys," he said gravely, turning to the crew, "Pat Travis rides again!" But they were already around him, pounding him on the back. He turned happily back to the screen, for the first time beginning to admire the view. By jing, he thought, what a lovely day!

That was his first mistake.

It was not a lovely day.

It was absolutely miserable.

*

Travis had his first pang of doubt when he stepped out of the ship.

The field was empty, not a native in sight. But Dahlinger was out before him, standing waist high in the grass and heaving deep lungfuls of the flower-scented air. He yelled that he could already smell the gold.

"I say, Trav," Trippe said thoughtfully from behind him, "where's the fatted calf?"

"In this life," Travis said warily, "one is often disappointed." A figure climbed out of a port over at the Mapping Command ship and came walking slowly toward them. Travis recognized him and grinned.

"Hey, Hort."

"Hey Trav," Horton replied from a distance. But he did not say anything else. He came forward with an odd look on his face. Travis did not understand. Ed Horton was an old buddy and Ed Horton should be happy to see him. Travis felt his second pang. This one went deep.

"Anybody beat us here?"

"No. You're the first, Trav."

Dahlinger whooped. Travis relaxed slightly and even the glacial Trippe could not control a silly grin.

Horton caught a whiff of air from the open lock.

"Burned generators? You must've come like hell." His face showed his respect. Between burning a generator and blowing one entirely there is only a microscopic distance, and it takes a very steady pilot indeed to get the absolute most out of his generators without also spreading himself and his ship over several cubic miles of exploded space.

"Like a striped-tailed ape," Dahlinger chortled. "Man, you should see the boss handle a ship. I thought every second we were going to explode in technicolor."

"Well," Horton said feebly. "Burned generators. Shame."

He lowered his eyes and began toeing the ground. Travis felt suddenly ill.

"What's the matter, Hort?"

Horton shrugged. "I hate like heck to be the one to tell you, Trav, but seein' as I know you, they sent me—"

"Tell me what?" Now Dahlinger and Trippe both realized it and were suddenly silent.

"Well, if only you'd taken a little more time. But not you, not old Pat Travis. By damn, Pat, you came in here like a downhill locomotive, it ain't my fault—"

"Hort, straighten it out. What's not your fault?"

Horton sighed.

"Listen, it's a long story. I've got a buggy over here to take you into town. They're puttin' you up at a hotel so you can look the place over. I'll tell you on the way in."

"The heck with that," Dahlinger said indignantly, "we want to see the *man*."

"You're not goin' to see the man, sonny," Horton said patiently, "You are, as a matter of fact, the last people on the planet the man wants to see right now."

Dahlinger started to say something but Travis shut him up. He told Trippe to stay with the ship and took Dahlinger with him. At the end of the field was a carriage straight out of Seventeenth Century England. And the things that drew it—if you closed your eyes—looked reasonably similar to horses. The three men climbed aboard. There was no driver. Horton explained that the 'horses' would head straight for the hotel.

"Well all right," Travis said, "what's the story?"

"Don't turn those baby browns on me," Horton said gloomily, "I would have warned you if I could, but you know the law says we can't show favoritism . . . ."

Travis decided the best thing to do was wait with as much patience as possible. After a while Horton had apologized thoroughly and completely, although what had happened was certainly not his fault, and finally got on with the tale.

"Now this here planet," he said cautiously, "is whacky in a lot of ways. First off they call it Mert. Mert. Fine name for a planet. Just plain Mert. And they live in houses strictly from Dickens, all carriages, no sewers, narrow streets, stuff like that. With technology roughly equivalent to seventeenth century. But now—see there, see that building over there?"

Travis followed his pointing finger through the trees. A large white building of blinding marble was coming slowly into view. Travis' eyes widened.

"You see? Just like the blinkin' Parthenon, or Acropolis, whichever it is. All columns and frescoes. In the middle of a town looks just like London. Makes no sense, but there it is. And that's not all. Their government is Grecian too, complete with Senate and Citizens. No slaves though. Well not exactly. You couldn't call them slaves. Or could you? Heck of a question, that—" He paused to brood. Travis nudged him.

"Yes. Well, all that is minor, next to the big thing. This is one of two major countries on the planet. There's a few hill tribes but these make up about 90 percent of the population, so you have to deal with these. They never go to war, well maybe once in a while, but not very often. So no trouble there. The big trouble is one you'd never guess, not in a million years."

He stared at Travis unhappily.

"The whole planet's run on astrology."

He waited for a reaction. Travis said nothing.

"It ain't funny," Horton said. "When I say run on astrology I mean really run. Wait'll you hear."

"I'm not laughing," Travis said. "But is that all? In this business you learn to respect the native customs, so if all we have to do—"

"I ain't finished yet," Horton said ominously, "you don't get the point. *Everything* these people do is based on astrology. And that means business too, lad, business too. Every event that happens on this cockeyed world, from a picnic to a wedding to a company merger or a war, it's all based on astrology. They have it down so exact they even tell you when to sneeze. You ought to see the daily paper. Half of it's solid astrological guidance. All the Senators not only have astrologers, they *are* astrologers. And get this: every man and woman and child alive on this planet was catalogued the day he was born. His horoscope was drawn up by the public astrologer—a highly honored office—and his future laid out according to what the horoscope said. If his horoscope indicates a man of stature and responsibility, he *becomes*, by God, a man of stature and responsibility. You have to see it to believe it. Kids with good horoscopes are sent to the best schools, people fight to give them jobs. Well, take the courts, for example. When they're trying a case, do they talk about evidence? They do not. They call in a legal astrologer—there's all kinds of branches in the profession—and this joker all by himself determines the guilt or innocence of the accused. By checking the aspects. Take a wedding. Boy meets girl. Boy likes girl. Does boy go see girl? No. He heads straight for an astrologer. The girl's horoscope is on file in the local city hall, just like everybody else. The astrologer compares the charts and determines whether the marriage will be a good one. He is, naturally, a marital astrologer. He gives the word. If he says no they don't marry.

"I could go on for hours. But you really have to see it. Take the case of people who want to have children. They want them born, naturally, at the time of the best possible aspects, so they consult an astrologer and he gives them a list of the best times for a baby to be conceived. These times are not always convenient, sometimes it's 4:18 in the morning and sometimes it's 2:03 Monday afternoon. Yet this is a legitimate excuse for getting out of work. A man goes in, tells his boss it's breeding time, and off he goes without a penny docked. Build a better race, they say. Of course the gestation period is variable, and they never do hit it right on the nose, and also there are still the natural accidents, so quite a few are born with terrible horoscopes—"

"Holy smoke!" Travis muttered. The possibilities of it blossomed in his mind. He began to understand what was coming.

"Now you begin to see?" Horton went on gloomily. "Look what an Earthman represents to these people. We are the unknown, the completely capital U Unknown. Everybody else is a certain definite quantity, his horoscope is on file and every man on Mert has access to all his potentialities, be they good, bad or indifferent. But not us. They don't know when we were born, or where, and even if they did it it wouldn't do them any good, because they haven't got any system covering Mars and Jupiter, the planets at home. Everybody else is catalogued, but not us."

"And just because they believe so thoroughly in their own astrology they've gotten used to the idea that a man is what his horoscope says he is."

"But us? What are we? They haven't the vaguest idea, and it scares hell out of them. The only thing they can do is check with one of the branches, what they call Horary Astrology, and make a horoscope of the day we landed. Even if that tells them nothing about us in particular at least it tells them, or so they believe, all about our mission to Mert. Because the moment our ship touched the ground was the birth date of our business here."

He paused and regarded Travis with woeful sympathy.

"With us, luckily, it was all right. The Mapping Command just happened to hit here on a good day. But you? Trav, old buddy, for once you came just too damn fast—"

"Oh my God," Travis breathed. "We landed on a bad day."

"Bad?" Horton sighed. "Man, it's *terrible*."

*

"You see," Horton said as they drove into the town, "not a soul on the streets. This is not only a bad day, this is one for the books. To-morrow, you see, there is an eclipse. And to these people there is nothing more frightening than an eclipse. During the entire week preceding one they won't do a darn thing. No business, no weddings, no anything. The height of it will be reached about tomorrow noon. Their moon—which is a tiny little thing not much bigger than our first space station—is called Felda. It is very important in their astrology. And for all practical purposes the eclipse is already in force. I knew you were riding in down the base so I checked it out. It not only applies to you, other things cinch it."

He pulled a coarse sheet of paper from his pocket and read from it in a wishful voice: "With Huck, planet of necessity, transiting the 12th house of endings and things hidden, squaring Bonken, planet of gain, in the ninth house of travellers and distant places, it is unquestionable that the visit of these—uh—persons bodes ill for Mert. If further proof is needed, one need only examine the position of Diomed, which is conjunct Huck, and closely square to Lyndal, in the third house of commerce, etc, etc. You see what I mean? On top of this yet an eclipse. Trav, you haven't got a prayer. If only you hadn't been so close. Two days from now would have been great. Once the eclipse ends—"

"Well, listen," Travis said desperately, "couldn't we just see the guy?"

"Take my advice. Don't. He has expressed alarm at the thought that you might come near him. Also his guards are armed with blunderbusses. They may be a riot to look at, but those boys can shoot, believe me. Give you a contract? Trav, he wouldn't give you a broom to sweep out his cellar."

At that moment they drew up before an enormous marble building vaguely reminiscent of a Theban palace. It turned out to be the local hotel. Horton stopped on the threshold and handed them two of the tiny Langkits, the little black memory banks in which the language of Mert had been transcribed for their use by the Mapping Command. Travis slipped his automatically into position behind his ear, but he felt no need to know the language. This one was going to be tough. He glanced at Dahlinger. The kid was wearing a stunned expression, too dulled even to notice the pantalooned customer—first Merts they'd seen—eyeing them fearfully from behind pillars as they passed.

Smell that gold, Travis remembered wistfully. Then, smell those generators. Oh, he thought sinkingly, smell those generators. They went silently on up to the room.

Travis stopped at the door as a thought struck him.

"Listen," he said cautiously, taking Horton by the arm, "haven't you thought of this? Why don't we just take off and start all over, orbit around for a couple of days, pick a good hour, and then come back down. That way we'll be starting all—"

But Horton was gazing at him reproachfully.

"They have a word for that, Trav," he said ominously, "they call it *vetching*. Worst crime a man can commit. Attempt to evade his stars. Equivalent almost to falsifying a horoscope. No siree, boy, for that they burn you very slowly. The first horoscope stands. All your subsequent actions, according to them, date from the original. You'll just be bearing out the first diagnosis. You'll be a vetcher."

"Um," Travis said. "If they feel that way, why the heck do they even let us stay?"

"Shows you the way the system works. This is a bad day for everything. Coming as well as going. They'd never think of asking you to start a trip on a day like this. No matter who you are."

Travis collapsed into an old, vaguely Chippendale chair. His position was not that of a man sitting, it was that of a man dropped from a great height.

"Well," Horton said. "So it goes. And listen, Trav, there was nothing I could do."

"Sure, Hort."

"I just want you to know I'm sorry. I know they've been kickin' you around lately, and don't think I don't feel I owe you something. After all, if you hadn't—"

"Easy," Travis said, glancing at Dahlinger. But the kid's ears perked.

"Well," Horton murmured, "just so's you know. Anyways I still got faith in you. And Unico will be in the same boat. If they get here tonight. So think about it. Let me see the old Pat Travis. Your luck has to change sometime."

He clenched a fist, then left.

Travis sat for a long while in the chair. Dahlinger muttered something very bitter about luck. Travis thought of telling him that it was not luck that had put them so close to Mert, but a very grim and expensive liaison with a ferociously ugly Mapping Command secretary at Aldebaran. She had told him that there was a ship in this area. But this news was not for Dahlinger's ears. And neither did he think it wise to explain to Dahlinger the thing he had done for Horton some years ago. Young Dolly was not yet ripe. Travis sighed and looked around for a bed. To his amusement he noted a four poster in the adjoining room. He went in and lay down.

Gradually the dullness began to wear off. There was a resiliency in Travis unequalled, some said, by spring steel. He began to ponder ways and means.

There was always a way. There had to be a way. Somewhere in the customs of this planet there was a key—but he did not have the time. Unico would be in tonight, others would be down before the week was out. And the one to land in two days, on the *good* day, would get the contract.

He twisted on the bed. Luck, luck, the hell with luck. If you were born with sense you were lucky and if a meteor fell on you, you were unlucky, but most of the rest of it was even from there on out. So if the legend was to continue . . . .

He became gradually aware of the clock in the ceiling.

In the ceiling?

He stared at it. The symbols and the time meant nothing, but the clock was embedded flat in the ceiling above the bed, facing directly down.

He pondered that for a moment. Then he exploded with laughter. By jing, of course. They would have to know what time the baby was conceived. So all over Mert, in thousands of homes, there were clocks in the bedrooms, clocks in the ceilings, and wives peering anxiously upward murmured sweetly in their husbands' ears: 4:17, darling, 4:17 and a half . . . .

The roar of his mirth brought Dolly floundering in from the other room. Travis sprang from the bed.

"Listen, son," he bellowed, "luck be damned! You get back to the ship. Get Mapping Command to let you look at its files, find out everything you can about Mert. There's a key somewhere, boy, there's an out in there someplace, if we look hard enough. Luck! Hah! Work, boy, work, there's a key!"

He shooed Dahlinger out of the room. The young man left dazedly, but he had caught some of Travis' enthusiasm. Travis turned back to the bed feeling unreasonably optimistic. No way out, eh? Well by jingo, old Pat Travis would ride again, he could feel it in his bones.

A few moments later he had another feeling in his bones. This one was much less delightful. He was pacing past a heavy drapery when something very hard and moving very fast struck him on the head.

*

The first thing Travis saw when he awoke was, unmistakably, the behind of a young woman.

His head was lying flat on the floor and the girl was sitting next to him, her back toward him very close to his face. He stared at it for a long while without thinking. The pain in his head was enormous, and he was not used to pain, not any kind of pain. The whiskey men drank nowadays left no hangovers, and for a normal headache there were instantaneously acting pills, so Travis on the floor was unused to pain. And though he was by nature a courageous man it took him a while to be able to think at all, much less clearly.

Eventually he realized that he was lying on a very hard floor. His arms and legs were tightly bound. He investigated the floor. It was brick. It was wet. The dark ceiling dripped water in the flickering light from some source beyond the girl. The brick, the dripping water, the girl, all combined to make it completely unbelievable. If it wasn't for the pain he would have rolled over and gone to sleep. But the pain. Yes the pain. He closed his eyes and lay still, hurting.

When he opened his eyes again he was better. By jing, this was ridiculous. Not a full day yet on Mert and in addition to his other troubles, now this. He did not feel alarmed, only downright angry. This business of the flickering light and being tied hand and foot was too impossible to be dangerous. He grunted feebly at the back of the girl.

"Ho," he said. "Now what in the sweet name of Billy H. Culpepper is this?"

The girl turned and looked down at him. She swiveled around on her hips and a rag-bound foot kicked him unconcernedly in the side. For the first time he saw the other two men behind her. There were two of them. The look of them was ridiculous.

The girl said something. It was a moment before he realized she was speaking in Mert, which he had to translate out of the Langkit behind his ear.

"The scourge awakes," one of the men said.

"A joy. It was my thought that in the conjunction was done perhaps murder."

"Poot. One overworries. And if death comes to this one, observe, will the money be paid? Of a surety. But this is bizarre."

"Truly bizarre," the girl nodded. Then to make her point, "also curious, unique, unusual. My thought: from what land he comes?"

"The cloth is rare," one of the men said, "observe with tight eyes the object on his wrist. A many-symboled engine—"

"My engine," the girl said positively. She reached down for his watch.

Travis jerked back. "Lay off there," he bawled in English, "you hipless—" The girl recoiled. He could not see her face but her tone was puzzled.

"What language is this? He speaks with liquid."

The larger of the two men arose and came over to him.

"Speak again scourge. But first empty the mouth."

Travis glared at the man's feet, which were wrapped in dirty cloth and smelt like the breezes blowing softly over fresh manure.

"Speak again? Speak again? Untie my hands, you maggoty slob, and I'll speak your bloody—" he went on at great length, but the man ignored him.

"Truly, he speaks as with a full mouth. But this is not Bilken talk."

"Nor is he, of clarity and also profundity, a hill man," the girl observed.

"Poot. Pootpoot," the young man stuttered, "the light! He is of *Them*!"

It took the other two a moment to understand what he meant, but Travis caught on immediately. May the Saints preserve us, he thought, they figured I was from Mert. He chuckled happily to himself. A natural mistake. Only one Earthman on this whole blinking planet, puts up at a good hotel, best in town, these boys put the snatch on me thinking I'm a visiting VIP, loaded, have no idea I'm just poor common trash like the rest of us Earthmen. Haw! His face split in a wide grin. He gathered his words from the Langkit and began to speak in Mert.

"Exactly, friends. With clarity one sees that you have been misled. I am not of Mert. I am from a far world, come here to deal with your Senate in peace. Untie me, then, and let us erase this sad but eraseable mistake with a good handshake all around, and a speedy farewell."

It did not have the effect he desired. The girl stepped back from him, a dark frown on her face, and the large man above him spoke mournfully.

"Where now is the ransom?"

"And the risk," the girl said. "Was not there great risk?"

"Unhappily," the tall man observed. "One risks. One should be repaid. It is in the nature of things that one is repaid."

"Well now, boys," Travis put in from the floor, "you see it yourselves. I'm flat as a—" he paused. Apparently the Merts had no word for pancake. "My pockets are—windy. No money is held therein."

"Still," the tall man mused absently, "this must have friends. On the great ships lie things of value. Doubt?"

"Not," the girl said firmly. "But I see over the hills coming a problem."

"How does it appear?"

"In the shape of disposal. See thee. Such as will come from the great ships, of value though it be, can it not be clarifiably identified by such pootian authorities as presently seek our intestines?"

"Ha!" the tall man snorted in anger. "So. Truth shapes itself."

"Will we not, then," continued the girl, "risk sunlight on our intestines in pursuing this affair?"

"We will," the young man spoke up emphatically. "We will of inevitability. Navel. Our risk is unpaid. So passes the cloud."

"But in freedom for this," the girl warily indicated Travis, "lies risk in great measure. Which way lie his ribs? Can we with profit slice his binds? He is of Them. What coils in his head? What strikes?"

They were all silent. Travis, having caught but not deciphered most of the conversation, glanced quickly from face to face. The girl had backed out into the light and he could see her now clearly, and his mouth fell open. She was thickly coated with dirt but she was absolutely beautiful. The features were perfect, lovely, the mouth was promising and full. Under the ragged skirt and the torn sooty blouse roamed surfaces of imaginable perfection. He had difficulty getting back to the question at hand. All the while he was thinking other voices inside him were whispering. "By jing, by jing, she's absolutely . . . ."

The two men were completely unlike. One was huge, from this angle he was enormous. He had what looked like a dirty scarf on his head, madonna-like, which would have been ridiculous except for the mountainous shoulders below it and the glittering knife stuck in his wide leather belt. The shaft of the knife flickered wickedly in the light. It was the only clean thing about him.

The other man was young, probably still in his teens. Curly-haired and blond and much cleaner than the other two, with a softness in his face the others lacked. But in his belt he carried what appeared to be—what was, a well-oiled and yawning barreled blunderbuss.

So they sat for a long moment of silence. He had time to observe that what they were sitting in was in all likelihood a sewer. It ran off into darkness but there was a dim light in the distance and other voices far away, and he gathered that this was not all of the—gang—that had abducted him. But it was beginning to penetrate, now, as he began to understand their words, that they were unhappy about letting him go. He was about to argue the point when the big man stepped suddenly forward and knelt beside him. He shut out the light, Travis could not see. The last thing he heard was the big man grunting as he threw the blow, like a rooting pig.

*

When he awoke this time the pain had moved over to the side of his neck. There was no light at all and he lay wearily for a long while in the blackness. He had no idea how much time had passed. He could tell from the brick wet below him that he was still in the sewer, or at least some other part of it, and, considering the last turn of the conversation, he thought he could call himself lucky to be alive.

But as his strength returned so did his anger. He began to struggle with his bonds. There was still the problem of the contract. He regarded that bitterly. He could just possibly die down here, but his main worry was still the contract. Allspace would be proud of him—but Allspace might never know.

He did nothing with the bonds, which he discovered unhappily were raw leather thongs. Eventually he saw a light coming down the corridor. He saw with a thrill of real pleasure that it was the girl. The young man was tagging along behind her but the big man was absent. The girl knelt down by him and regarded him quizically.

"Do you possess pain?"

"Maiden, I possess and possess unto the limits of capacity."

"My thought is sorrow. But this passes. Consider: your blood remains wet."

Travis caught her meaning. He swore feebly.

"It was very nearly let dry," the girl said. "But solutions conjoined. It was noted at the last, even as the blade descended, that such friends as yours could no doubt barter for Mertian coin, untraceable, thus restoring your value."

"Clever, clever. Oh, clever," Travis said drily.

To his surprise, the girl blushed.

"Overgracious. Overkind. Speed thanks awry of this windy head, aim at yon Lappy"—she indicated the boy who stood smiling shyly behind her—"it was he who thought you alive, he my brother."

"Ah," Travis said. "Well, bless you, boy." He nodded at the boy, who very nearly collapsed with embarrassment. Travis wondered about this 'brother' bit. Brother in crime? The Langkit did not clarify. But the girl turned back on him a smile as glowing as a tiny nova. He gazed cheerfully back.

"Tude and the others sit now composing your note. A matter of weight, confounded in darkness." She lowered her eyes becomingly. "Few of us," she apologized, "have facility in letters."

"A ransom note," Travis growled. "Great Gods and Little—Tude? Who is Tude?"

"The large man who, admittedly hastening before the horse, did plant pain in your head."

"Ah," Travis said, smiling grimly. "We shall presently plow his field—"

"Ho!" the girl cried, agitated. "Speak not in darkness. Tude extends both north and south, a man of dimension as well as choler. He boasts Fors in the tenth in good aspect to Bonken, giving prowess at combat, and Lyndal in the fourth bespeaks a fair ending. Avoid, odd man, foreordained disaster."

In his urge to say a great many things Travis stammered. The girl laid a cool grimy hand lightly on his arm and tried to soothe him.

"With passivity and endurance. The night shall see you free. Tude comes in close moment with the note. Quarrel not at the price, sign, and there will be a conclusion to the matter. We are not retrograde here. As we set our tongues, so lie our deeds."

"Yes, well, all right," Travis grumbled. "But there will come—all right all right. My name shall be inscribed, let your note contain what it will. But I would have speed. There are matters of gravity lying heavily ahead."

The girl cocked her head oddly to one side.

"You sit on points. A rare thing. Lies your horoscope in such confusion that you know not the drift of the coming hours?"

Travis blinked.

"Horoscope?" he said.

"Surely," the girl said, "the astrologers of your planet did preach warning to you of the danger of this day, and whether, in the motions of your system, lay success or failure. Or is it a question of varying interpretations? Did one say you good while the other—"

Travis grinned broadly. Then he sobered. It would quite logically follow that these people, primitive as they were, might not be able to conceive of a land where astrology was not Lord over all. A human trait. But he saw dangerous ground ahead. He began very cautiously and diplomatically to explain himself, saying that while astrology was practiced among his own people, it had not yet become as exact an art as it was on Mert, and only a few had as yet learned to trust it.

The effect on the girl was startling. She seemed for a moment actually terrified when it was finally made clear to her. She abruptly retreated into a corner with her brother and mumbled low frantic sounds. Travis grinned to himself but kept his face stoically calm. But now the girl was out in the light and he could examine her clearly for the first time, and he forgot about astrology entirely.

She was probably in her early twenties. She was dirtier than a well-digger's shoes. She ran with a pack of cutthroats and thieves in what was undoubtedly the lowest possible level of Mertian society. But there was something about her, something Travis responded to very strongly, which he could not define. Possibly something about the set of her hair, which was dark and very long, or perhaps in the mouth—yes the mouth, now observe the mouth—and also maybe in the figure . . . . But he could not puzzle it out. A girl from the gutter. But—perhaps that was it, there seemed to be no gutter about her. There was real grace in her movements, a definite style in the way she held her head, something gentle and very fine.

Now watch that, Travis boy, he told himself sharply, watch that. A psychological thing, certainly. She probably reminds you of a long forgotten view of your mother.

The girl arose and came back, followed this time by the young man. She had become suddenly and intensely interested in his world—she had apparently taken it for granted that it was exactly like hers, only with space ships—and Travis obliged her by giving a brief sketch of selected subjects: speeds, wonders, what women wore, and so on. Gradually he worked the conversation back around to her, and she began to tell him about herself.

Her name was, euphonically, Navel. This was not particularly startling to Travis. Navel is a pretty word and the people of Mert had chosen another, uglier sound for use when they meant 'belly button,' which was their right. Travis accepted it, and then listened to her story.

She had not always been a criminal, run with the sewer packs. She had come, as a matter of proud record, from an extremely well-to-do family which featured two Senators, one Horary Astrologer, and a mercantile tycoon—which accounted, Travis thought, for her air of breeding. The great tragedy of her life, however, the thing that had brought her to her present pass, was her abysmally foul horoscope. She had not been a planned baby. Her parents felt great guilt about it, but the deed was done and there was no help for it. She had been born with Huck retrograde in the tenth house, opposing Fors retrograde in the fourth, and so on, and so on, so that even the most amateur astrologer could see right at her birth that she was born for no good, destined for some shameful end.

She told about it with an air of resigned cheerfulness, saying that after all her parents had really done more than could be expected of them. Both with her and her similarly accidental brother Lappy—now *there*, Travis thought, was a careless couple—whose horoscope, she said dolefully, was even worse than her own. The parents had sent her off to school up through the first few years, and had given her a handsome dowry when they disowned her, and they did the same with Lappy a few years later.

But Navel held no bitterness. She was a girl born inevitably for trouble—her horoscope forecast that she would be a shame to her parents, would spend much of her life in obscure, dangerous places, and would reflect no credit on anyone who befriended her. So, for a child like this, what reasonable citizen would waste time and money and love, when it was certain beforehand that the child grown up would be as likely as not to end up a murderess? No, the schools were reserved for the children of promise, as were the jobs and the parties and the respect later on. The only logical course, the habitual custom, was for the parents to disown their evilly aspected children, hoping only that such tragedies as lay in the future would not be too severe, and at least would not be connected with the family name.

And Navel was not bitter. But there was only one place for her, following her exile from her parents' home. A career in business was of course impossible. Prospective employers took one look at your horoscope and—zoom, the door. The only work she could find was menial in the extreme—dish-washing, street cleaning, and so on. So she turned, and Lappy turned, as thousands of their ill-starred kind had turned before them for generations, to the wild gangs of the sewers.

And it was not nearly so bad as it might have seemed. The sewer gangs were composed of thousands of people just like herself, homeless, cast out, and they came from all levels of society to found a society of their own. They offered each other what none of them could have found anywhere else on Mert: appreciation, companionship, and even if life in the sewers was filthy, it was also tolerable, and many even married and had children—the luckiest of whom quickly disowned their parents and were adopted by wealthy families.

But the thing which impressed Travis most of all was that none of these people were bitter at their fate. Navel could not recall ever hearing of any organized attempt at rebellion. Indeed, most of the sewer people believed more strongly in the astrology of Mert than did the business men on the outside. For each day every one of them could look at the dirt of himself, at the disease of his surroundings, and could see that the message of his horoscope was true: he was born to no good end. And since it had been drummed into these people from their earliest childhood that only the worst could be expected of them, they gave in, quite humanly, to the predictions, and went philosophically forth to live up to them. They watched the daily horoscopes intently for the Bad Days, realizing that what was bad for the normal people must be a field day for themselves, and they issued out of the sewers periodically on binges of robbery, kidnapping, and worse. In this way they lived up to the promise of their stars, fulfilled themselves, and also managed to eat. And few if any ever questioned the justice of their position.

Travis sat listening, stunned. For a long while the contract and how to get out of here and all the rest of it was forgotten. He sat watching the girl and her shy brother as they spoke self-consciously to him, and began to understand what they must be feeling. Travis was from outside the sewers, he had stayed at the grand hotel—his horoscope, whether he believed it or not, must be very fine. And so they did him unconscious homage, much in the manner of low caste Hindus speaking to a Bramin. It was unnerving.

Gradually the boy Lappy began to speak also, and Travis realized with surprise that the boy was in many ways remarkable. As Navel's brother—Navel, Travis gathered with a twinge of deep regret, was the big Tude's 'friend', and Tude was the leader of this particular gang—young Lappy had a restful position. He was kept out of most of the rough work end allowed to pursue what he shamelessly called his 'studies', and he guessed proudly that he must have stolen nearly every book in the Consul's library. His particular hobbies, it turned out, were math and physics. He had a startling command of both, and some of the questions he asked Travis were embarrassing. But the boy was leaning forward, breathlessly drinking in the answers, when Tude came back.

The big man loomed over them suddenly on his quiet rag-bound feet, frightening the boy and causing the girl to flinch. He made a number of singularly impolite remarks, but Travis said nothing and bided his time. He regarded the big man with patient joy, considering with delight such bloodthirsty effects as judo could produce on this one—Fors and Bonken be damned—if they ever untied his hands.

Eventually, unable to get a rise out of him, the big man shoved a paper down before his nose and told him to sign it. He pulled out that wickedly clean knife and freed Travis' hand just enough for him to move his wrist. Hoping for the best, Travis signed. Tude chuckled, said something nastily to the girl, the girl said something chilling in return, and the big man cuffed her playfully on the shoulder. Then he lumbered away.

Travis sat glaring after him. The contract, the need to escape flooded back into his mind. The eclipse might be ending even now. Unico would already be here, probably one or two others as well. And this ransom business might take a week. He swore to himself. Pat Travis, the terror of the skies, held captive by a bunch of third rate musical comedy pirates while millions lay in wait in the city above. And oh my Lord, he thought, stricken, what will people say when they hear—he had to get out.

He glanced cautiously at the girl and the boy, who were gazing at him ingenuously. He saw instantly that the way, if there was a way, lay through them. But the plan had not yet formed when the boy leaned forward and spoke.

"I have an odd thing in my head," Lappy said bashfully, "that nevertheless radiates joy to my mind. In my reading I have seen things leap together from many books, forming a whole, and the whole is rare. Can you, in your wisdom, confirm or deny what I have seen? It is this—"

He spoke a short series of sentences. Navel tried to shush him, embarrassed, but he doggedly went on. And Travis, stricken, found himself suddenly paying close attention.

For the words Lappy said, with minor variations, were Isaac Newton's Laws of Motion.

*

"There are the seven planets," Navel was saying gravely, "and the two lights—that is, the sun and the moon. The first planet, that nearest the sun, is called Rym. Rym is the planet of intellect, of the ordinary mind. Second, is Lyndal, the planet of love, beauty, parties, marriage, and things of a gentle nature. Third is Fors, planet of action, strife. Fourth is Bonken, planet of beneficence, of gain, money, health. Next comes Huck, orb of necessity, the Greater Infortune, which brings men most trouble of all. Then Weepen, planet of illusion, of dreamers and poets and, poorly aspected, liars and cheats. And finally there is Sharb, planet of genius, of sudden cataclysms."

"I see," Travis murmured.

"But it is not only these planets and their aspects which is important, it is also to be considered such houses and signs as through which these planets transit . . . ."

She went on, but Travis was having difficulty following her. He could not help but return to Newton's Laws. It was incredible. Here on this backward planet, mired in an era roughly equivalent to the time of the Renaissance, an event was taking place almost exactly at the same time as it had happened, long ago, on Earth. It had been Isaac Newton, then. It was, incredibly, this frail young man named Lappy now. For unless Travis was greatly mistaken, Navel's kid brother was an authentic genius. And such a genius as comes once in a hundred years.

So, naturally, Lappy would have to come home with Travis. The boy was hardly college age as yet. Sent to school by Allspace, given a place in the great Allspace laboratories at Aldebaran, young Lappy might eventually make the loss of the contract at Mert seem puny in comparison to the things that head of his could produce. For Lappy was a natural resource, just as certainly as any mine on Mert, and since the advent of Earth science meant Mert would no longer be needing him, Lappy could go along with Travis and still leave him a clear conscience.

But the question still remained: how? He could not even get himself out, yet, let alone Lappy. And the girl. What about the girl?

He brooded, groping for an out. But in the meanwhile he listened while the girl outlined Mert's system of astrology. He had realized finally that the key to the business lay there. Astrology was these people's most powerful motivating force. If he could somehow turn it to his advantage—He listened to the girl. And eventually found his plan.

"Ho!" he said abruptly. Startled, the girl stared at him.

"Lightning in the brain," Travis grinned, "solutions effervesce. Attend. Of surety, are not *places* on Mert also ruled by the stars? Is it not true that towns and villages do also have horoscopes?"

Navel blinked.

"Why, see thee, it is in the nature of things, odd man, that all matter is governed by the planets. How else come explanations, for example, of natural catastrophes, fires, plagues, which affect whole cities and not others? And consider war, does not one country win, and the other lose? Of a surety different aspects obtain . . . ."

"Joy then," Travis said. "But do further observe. Is it not so, in your astrology, that a man's horoscope may often conflict with that of the place wherein he dwells? Is it not so that, often, a man is promised greater success in other regions, where the ruling stars more closely and friendlily conjoin his own?"

"Your mind leaps obstacles and homes to the truth," Navel said approvingly. "Many times has it been made clear that a man's fortune lies best in places ruled by his Ascendant, as witness, for example, those who are advised to take to the sea, or to southern lands . . . ."

"Intoxication!" Travis cried out happily, "then is our goal made known. Consider: from your poor natal horoscope, in this city, this land, no fortune arises. You doom yourself, with Lappy, by remaining here. But what business is this? Seek you not better times? Could you not go forth to another place, and so become people of gravity, of substance, of moment?"

The girl regarded for a moment, puzzled, then caught his point and shook her head sadly.

"Odd man, without profit. You misconstrue. Such as we, my brother and I, are not condemned by place, but by twistings of the character. My natal Huck, retrograde in the tenth, gives an untrustworthy, criminous person. It would be so here, there, anywhere. My pattern is set. Such travels as you describe are for those who conflict only with place. I, and my brother, it is our sad fortune to conflict with *all*."

"But this is the core," Travis insisted. "The conflict is with *Mert*! Consider, such travail as is yours stems from the radiations of Huck, of Weepen, of Scharb. But should you remove yourself beyond their reach, across great vastnesses of space to where other planets subtend—and in their alien radiation extinguish and nullify those of Huck—what fortune comes then? What rises, what leaps in joy?"

The girl sat speechless, staring at Travis with great soft eyes. The boy Lappy, who until that moment had been grinning happily over the news that his laws were true, suddenly understood what Travis was saying and let his mouth fall open.

But the girl sat without expression. Then, to Travis' dismay, a slow dark look of disgust came over her face.

"This," she said ominously, "this smacks of *vetching*."

The word fell like a sudden fog. Lappy, who had begun to smile, cut it sharply off. Travis, remembering what vetching meant to these people, gathered his forces.

"Woman," he said bitingly, "you speak in offense, but with patience and kindness I heal your insult. I control my choler, but my blood flows hot, therefore fasten your tongue. Tell me not that I have overvalued you, for your brain is clear, your courage thick. Wherefore speak of vetch? What vetch is there in travel? He vetches who leaves a certainty for another certainty, who attempts to avoid his starry fate. But you go from a certain end to an end not certain at all, to places of dark mystery, of grim foreboding. It may be that you perish, or pain in the extreme, as well as gain fortune. The end is not clear. This then is not vetching. Now retreat your words, and reply to me as one does to a friend, a companion, one who seeks your good."

He sat tautly while the girl thought it out. Eventually she dropped her eyes in submission and he sighed inwardly with relief. It was accomplished. He would have to shore it up perhaps with a little elaboration, but it was accomplished.

Ten minutes later he was standing free and unbound in the passageway. It was just barely in time. Down the round dark tunnel two men came.

*

Navel stopped gingerly over the bodies and gazed at Travis with awestruck admiration.

"A rare skill," she murmured, "they did flip and gyrate as dry leaves in the wind."

"Observe then," Travis said ominously, inspecting meanwhile the long slash down his arm with which Tude had nearly gotten him "and learn. And in the future receive my words with planetary respect."

"I will."

"And I," added Lappy, shaken.

"Fair. Bright. Now attend. How lies the path?"

"Through more such as these, I fear. This place in which we trouble lies at a dead end. We must proceed through great halls where many sit waiting, ere we arrive at the light."

"No other way? Think now."

"None."

Travis sighed.

"And they talk about luck. Well boy," he turned to Lappy, "give me your blunderbuss. Obtain that one's knife"—he indicated the sleeping Tude—"and let us carve our way out into the sunshine."

But as it turned out, the getting free was much easier than he had anticipated. There was only one band, the girl's own, between them and the opening, and these had fortunately just finished their evening meal when Travis stalked, black, gaunt and murderous, out of the tunnel into their large round room. Part of it was the surprise, part of it was the sudden knowledge that big Tude and the other man had already tried to stop him, but most of it was simply the look of him. He was infinitely ready. They were not, had no reason to be, and they took it automatically for granted that a man this confident must have the stars behind him. They regarded him thoughtfully as he went on by. No one moved. They were a philosophical people. When he had gone, taking the boy and girl with him, they discussed it thoroughly.

Out under the sky at last it was pitch black and the stars were shining. Travis realized that he had been in the sewer almost a full 24 hours. That meant that the eclipse was done, tomorrow would be a good day. There was not much time.

He commandeered the first carriage to come by, routing three elegantly dressed but unwarlike young men who fled in terror. He saw with relief that they thought him only another sewer rat, for if word of an Earthman robbing the local citizens ever got out there would be hell to pay, and in addition to his other troubles he could not abide that. He told Navel to head for the field where old 29 rested. Thoroughly bushed and beginning now to feel a woeful hunger, he sat back to brood.

At the ship young Trippe greeted him with haggard astonishment. He jumped forward joyfully.

"Trav! By jig, Trav, I thought we'd lost you. Old Dolly's over at the local police sta—" He stopped abruptly and stood slack-jawed as Navel and Lappy clambered fearfully through the lock. Travis glanced back. No spectators. Good.

"Now what in the sweet silly name—" Trippe began, but Travis stopped him.

"Russ, be a good kid. See if you can get me something to eat. Haven't had a bite in 24 hours."

"Sure, Trav, sure, only—what's with the Lower Depths here?"

"You might show them the showers," Travis grinned. "Or at least turn on the air conditioning. But listen, anything new on the contract?"

Trippe's face fell. "Not a thing. Even worse. Let me tell you. But ho, the food." He dashed off. Travis collapsed into a chair. A few moments later Trippe came back bearing food, but his eyes by now had begun to penetrate the dirt of the girl, and he stood watching her, bemused. Then suddenly he began to look happier than he had in several days. Travis told him briefly what had happened in the sewer, also about the brains of Lappy. Trippe was impressed. But he continued to regard the girl.

"Well," Travis said, munching, "fill me in on what's been going on. The eclipse come off?"

Trippe jerked. He focussed on Travis unhappily.

"Oh boy, did it come off. Wait'll you hear. Listen, you know the way it is now, I think they're going to kick *all* Earthmen off this planet. The M.C. says we may have to leave and come back a hundred years from now. Not anybody going to get a contract now."

"What happened?"

"Well, you wouldn't believe it. You have to understand these people's astrology. You know the little moon these people have—Felda, they call it—it's only a tiny thing, really only a few hundred yards wide. Well, when the Mapping Command first came by here they set down on that Moon and set up a listening post before landing, you know, the way they always do, to size up the situation through telescopes, radio, all that. Mostly they just orbit but this time they landed. God knows why. And took off again, naturally, throwing in the star drive. So today the eclipse comes off all right, but it comes off late."

He could not help smiling.

"You see what happened. A star drive is a hell of a force. It altered the orbit of the moon. Not enough to make any real difference, just a few hours a year, only minutes a day, but boy, you want to hear these people howl. And I guess you can see their point. Every movement that damn moon makes is important to them, they know where it should be to the inch. And now not only is it slightly off course, but so is every ephemeris printed on Mert. And they have them printed up, I understand, for the next thousand years. Which runs into money. We offered to pay, of course, but paying isn't going to help. It seems we've also messed up interpretations, predictions, the whole doggone philosophy. Oh it's a real ding dong. But contract? Not in a million years."

Travis sighed. That seemed to put the cap on it, all right. After all, when you start pushing people's moons around, where will it end? He brooded, his appetite gone. But he made a last effort.

"Did you discover anything at all we could use?"

"Nope. Not a thing. I finally figured the only thing to do was work on the astrology end of it, you know, maybe we could argue about interpretations. These people love to argue about interpretations. But no soap. It's too complicated. To learn enough

77

even to argue would take a couple of years. And besides Unico is here, and also Randall, and they all have the same idea. Anyway, I don't think it would work. The eclipse is too definite. You can't argue the eclipse."

"Well," Travis said with approval, "you were on the right track. You did what you could. At least we got *something* out of the deal." He indicated Lappy, who was at that moment fervidly examining the interior of the viewscreen.

Trippe nodded, but his eyes were on Navel.

"By jing," he said suddenly, "your luck holds good, no matter what. I never saw the beat of it—"

"Luck?" Travis fumed, "what luck?"

"Look, Trav, what else could you call it! You fall in a sewer, you come up with Isaac Newton and a gorgeous doll. It's uncanny, that's what it is, uncanny."

Travis lapsed into wordless musing on Navel, planets, people.

Come to think of it, he thought, it *is* uncanny.

At that moment there was a pounding on the lock. Travis quickly shooed Navel and Lappy into hiding, then cautiously went to the door. He relaxed. It was Ed Horton.

"I saw you come back, Trav. Mighty glad. But I knew you'd make it. Old Pat Travis always comes through. Aint that right, Pat?"

He tottered in the doorway. Travis caught the sweet scent of strong brew. He stepped forward to help him but Horton stood up grandly, waving him away. His mouth creased in an amiable grin.

"Diomed," he announced proudly, "is a nine planet system."

After which he fell backwards out of the door.

Trav ran to the door, stared down into the dark. Horton sat upright at the foot of the ladder.

"Sall right ole buddy. Dint mean to stay. Only thought you'd like to know natural sci-yen-tiffy fack. Diomed is nine plan' system."

He rose on wobbly but cheerful legs.

"No favoritism there, hey? Science. I just tell you a fack, you take it from there. No favoritism tall."

He lurched away mumbling cheerily, his obligation fulfilled.

Travis stared after him, wheels turning in his brain. Fack? A nine planet system. It jelled slowly, then broke.

Nine planets.

The key.

He turned slowly on Trippe, his eyes swivelling like twin dark cannon.

"What's he say?" Trippe said, half-smiling. "Boy, he was sure—"

"Did you know this was a nine planet system?"

"Why . . . sure, Trav. But what—"

"And did you take the trouble to examine their astrology?"

"Certainly. What the heck—"

"And you call it luck." Travis sighed, then broke into a radiant grin. "Why there's your bloomin' answer, you sad silly dreamin'—there's your bloomin' answer!" He sailed over to a drawer, grabbed a batch of fresh contracts, then flashed toward the door.

"Hold the fort," he bawled over his shoulder, "break out a big bottle and small glasses! We got a contract, lad, we got a contract!"

He vanished triumphantly into the night.

*

Old 29 was homing. Travis felt the great soft peace of deep space close over him. All was right with the world. A clean and sparkling Navel, well-bathed now and almost frighteningly beautiful, sat worshipfully at his feet dressed in a pair of Dahlinger's pajamas. Both Trippe and Dahlinger were regarding him with wonder and delight, and as he sat gazing down at them fondly he recalled with pleasure the outraged faces of the men from Unico, that robber outfit.

"Pat Travis," he chuckled, patting the fat contract in his pocket, "the luckless Pat Travis rides again." He turned an eye on the staring Trippe.

"My boy," he said paternally, "speaks me no speaks about luck, from this day forth. All the material was in your hands, there was no luck involved. All you had to do was use it."

"But Trav, I still don't get it. I've been thinkin' all night, all the while you were gone . . . ."

"The planet Pluto," Travis said evenly, "was discovered by Earthmen, finally, in the year 1930. At that time we were approximately 300 years ahead, technologically, of the people of Mert. A similar case exists for Neptune, which was not discovered, although adequate telescopes had long been in use, until 1846." He paused and gazed happily around. "Does the light dawn?"

"Holy cow!"

"Exactly. Diomed is a nine planet system. For which 'fack' thank old Ed Horton, who returned a favor done many years ago. Luck? Only if doing favors for people is lucky. Which I suppose you could make a case for. But in the astrology of Diomed III—an astrology I took great pains to understand—how many planets are considered? Let us examine. Rym, Fors, Lyndal, Bonken, Huck, Weepen, and Sharb. And then there are also the two 'lights,' that is, the sun and the moon. But how many *planets* are there? Counting Mert as one, add them up. It comes out eight. Not nine. Eight.

But Diomed is a nine planet system. Bless Ed Horton. What happened to the missing planet?"

Dahlinger whooped. "They didn't know they had one!"

Travis grinned. "With surety. They didn't know it existed. If they had their astrology would certainly have shown it. So it had obviously, like our own Pluto at a similar time, never been discovered."

He paused once again while Dahlinger and Trippe regarded him with delight.

"And you," Trippe said, "you showed them where it was."

Travis clucked. "I did not. For one thing, I didn't know where it was. I simply told him, very regretfully, that there *was* one, but the situation being what it was, I couldn't allow him to use our telescopes to plot its orbit. Unless, you see, there existed a concrete agreement between us.

"I added that I had heard that Earthmen would shortly be leaving his planet. Very unhappily I told him he could not expect to produce a telescope of the necessary power within at least the next hundred years. And even then, it would be many more years before they actually found it. I was very sorry about the whole business, so I just thought I'd drop by to offer my regrets."

"And he leaped at the chance."

"No. You rush to conclusions. He did not leap at the chance. He sat very quietly thinking about it. It was a gruesome sight. I could sympathize with him. On the one hand he had us, the unknown, moon-moving Us, with which he wanted no traffic whatever. But on the other side there was the knowledge of that planet moving all unwatched out in the black, casting down its radiations, be they harmful or good, and no way to know in what sign the thing was, or what house, or what effect it would have on him,*was having* on him, even as he sat there. Oh he struggled, but I knew I had him. He signed the contract. I think I may say, that it is among the most liberal contracts we have ever signed."

There was a long moment of silence in the ship. The young men sat grinning foolishly.

"So let me hear no more about luck," said Travis firmly. "In the future, sons, put your shoulders to the wheel . . . ."

But the attention of the two was already wandering. They were both beginning to gaze once more upon the lovely Navel, who was quite shyly but very womanly gazing back. He saw Trippe look at Dahlinger, Dahlinger glare at Trippe, their hackles rising. He looked down at Navel in alarm.

Born to cause trouble?

Oh no, he thought abruptly, seeing a whole new world beginning to open up, oh no, oh no . . . .

RESCUE SQUAD

by Thomas J. O'Hara

When Mr. O'Hara won the prize story contest recently conducted by THE FANTASY WRITERS' WORKSHOP *at the College of the City of New York, in conjunction with* FANTASTIC UNIVERSE, *it was the unanimous opinion of the judges that a second story by Mr. O'Hara,* RESCUE SQUAD, *deserved honorable mention. We think you'll agree with that decision when you've read this documentary-type science-fiction yarn, which so excitingly combines realistic characterization with the mystery, suspense and terror of the near future's exploration of space and a lone pilot's struggle to survive.*

Stark disaster to a brave lad in space may—to the mind that loves—be a tragedy pridefully concealed.

THE MAIL SHIP, MR4, spun crazily through space a million miles off her trajectory. Her black-painted hull resembled a long thermonuclear weapon, and below her and only a scant twenty million miles away burned the hungry, flaming maw of the Sun.

The atomic-powered refrigeration units of the MR4 were working full blast—and still her internal and external temperatures were slowly and inexorably rising. Her atomic engines had been long since silenced—beaten by the inexhaustible, fiery strength of the invincible opponent waiting patiently a narrowing twenty million miles "below."

Hal Burnett twisted painfully on the narrow space-bunk, his tormented body thrusting desperately against the restraining bands of the safety straps that lashed him in against the dangers of non-gravity.

He moaned, and twisted sideways, while his half-asleep mind struggled on an almost instinctive level against a dimly-remembered, utterly intolerable reality.

It was a losing battle. He was suddenly wide awake, staring in horror at the vibrating bulkheads of the deserted little mail ship. For a moment his conscious barriers against reality were so completely down that he felt mortally terrified and overwhelmed by the vast emptiness about him. For a moment the mad idea swept into his mind that perhaps the universe was just another illusion, an echo of man's own inner loneliness.

Realizing his danger, Burnett quickly undid the restraining safety straps, sat up and propelled himself outward from the edge of his bunk. The sudden surge of physical action swept the cobwebs from his mind.

He thought of his father—and there was bitterness in his heart and frustration, and a rebellious, smouldering anger. The old man would never know how close he had come to cracking up.

For a moment he wondered fearfully if his father's cold and precise appraisal of his character and courage had been correct. Suppose he *was* unable to stand the rigid strains and pressures of a real emergency. Suppose— He tightened his lips in defiant self-justification. What did they expect of a twenty-year-old kid anyway? He was, after all, the youngest and probably the greenest mail pilot in the entire Universal Run.

Suddenly the defensive barriers his mind had thrown up against the grievous flaw in his character, which made him feel uncertain of himself when he should have felt strong and capable, crumbled away completely. He could no longer pretend, no longer deceive himself. He hated his father because the elder Burnett had never known a moment of profound self-distrust in his entire life.

He remembered his father's favorite line of reasoning with a sudden, overwhelming resentment. "Fear can and must be controlled. If you have your objective clearly in mind a new experience, no matter how hazardous, will quickly become merely a routine obstacle to be surmounted, a yardstick by which a man can measure his own maturity and strength of purpose. You'll find peace of mind in doing your work ably and well and by ignoring all danger to yourself."

It was so easy to say, so hard to live up to. How, for instance, could a twenty-year-old kid on his *first* mail run hope to completely outwit fatigue, or even forget, for a single moment, that it *was* his first run. Fatigue had caused his undoing, but had he been completely fearless he might have found a way to save himself, might have managed somehow to prevent the small, navigational errors from piling up until they had carried him past the point of no return.

A constant re-checking of every one of his instruments might have saved him. But he had been too terrified to think straight, and too ashamed of his "first-run" inexperience to send out a short wave message requesting emergency instructions and advice. Now he was hopelessly off his course and it was too late. Too late!

He could almost feel the steadily-growing pull of his mindless enemy in the distant sky. Floating and kicking his way over to the Tele-screen, he quickly switched the instrument on. Rotating the control dials, he brought the blinding white image of the onrushing solar disk into perfect focus. Automatically he adjusted the two superimposed polaroid filters until the proper amount of light was transmitted to his viewing screen. They really built ships and filters these days, he reflected wryly. Now if they could only form a rescue squad just as easily—

Even through the viewing screen he could almost feel the hot blast of white light hit his face with the physical impact of a baseball bat. With what was almost a whimper of suppressed fear he rocked backward on his heels.

The Sun's ghastly prominences seemed to reach beckoning fingers toward him, as its flood of burning, radiant light seared through the incalculable cold of space, and its living corona of free electrons and energy particles appeared to swell and throb menacingly.

Fearfully he watched the flaming orb draw closer and closer, and as its pull grew more pronounced he wondered if it were not, in some nightmarishly fantastic fashion becoming malignantly aware of him. It resembled nothing so much as a great festering sore; an infection of the very warp-and-woof stuff of space.

He flipped off the power control on the Tele-screen and watched the image fade away with a depleted whine of dying energy. That incandescent inferno out there— Grimly he tried to recall the name of the man who had said that, philosophically, energy is not actually a real thing at all.

He knew better than to waste time trying the pilot controls again. They were hopelessly jammed by the great magnetic attraction of the Sun. They had been jammed for hours now. He forced his way back to his bunk, and securely lashed himself to it again. Sleep was his only hope now, his only real escape from the growing, screaming hysteria within him.

He flung an arm across his tired face. His thin features trembled as he remembered the continuous alterations in his trajectory that had brought him within range of the Sun's mighty pull. He remembered also every detail of the last and gravest of the series of miscalculations that had swept him from the established route of the regular Venus-Mercury mail run, and threatened him with a violent, flaming end.

Greatly off course, he had been approaching Mercury, a routine thirty-six million miles from the Sun. On this, the final leg of his long journey, he had deviated just far enough from the extreme limits of safety to find himself and his ship gripped inexorably in the mighty magnetic fields of the Sun's passage . . . .

He remembered a name— Josephine.

There would be no lover's meeting now on the green fields of Earth in the dusk of a summer evening. There would be no such meeting now. Not unless the prayers and dreams a boy and a girl had shared had followed him, plunging senselessly into the cold glacial heart of interstellar space.

His false bravado began to break and he began to weep quietly. He began to wish with all his heart that he had never left home.

The sudden crackling of the almost static-jammed ultra-wave radio snapped through to his mind. Quickly he began to free himself from the bunk.

"MR4, come in, MR4."

An eternity seemed to pass as he floated across the room, deliberately disregarding the strategically-placed hand-grips on the walls, floor, and ceiling. It seemed aeons before he reached the narrow little control compartment, and got the ultra-wave radio into action, nearly wrecking it in his clumsy-fingered haste.

"MR4 to Earth. Over."

He waited a few moments and then repeated the message as no acknowledgment came through. Then he abruptly remembered the nearby presence of the Sun and its interference with radio transmission and reception. He was white and shaken by the time his message was received and his report requested and given.

He gave the whole tragic picture in frantic short wave. The amount of atomic fuel left in the ship, the internal and external temperatures, the distance from the Sun, and the strength of the solar disk's magnetic field and his rate of drift toward it—along with a staggering list of other pertinent factors.

At last it was over and he stood by awaiting the decision from Earth headquarters. It came at last.

"MR4." The growling voice was Donnelly's, the huge space-engineer in charge of the smaller mail-rocket units. "You're in a tough spot but we've got an expert here from the Government. He's worked on deals like this with me before and he's got an idea.

"Here's the substance of it. We're going to send out a space tug from Mercury to see if we can haul you in. It's a new, experimental tug and it's been kept under wraps until now. But it's been designed for jobs like this and we figure it can sure as hell do it.

"There's just one hitch, though, kid. It's a mighty powerful ship so there's going to be a terrific shock when it contacts you and the magnetic grapples set to work. In your medicine kit you'll find a small hypo in a red-sealed plastic box. Take the shot that's in it immediately and we'll have the tug out there as soon as we can. It will probably take about twelve hours."

Donnelly's voice broke and he hesitated strangely for a moment. "You'll be out fast," he went on. "So you won't feel a thing when the shock wave hits you. There's less chance of injuries, this way."

*

"It's a lousy thing to do," cried Donnelly as he snapped off the set. "A rotten, heartless way of giving the lad false hopes. But then you don't give a damn about anybody's feelings but your own, do you, Doc?"

"Take it easy, Joe—"

"Shut up, Williams. I'm talking to this little Government time-server over here, not to you."

The psychiatrist shrugged wearily. "I don't care what you think. I've worked with you both on cases similar to this before, though I'll admit that none of them were quite as hopeless. In any case, I'll do it my way, or not at all."

"Maybe you will, maybe you will," said Donnelly. "But if I had to wait thirty days in that thing and somebody told me it was only a matter of hours—"

"I know what I'm doing even if you think that I don't. The Government has developed a set approach in matters like this. Fortunately, there aren't many of them. Perhaps if there were—"

"Let me take over, Doc," broke in Donnelly. "I'm a space-engineer and that makes me far better qualified to handle this than you are. Why the hell they ever put a psychiatrist on this job in the first place is something I'll never know, if I live to be a hundred and ten. It's a job for an engineer, not a brain washer."

"There's a lot of things you'll never know, Donnelly," the gaunt, thin little man sighed wearily. He sat down at the long mahogany table in the Radio Room. With a careless wave of one arm, he swept a pile of papers and magazines to the floor.

"Try and get this through your head, Donnelly. There's not too much you can do by yourself for that boy up there. You just don't know how to cope with the psychological intangibles. That's why they have me here—so that we could work together as a team.

"Now the sooner you get on that radio and follow my instructions for the pilot the sooner we'll get this over with. Then maybe I can go home and spend a hundred years trying to forget about it. Until then please try and keep your personal opinions to yourself. Please."

Donnelly's face flushed a still deeper red. His fists clenched and, as a muscle started to twitch warningly in his cheek, he started to get up. He stopped for a moment—frozen in silence. Then he relaxed and pushed back his chair. With a heavy sigh, he maneuvered his huge bear of a body to its feet.

He rumbled something disgustedly in his throat and then spat casually on the floor. "Williams," he thundered. "Get the hell out of here and get us some coffee."

He waited a moment until the only witness had left the room and then, with grim determination, he turned to the little psychiatrist seated at the table.

"You, Doc," he said coldly and with deliberate malice, "are a dirty, unclean little—"

*

Williams, when he eased his slight body through the door a few minutes later, found a suspicious scene. The little doctor, his face flushed and rage-twisted, his effortless and almost contemptuous composure shaken for once, was on his feet. Speechless, he faced the grinning space-engineer who was waving a huge and warning finger in his face.

"Easy, Doc," Donnelly roared in a friendly voice. "I might take advantage of it if you keep on giving me a good excuse. Then where would all your psychiatry and your fine overlording manners get you?"

"Joe," yelled Williams in explosive sudden fright. "Leave him alone. You're liable to have the Government Police down on us."

"Sure, Williams. The police and the newspapers too. They'd just love to have the taxpayers find out what they're doing to those kids out in deep space. What would they call it, Doc? Just an interesting psychological experiment? Is that what it's meant to be, eh, Doc?"

He chuckled suddenly as the little doctor flinched under his virulent attack. "I really hit the spot that time, didn't I, Doc? So that's what the Government's so scared and hush-hush about. They're really scared to hell and back, aren't they? I wonder what's really going on behind all this?"

He leaned forward, suddenly roaring and ferocious. "Why are Williams and I followed everywhere we go when we leave here? To see who we talk to? Is that the way of it? Why do quite a few of the ships you and I and Williams have rescued in the past few years never show up again? Just where are they? I don't see them reported missing in the newspapers, either."

He leaned back in exhausted satisfaction at the look on the little doctor's face. "Yeah, Doc, the only way to get anything out of you is to blast it out, isn't it?"

Pale and frightened, Williams hurried across the room to the table and, with shaky hands, took out three containers of coffee from the paper bag and passed them out.

Nobody bothered to thank him.

The hidden tension in the room had begun to mount steadily, so Donnelly helped it out a little.

"Is this the first time you've ever been on the defensive, Doc?" he asked.

Williams jumped in before the explosion. "When will the rocket get to the kid's ship, Doctor?" he asked.

"In about thirty days," the little man answered, coldly and deliberately.

Williams blinked in surprise. "Good Lord," he said. "I thought it was supposed to be in twelve hours or so?"

"That's the whole point," snapped Donnelly. "That's what I'm so fighting mad about. Think of it yourself, Williams. Suppose you had a son or a brother up there, how would you feel about this whole infernal, lying business?

"I don't get it," he went on. "I just don't get the big central idea behind it. Don't all these tugs we send out ever get there? First they tell the kid he'll have his life saved in twelve hours or so. Then they get him to take a shot so his mind won't crack up while he's waiting.

"Now they know very well the shot won't last for thirty days. If it did he'd starve to death. So what have they accomplished? Nothing. As a matter of fact they've made things worse instead of better. What's going to happen to that poor kid when he wakes up in twelve hours and finds out he still has to wait for thirty more days? What's going to happen to him then, Doc? Don't you think that kid will really go off his rocker for sure?"

Donnelly and Williams both looked at the little psychiatrist. He sat again at his former place at the table, white and shaken. His face was once again buried in one hand.

"Come on, Doc," whispered Williams, quietly. "What's going on here, anyway?"

"That's enough," cried the doctor, suddenly. He sprang up and strode toward the door. "Leave me alone," he exclaimed, almost in tears. "By heaven, I've had enough of this. I've had all I can stand."

Donnelly moved to block the door and the psychiatrist came abruptly to a halt. "That ain't enough, Doc. You get out after you talk."

"For God's sake, Joe."

"Shut up, Williams, I'm warning you for the last time."

"Let me by. I warn you, Donnelly. Let me by."

Williams moved in, regaining a sudden spurt of assurance. "What about that kid up there, Doc? Nobody's letting him by, are they, Doc?"

A look of utter weariness swept across the doctor's face.

"All right," he said. "You may as well know the truth then. You won't like or understand it, but here it is anyway. You see, there isn't any tug up there, experimental or otherwise. There was only our need for a good excuse—in this present case—to get him to take the drug. You're a space-engineer and a good one, Donnelly. That's why you were chosen for this job. If anybody could help those kids, you could."

Donnelly's face tightened warningly and the doctor hurried on. "You would have known about it if there had been any experimental models developed even if they had been secret. As a matter of fact, with your standing, you would probably have been working on them."

"Why all this, then, Doc? Why?"

"Because," the little doctor hesitated—and then shrugged. "I may as well tell you. It's not going to make any difference now, anyway. It was all done to put him out for several hours until—"

"Until what, Doc?" Donnelly's tone was harsh and uncompromising.

"You must understand that I'm under orders. I'm doing what is done in all these cases. Though heaven help me, I wish I didn't have to—"

"Doc," Donnelly roared. "You have been contradicting yourself all along and I intend to find out why."

"There isn't much more to find out . . . . Wait."

The doctor strode quickly over to the radio, and glanced at his wristwatch. His face haggard with strain, he turned to Williams. "Will you contact the MR4, please?"

He held up a silencing hand to Donnelly. "There's a reason behind all this. Just wait for a moment, please. Just wait and listen—"

*

It was a fumbling-fingered ten minutes later, after Donnelly had signed off, that Hal Burnett finally found the tiny red plastic box in the little emergency medical kit. Trembling he held it in his hand as he floated in free fall.

It was a little red key—a key to Earth, to life and to the chance to ram every cold, precise, contemptuous word down his father's over-analytical mouth.

He didn't really hate the old man but he knew that he feared him. He feared also that his father might be right about him after all. Who in his own mind, he thought bitterly, should know a son better than that son's own father.

A quick surge of elation swept over him as he swam quickly to the Tele-screen and switched it on. It wasn't a bit like saying good-bye to an old friend, he thought, as he gazed at the flaming prominences not so far below him. After a while he switched the instrument off and swam triumphantly back to his bunk.

There were some tri-dimensional color slides in the ditty bag hanging by his bunk. He took them out and looked at them. None of them were of his father.

The girl was there, though. She was a small, cute girl with a rainbow of laughter wreathed about her. She hadn't been really important before, but she sure was important now that he was going to live. His old man had foretold that, too.

After a little while he put the slides back in the portable holder and broke open the plastic box. It contained a gleaming hypo filled with what looked like a small quantity of water. There was an odd peppermint-like odor about it.

There were no instructions. Just the needle and the little red box.

He wondered how many hours he would have to wait before help would come. But that didn't matter. He would be asleep, anyway.

The temperature had climbed. It was burning, roaring hot.

Gently he slid the needle into his arm and depressed the plunger . . . .

*

The MR4 continued to spin even more lazily in space. Her sun-blackened hull, pitted by the glancing blows of by-passing meteor fragments, was slowly overheating. Her refrigeration units were gradually breaking down under their tremendous overload.

She was inching in ever-shortening circles always in the direction of the massive, molten globe not so far below . . . .

Sometime later, Hal Burnett awakened slowly, as if from some distant and dimly-remembered dream. The haze of a deep and foggy sleep clung to the unfamiliar mass that was his mind.

A distant alarm bell had rung deep within the primitive, subcortical levels of his brain. It had rung—but not loudly nor insistently enough. It had failed to cut through the eddying fog that was rising slowly into his ebbing consciousness.

He did not remember undoing the straps with benumbed and aching fingers. He did not remember the befogged and stumbling "walk" into the Control Room. Dimly, as if viewing himself and the room from a distant world, he switched on the dying hum of the radio and tried futilely to transmit a message.

The faint crackle of the radio grew more distant. He slumped forward in the bucket seat, his head striking the controls in front of him—and, for him, the sounds of the muted radio died out completely.

The burning heat seared into the metal hull of the MR4. Its outer hull was almost at the boiling point. Inside, it was a burning, suffocating hell. Perhaps it was the heat that aroused Hal Burnett once again. Somehow he managed to stumble to the Telescreen. With the last vestige of a waning strength, he managed to switch it on and hold himself erect.

The stupendous white blast of the Sun struck across his staring eyes, but he did not flinch. Unconscious, his hands clutched at the control knobs as his sagging legs let him drift weightlessly toward the floor. He was like a drowning swimmer, out of control and helplessly floating under water.

He seemed to become aware for a moment as a last flicker of consciousness crossed his mind. He mouthed something unintelligible—a last, forgotten word.

Anchored only by his grip on the control knobs, his weightless body floated aimlessly in the almost steaming cabin as the awful stillness re-echoed throughout the hollow vault of the ship.

Down below, with ever-growing closeness, the Sun waited patiently, like a bright and hovering vulture.

The MR4 swung and pivoted gently like a ship at sea straining at its anchor in the first, fresh breezes of a gathering storm. For a moment it seemed to hesitate like a coy maiden on the verge of some unknown threshold. Then, abruptly, she climaxed her voyage and plunged directly toward the waiting Sun some twenty million miles below, carrying with her only her dead cargo; her pilot—

*

The radio crackled noisily after Hal Burnett's last incoherent transmission. It crackled aimlessly for a few moments—and then was still.

"Something's wrong," said Williams, a thin thread of moisture shining down his face. "Something's gone wrong up there!"

"It sure has," said Donnelly, quietly. "And I know who I'm going to ask about it."

The little doctor said nothing. His face was an embittered parchment mask. "It's happened. God help me. It's happened. He's gone," he muttered, almost inaudibly.

Donnelly sighed heavily, a look almost of defeat sweeping momentarily across his features. "See here, Doc," he said exhaustedly. "Don't be so heartless about people. You've got a son of your own in space, so you ought to understand how other people feel. What kind of a father would do a thing like this to another man's son anyway?"

"Look, Donnelly," said the little man with bitter weariness. "Do me a favor will you? You fill out the reports tonight. Somehow or other I just don't feel up to it."

"Maybe it's your conscience," said Donnelly, sarcastically. "But I'll be damned if I'll do it for you. You don't like to do your own dirty work, do you, Doc? I thought you just loved to fill out Government reports."

"Donnelly, Donnelly," cried the doctor in sudden anguish. "Can't you understand yet. Even an undertaker's job is unpleasant but somebody's got to do it. Don't you see yet? *It has to be done!*"

With a muffled groan of disgust, Donnelly sprang to the radio once again, pushing Williams roughly aside. Futilely, and in desperation he strained at the controls for a moment and then, with a roar of fury, he turned back to the doctor.

"Now see here, Doc—" he thundered, and then stopped in amazement.

The door to the dim and ill-lighted outer hallway of the lab was standing open. And at the far end, the outer door was quietly closing behind the disappearing figure of the bent-shouldered little man.

Donnelly started to spring after him, and then abruptly stopped. His huge figure slumped in sudden despairing futility as he recognized the tragic hopelessness of the situation.

"Let him go," rasped Williams. "There's nothing we can do now anyway, Joe."

"Yeah, yeah. Let's write the report up ourselves. That's real important, you know. The Government needs it."

He sat down at the typewriter, his heavy features twisted in hopeless bitterness and anger. He started typing, and then stopped for a moment.

"What was this kid pilot's full name, Williams?"

Williams checked the Government order sheet. "Hell," he said. "Strangely, it's the same as the doctor's, Dr. Alfred Burnett. Only the kid's name is Harold Burnett."

Donnelly sat, suddenly transfixed, staring at his typewriter. A peculiar look flashed across his face. Then he shook his massive head in an unbelieving gesture of agonized understanding.

"Hell, no," he muttered to himself. "It couldn't be. It just couldn't be. It just isn't possible. Burnett! *Burnett!*"

Swiftly he was on his feet and moving through the door after the vanished figure of the little doctor, his face a mask of grim remorse.

"It was merciful," he muttered. "Yes, it *was* merciful. It was the only thing Doc Burnett could have done."

Williams stared after Donnelly's disappearing figure in frank and open-mouthed amazement.

"Hey, Joe," he yelled. "Where the hell are you going?"

The outer door slammed shut on the departing echo of his words. "Well, I'll be hung for an ugly son!" he muttered to himself. "Nobody makes sense around this place, any more."

He shrugged half to himself and then began to type out the rest of the report.

"I don't get it," he mumbled to himself. "I just don't get it at all. There's no logic in it."

THE SHINING COW

by Alex James

This is NOT a story about sinister aliens from outer space. This is simply the story of what happened to poor Junius when she found herself much too close to a Flying Saucer, long enough so she could be analyzed and long enough to cause some strange happenings on that farm.

Robbie whined and acted like his eyes were burning, as if he'd gotten dust or something even stranger into them . . . .

ZACK STEWART stared sleepily into the bottom of his cracked coffee cup as his wife began to gather the breakfast dishes.

Mrs. Stewart was a huge, methodical woman, seasoned to the drudgery of a farm wife. Quite methodically she'd arise every morning at 4:00 A.M. with her husband and each would do their respective chores until long after the sun had set on their forty-acre farm.

"You've jest got to find Junius today, Zack," Mrs. Stewart spoke worriedly, "Lord only knows her condition, not being milked since yesterday morning."

"Yeah, I know, Ma," Zack said wearily as he rose from the table, "I'll search for her again in the north woods, but if she ain't there this time, I give up."

A dog suddenly howled outside. There was a brief instant when neither moved, then Zack suddenly exclaimed, "It's Robbie!" and dashed outside.

In the light from the open doorway Zack saw the dog creeping along on his haunches, howling and whining, and scratching frantically at his tear-streaming eyes.

"Skunk finally got ya, eh boy?" Zack spoke sympathetically as the dog, fawning, came closer.

"Stay away, Robbie, stay away now!" he ordered the dog. Robbie whined and scratched again, furiously. Zack sniffed cautiously, expecting any moment the pungent smell of skunk fluid to hit his nostrils. He sensed nothing but the clean, fresh smell of the morning air, so he leaned closer. Within a foot of Robbie, he sniffed again. Nothing. He realized it wasn't a skunk that caused Robbie's eyes to burn. He knelt down and took the dog's head tenderly in his rough, calloused hands and examined his eyes. They were bloodshot and watery. He took some water from the well and dashed it into the dog's eyes as Robbie struggled.

"Hold still, boy, I'm trying to help ya," Zack soothed. He took out a blue work bandanna and wiped tenderly around Robbie's eyes.

"What did it, boy? How did it happen?" Zack asked. Robbie merely whined.

"What's wrong with him?" Mrs. Stewart, broom in hand, asked from the doorway.

"Don't rightly know," Zack patted the dog, "acts like he got something in his eyes."

"Skunk?"

"Naw," Zack shook his head. "He don't smell. Something else."

"Cat?"

"No scratches, either. He acts like they're burnin' him, like he got dust or somethin' in 'em."

"Well, take him out to the barn and you better get after Junius."

"Yeah, Ma. Come on, Robbie." He led Robbie to the barn and made him lie on a bed of hay in one of the stalls then returned to the kitchen for his lantern. He put on his thick denim jacket and work cap and turned to his wife.

"If she ain't in the woods, I'll come back and git the truck and drive over to the Leemers and see if he seen her."

He left the kitchen and shone the lantern around in the farmyard to get his bearings, then headed for the north end of his farm. He could see the faint glimmer of dawn in the east, more pronounced in the northeast, and even more so due north. He rubbed his eyes. A much brighter glow outlined the treetops in the north woods, that made the dawn on the eastern horizon look like a dirty gray streak. His first thought was of fire, but there was no smoke, no flame.

Zack walked dazedly toward the woods, his eyes glued to the light above the trees. Soon he was in the woods, and he could see the brightness extended down through the trees from the sky, on the other side of the woods. He approached cautiously as the light grew brighter, and came to the clearing where it was most intense. A thick bush obstructed his view, and Zack moved it aside then uttered a hoarse gasp, as he clutched at his eyes.

For a moment he felt he was dreaming. He squinted between the slits of his fingers. The glow was still piercing, but he could see the brightly lit Junius, radiating blue-white light, nibbling at the sparse grass in the clearing. Zack stood transfixed, his eyes widening behind his fingers. He felt the tears and the burning sensation, and squinted tightly, turning his head from the unbelievable scene.

*

Zack didn't remember his return to the farmhouse, or incoherently trying to explain to his wife the scene he had witnessed. A stiff jolt of elderberry wine drove off the jitters and reasoning returned. His wife sat patiently, eyeing him oddly, as Zack muttered over and over again, "It's unbelievable! It's unbelievable!"

Mrs. Stewart rose. "I'm going out and see fer myself. And, Zack, if yer lying to me—"

Zack jumped from the chair, barring her way.

"Believe me, maw, it's true. Don't go out there. It might be too much fer ya."

"It's the craziest thing I ever heard," Mrs. Stewart scoffed. "A cow that shines like the sun!"

"Look, maw, will ya jest come with me as fer as the pasture, you can see the glow from there, and mebbe that might convince ya."

"Yes, yes, I will." Mrs. Stewart jerked off her apron. "I declare, Zack, I think these chores are getting the best of ya."

They walked to the pasture, their eyes on the treetops of the north woods. A faint glow began to appear.

"See! See!" Zack pointed, laughing crazily.

"Let's get closer, looks like a fire," Mrs. Stewart said.

"Ain't no fire." Zack's tone was angry. "It's Junius and she's all lit up like a Christmas tree."

"Zack, now you stop that kinda crazy talk. There's a reason behind everything, and I'm sure there's one fer this."

"There is a reason, maw. Junius. She's got the whole clearing lit up like the noonday sun. Lord only knows how she got that way, but she's shining out there like a great big light bulb, only brighter."

Mrs. Stewart quickened her pace towards the clearing.

"I'm going to see fer myself," she said determinedly, "and put an end to this foolish nonsense."

"Alright, maw," Zack spoke resignedly, "if yer mind's set. But I'm warning ya, ya better squint yer eyes tight. She's too bright to look at. Poor Robbie must have got too good a look at her."

Mrs. Stewart approached the clearing ahead of her husband, and moved the same bush aside that had obstructed her husband's view. Her gaze caught the brightly radiating figure of Junius, and Mrs. Stewart screamed, clasping her face with her hands. Zack had his head turned, but he groped for his wife, grasped her arm and led her from the clearing.

"It's too crazy to believe, Zack," she whispered in awe; "What are we going to do? What has happened to poor Junius?"

"I don't know what happened to her," Zack answered, "but I know what I'm going to do about it. I'm going to call the University and git them scientist fellas down here."

"You suppose they can git close enough to milk the poor thing?" Mrs. Stewart clasped her hands in frustration. "She's probably in misery."

Zack shook his head. "Ain't no tellin' what they're liable to do after they seen her. Most likely they'll want to ship her to the University to examine her and see how she got that way."

"Why don't we call the Vet'nar'n?" Mrs. Stewart asked. "It might be some kind of new disease."

"It ain't no disease, maw. It's something nobody in the whole world ever seen or heard of before. I jest hope I can convince them University fellas to come down here."

"Don't you think you better tie Junius so she won't stray?"

"Better wait and see what them scientists say. Besides, if she strays, all we gotta do is follow the light!"

*

Zack did the most important chores and at eight A.M. on the dot he called the State University.

The operator at the switchboard answered sleepily.

"Good morning, State University."

"Mornin', ma'am. I'd like to talk to one of them scientist fellas."

"To whom in particular did you wish to speak?"

"Any of 'em that ain't busy. I got somethin' important to tell 'em."

"If I knew what it was about," the operator was becoming irritated, "I'd connect you with the right party."

Zack hesitated, reluctant to give his startling news to a mere operator. Instead, he hedged. "Well, who would have charge of things that light up?"

"Oh, you want the electrical engineering lab. Just a moment, sir."

There was a series of clicks and buzzes in the earpiece then Zack heard a man's deep voice.

"Hello."

"Hello," Zack replied, "this the electrical engineering lab?"

"Yessir, that's right."

"Well, my name is Zack Stewart and I own a forty-acre farm on the Canal Road just outside of Smithville."

"I'm Professor Donnell, can I help you?"

"Yeah," Zack took a deep breath then began, "my cow Junius was missing since yesterday morning and this morning when I went out to search for her again, I found her."

"Mr. Stewart," Professor Donnell's voice was impatient, "I'm a very busy man with a heavy class schedule. Why in the world would I care if you found your cow or not?"

"You'd care if you knew how I found her."

"Alright, Mr. Stewart, how did you find your cow, with some new kind of radar?"

"Nossir, I found her by following the bright light in the north wood and when I got there, there was Junius lit up like a neon sign."

"Mr. Stewart, are you drunk?"

"I knew you wouldn't believe me. All I can say is, come see for—"

Zack heard a sudden click then an immediate buzzing. Professor Donnell had hung up.

*

He had no sooner replaced the phone when there was a pounding on the door. He opened it and saw six state troopers and four important-looking gentlemen in civilian dress. A trooper who looked as though he might be in charge, spoke to Zack.

"Sir, we don't want you or your wife to get panicky, but we have reason to believe that something strange is going on in your woods. These men are from the atomic research laboratory at the University and they are convinced that a flying saucer has landed out there."

"It ain't no flying saucer," Zack spoke wearily.

"It isn't?" one of the gentlemen asked, disappointed, "then what is it?"

"It's Junius, my cow."

"Your—WHAT?" the state trooper exclaimed incredulously. "Are you nuts?"

Angrily, Zack jerked his thumb in the direction of the north woods.

"Jest go out there and see fer yourself and then tell me I'm nuts."

They hurriedly left the house, looking back skeptically at Zack.

Zack and his wife stood in the doorway, watching them until they were out of sight in the woods.

"You watch 'em come busting back here in a minute, maw."

In a few moments they saw the men scrambling out of the woods, rushing madly for the house, holding their eyes.

"Now I don't have to convince anybody," Zack smirked.

By the time they reached the porch, they were all talking excitedly and rubbing their eyes. The state trooper in charge pulled Zack aside.

"Mister," he asked ominously, "what the hell happened to that cow?"

"I don't know," Zack spoke with sarcasm, "jest the way I found her."

The important-looking civilian bustled past the patrolman and confronted Zack.

"I'd like to use your phone," his hands moved nervously, "where is it?"

Zack showed him and the man rushed to it and hastily dialed a number.

"This is Professor Jonathon Sims, Nuclear Physicist at State University. Put me through immediately to the Governor. It's very important."

There was a slight pause as Sims drummed impatiently on the phone.

"Hello! Hello, Governor? Professor Sims. I'd like a contingent of National Guardsmen around the farm of Zack Stewart on the old Canal Road. A most astounding thing has happened out here. For the welfare of the Public, I urgently request this farm be placed under tight security check at once and the Federal Government notified immediately."

"Hey now, wait a minute, Mister—" Zack protested.

Sims motioned him into silence, his ear glued to the phone.

"Sir," he hesitated, glancing at the group sideways, "you won't believe this until you see it. But we have positive proof a saucer has landed here. Mr. Stewart's cow is radiating intense blue and white light, the kind that has been associated with the glow of flying saucers."

Sims paused, listening to the Governor. Zack saw him fidget and stick a forefinger in his collar.

"Honestly, Sir! I am not drunk! The cow is radiating light."

"See?" Zack grinned at him. "Now ya know how I felt."

Sims ignored him, concentrating on the phone.

"Yessir, there is a state trooper here." He turned to the one in charge. "He wants to speak to you." The trooper took the receiver.

"Hello, Governor. Sgt. Les Johnson of the Highway Patrol." Pause. "That's right, sir. There's a number of people here who can swear to it. Yessir." This time the trooper fidgeted. "I seen it too. Blue-white light, yessir. Nossir, we are not having a drinking party. The light was reported by the pilot of the Continental Airways early this morning and we investigated. Yessir." He held the receiver towards Sims. "He wants to talk to you again."

The Governor was finally convinced something indeed strange was happening at the Stewart place, but being a solid citizen and faithful servant of the people who elected him, he couldn't believe the fantastic story the professor and the trooper told him. He decided to see for himself and rang for his chauffeur after his telephone conversation with Professor Sims.

Meanwhile, Mrs. Stewart turned to Sims.

"Will you please tell us if Junius can be milked?"

"I really don't know yet, Mrs. Stewart. I'll have to investigate the area for harmful radio-activity first, then I'll have to check the cow, herself. Pardon me." He turned to the phone again.

Trying to keep his voice and emotion under control, Professor Sims called his laboratory at the University and ordered among other technical equipment, a Geiger counter, a gamma-ray detector, a portable lead shield, body and temperature thermometers, a portable X-ray machine, and a dozen pairs of smoked glasses.

The equipment arrived within the hour, and Professor Sims distributed it among his assistants with his instructions. It was understood that he alone would approach Junius, wearing his smoked glasses and carrying the protective lead shield, to make the initial test. If his tests proved that Junius could be safely approached, he would go back for the others.

"You look like one of them flying saucer fellas, yerself," Zack laughed, seeing Professor Sims donned in the lead shield and the dark glasses.

Sims waved at the crowd in the farmyard and walked awkwardly toward the glow in the north wood, less pronounced now in the daylight. They watched until his retreating figure disappeared into the woods, and they were still watching the spot for what seemed a long time afterward. One of the assistants fidgeted and looked at his watch.

"He's been in there twenty minutes. Wonder what he's doing?"

"I hope he's milking her," Mrs. Stewart said hopefully.

Zack chuckled as a thought struck him.

"What's so funny, Zack?" his wife asked.

"Junius," Zack's chuckle bubbled into laughter, "will be the first cow to give radiated milk."

*

Finally, after another fifteen minutes, they saw Professor Sims emerge from the woods. As he came across the pasture they could see that his smoked glasses were propped above his eyebrows and he was concentrating on a small notebook in his hand, shaking his head from time to time.

When he finally joined the waiting group, he was flooded with questions.

He gestured them into silence.

"Please, I cannot answer any questions as yet until I have consulted with my assistants. Sgt. Johnson, will you please have your men guard the clearing while we hold a conference?"

"Is it safe to get that close to her?" the trooper asked, unbelieving.

"I can assure you that it is. There is just a negligible amount of radio-activity present, and no more ultra-violet rays then there are in an average sun lamp. But you must wear your glasses." Turning to his aides he said, "Come gentlemen," and they followed him into the farmhouse.

"Can she be milked?" Mrs. Stewart wailed after them.

"What a gadawful situation," Zack muttered, grabbing a pitchfork and heading for the barn.

The scientists seated themselves around the big dining-room table and faced Professor Sims.

"Gentlemen, it's the most amazing thing that ever happened. That cow is glowing out there like a miniature atomic pile, and under the circumstances as we know them, should be deader than a door nail, but there she stands, shining like the morning sun, chewing her cud and just mooing away as if nothing happened."

"What is your theory, Professor?" one of the assistants asked.

"I have one, but it's utterly fantastic," Sims answered.

"So is that cow out there. Let's hear it!"

"Do you remember how much more frequent saucer sightings were reported in this area alone?" Sims asked. All the assistants nodded their heads.

"Well," Sims went on, "I am of the opinion that a saucer actually landed out there and they came across the cow by accident. They either shot her with some sort of radium ray gun, or some luminous substance unknown to us."

"Why didn't Junius die?" one of the assistants asked.

Sims shook his head. "They wished to examine her. You see, gentlemen, whatever it was, it served a threefold purpose. It made her luminous, immobile and—" Sims placed both hands on the table and leaned forward for emphasis, "transparent."

There was a gasp and exclamations.

"Transparent? How?—"

"I was within a foot of the cow, felt her hide, and through the glasses I could see the skeletal frame, the chest cavity, the heart beating within, the entire intestinal tract, much, much more clearly than could be seen by the best X-ray."

As if on command, the assistants all rose simultaneously.

"Sit down, gentlemen, the cow isn't going anywhere. We shall have to face this situation with sound scientific reasoning. There will be a closed van here soon to pick up Junius and haul her to the laboratory where we can examine her more thoroughly. Now my belief is that the saucer took off in haste, such great haste that they forgot to extinguish poor Junius. I believe they will be back looking for her, therefore we shall have to return her tonight and conceal ourselves around the area and watch."

"Splendid idea, Professor Sims!" one of the assistants exclaimed.

Yelling voices in the farmyard caught their attention. They saw Sgt. Johnson through the dining-room window, coming across the yard, yelling and pointing to the sky. Sims rushed from the house, met Johnson, grasped him by the shoulders, shaking him.

"What happened, man, what happened?" Sims asked.

"Black light, black light!" Johnson shouted, pointing skyward. Sims looked up. Nothing but the serene blue of the summer sky and an occasional bird caught his eye.

Sims shook him again, more roughly.

"Speak, man, what happened?"

"Black light flashed down on the cow! Blackest light you ever saw!"

The group gathered around him in the yard, trying to make sense out of what he said. So engrossed were they with his babblings, that none but Mrs. Stewart was aware of the fact that Junius had entered the farmyard and was eyeing them curiously.

"Junius!" she exclaimed.

"Moooo!"

The crowd looked up to see the ordinary, unlit Junius standing calmly by the gate.

"Hurry and get the milk pail, Zack, Junius is all right now!" Mrs. Stewart yelled happily to her husband, as Professor Sims and his assistants led the hysterical trooper into the house.

High over the horizon, a faint, silvery disc was disappearing at fantastic speed into outer space.

OF TIME AND TEXAS

by William F. Nolan

Twenty-eight-year-old William Nolan, another newcomer to the field, introduces us to the capricious Time Door of Professor C. Cydwick Ohms, guaranteed to solve the accumulated problems of the world of the year 2057.

Open the C. Cydwick Ohms Time Door, take but a single step, and—

"IN ONE fell swoop," declared Professor C. Cydwick Ohms, releasing a thin blue ribbon of pipe-smoke and rocking back on his heels, "—I intend to solve the greatest problem facing mankind today. Colonizing the Polar Wastes was a messy and fruitless business. And the Enforced Birth Control Program couldn't be enforced. Overpopulation still remains the thorn in our side. Gentlemen—" He paused to look each of the assembled reporters in the eye. "—there is but *one* answer."

"Mass annihilation?" quavered a cub reporter.

"Posh, boy! Certainly not!" The professor bristled. "The answer is—TIME!"

"Time?"

"Exactly," nodded Ohms. With a dramatic flourish he swept aside a red velvet drape—to reveal a tall structure of gleaming metal. "As witness!"

"Golly, what's *that* thing?" queried the cub.

"This *thing*," replied the professor acidly, "—is the C. Cydwick Ohms Time Door."

"Whillikers, a Time Machine!"

"Not so, not so. *Please*, boy! A Time Machine, in the popular sense, is impossible. Wild fancy! However—" The professor tapped the dottle from his pipe. "—by a mathematically precise series of infinite calculations, I have developed the remarkable C. Cydwick Ohms Time Door. Open it, take but a single step—and, presto! The Past!"

"But, *where* in the past, Prof.?"

Ohms smiled easily down at the tense ring of faces. "Gentlemen, beyond this door lies the sprawling giant of the Southwest—enough land to absorb Earth's overflow like *that*!" He snapped his fingers. "I speak, gentlemen, of Texas, 1957!"

"What if the Texans *object*?"

"They have no choice. The Time Door is strictly a one-way passage. I saw to that. It will be utterly impossible for anyone in 1957 to re-enter our world of 2057. And now—the Past awaits!"

He tossed aside his professorial robes. Under them Cydwick Ohms wore an ancient and bizarre costume: black riding boots, highly polished and trimmed in silver; wool chaps; a wide, jewel-studded belt with an immense buckle; a brightly checked shirt

101

topped by a blazing red bandana. Briskly, he snapped a tall ten-gallon hat on his head, and stepped to the Time Door.

Gripping an ebony handle, he tugged upward. The huge metal door oiled slowly back. "Time," said Cydwick Ohms simply, gesturing toward the gray nothingness beyond the door.

The reporters and photographers surged forward, notebooks and cameras at the ready. "What if the door swings shut after you're gone?" one of them asked.

"A groundless fear, boy," assured Ohms. "I have seen to it that the Time Door can never be closed. And now—good-bye, gentlemen. Or, to use the proper colloquialism—*so long, hombres!*"

Ohms bowed from the waist, gave his ten-gallon hat a final tug, and took a single step forward.

And did *not* disappear.

He stood, blinking. Then he swore, beat upon the unyielding wall of grayness with clenched fists, and fell back, panting, to his desk.

"I've failed!" he moaned in a lost voice. "The C. Cydwick Ohms Time Door is a botch!" He buried his head in trembling hands.

The reporters and photographers began to file out.

Suddenly the professor raised his head. "*Listen!*" he warned.

A slow rumbling, muted with distance, emanated from the dense grayness of the Time Door. Faint yips and whoopings were distinct above the rumble. The sounds grew steadily—to a thousand beating drums—to a rolling sea of thunder!

Shrieking, the reporters and photographers scattered for the stairs.

Ah, another knotty problem to be solved, mused Professor Cydwick Ohms, swinging, with some difficulty, onto one of three thousand Texas steers stampeding into the laboratory.

THE HELPFUL ROBOTS

by Robert J. Shea

Robert J. Shea, of Rutgers University, makes an interesting contribution to robotics with this story of Rankin, who prided himself on knowing how to handle robots, but did not realize that the robots of the Clearchan Confederacy were subject to a higher law than implicit obedience to man.

They had come to pass judgement on him. He had violated their law—wilfully, ignorantly, and very deliberately.

"OUR people will be arriving to visit us today," the robot said.

"Shut up!" snapped Rod Rankin. He jumped, wiry and quick, out of the chair on his verandah and stared at a cloud of dust in the distance.

"Our people—" the ten-foot, cylinder-bodied robot grated, when Rod Rankin interrupted him.

"I don't care about your fool people," said Rankin. He squinted at the cloud of dust getting bigger and closer beyond the wall of *kesh* trees that surrounded the rolling acres of his plantation. "That damned new neighbor of mine is coming over here again."

He gestured widely, taking in the dozens of robots with their shiny, cylindrical bodies and pipestem arms and legs laboring in his fields. "Get all your people together and go hide in the wood, fast."

"It is not right," said the robot. "We were made to serve all."

"Well, there are only a hundred of you, and I'm not sharing you with anybody," said Rankin.

"It is not right," the robot repeated.

"Don't talk to me about what's right," said Rankin. "You're built to follow orders, nothing else. I know a thing or two about how you robots work. You've got one law, to follow orders, and until that neighbor of mine sees you to give you orders, you work for me. Now get into those woods and hide till he goes away."

"We will go to greet those who visit us today," said the robot.

"Alright, alright, scram," said Rankin.

The robots in the fields and the one whom Rankin had been talking to formed a column and marched off into the trackless forests behind his plantation.

A battered old ground-car drove up a few minutes later. A tall, broad-shouldered man with a deep tan got out and walked up the path to Rankin's verandah.

"Hi, Barrows," said Rankin.

"Hello," said Barrows. "See your crop's coming along pretty well. Can't figure how you do it. You've got acres and acres to tend, far's I can see, and I'm having a hell of

103

a time with one little piece of ground. I swear you must know something about this planet that I don't know."

"Just scientific farming," said Rankin carelessly. "Look, you come over here for something, or just to gab? I got a lot of work to do."

Barrows looked weary and worried. "Them brown beetles is at my crop again," he said. "Thought you might know some way of getting rid of them."

"Sure," said Rankin. "Pick them off, one by one. That's how I get rid of them."

"Why, man," said Barrows, "you can't walk all over these miles and miles of farm and pick off every one of them beetles. You must know another way."

Rankin drew himself up and stared at Barrows. "I'm telling you all I feel like telling you. You going to stand here and jaw all day? Seems to me like you got work to do."

"Rankin," said Barrows, "I know you were a crook back in the Terran Empire, and that you came out beyond the border to escape the law. Seems to me, though, that even a crook, any man, would be willing to help his only neighbor out on a lone planet like this. You might need help yourself, sometime."

"You keep your thoughts about my past to yourself," said Rankin. "Remember, I keep a gun. And you've got a wife and a whole bunch of kids on that farm of yours. Be smart and let me alone."

"I'm going," said Barrows. He walked off the verandah and turned and spat carefully into the dusty path. He climbed into his ground-car and drove off.

Rankin, angry, watched him go. Then he heard a humming noise from another direction.

He turned. A huge, white globe was descending across the sky. A space ship, thought Rankin, startled.

Police? This planet was outside the jurisdiction of the Terran Empire. When he'd cracked that safe and made off with a hundred thousand credits, he'd headed here, because the planet was part of something called the Clearchan Confederacy. No extradition treaties or anything. Perfectly safe, if the planet was safe.

And the planet was more than safe. There had been a hundred robots waiting when he landed. Where they came from he didn't know, but Rankin prided himself on knowing how to handle robots. He'd appropriated their services and started his farm. At the rate he was going, he'd be a plantation owner before long.

That must be where the ship was from. The robot said they'd expected visitors. Must be the Clearchan Confederacy visiting this robot outpost. Was that good or bad?

From everything he'd read, and from what the robots had told him, they were probably more robots. That was good, because he knew how to handle robots.

The white globe disappeared into the jungle of *kesh* trees. Rankin waited.

A half hour later the column of his robot laborers marched out of the forest. There were three more robots, painted grey, at the head. The new ones from the ship, thought Rankin. Well, he'd better establish who was boss right from the start.

"Stop right there!" he shouted.

The shiny robot laborers halted. But the three grey ones came on.

"Stop!" shouted Rankin.

They didn't stop, and by the time they reached the verandah, he cursed himself for having failed to get his gun.

Two of the huge grey robots laid gentle hands on his arms. Gentle hands, but hands of superstrong metal.

The third said, "We have come to pass judgement on you. You have violated our law."

"What do you mean?" said Rankin. "The only law robots have is to obey orders."

"It is true that the robots of your Terran Empire and these simple workers here must obey orders. But they are subject to a higher law, and you have forced them to break it. That is your crime."

"What crime?" said Rankin.

"We of the Clearchan Confederacy are a race of robots. Our makers implanted one law in us, and then passed on. We have carried our law to all the planets we have colonized. In obeying your orders, these workers were simply following that one law. You must be taken to our capital, and there be imprisoned and treated for your crime."

"What law? What crime?"

"Our law," said the giant robot, "is, *Help thy neighbor*."

THE FLYING CUSPIDORS

by V. R. Francis

A trumpet-tooter in love can be a wonderful sight, if Local 802 will forgive our saying so; when extraterrestrials get involved too—oh brother! V. R. Francis, who lives in California and has previously appeared in men's magazines, became 21 and sold to FANTASTIC UNIVERSE *all in the same week.*

This was love, and what could be done about it? It's been happening to guys for a long time, now.

HOTLIPS GROGAN may not be as handsome and good-looking like me or as brainy and intellectual, but in this fiscal year of 2056 he is the gonest trumpet-tooter this side of Alpha Centauri. You would know what I mean right off if you ever hear him give out with "Stars Fell on Venus," or "Martian Love Song," or "Shine On, Harvest Luna." Believe me, it is out of this world. He is not only hot, he is radioactive. On a clear day he is playing notes you cannot hear without you are wearing special equipment.

That is for a fact.

Mostly he is a good man—cool, solid, and in the warp. But one night he is playing strictly in three or four wrong keys.

I am the ivory man for this elite bunch of musicians, and I am scooping up my three-dee music from the battered electronic eighty-eight when he comes over looking plenty worried.

"Eddie," he says, "I got a problem."

"You got a problem, all right," I tell him. "You are not getting a job selling Venusian fish, the way you play today."

He frowns. "It is pretty bad, I suppose."

"Bad is not the word," I say, but I spare his feelings and do not say the word it is. "What gives?"

He looks around him, careful to see if anybody in the place is close enough to hear. But it is only afternoon rehearsal on the gambling ship *Saturn*, and the waiters are busy mopping up the floor and leaning on their long-handled sterilizers, and the boys in the band are picking up their music to go down to Earth to get some shut-eye or maybe an atomic beer or two before we open that night.

Hotlips Grogan leans over and whispers in my ear. "It is the thrush," he says.

"The thrush?" I say, loud, before he clamps one of his big hands over my kisser. "The thrush," I say, softer; "you mean the canary?"

He waves his arms like a bird. "Thrush, canary—I mean Stella Starlight."

106

For a minute I stand with my mouth open and think of this. Then I rubber for the ninety-seventh time at the female warbler, who is standing talking to Frankie, the band leader. She is a thrush new to the band and plenty cute—a blonde, with everything where it is supposed to be, and maybe a little extra helping in a couple spots. I give her my usual approving once-over, just in case I miss something the last ninety-six approving once-overs I give her.

"What about her?" I say.

"It is her fault I play like I do," Hotlips Grogan tells me sadly. "Come on. Leave us go guzzle a beer and I will tell you about it."

Just then Frankie comes over, looking nasty like as usual, and he says to Grogan, "You are not playing too well today, Hotlips. Maybe you hurt your lip on a beer bottle, huh?"

As usual also, his tone is pretty short on sweetness and light, and I do not see why Grogan, who looks something like a gorilla's mother-in-law, takes such guff from a beanpole like Frankie.

But Grogan only says, "I think something is wrong with my trumpet. I have it fixed before tonight."

Frankie smirks. "Do that," he says, looking like a grinning weasel. "We want you to play for dancing, not for calling in Martian moose."

Frankie walks away, and Hotlips shrugs.

"Leave us get our beer," he says simply, and we go to the ferry.

We pile into the space-ferry with the other musicians and anyone else who is going down to dirty old terra firma, and when everybody who is going aboard is aboard, the doors close, and the ferry drifts into space. Hotlips and I find seats, and we look back at the gambling ship. It is a thrill you do not get used to, no matter how many times you see it.

The sailor boys who build the *Saturn*—they give it the handle of *Satellite II* then—would not know their baby now, Frankie does such a good job of revamping it. Of course, it is not used as a gambling ship then—at least not altogether, if you know what I mean. Way back in 1998 when they get it in the sky, they are more interested in it being useful than pretty; anybody that got nasty and unsanitary ideas just forgot them when they saw that iron casket floating in a sky that could be filled with hydrogen bombs or old laundry without so much as a four-bar intro as warning.

Frankie buys *Satellite II* at a war surplus sale when moon flights become as easy as commuters' trips, and he smoothes out its shape so it looks like an egg and then puts a fin around it for ships to land on. After that, it does not take much imagination to call it the *Saturn*. Then he gets his Western Hemisphere license and opens for business.

My daydreaming stops, for suddenly Hotlips is grabbing my arm and pointing out the window.

"What for are you grabbing my arm and waving your fist at the window, Hotlips?" I inquire politely of him.

"Eddie," he whispers, all nervous and excited from something, "I see one."

I give him a blank stare. "You see one what?"

"One flying cuspidor," he says, his face serious. "I see it hanging out there by the *Saturn* and then suddenly it is gone. Whoosh."

"Hallucination," I tell him. But I look out hard and try to see one too. I don't, so I figure maybe I am right, after all.

I do not know about this "men from space" gimmick the science-fiction people try to peddle, but lots of good substantial citizens see flying cuspidors and I think to myself that maybe there is something to it. So I keep looking back at the *Saturn*, but nothing unusual is going on that I can see. My logic and super-salesmanship evidently convinces Hotlips, for he does not say anything more about it.

Anyway, in a few minutes we joggle to a stop at Earthport, pile out, wave our identification papers at the doorman with the lieutenant's bars, and then take off for the *Atomic Cafe* a block away.

Entering this gem of a drinking establishment, we make our way through the smoke and noise to a quiet little corner table and give Mamie the high-sign for two beers. A few minutes later she comes bouncing over with the order and a cheery word about how invigorating it is to see us high-class gentlemen instead of the bums that usually hang around a joint like this trying to make time with a nice girl like her.

"That is all very nice," I say to her politely, "and we are overjoyed beyond words to see you too, Mamie, but Hotlips and I have got strange and mysterious things to discuss, so I would appreciate it if you would see us later instead of now." With this, I give her arm a playful pat, and she blushes and takes the hint.

When we are alone, I ask Hotlips, now what is the trouble which he has.

"Like I tell you before," Hotlips says, "I have a problem. So here it is." He takes a deep breath and lets fly all at once. "I am in love of the thrush, Stella Starlight."

I am drinking my beer when he says this, and suddenly I get a snootful and start coughing, and he whams me on the back with his big paw so I stop, more in self-defense than in his curing me. Somehow, the idea of a big bruiser like Hotlips Grogan in love of a sweet fluffy thing like Stella Starlight seems funny.

"So?" I say.

"So that is why I play so bad tonight," he says. Seeing I do not quite catch on to the full intent of his remarks, he continues. "I am a happy man, Eddie. I got my trumpet, a paid-for suit of clothes, a one-room apartment with green wallpaper. Could a man ask for much more?"

"Not unless he is greedy," I agree.

Hotlips Grogan is staring at his beer as though he sees a worm in it and looking sadder than ever. "It is a strange and funny thing," he says, dreamy-like. "There she is singing, and there I am giving with the trumpet, and all of a great big sudden—whammo!—it hits me, and I feel a funny feeling in my stomach, like maybe it is full of supersuds or something, and my mouth is dry just like cotton candy."

"Indigestion," I suggest.

He shakes his big head. "No," he says, "it is worse than indigestion." He points to his stomach and sighs. "It is love."

"Fine," I say, happy it is not worse. "All you got to do is tell her, get married and have lots and lots of kids."

Hotlips Grogan's big eyebrows play hopscotch around his button nose, so I can tell he does not think I solve all his troubles with my suggestion.

"You are a good man, Eddie," he tells me, "but you are too intellectual. This is an affair of the heart." He sighs again. "I am never in love of a girl before," he goes on, more worried, "and I do not know how to act. Besides, the thrush is with us only a day, and Frankie already is making with the eyes."

"So what should I do, give you lessons?" The idea is so laughable I laugh at it. "Anyway, Frankie always makes with the eyes at thrushes."

"Yes," Hotlips Grogan admits, "but never before have I been in love of any of the thrushes Frankie has made with the eyes at. Frankly, Eddie, I am worried like all get out about this."

"Sometimes I do not even understand the way you play even before the thrush comes, Hotlips," I admit. "Like for instance yesterday when we play 'A Spaceship Built for Two.' This is a song, as you know, that does not have in it many high notes, but even when you play the low notes they sound somewhat like they maybe are trying to be high notes. It is a matter which is perplexing to one of my curious nature."

Hotlips looks sheepish for a minute and then he says, "It is a physical disability with me, Eddie. When I am young and practicing with my trumpet one day, I have an accident and get my tongue caught in the mouthpiece, and it is necessary for the doctor to operate on my tongue and cut into it like maybe it is chopped liver."

"I am sorry to hear this, Hotlips," I say.

"I do not tell anyone this before, Eddie," Hotlips confesses. "But afterward when I play the trumpet, I play two notes at one time, which at first is pretty embarrassing."

"This is great, Hotlips," I proclaim as a big idea hits me; "you can play your own harmony. With talent like that, and my brain—"

But Hotlips is shaking his head. "No, Eddie," he says. "The other note is way off in the stratosphere someplace and no one can hear it, even when the melody note is low. And the higher the note is you can hear, the higher the other note is you cannot hear. Besides, now I cannot even play what I am supposed to play, what with the thrush around."

I sit there with my beer in my hand and think about it for a while, while Hotlips looks at me like a lost sheepdog. I scratch my head but I do not even come up with dandruff.

Finally, I say, "Well, thrush or not, if you play no better than you do this afternoon, Frankie will make you walk back home without a spacesuit."

"That is for positive," Hotlips agrees sadly. "So what can I do?"

I am forced to admit that I do not know just what Hotlips can do. "However," I say, "I have an idea." And I call Mamie over and tell her the problem. "So you are a woman and maybe you know what my musician friend can do," I suggest.

Mamie sighs. "I am at a loss for words concerning what your friend can do, but I know just how he feels, for it is like that with me, too. I am in love of a handsome young musician who comes in here, but he does not take notice of me, except to order some beer for him and his friend."

I click my teeth sympathetically at this news.

"And I am too shy and dignified a girl to tell him," Mamie continues sadly. "So you see I have the same problem as your friend and cannot help you."

"See," I whisper to Hotlips, "it is perfectly normal."

"Yes," he hisses back. "But I am still miserable, and the only company I desire is that of Stella Starlight."

"Maybe it really is your trumpet," I suggest, not very hopeful, though.

Hotlips shakes his head. "Look," he says and takes the trumpet from his case and puts it to his lips, "and listen to this."

Inwardly, I quiver like all get out, because I figure that is just what the management will tell us to do, once Hotlips lets go. Hotlips puffs out his cheeks and a soft note slides from the end of the trumpet—low, clear, and beautiful, without a waver in a spaceload. Only a few people close by can hear the note and they do not pay us any attention, except to think that maybe we are a little nuttier than is normal for musicians.

From his first note, Hotlips shifts to a higher note which is just as pretty. Then he goes on to another one and then to another, improvising a melody I do not hear before and getting higher all the time. After a while I can hardly hear it, it is so high, but I can feel the glass in my hand vibrating like it wants to get out on the floor and dance. I hold on to it with both hands, so my beer will not slosh over the side. Then there is no sound at all from the trumpet, but Hotlips' cheeks are puffed out and he is still blowing for all he is worth—which is plenty, if he can play like this when Stella Starlight is around.

I tap Hotlips on the shoulder. "Hotlips, that is all very well for any bats in the room which maybe can hear what you play, but—" He does not pay me any attention.

Suddenly there is a large crinkle-crash of glass from the bar and a hoarse cry from the bartender as he sees his king-size mirror come down in little pieces. At the same time, glasses pop into fragments all over the room and spill beer over the people holding them. Even my own glass becomes nothing but ground glass and the beer sloshes over the table. At the moment, however, I do not worry about that.

There are other things to worry about which are more important—like Hotlips' and my health, for instance, which is not likely to be so good in the near future.

Like I say, Hotlips does not play loud and it is noisy in the place, so there are not too many who hear him. But they look around, all mad and covered with beer, and see him there with the trumpet in his hand and a funny look on his big face, and they put two and two together. I can see they figure the answer is four. And what makes things worse, they are between us and the front door, so we cannot sneak past like maybe we are just tourists.

"Hotlips," I say to him, my voice not calm like is usual, "I think it is a grand and glorious idea that we desert here and take ourselves elsewhere."

Hotlips agrees. "But where?" he wants to know.

I am forced to admit to myself that he comes up with a good question.

"Over here," Mamie said suddenly, and we look across the room to see her poking her nose through a side door.

We do not wait for a formal invite but zoom across the floor and through the door into another, emptier room. Mamie slams the door and locks it just as two or three bodies thump into it like they mean business.

"The manager is out there and is not completely overjoyed with your actions of a short while ago," Mamie informs us, explaining, "I recognize the thump the character makes."

"Evidently," I surmise, "he is in no mood to talk to concerning damages and how we can get out of paying them, so we will talk to him later instead of now."

"See what I mean, though, Eddie," Hotlips says. "I play fine when Stella Starlight is not in the place. Like I say, it is love and what can I do about it."

"It is a problem," I say. "Even if you *do* play, you will no doubt be fired and cannot pay for the damages to the bar room and to the customers' clothing." Already there are holes in my plastic clothing where the beer splashes. "If you can only give out on the *Saturn* like you play here," I sigh, "we can break all records and show Frankie—"

Suddenly Mamie is tugging at my arm.

"Mamie," I inquire politely of her, "why are you tugging at my arm?"

"That is it," she informs me and leans forward and whispers in my ear.

"But—" I say.

"Hurry," she says, pushing us out another door. "You have only got this afternoon to do it."

"But—" I say again, and Hotlips and I are in the alley looking at the door which Mamie closes in our face.

"What does Mamie say?" Hotlips wants to know eagerly. "Can she fix it up with me and Stella Starlight?"

I scratch my head. "That I do not know, Hotlips, but she does give me an idea which is so good I am surprised at myself I do not think of it alone."

Hotlips gives me a blank stare. "Which is?"

"Come on," I say mysteriously. "You and me have got things to do."

It is hard to say who is more nervous that night, Hotlips or a certain piano player with my name. Frankie is smirking like always, and Stella Starlight is sitting and looking beautiful while she waits for her cue. Hotlips is fumbling with his trumpet like maybe he never sees one before. And I—even I am not exactly calm like always.

The band begins to warm up, but we do not knock ourselves out because there are still no customers to speak of. Frankie's license makes it plain that he has to stay over the western hemisphere so he has to wait until it gets dark enough there for the people to want to go night-clubbing, even though it is not really night on the *Saturn*, or morning or anything else.

We play along like always, and Hotlips has his trumpet pressed into his face, and nothing but beautiful sounds come from the band. I do not know if Frankie is altogether happy about this, for he does not like Hotlips and would like this chance to bounce him. But what surprises me most is that the thrush, Stella Starlight, keeps looking back at Hotlips like she notices him for the first time and is plenty worried by what she sees.

We have a short break after a while and I am telling Hotlips that the idea goes over real great, when Stella Starlight waltzes over. Hotlips' big eyes bug out and I can see him shaking and covered with goosebumps.

"You do not play like that before, Hotlips," she coos. "What did you do?"

Hotlips blushes and stammers, "Eddie and I fix—" But I give him a kick in his big shins before he gives the whole thing away.

"Hotlips does some practicing this afternoon," I tell her, "to get his lip in shape for tonight."

She looks at me like she is looking through me, and then she turns back to Hotlips and says, soft and murmuring: "Please do not play too high, Hotlips. I am delicate and am disturbed by high sounds."

She waltzes away, and I scratch my head and try to figure out what this pitch is for. Hotlips is not trying to figure out anything; he just sits there looking like he has just got his trumpet out of hock for the last time.

"Hotlips," I say to him.

"Go away, please, Eddie," he tells me. "I am in heaven."

"You will be in the poorhouse or maybe even in jail if you tell somebody how we fix your playing," I warn him.

"I still feel funny feelings though, Eddie," he tells me, frowning, "like I cannot hit high notes now if I try."

"Then do not try," I advise. "One problem at a time is too much."

There is a commotion at the entrance on the other side of the dance floor, where some people all dressed up come in. A woman is holding her head and moaning and threatening to faint all over the place.

Frankie hurries over to us, running fidgety hands through his hair. "For goodness sake, play something," he almost begs.

"What gives?" I inquire.

"Flying cuspidors," Frankie says in a frantic tone. "They are all around the place, like they are maybe mad at something, and a few minutes ago they buzz the ferry and get the passengers all nervous and upset. If they do that again, business will be bad; maybe even now it will be bad. Play something!"

He hops out in front with his baton and gives us a quick one-two, and we all swing into "Space On My Hands," real loud so as to get people's minds off things which Frankie wants to get people's minds off of.

Stella Starlight gets up to sing, but she looks more like she would rather do something else. She stares at Hotlips and at the trumpet on his lips and begins to quiver like she is about to do a dance.

I remember she says she does not like high notes, and this song has some pretty well up in the stratosphere, especially for the trumpet section, which is Hotlips.

She is frowning like maybe she is thinking real hard about something and is surprised her thoughts do no good. Her face becomes waxy and there is a frightened look on it.

She quivers some more, as the notes go up and up and up. Then she lets out a shriek, like maybe she is going to pieces.

And then she does. Actually.

Right before our popping eyeballs she goes to pieces.

As each one in the band sees what is going on, he stops playing, until finally Hotlips is the only one. But the trumpet is in Hotlips' hand, and the music is coming from the recording machine we place under his chair. The notes are clear and smooth, and you can almost feel the air shaking with them.

But nobody notices the music or where it comes from. They are too busy watching the thrush, Stella Starlight.

She stands there, her face as white as clay, shaking like a carrot going through a mixmaster. And then tiny cracks appear on her face, on her arms, even in her dress, and then a large one appears in her forehead and goes down through her body. She splits in the middle like a cracked walnut, and there in the center, floating three feet from the floor is a small flying cuspidor.

Nobody in the room says anything. They just stand there, bug-eyed and frightened like anything. Somewhere, across the room, a woman faints. I do not feel too well myself, and I am afraid to look to see how Hotlips takes this.

There is no sound, but I hear a voice in my mind and know that the others hear it too. The voice sounds like it is filled with wire and metal and is not exactly human. It says:

"*You win, Hotlips Grogan. I, as advance agent in disguise, tell you this. We will go away and leave you and your people alone. We place a mental block in your mind, but you outsmart us, and now you know our weakness. We cannot stand high sounds which you can play so easy on your trumpet. We find ourselves a home someplace else.*"

With that, the cuspidor shoots across the room and plows right through the wall.

"That's the engine room!" Frankie wails.

There is a sudden explosion from the other side of the wall, and everybody decides all at once they would like to be someplace else, and they all pick the same spot. The space ferry is pretty crowded, but we jam aboard it and drift away from the *Saturn*—musicians, waiters and paying customers all sitting in each other's laps.

The *Saturn* is wobbling around, with flames shooting out at all angles, and Frankie is holding his head and moaning. In the distance, you can just about make out little specks of cuspidors heading for the wild black yonder.

So all is well that ends well, and this is it.

Frankie uses his insurance money to open a rest home on Mars for ailing musicians.

Hotlips is all broken up, in a manner of speaking, over Stella Starlight's turning out to be not human, but he consoles himself with a good job playing trumpet in a burlesque house where the girls wear costumes made of glass and other brittle stuff.

*

As for me, Mamie gets me a job playing piano at the place where she works, and everything is okay except for one thing. When Mamie is around I cannot seem to concentrate on my playing. I feel a funny feeling in my stomach, like maybe it is full of supersuds or something, and my mouth is dry like cotton candy.

I think maybe it is indigestion.

THE PSILENT PARTNER

by Edward S. Staub and John Victor Peterson

Without stressing the technological aspects of the strange powers of the widely-talented ones—the psis, espers, telepaths which have been so painstakingly forecast by Stapledon, van Vogt, Weinbaum, Vance and others—Messieurs Peterson and Staub have whipped fantasy, forecasts and facts into a stirring and mentally titillating story of a too-imaginative mind.

A pstrange probing mind that crossed pstate lines, the pseas, even high in the psky—to bring psomething new to Wall Pstreet.

He had never cast his consciousness so far before. It floated high above New York, perceiving in the noonday sky the thin, faint crescent of a waning moon. He wondered if one day he might cast his mind even to the moon, knew with a mounting exultation that his powers were already great enough.

Yet he was as afraid to launch it on that awesome transit as he still was to send it delving into the tight subway tunnels in the rock of Manhattan. Phobias were too real now. Perhaps it would be different later . . . .

He was young, as a man, younger as a recognized developing psi. As his consciousness floated there above the bustling city, exultant, free, it sensed that back where his body lay a bell was ringing. And the bell meant it—his consciousness—must return now to that body . . . .

*

Dale V. Lawrence needed a lawyer urgently. Not that he hadn't a score of legal minds at his disposal; a corporation president must maintain a sizable legal staff. You can't build an industrial empire without treading on people's toes. And you need lawyers when you tread.

He sat behind his massive mahogany desk, a stocky, slightly-balding, stern-looking man of middle age who was psychosomatically creating another ulcer as he worried about the business transaction which he could not handle personally because of the ulcer operation he was about to have. Neither the business transaction nor the operation could be delayed.

He needed a particularly clever lawyer, one not connected with the corporation. Not that he had committed or that he contemplated committing a crime. But the eyes of the law and the minds of the psis of the government's Business Ethics Bureau were equally keen. Anyone in the business of commercially applied atomics was automatically and immediately investigated in any proposed transaction as soon as BEB had knowledge thereof. There was still the fear that someone somewhere might attempt, secretly, to build a war weapon again.

116

Lawrence had an idea, a great, burning, impossible-to-discard idea. Lawrence Applied Atomics, Inc., had been his first great idea—the idea that had made him a multi-millionaire. But through some devious financing he had lost control of the corporation. And although his ideas invariably realized millions, the other major stockholders were becoming cautious about risking their profits. Overly cautious, he thought. And on this new idea he knew they would never support him. They'd consider it a wild risk. He could blame BEB with its psis for that. BEB was too inquisitive. A business man just couldn't take a decent gamble any longer.

The real estate firm in Los Angeles was secretly securing options from individual landowners. Fortunately the firm employed a psi, one of the few known psis not in government service. Lawrence had wondered why this psi was not working for the government, but decided the 'why' didn't matter if there were positive results.

Lawrence knew a little about psis. He knew, of course, what was commonly known—that they possessed wide and very varied talents, that they were categorized as plain psis, psi-espers, esper-psis, telepaths and other things. They weren't numerous; the Business Ethics Bureau which employed at least sixty percent of the known psis showed thirty on the payroll for this fiscal year.

Despite their rumored emotional instability, he knew that they were clever and he would steer clear of them in the present stages of his transaction. Although his idea wasn't unethical, the so far closely kept secret would be out if BEB investigated. Then anybody could cut in. BEB advertised whatever it did on its video show, "Your Developing Earth."

So, he needed a lawyer who could act for him personally, now, and steer his project clear of the government service psis. But where to find a psis . . . .

*

Of course! Bob Standskill! Standskill had helped him once years before when he had had that trouble with the Corporation Stock Control Board over a doubtful issue of securities he had floated to build Mojave City out of desert wastes. Without Standskill's techniques he never would have put that issue across. Standskill could handle this if anyone could.

Lawrence reached to the visiphone, punched the button sequence of Standskill's office number. The bell rang interminably before a rather bored young voice said, "Offices of Standskill and Rich, Attorneys-at-Law."

"I know," Lawrence said harshly. "I don't button wrong numbers. Is Standskill there? And where's your courtesy? There's no visual."

The picture came in then. Lawrence caught a flash of long, skinny legs going down behind the desk at the other end of the circuit; then he saw a most remarkable thing—the open collar of the young man's shirt seemed suddenly to button itself and the knot of the gaudy tie to tighten and all the while the fellow's hands were lying immobile on the desk!

Impossible! Lawrence thought. *I'm cracking up! Too many worries about the psis . . . I think I see them everywhere!*

As the youth gulped as though the tie was knotted too tightly, Lawrence was sure that he saw the knot relax itself!

"I'm sorry, Mr. Lawrence, Mr. Standskill's on vacation and Mr. Rich is in court. May I help you, sir, or take a message?"

Undoubtedly the fellow had recognized him from news fotos.

"Well, who are you, the office boy?"

A frown of annoyance crossed the young man's thin, dark features. He snapped, "Are corporation presidents exempt from common courtesy? My name is Black—Martin J. Black. I'm not connected with this firm. I answered as a courtesy. Shall we disconnect?"

Lawrence was silent for a moment. He thought of the shirt-tie business and said, "You're a trainee psi, aren't you? A prospective service psi?"

"I'm afraid so. I wish I weren't. It's not a pleasant prospect."

"What do you mean?"

"Would you like to probe minds for a living? And it has its other drawbacks. You can't live normally and you'll have very few friends. Unfortunately no two psis are alike, which makes the job more complicated. I'm un-normal, abnormal, subnormal or some other normal they haven't prefixed yet."

"Any special talents?"

"I'm afraid so."

"Rather young," Lawrence mused. Then said, "Are you economically stable?"

The young man hesitated, then said hastily, "Oh, yes, of course. Economically, yes. Somewhat more stable than most, I think. I'm in final training now. The legal phase comes last, you know."

"Then you're not committed yet? You've not taken the Oath of Anterhine?"

"No. I won't until the training is done. Wish I didn't have to then."

"And your training?"

"Complete except for criminal psychology."

"Would you like to make a hundred thousand dollars?"

Black said, "Your firm bought out Black Controlled Atomics, remember? That was my dad, and that was the end for him." He hesitated. "Let's say I'm vaguely interested. What's your proposition?"

Lawrence was silent for a moment. At length he said, "Being a psi your ultimate destiny is to aid in the development of the world whether you like to look forward to it or not. But would you not like to see desert areas developed through applied atomics as Mojave City, Sanup Plateau City and Quijotoa City were?"

"Certainly," Black said quickly. "It's in my blood. The old man did well at such developments; in fact, he started Quijotoa. Sometimes I wish Standskill hadn't liquidated our estate, but my mother's will made it mandatory."

"How much do you know about Standskill's techniques?"

"I'm a psi," Black said. "I can find out anything I want to know."

"Where *is* Standskill?"

"Paris. His first vacation in years. Going to be away quite a while."

"Will you come to my office?"

"Why?"

"I'd like to discuss a business proposition."

"What's wrong with doing it over the visiphone?"

"This is confidential," Lawrence said.

"Something not exactly legal?" Black asked. "Big deal, eh? The Control Board again—oh, oh! You'd better see Standskill!"

Lawrence felt uneasy. "Are you—are you reading my mind?" he stammered.

"Sorry," the young man said, smiling faintly. "It's easier that way. I dislike physical movement on such warm days as this. And it's easier for me to pick up your proposal this way than to go through that beastly traffic."

"Then you know?"

"Certainly. I'm a psi so I can read your mind."

"Do you accept the job?"

"Well, people in that area and the country in general would certainly benefit from the development. I don't know about that lawyer from Los Angeles though. They teach us in Service Psi School that non-service psis are not to be trusted. In fact, service psis are forbidden to associate with non-service psis. They're considered unethical."

"You're not in service yet, Black, and you must realize that the psi-ethics as taught in your school are much more strict than business ethics. If Standskill were here he'd certainly help me, and you know he has a fine code of ethics. It's desperate, Black. I need your services urgently. Won't you please accept the job?"

*

"I suppose so," the young man said wearily, resignedly. "Standskill would agree, I'm sure. But, as a trainee, I'm not supposed to meddle in business transactions. However,

I'd hate to see you lose out on this because I know Standskill would unhesitatingly help you if he were here. Also, I'm curious to meet that psi from Los Angeles." His sharp chin grew resolute. "I'll try, Mr. Lawrence. And my conscience will be clear; I haven't yet taken the Oath."

"Will you need anything—any physical help, any tangible thing?"

"I'll need your power-of-attorney."

"You'll have it before I go to the hospital."

"And, Mr. Lawrence," Black said softly. "About the surgery—don't worry, you'll be okay. It's chiefly psychosomatic, you know. In a couple of weeks you'll be fine. You couldn't have picked a better doctor than Summers."

Lawrence felt better already, a result of his talk with this brash young man.

"Thank you, Black," he said. "Thank you very much. But, look—as a psi, can you assure me that my idea is not slightly lunatic? I've begun to doubt that it will work."

Lunatic . . . . Mentally unsound . . . . Luna . . . . Moon . . . . The crescent of the moon in the noonday sky. Yes, he could go now . . . . The transit was brief . . . . No! He must go back, must bear the consciousness that was Martin Black back from this airless, cratered sphere! Panic seized him. He fled.

Lawrence was astounded to see the young man at the other end of the visiphone seemingly fall into a deep sleep, his head down suddenly on the desk.

"Black," he cried, "are you all right? Shall I send a doctor to—"

"*No!*"

The young man raised his head. "I'm quite all right, Mr. Lawrence, though slightly exhausted. Didn't sleep well last night. Sorry! I'll ring you after I contact Dick Joyce."

"No names, please," Lawrence said. "I go into the hospital this afternoon, Black. You'd better not contact me there. The doctor said no business while I'm there. From now on you're on your own."

Your own! He was drifting! He fought it . . . .

"Right, Mr. Lawrence. Goodbye!"

II

Martin Black *was* tired. His consciousness had almost drifted off to home again, back to that old mansion on the Hudson River which Standskill had sold as directed under Black's mother's will. The old house in which he was born, where he had first found that he could sit in his room and send his consciousness questing down the hall to meet his father when he came home, pry into what his father had brought for him and surprise his parents later by invariably guessing correctly.

Sometimes now he wished that he hadn't "guessed" correctly so often in those days. Then his uncle Ralph wouldn't have mentioned his unusual ability to the Business

Ethics Bureau and the psis wouldn't have investigated him. Once they found that he had such mental qualifications he had been sent to the Service Psi School, a virtual prison despite his family's social status.

Anger suddenly choked him at the thought of what his uncle Ralph had brought upon him. The psi training had been so rigid, so harsh at times.

Well, of course they have to be sure that psis develop into useful members of society. But couldn't they treat you more normally, more humanly?

Now, perhaps he'd show them, repay them for the cruel years of a lonely, bitter youth. He hadn't taken the Oath yet, and if he were clever enough he'd never have to! The real estate lawyer in Los Angeles with whom Lawrence was making a deal had evaded service somehow, apparently. So it was possible.

He had learned long ago that money wouldn't buy him out of service. He'd tried also to purchase certain liberties at school. Some of the less scrupulous teachers had taken his allowance, but only one of them had ever given him anything in return. And of course he couldn't protest when he had violated Ethics to give the bribes. In any event, no one would take the word of an untrained psi over the word of a stable, normal human being.

During the stabilization course one professor had permitted him to skip some classes. Now he wished that he hadn't missed them; he probably wouldn't have this semantic instability to contend with now. Oh, well . . . .

He *was* tired. He'd spent the previous night, or most of it, worrying about the miserable state of his finances. He needed money, a lot of money. But he wouldn't, of course, admit that to Lawrence.

Lawrence would have understood why he needed money—even more than the hundred thousand he had offered. But then Lawrence might mistrust his motives in accepting the proposal so readily if he knew.

A year before Black had invested too much of his own money in a "sure thing" upon the advice of a fellow psi trainee who, he subsequently and sadly found out, had *economic* instability. Semantic instability was bad enough!

Not that Martin Black didn't have a hundred thousand dollars. He was, indeed, a rather wealthy young man, thanks to his mother who had been, to her son's knowledge—and to his alone—a psi with definite powers of pre-vision and persuasion.

He recalled the tale Mom had told him of her first meeting with Dad, of how she'd lingered over Dad's well groomed nails three times longer than desire for a good tip made necessary, while she'd gently insinuated into his mind an idea that was next day translated into action on the stock market, with a modest investment from a modest purse that brought the young man a small fortune. After the wedding Martha Black dedicated herself to further improvements in the same direction.

As for Martin's father, his chief business assets had been an unswerving adoration of his wife and complete willingness to do with his money as she saw fit. The combination had been unbeatable.

When Martin's father was laid to rest, Martha Black, concerned over the future of her somewhat unusual son and fearing that economic instability might beset him, continued to improve the fortune he would some day inherit.

Long before the death of his mother five years before, Black Controlled Atomics, Inc., had grown sufficiently important to command the services of a lawyer of Standskill's caliber. Gradually Standskill had become general counsel to the Black enterprises and at the same time a close friend of Martha Black and her son.

It was chiefly in the latter capacity that the widow consulted Standskill as she approached the end of her life. Her Last Will and Testament, duly signed, sealed, published and declared, left one-half of the immediately-to-be-liquidated estate to her son outright. The other half was put in trust.

Under the trust Martin was to receive the income until he was thirty. If then an audit showed that his net worth, exclusive of the trust, had increased by thirty percent the trust was to end and Martin was to receive the principal. If not, the trust would end and the full amount thereof would go to his uncle Ralph, a prospect which caused Martin completely to lose his stability whenever he allowed himself to think of it. He just *had* to make the thirty percent!

R. W. Standskill was trustee, and the will gave him full power to invest the trust estate as he saw fit and without liability if his investments went bad and without any bond or security required of him whatsoever. More in token of appreciation of his services than anything else, Standskill was to receive one percent of the trust as long as he was trustee.

Martin Black's mind dwelled on the thought of the thirty percent increase. After five years of conservative investing he had taken some bad advice in the past year. And now he had to make some money fast in order to catch up to the quota which was necessary if he were to achieve his goal.

The Lawrence deal would give him his chance. But not if Standskill knew about it. The Lawrence deal seemed a good thing, but perhaps it was only a *sure* thing if he kept to himself, for the time being at least.

He was so tired . . . . *Fatigué*. The French for tired. Funny, he did remember some of the French from school. Standskill was in Paris. Association. *Fatigué*. The word stuck. That club—Bob Standskill's favorite—*Le Cheval Fatigué* in Montmartre. The Tired Horse. Tired . . . .

Sleep closed in . . . . He drifted . . . and came to with a sudden start as a hand roughly shook his shoulder. It seemed as though he had been hovering mentally in a dimly-lighted cellar cafe, where there was a babel of voices speaking continental languages, and Standskill was there.

But, *no!* he couldn't have been in Paris any more than he had been on the meteor-pounded wastes of the moon! It was ridiculous. As far as he knew, no psi had ever been known consciously to flit to the moon—or unconsciously, for that matter—or to the other side of an ocean!

Standskill's partner, G. D. Rich, was shaking his shoulder. "What's the matter, Marty? Big night?"

"Big day," Black said. "Why don't you fellows stick around and take care of your business? I'm not even supposed to answer the telephone, you know, but someone has to!"

"Can I help it that the Legal Secretaries Guild has called a three-day convention? There's not a secretary present in any law office in New York right now! I personally cut the phone in to the answering service before I left for court."

"Inadvertence, I guess," Black said thoughtfully.

"Inadvertence?" Rich said quickly.

"Mine. I must have cut it back."

He didn't tell Rich that he hadn't stirred from the desk since Rich had left. The switch was in the outer office. Had he with his consciousness floating high over New York sensed subconsciously that Lawrence was about to call and so cut in the switch? Had he built into himself something of the pattern of his mother, something of pre-vision or prescience, or call it what you will? Was a latent hunch power coming out in him now, something that would manifest itself by acts not consciously controlled? He hoped not! Semantic instability was bad enough!

III

Sleep evaded Martin Black again that night . . . . There was no doubt that Lawrence had a great idea.

Lawrence held forty-five percent of the company's stock. He wanted control. In fact, he wanted outright ownership, but this was not possible because the other major stockholders, holding forty-five percent, seemed to be perfectly satisfied with their lucrative investment. Cautious inquiries had failed to disclose any inclination on their respective parts to sell.

There were, however, enough independent shares outstanding to give Lawrence control if they were added to his own. The thing to do was to figure a way to buy them. The problem was that no matter how secret his operations, news or rumors of them would certainly leak out. The shares would then undoubtedly jump to outrageous highs. Lawrence couldn't risk that. He'd not be able to buy sufficient shares if the price rose.

His corporation had completed Quijotoa City and had built Mojave City and Sanup Plateau City, had through applied atomics created verdant and lovely places out of wasteland and desert. It still owned the atomic piles that provided power for the cities and the profits therefrom were enormous.

Lawrence was progressive. He was at heart a humanitarian. He wanted to develop other areas more from the humanitarian view than the profit motive. He had learned long ago that the profits would take care of themselves.

In probing the man's mind, Black sensed Lawrence's great desire for adulation, his great desire to be remembered as a public benefactor.

Now if only he, Martin J. Black, could benefit financially from this new deal—if he could corner enough of those independent shares, he could and certainly would vote them Lawrence's way. Then, perhaps the possibility of making the thirty percent he needed would approach probability, would reach it. With Lawrence's Midas touch the corporation would also realize millions in profits if the deal went through.

Figures revolved in Black's mind. If Lawrence—or if he—could corner six percent of the stock . . . . Could some of the independents be persuaded to sell, *psionically persuaded*? Or one of the other major stockholders? No, that would be unethical and the strongest part of a psi's training was a fine code of ethics.

Black began to doze—and felt something ever so softly probing at his mind. A *probe*! Probably a service psi checking on him. *Why*? Just the usual check? No, it wasn't due.

He knew what to do. He had been probed before. Probing was part of the training at psi school but he had never revealed—and his tutors had never guessed—that he could create a block that could not be sensed by the prober. A block which could close off whatever thoughts he wished to conceal.

He blocked his thoughts of Lawrence and the deal now, and opened freely that part of his mind which held the routine thoughts of the law offices. He felt that feather of thought brushing lightly through his brain, then it was gone as quickly as it had come.

There was a cold sweat over him but he knew that he had passed the test. Why the probe? Perhaps a BEB psi had wind of Lawrence's deal and by probing Lawrence's mind—or the mind of someone in the West Coast realty outfit—had somehow learned of Black's association with the industrialist. If that were the case there would be more probes. One time or another a probe might come at a moment of nervous tension or stress and the information would be gleaned from his mind before he could block!

He must work fast.

He arose and went to the visiphone, placed a person-to-person call to Los Angeles.

"Dick Joyce?" he asked before the visual contact was complete, and only his voice went out.

The face that came in sync on the screen was round, jovial. "Well, hello, Marty!"

Lawrence must have called him, or else he plucked the name from my mind. But he didn't probe—or did he?

"Dick, do you register?" *With the mind now—cautiously!*

"Yes, Marty."

Pretend you're my personal friend, Dick. There's no psi on us but we may be wiretapped by BEB—lots of law offices are and trainees connected with them. Can a definite date be set for the picking-up of the options?

"It's good to see you again, Marty! When will you be coming out for another visit?" *Yes, the options are in the bag. My agents have them all lined up. Confidentially, they couldn't miss. The only trouble they ran into was that some of the landowners thought they were insane to be interested in the property and one of them actually suffered a sprained wrist from the hand-shaking of an overly thankful owner.*

"Soon. That's why I called you. Thought we should get together after all these years." *What's the latest date for signing?*

Tomorrow night.

Tomorrow night! That doesn't give much time! Since I'm acting for Lawrence I have to see what we're getting.

Well, Lawrence told us to work fast. But I agree that it's a good idea that you see the properties. "How about this weekend?" His voice was casual.

Tomorrow evening local time it is then. But where will we make psi-contact?

A mental picture of a map. Desolation . . . . Oklahoma . . . .

"Okay, Dick. See you then. Regards to the family!"

"Goodbye, Marty."

He rang off.

He was tired. He went to bed and sought sleep, praying that the block his fatigued mind had set would remain firm.

IV

Martin Black passed a very bad night. Maintaining a mental block when asleep is a major feat, especially when one has semantic instability and a dream can so often be so realistic as to bring one's consciousness awake and mentally screaming miles from the physical being it has involuntarily left.

He dreamed with incredible regularity, waking five times out of nightmares, five times strangely on the hour as though he had tied some part of his mental being to the irresistibly moving, luminescent minute hand of his electric clock. *Time is of the essence*, he had told himself during the psi-visiphone contact with Joyce. *Association!*

Two A.M. He had dreamt of Joyce, dreamt that Joyce had somehow revealed the proposed transaction to BEB, putting Dodson on his trail. Wide awake now, he forced himself to think of the options which must be picked up the following night, options drawn so that not only the landowners must sign them but both the realty outfit and he, as Lawrence's attorney-in-fact, as well. Could he sign for Lawrence if Joyce had spilled?... No, it was only a dream. Joyce was so *very* stable!

Three A.M. He had dreamt of Standskill, tall, lean Standskill striding through the lovely early morning along the Champs Élysées, moving purposefully. He had even dreamt he had for a moment invaded Standskill's mind and caught the lawyer's pounding thought, "Lawrence! *Buy*, Lawrence!" Oh, but that would never do. The service psis would catch Standskill, would test the ethics of it now that Joyce had spilled, would cause Standskill to be disbarred. But Standskill didn't know! A dream. A *lunatic dream.*

Four A.M. The coincidence of the timing of his wakings struck him then. For a moment the latest dream eluded him and then the sense of airless cold, a bleak, cratered landscape, stark stars staring in a lunar night swept coldly across his mind. He shivered, drew the blanket over him, thought: *How many shares? Six thousand? I can do it. I'll contact the broker in the morning. Six thousand at two hundred per. One million two hundred thousand dollars.*

But that would raise the price, the attempt to buy so many shares. You can't buy a million plus in one stock without driving the price up—*unless you manage to buy all the shares at once!* If only he could persuade—psionically persuade—but he couldn't! It wasn't ethical.

His mind drifted . . . . I'll call the broker in the morning. Perhaps he can start picking up some of the independent shares when the market opens. If only he could snag the four thousand that—what was that name in Lawrence's mind?—yes, Redgrave! The four thousand that Redgrave has! That would be a start!

Redgrave had always fought Lawrence tooth and nail. Lawrence would derive vast personal satisfaction from seeing Redgrave an *ex*-stockholder. Thankless cad! Investment in the corporation had helped make Redgrave a very wealthy man.

Lawrence stock was only part of his vast holdings. Redgrave was definitely out of the red!

Black chuckled, then told himself that this was a grave and not a laughing matter. Sleep was coming again . . . . *Out of the red. Grave. Redgrave!*

Five A.M. He awoke in a cold sweat . . . . This time the dream came back slowly, drenching him with fear as it came. It was sheer madness, this dream! To have even considered investing in Lawrence Applied Atomics! The Government would never condone the deal Lawrence was contemplating—the Applied Atomics Corporation was nearly insolvent, the BEB psis were investigating it . . . .

Black tossed fitfully on the bed, seeking sleep desperately, seeking to escape the black night pressing in, to evade the imagined—or was it real?—probing minds of service psis.

Six A.M. He almost forgot the fears that had assailed him an hour before. He realized then that in the last few minutes or seconds or however long the latest transient phantasm had been in his mind he had dreamt of his broker pacing a dimly-lighted chamber, muttering, "The man's out of his mind. Economic instability, that's certain. Thinking of selling good stock to invest in Lawrence Applied Atomics! Not that Lawrence stock isn't fairly good, but he'll never make enough out of the corporation's piles; the returns are not that great!"

8 A.M. Black stretched, felt strangely relaxed. He realized then that as he had slept and, despite the fitfulness of his sleeping, his mind had apparently gone on analyzing the possible reactions to the big deal.

He arose, took a shower, shaved, ate breakfast. Then he went to the visiphone and buttoned Charles Wythe, his broker, at his office.

"Charlie," Black said to the cadaverous looking man who answered. "Where's the boss?"

"Went to see a psychiatrist."

"Why?"

"I don't know. What's on your mind?"

"I want you to do some selling and buying for me. Sell whatever you like, but buy Lawrence Applied Atomics."

"Look, Marty, let's not go off half-cocked. Last year you had a sudden brainstorm and remember what happened. Lawrence may be a good stock, but it won't help you to build up to that thirty percent you need. Not in the time you have to do it in. It's bad enough for you to take a big licking once. Let's not be stupid again."

"Now, Charlie, don't be nasty. I want you to buy Lawrence as quietly as you can. I want six thousand shares at the current price. Get them for me."

"Are you shaken loose from your psyche or id or whatever?" Wythe cried. "Do it quietly, the man says, do it quietly! You can do it about as quietly as they launched the space station. Where do you think I can get six thousand shares of Lawrence?"

"Why, you buy them!" Black answered innocently. "Isn't that what you do down at the Stock Exchange?"

The broker groaned. "Sure, that's all I do. Buy, that is. But not Lawrence. Look, Marty, see this chart? Yesterday was a big day for Lawrence Applied Atomics. It was unusually active. Three hundred shares changed hands. The day before it was one hundred. Once in my memory Lawrence had a four thousand share day. That must have been when Redgrave bought in. Now you tell me how I'm going to get you six thousand shares, get them quietly, and get them at the current price!"

"Start buying," Black said, "because I've got a hunch you'll find them. My mother had hunches, didn't she? Did she ever tell you or the boss to buy the wrong stocks? Did she—"

"That was your mother, Marty. What about that hunch you had last year, the one that cost you a couple of hundred thou—"

"That was last year!"

"So, what's changed?" asked Wythe.

"Maybe *I've* changed, Charlie. Do it; that's all I ask."

"Okay, Marty. But I think you're out of your mind, especially with what was on the morning news."

"And what was that?"

"Lawrence is in bad shape. He's not likely to pull through. They operated last night, in case you didn't know."

"But that should drive the stock down!"

"Why? It won't affect the profits from the corporation's piles."

"No. I agree. But that's not the only thing that keeps the price up. What about Lawrence's reputation?"

"Well, there's also a rumor about a government investigation of the corporation," Wythe admitted. "That might have some downward effect."

"Buy, Charlie, buy! I'll ring you later."

Black rang off. He felt an overwhelming confidence. He had only one small doubt in his mind—during or following one of those disturbing dreams had he been sufficiently overwrought to have relaxed his mental block, thereby letting in a fleeting probe from a service psi who would then have gleaned, in a moment, knowledge of the proposed transaction?

The unease waned. The exuberant confidence was in him again. The prescience of Martha Black?

He went out and caught a heli-cab to the law offices. He'd be a good trainee to the eyes and minds of anyone who might check. If the service psis were on his trail, he'd show them how good a trainee he was. He could check with Charlie Wythe later.

V

At ten A.M., Standskill's partner, G. D. Rich left the office to attend court.

At ten-thirty A.M., a contact call came whispering to Black's mind. He thought it at first a probe and blocked part of his mind; then relaxed as it realized it was a psi asking with overbearing politeness for him to connect the visiphone circuit. The mental touch seemed somehow familiar, but it wasn't Joyce. He knew it wasn't Joyce; there was something unsure and tentative about the whisper of thought.

Black psionically cut in the outer office visiphone connection. The bell rang almost immediately. He switched on the inner office instrument and a familiar face came in sync on the screen—that of Peter Dodson, the principal administrative officer of the BEB psis.

Dodson's blondly handsome face showed concern. He said, "I wanted visiphone contact, Black, because of an unfavorable report I've received on you. I'll get to that in a minute. First, I'd like to explain the background. As you may have learned from the news this morning, we're investigating Lawrence Applied Atomics because of a tip we'd received from Los Angeles that Lawrence is engaged in a venture which will eventually affect corporation funds without proper advance authorization.

"Finding that Lawrence had some dealings with Standskill in the past, we thought that Standskill might be able to shed some light on the new venture. When we were unable to contact Standskill, we sought to contact you psionically last night, but found that your mind was a completely unreadable jumble of nightmares, filled with phobias and instabilities. We stopped probing then, realizing that you might be seriously ill."

Apparently visual examination had convinced Dodson that Black wasn't as ill as had been thought. Black felt the feather touch of a probe coming now and he blocked, his thin face expressionless.

"I did have a rather bad night," Black said. "Association. Semantic instability." He felt the tentacle of thought that was sweeping across his mind.

"Well," Dodson said, his eyes probing from the screen, "it's obvious *you* know nothing of the Lawrence deal. Strange, though, since there's a record of a call placed to that office by Lawrence yesterday, and as far as we have been able to determine only you were there and only you could have answered. How do you explain that?"

Easy now! The block is most difficult to maintain when you're lying. Easy . . . .

"There was a call," Black admitted, "from someone I don't know, a fellow who wanted Standskill. Wouldn't say why or give his name. The moment I told him Standskill was in Paris he said with some reluctance that he would have to contact another law firm. The caller was probably Lawrence. If you could describe him—"

"So Standskill's in Paris! The answering service didn't know that. Well, that rules him out. Thank you, Black. Are you sure you're all right?"

"Rather tired," Black said. "Overwork, I expect. The training is rather strenuous, and I do wish you wouldn't probe. As you found in psi school, my powers have a very delicate balance."

The probe withdrew hastily.

"Sorry, Black. Very sorry. Perhaps you need a rest. I'll be only too glad to send through an order—"

"Oh, thank you, sir," Black said, trying to make it sound fervent and properly subservient. He sent a thought of thankfulness after his words, a weak one. He must not appear too strong.

Dodson rang off.

The coast was clear! They would not probe again soon!

Black immediately called Charles Wythe, found his broker's cadaverous face puzzled.

"Marty, the market's crazy! I managed to pick up four thousand shares within ten minutes after the market opened. One purchase. The broker from whom I obtained them represented Dan Redgrave—"

"Redgrave!" Black almost shouted.

"Yes, Redgrave. He said Redgrave is plain cuckoo. Ordered him to sell at one hundred fifty. Said he'd bought them at that and would sell them at that. No profit wanted. Glad to get out in time to recoup his original investment. What's cuckoo about it is that, except for the momentary flurry when we picked up the Redgrave shares, the stock has been rising all morning. It's up to two twenty-five as of this moment.

"Lawrence must have someone else buying regardless of the price. Three concerns are still trying to buy at the present price. Ethics forbids me to ask who their clients are. Not that they'd tell me anyway! Now, look, Marty, do you want me to buy at that price, if I can, that is?"

"Well, I must have six thousand, unless Lawrence is buying and I'm quite sure he isn't. See if you can find out who the buyer is, won't you?"

"Everybody's crazy today," the broker said. "I'll call you back."

Wythe did, a few minutes later.

"I'm afraid it's no use, Marty. There's not another share to be had. There's been news from the hospital. Lawrence has rallied. Although he's still in a coma, his chances are good for recovery. Not only that, but the Business Ethics Bureau has issued a statement to the effect that the tip they'd received about Lawrence and a deal has not been proved to have a foundation in fact. Those things have put the stock way up. Everybody wants to buy Lawrence but nobody wants to sell—except me! Let's sell, Marty!"

"Not on your life," Black said decisively. "And, look, we *must* get two thousand more shares! Get them, Charlie!"

He clicked off again.

So Dan Redgrave had sold at a ridiculously low price! Had his consciousness wandered in those dreams? Had he psionically persuaded Redgrave to sell? That wouldn't be ethical. But do ethics apply to *involuntary* acts?

His mind was in turmoil. He dared not exercise his psi powers again just now. He feared above all the wrath of Dodson and the other service psis. If they came to suspect that he had persuaded Redgrave—that he had, according to Ethics, misused his powers . . . he knew only too well that there are ways of banishing psi powers, insulin shock and other treatments.

And for all his present aloneness he was beginning to realize his latent powers—powers which, when fully developed, would doubtlessly bring him into contact with others like himself, with someone who could share the fierce ecstasy of probing with the consciousness to the moon, or even farther, at the speed of light at which thought moved. No, perhaps he need not always be alone . . . .

He went out to lunch, returned, called his broker. Wythe told him there was no activity in Lawrence. The afternoon wore. A few minutes before the exchange closed the broker called.

"It's hopeless, Marty," said Wythe. "Let's sell. The price is still two twenty-five and nothing for sale. How about it? Three hundred thousand profit in one day."

It sounded attractive. Black hesitated, then thought of Lawrence, good, old would-be humanitarian and philanthropist D. V. Lawrence lying in coma. Lawrence, whose dreams were in his hands now. He had come to like Lawrence, the trail-blazer where there were so few trails to be blazed. He had to help him. If worse came to worse he would cast Ethics to the winds. He'd have to! His conscience couldn't permit him to do anything else. He would psionically persuade at least one of the other stockholders to vote Lawrence's way.

Well, at least his mind was made up. Lawrence would have his options. And with forty-nine percent of the stock between them they could gamble on getting a favorable vote.

"What about it, Marty?" the broker asked impatiently.

"Sorry," Black said. "The answer is no, Charlie! I want that stock."

He rang off.

Moments later his consciousness was on its way to keep the rendezvous with Joyce high in the evening sky over Oklahoma, up where the blue of the atmosphere turned to the black of infinity.

And moments later lights blazed over a table in a realty office in Los Angeles where no one sat. But pens lifted and wrote . . . .

"*D. V. Lawrence by Martin J. Black, his attorney-in-fact.*"

"*J. F. Cadigan Realty Corporation by Richard Joyce, Vice-President.*"

Another pen lifted with the invisible but delicate twist of a feminine psi-touch.

"*Before me this ninth day of September in the year Nineteen Hundred and Seventy-six Anno Domini psionically appeared . . . .*"

The options were psigned, come what may!

VI

An oak-panelled conference room. Lawrence's first vice-president reading the proposal. The board of directors. The major stockholders. Smaller ones. Attorneys-in-fact for both Lawrence and Black.

And *Bob Standskill!*

What was Standskill doing here?

But the first vice-president had finished reading the proposal and was asking for a vote.

Lawrence—forty-five thousand shares—*yes!*

Maryk—twenty thousand shares—*no!*

Carrese—nine thousand shares—*no!*

Tonemont—seven thousand shares—*no!*

Black—four thousand shares—*yes!*

Turitz—five thousand shares—*no!*

And the smaller stockholders, one by one—*no, no, no!*

Forty-nine thousand shares—*no!* Forty-nine thousand shares—*yes!*

Black felt ill. His hovering consciousness almost fled from its invisible vantage point above the conference table back to the mansion on Riverside Drive, back where the memories of Martha Black remained . . . . But it wavered, stabilized . . . .

Standskill rising, so implacable, so sure and saying, "Two thousand shares—*yes!*"

Black probed Standskill's mind almost involuntarily then, realizing instantly that he should have disregarded Ethics and probed before. Standskill was a psi, a *non-service psi*! And Black knew then that when his consciousness had flitted through association to *Le Cheval Fatigué* in Montmarte, Paris, and had fixed there for a brief unstable moment it had yielded to Standskill all knowledge of the Lawrence deal, persuading Standskill to order his brokers to buy the corporation's stock for the trust . . . .

Black's consciousness sped to join Joyce's in a law office in Oklahoma. It watched the landowners signing the deeds even as it signed psionically the checks which represented the good and valuable considerations.

The deal was closed.

VII

Joyce, tell me—did you, to your knowledge, tip off the BEB psis?

Yes. Inadvertently, of course. I had a nightmare. I'm afraid I'm sometimes unstable, anonymously so, when asleep. Only then, though, thank Heaven!

And, Joyce, why aren't you in service?

For the same reason you can't be.

Confusion.

What do you mean?

Your mother knew.

My mother?

Yes, Marty, don't you realize that only unstable psis are taken into service? Stability is the mark of the superman. Do the majority of men want the minority—the supermen—running their world even though the supermen are their brothers, sisters and children? And they must surely realize that all mankind will evolve to psis one day. Marty, you were in psi school. So was I. Did you complete Stabilization?... I see you didn't. No psi does! They let you think you're getting away with something when you skip classes, but you're not!

Fortunately, if you are strong enough, you stabilize on your own. Perhaps you'll realize now that your mother gave you the incentive: the thirty percent angle, realizing that an uncle you definitely did not like would inherit if you didn't strive to the utmost. It worked.

They can't touch me, Marty, and they can't touch you! We can elude them mentally and physically. They know they can't touch us; so they just have to tolerate us! I can read in your mind that you've stabilized. You can fit physically now. Why don't you try? Lawrence is waiting . . . .

Black's consciousness sped back to his body. His body lifted and sped to a hospital room.

Lawrence was awake. He viewed Black's materialization with incredulity.

"The deal is closed," Black said.

"But—you—" Lawrence stammered. "Closed?"

"Yes. And, considering the shares I hold, I guess that makes me something of a psilent partner of yours!"

A brash young man, Lawrence thought. A very brash young man!

Black grinned. *Thirty percent? He couldn't miss!*

They shook hands.

It was a deal. Psigned, sealed and delivered!

.

HAPPY ENDING

by Mack Reynolds and Fredric Brown

A world had collapsed around this man—a world that would never shout his praises again. The burned-out cities were still and dead, the twisted bodies and twisted souls giving him their last salute in death. And now he was alone, alone surrounded by memories, alone and waiting . . .

Sometimes the queerly shaped Venusian trees seemed to talk to him, but their voices were soft. They were loyal people.

THERE were four men in the lifeboat that came down from the space-cruiser. Three of them were still in the uniform of the Galactic Guards.

The fourth sat in the prow of the small craft looking down at their goal, hunched and silent, bundled up in a greatcoat against the coolness of space—a greatcoat which he would never need again after this morning. The brim of his hat was pulled down far over his forehead, and he studied the nearing shore through dark-lensed glasses. Bandages, as though for a broken jaw, covered most of the lower part of his face.

He realized suddenly that the dark glasses, now that they had left the cruiser, were unnecessary. He slipped them off. After the cinematographic grays his eyes had seen through these lenses for so long, the brilliance of the color below him was almost like a blow. He blinked, and looked again.

They were rapidly settling toward a shoreline, a beach. The sand was a dazzling, unbelievable white such as had never been on his home planet. Blue the sky and water, and green the edge of the fantastic jungle. There was a flash of red in the green, as they came still closer, and he realized suddenly that it must be a *marigee*, the semi-intelligent Venusian parrot once so popular as pets throughout the solar system.

Throughout the system blood and steel had fallen from the sky and ravished the planets, but now it fell no more.

And now this. Here in this forgotten portion of an almost completely destroyed world it had not fallen at all.

Only in some place like this, alone, was safety for him. Elsewhere—anywhere—imprisonment or, more likely, death. There was danger, even here. Three of the crew of the space-cruiser knew. Perhaps, someday, one of them would talk. Then they would come for him, even here.

But that was a chance he could not avoid. Nor were the odds bad, for three people out of a whole solar system knew where he was. And those three were loyal fools.

The lifeboat came gently to rest. The hatch swung open and he stepped out and walked a few paces up the beach. He turned and waited while the two spacemen who had guided the craft brought his chest out and carried it across the beach and to the corrugated-tin shack just at the edge of the trees. That shack had once been a space-radar relay station. Now the equipment it had held was long gone, the antenna mast taken down. But the shack still stood. It would be his home for a while. A long while. The two men returned to the lifeboat preparatory to leaving.

And now the captain stood facing him, and the captain's face was a rigid mask. It seemed with an effort that the captain's right arm remained at his side, but that effort had been ordered. No salute.

The captain's voice, too, was rigid with unemotion. "Number One . . . "

"Silence!" And then, less bitterly. "Come further from the boat before you again let your tongue run loose. Here." They had reached the shack.

"You are right, Number . . . "

"No. I am no longer Number One. You must continue to think of me as *Mister Smith*, your cousin, whom you brought here for the reasons you explained to the under-officers, before you surrender your ship. If you *think* of me so, you will be less likely to slip in your speech."

"There is nothing further I can do—Mister Smith?"

"Nothing. Go now."

"And I am ordered to surrender the—"

"There are no orders. The war is over, lost. I would suggest thought as to what spaceport you put into. In some you may receive humane treatment. In others—"

The captain nodded. "In others, there is great hatred. Yes. That is all?"

"That is all. And, Captain, your running of the blockade, your securing of fuel *en route*, have constituted a deed of high valor. All I can give you in reward is my thanks. But now go. Goodbye."

"Not goodbye," the captain blurted impulsively, "but *hasta la vista, auf Wiedersehen, until the day* . . . you will permit me, for the last time to address you and salute?"

The man in the greatcoat shrugged. "As you will."

Click of heels and a salute that once greeted the Caesars, and later the pseudo-Aryan of the 20th Century, and, but yesterday, he who was now known as *the last of the dictators*. "Farewell, Number One!"

"Farewell," he answered emotionlessly.

*

Mr. Smith, a black dot on the dazzling white sand, watched the lifeboat disappear up into the blue, finally into the haze of the upper atmosphere of Venus. That eternal haze that would always be there to mock his failure and his bitter solitude.

The slow days snarled by, and the sun shone dimly, and the *marigees* screamed in the early dawn and all day and at sunset, and sometimes there were the six-legged*baroons*, monkey-like in the trees, that gibbered at him. And the rains came and went away again.

At nights there were drums in the distance. Not the martial roll of marching, nor yet a threatening note of savage hate. Just drums, many miles away, throbbing rhythm for native dances or exorcising, perhaps, the forest-night demons. He assumed these Venusians had their superstitions, all other races had. There was no threat, for him, in that throbbing that was like the beating of the jungle's heart.

Mr. Smith knew that, for although his choice of destinations had been a hasty choice, yet there had been time for him to read the available reports. The natives were harmless and friendly. A Terran missionary had lived among them some time ago—before the outbreak of the war. They were a simple, weak race. They seldom went far from their villages; the space-radar operator who had once occupied the shack reported that he had never seen one of them.

So, there would be no difficulty in avoiding the natives, nor danger if he did encounter them.

Nothing to worry about, except the bitterness.

Not the bitterness of regret, but of defeat. Defeat at the hands of the defeated. The damned Martians who came back after he had driven them halfway across their damned arid planet. The Jupiter Satellite Confederation landing endlessly on the home planet, sending their vast armadas of spacecraft daily and nightly to turn his mighty cities into dust. In spite of everything; in spite of his score of ultra-vicious secret weapons and the last desperate efforts of his weakened armies, most of whose men were under twenty or over forty.

The treachery even in his own army, among his own generals and admirals. The turn of Luna, that had been the end.

His people would rise again. But not, now after Armageddon, in his lifetime. Not under him, nor another like him. The last of the dictators.

Hated by a solar system, and hating it.

It would have been intolerable, save that he was alone. He had foreseen that—the need for solitude. Alone, he was still Number One. The presence of others would have forced recognition of his miserably changed status. Alone, his pride was undamaged. His ego was intact.

*

The long days, and the *marigees'* screams, the slithering swish of the surf, the ghost-quiet movements of the *baroons* in the trees and the raucousness of their shrill voices. Drums.

Those sounds, and those alone. But perhaps silence would have been worse.

For the times of silence were louder. Times he would pace the beach at night and overhead would be the roar of jets and rockets, the ships that had roared over New Albuquerque, his capitol, in those last days before he had fled. The crump of bombs and the screams and the blood, and the flat voices of his folding generals.

Those were the days when the waves of hatred from the conquered peoples beat upon his country as the waves of a stormy sea beat upon crumbling cliffs. Leagues back of the battered lines, you could *feel* that hate and vengeance as a tangible thing, a thing that thickened the air, that made breathing difficult and talking futile.

And the spacecraft, the jets, the rockets, the damnable rockets, more every day and every night, and ten coming for every one shot down. Rocket ships raining hell from the sky, havoc and chaos and the end of hope.

And then he knew that he had been hearing another sound, hearing it often and long at a time. It was a voice that shouted invective and ranted hatred and glorified the steel might of his planet and the destiny of a man and a people.

It was his own voice, and it beat back the waves from the white shore, it stopped their wet encroachment upon this, his domain. It screamed back at the *baroons* and they were silent. And at times he laughed, and the *marigees* laughed. Sometimes, the queerly shaped Venusian trees talked too, but their voices were quieter. The trees were submissive, they were good subjects.

Sometimes, fantastic thoughts went through his head. The race of trees, the pure race of trees that never interbred, that stood firm always. Someday the trees—

But that was just a dream, a fancy. More real were the *marigees* and the *kifs*. They were the ones who persecuted him. There was the *marigee* who would shriek "*All is lost!*" He had shot at it a hundred times with his needle gun, but always it flew away unharmed. Sometimes it did not even fly away.

"*All is lost!*"

At last he wasted no more needle darts. He stalked it to strangle it with his bare hands. That was better. On what might have been the thousandth try, he caught it and killed it, and there was warm blood on his hands and feathers were flying.

That should have ended it, but it didn't. Now there were a dozen *marigees* that screamed that all was lost. Perhaps there had been a dozen all along. Now he merely shook his fist at them or threw stones.

The *kifs*, the Venusian equivalent of the Terran ant, stole his food. But that did not matter; there was plenty of food. There had been a cache of it in the shack, meant to restock a space-cruiser, and never used. The *kifs* would not get at it until he opened a can, but then, unless he ate it all at once, they ate whatever he left. That did not matter. There were plenty of cans. And always fresh fruit from the jungle. Always in season, for there were no seasons here, except the rains.

But the *kifs* served a purpose for him. They kept him sane, by giving him something tangible, something inferior, to hate.

Oh, it wasn't hatred, at first. Mere annoyance. He killed them in a routine sort of way at first. But they kept coming back. Always there were *kifs*. In his larder, wherever he did it. In his bed. He sat the legs of the cot in dishes of gasoline, but the *kifs* still got in. Perhaps they dropped from the ceiling, although he never caught them doing it.

They bothered his sleep. He'd feel them running over him, even when he'd spent an hour picking the bed clean of them by the light of the carbide lantern. They scurried with tickling little feet and he could not sleep.

He grew to hate them, and the very misery of his nights made his days more tolerable by giving them an increasing purpose. A pogrom against the *kifs*. He sought out their holes by patiently following one bearing a bit of food, and he poured gasoline into the hole and the earth around it, taking satisfaction in the thought of the writhings in agony below. He went about hunting *kifs*, to step on them. To stamp them out. He must have killed millions of *kifs*.

But always there were as many left. Never did their number seem to diminish in the slightest. Like the Martians—but unlike the Martians, they did not fight back.

Theirs was the passive resistance of a vast productivity that bred *kifs* ceaselessly, overwhelmingly, billions to replace millions. Individual *kifs* could be killed, and he took savage satisfaction in their killing, but he knew his methods were useless save for the pleasure and the purpose they gave him. Sometimes the pleasure would pall in the shadow of its futility, and he would dream of mechanized means of killing them.

He read carefully what little material there was in his tiny library about the *kif*. They were astonishingly like the ants of Terra. So much that there had been speculation about their relationship—that didn't interest him. How could they be killed, *en masse*? Once a year, for a brief period, they took on the characteristics of the army ants of Terra. They came from their holes in endless numbers and swept everything before them in their devouring march. He wet his lips when he read that. Perhaps the opportunity would come then to destroy, to destroy, *and destroy*.

Almost, Mr. Smith forgot people and the solar system and what had been. Here in this new world, there was only he and the *kifs*. The *baroons* and the *marigees* didn't count. They had no order and no system. The *kifs*—

In the intensity of his hatred there slowly filtered through a grudging admiration. The *kifs* were true totalitarians. They practiced what he had preached to a mightier race, practiced it with a thoroughness beyond the kind of man to comprehend.

Theirs the complete submergence of the individual to the state, theirs the complete ruthlessness of the true conqueror, the perfect selfless bravery of the true soldier.

But they got into his bed, into his clothes, into his food.

They crawled with intolerable tickling feet.

Nights he walked the beach, and that night was one of the noisy nights. There were high-flying, high-whining jet-craft up there in the moonlight sky and their shadows dappled the black water of the sea. The planes, the rockets, the jet-craft, they were what had ravaged his cities, had turned his railroads into twisted steel, had dropped their H-Bombs on his most vital factories.

He shook his fist at them and shrieked imprecations at the sky.

And when he had ceased shouting, there were voices on the beach. Conrad's voice in his ear, as it had sounded that day when Conrad had walked into the palace, white-faced, and forgotten the salute. "There is a breakthrough at Denver, Number One! Toronto and Monterey are in danger. And in the other hemispheres—" His voice cracked. "—the damned Martians and the traitors from Luna are driving over the Argentine. Others have landed near New Petrograd. It is a rout. All is lost!"

Voices crying, "Number One, *hail*! Number One, *hail*!"

A sea of hysterical voices. "Number One, *hail*! Number One—"

A voice that was louder, higher, more frenetic than any of the others. His memory of his own voice, calculated but inspired, as he'd heard it on play-backs of his own speeches.

The voices of children chanting, "To thee, O Number One—" He couldn't remember the rest of the words, but they had been beautiful words. That had been at the public school meet in the New Los Angeles. How strange that he should remember, here and now, the very tone of his voice and inflection, the shining wonder in their children's eyes. Children only, but they were willing to kill and die, *for him*, convinced that all that was needed to cure the ills of the race was a suitable leader to follow.

"*All is lost!*"

And suddenly the monster jet-craft were swooping downward and starkly he realized what a clear target he presented, here against the white moonlit beach. They must see him.

The crescendo of motors as he ran, sobbing now in fear, for the cover of the jungle. Into the screening shadow of the giant trees, and the sheltering blackness.

He stumbled and fell, was up and running again. And now his eyes could see in the dimmer moonlight that filtered through the branches overhead. Stirrings there, in the branches. Stirrings and voices in the night. Voices in and of the night. Whispers and shrieks of pain. Yes, he'd shown them pain, and now their tortured voices ran with him through the knee-deep, night-wet grass among the trees.

The night was hideous with noise. Red noises, an almost *tangible* din that he could nearly *feel* as well as he could see and hear it. And after a while his breath came raspingly, and there was a thumping sound that was the beating of his heart and the beating of the night.

And then, he could run no longer, and he clutched a tree to keep from falling, his arms trembling about it, and his face pressed against the impersonal roughness of the bark. There was no wind, but the tree swayed back and forth and his body with it.

Then, as abruptly as light goes on when a switch is thrown, the noise vanished. Utter silence, and at last he was strong enough to let go his grip on the tree and stand erect again, to look about to get his bearings.

One tree was like another, and for a moment he thought he'd have to stay here until daylight. Then he remembered that the sound of the surf would give him his directions. He listened hard and heard it, faint and far away.

And another sound—one that he had never heard before—faint, also, but seeming to come from his right and quite near.

He looked that way, and there was a patch of opening in the trees above. The grass was waving strangely in that area of moonlight. It moved, although there was no breeze to move it. And there was an almost sudden *edge*, beyond which the blades thinned out quickly to barrenness.

And the sound—it was like the sound of the surf, but it was continuous. It was more like the rustle of dry leaves, but there were no dry leaves to rustle.

Mr. Smith took a step toward the sound and looked down. More grass bent, and fell, and vanished, even as he looked. Beyond the moving edge of devastation was a brown floor of the moving bodies of *kifs*.

Row after row, orderly rank after orderly rank, marching resistlessly onward. Billions of *kifs*, an army of *kifs*, eating their way across the night.

Fascinated, he stared down at them. There was no danger, for their progress was slow. He retreated a step to keep beyond their front rank. The sound, then, was the sound of chewing.

He could see one edge of the column, and it was a neat, orderly edge. And there was discipline, for the ones on the outside were larger than those in the center.

He retreated another step—and then, quite suddenly, his body was afire in several spreading places. The vanguard. Ahead of the rank that ate away the grass.

His boots were brown with *kifs*.

Screaming with pain, he whirled about and ran, beating with his hands at the burning spots on his body. He ran head-on into a tree, bruising his face horribly, and the night was scarlet with pain and shooting fire.

But he staggered on, almost blindly, running, writhing, tearing off his clothes as he ran.

This, then, was *pain*. There was a shrill screaming in his ears that must have been the sound of his own voice.

When he could no longer run, he crawled. Naked, now, and with only a few *kifs* still clinging to him. And the blind tangent of his flight had taken him well out of the path of the advancing army.

But stark fear and the memory of unendurable pain drove him on. His knees raw now, he could no longer crawl. But he got himself erect again on trembling legs, and staggered on. Catching hold of a tree and pushing himself away from it to catch the next.

Falling, rising, falling again. His throat raw from the screaming invective of his hate. Bushes and the rough bark of trees tore his flesh.

*

Into the village compound just before dawn, staggered a man, a naked terrestrial. He looked about with dull eyes that seemed to see nothing and understand nothing.

The females and young ran before him, even the males retreated.

He stood there, swaying, and the incredulous eyes of the natives widened as they saw the condition of his body, and the blankness of his eyes.

When he made no hostile move, they came closer again, formed a wondering, chattering circle about him, these Venusian humanoids. Some ran to bring the chief and the chief's son, who knew everything.

The mad, naked human opened his lips as though he were going to speak, but instead, he fell. He fell, as a dead man falls. But when they turned him over in the dust, they saw that his chest still rose and fell in labored breathing.

And then came Alwa, the aged chieftain, and Nrana, his son. Alwa gave quick, excited orders. Two of the men carried Mr. Smith into the chief's hut, and the wives of the chief and the chief's son took over the Earthling's care, and rubbed him with a soothing and healing salve.

But for days and nights he lay without moving and without speaking or opening his eyes, and they did not know whether he would live or die.

Then, at last, he opened his eyes. And he talked, although they could make out nothing of the things he said.

Nrana came and listened, for Nrana of all of them spoke and understood best the Earthling's language, for he had been the special protege of the Terran missionary who had lived with them for a while.

Nrana listened, but he shook his head. "The words," he said, "the words are of the Terran tongue, but I make nothing of them. His mind is not well."

The aged Alwa said, "Aie. Stay beside him. Perhaps as his body heals, his words will be beautiful words as were the words of the Father-of-Us who, in the Terran tongue, taught us of the gods and their good."

So they cared for him well, and his wounds healed, and the day came when he opened his eyes and saw the handsome blue-complexioned face of Nrana sitting there beside him, and Nrana said softly, "Good day, Mr. Man of Earth. You feel better, no?"

There was no answer, and the deep-sunken eyes of the man on the sleeping mat stared, glared at him. Nrana could see that those eyes were not yet sane, but he saw, too, that the madness in them was not the same that it had been. Nrana did not know the words for delirium and paranoia, but he could distinguish between them.

No longer was the Earthling a raving maniac, and Nrana made a very common error, an error more civilized beings than he have often made. He thought the paranoia was an improvement over the wider madness. He talked on, hoping the Earthling would talk too, and he did not recognize the danger of his silence.

"We welcome you, Earthling," he said, "and hope that you will live among us, as did the Father-of-Us, Mr. Gerhardt. He taught us to worship the true gods of the high heavens. Jehovah, and Jesus and their prophets the men from the skies. He taught us to pray and to love our enemies."

And Nrana shook his head sadly, "But many of our tribe have gone back to the older gods, the cruel gods. They say there has been great strife among the outsiders, and no more remain upon all of Venus. My father, Alwa, and I are glad another one has come. You will be able to help those of us who have gone back. You can teach us love and kindliness."

The eyes of the dictator closed. Nrana did not know whether or not he slept, but Nrana stood up quietly to leave the hut. In the doorway, he turned and said, "We pray for you."

And then, joyously, he ran out of the village to seek the others, who were gathering bela-berries for the feast of the fourth event.

When, with several of them, he returned to the village, the Earthling was gone. The hut was empty.

Outside the compound they found, at last, the trail of his passing. They followed and it led to a stream and along the stream until they came to the tabu of the green pool, and could go no farther.

"He went downstream," said Alwa gravely. "He sought the sea and the beach. He was well then, in his mind, for he knew that all streams go to the sea."

"Perhaps he had a ship-of-the-sky there at the beach," Nrana said worriedly. "All Earthlings come from the sky. The Father-of-Us told us that."

"Perhaps he will come back to us," said Alwa. His old eyes misted.

*

Mr. Smith was coming back all right, and sooner than they had dared to hope. As soon in fact, as he could make the trip to the shack and return. He came back dressed in clothing very different from the garb the other white man had worn. Shining leather boots and the uniform of the Galactic Guard, and a wide leather belt with a holster for his needle gun.

But the gun was in his hand when, at dusk, he strode into the compound.

He said, "I am Number One, the Lord of all the Solar System, and your ruler. Who was chief among you?"

Alwa had been in his hut, but he heard the words and came out. He understood the words, but not their meaning. He said, "Earthling, we welcome you back. I am the chief."

"You were the chief. Now you will serve me. I am the chief."

Alwa's old eyes were bewildered at the strangeness of this. He said, "I will serve you, yes. All of us. But it is not fitting that an Earthling should be chief among—"

The whisper of the needle gun. Alwa's wrinkled hands went to his scrawny neck where, just off the center, was a sudden tiny pin prick of a hole. A faint trickle of red coursed over the dark blue of his skin. The old man's knees gave way under him as the rage of the poisoned needle dart struck him, and he fell. Others started toward him.

"Back," said Mr. Smith. "Let him die slowly that you may all see what happens to—"

But one of the chief's wives, one who did not understand the speech of Earth, was already lifting Alwa's head. The needle gun whispered again, and she fell forward across him.

"I am Number One," said Mr. Smith, "and Lord of all the planets. All who oppose me, die by—"

And then, suddenly all of them were running toward him. His finger pressed the trigger and four of them died before the avalanche of their bodies bore him down and overwhelmed him. Nrana had been first in that rush, and Nrana died.

The others tied the Earthling up and threw him into one of the huts. And then, while the women began wailing for the dead, the men made council.

They elected Kallana chief and he stood before them and said, "The Father-of-Us, the Mister Gerhardt, deceived us." There was fear and worry in his voice and apprehension on his blue face. "If this be indeed the Lord of whom he told us—"

"He is not a god," said another. "He is an Earthling, but there have been such before on Venus, many many of them who came long and long ago from the skies. Now they are all dead, killed in strife among themselves. It is well. This last one is one of them, but he is mad."

And they talked long and the dusk grew into night while they talked of what they must do. The gleam of firelight upon their bodies, and the waiting drummer.

The problem was difficult. To harm one who was mad was tabu. If he was really a god, it would be worse. Thunder and lightning from the sky would destroy the village. Yet they dared not release him. Even if they took the evil weapon-that-whispered-its-death and buried it, he might find other ways to harm them. He might have another where he had gone for the first.

Yes, it was a difficult problem for them, but the eldest and wisest of them, one M'Ganne, gave them at last the answer.

"O Kallana," he said, "Let us give him to the *kifs*. If *they* harm him—" and old M'Ganne grinned a toothless, mirthless grin "—it would be their doing and not ours."

Kallana shuddered. "It is the most horrible of all deaths. And if he is a god—"

"If he is a god, they will not harm him. If he is mad and not a god, we will not have harmed him. It harms not a man to tie him to a tree."

Kallana considered well, for the safety of his people was at stake. Considering, he remembered how Alwa and Nrana had died.

He said, "It is right."

The waiting drummer began the rhythm of the council-end, and those of the men who were young and fleet lighted torches in the fire and went out into the forest to seek the*kifs*, who were still in their season of marching.

145

And after a while, having found what they sought, they returned.

They took the Earthling out with them, then, and tied him to a tree. They left him there, and they left the gag over his lips because they did not wish to hear his screams when the *kifs* came.

The cloth of the gag would be eaten, too, but by that time, there would be no flesh under it from which a scream might come.

They left him, and went back to the compound, and the drums took up the rhythm of propitiation to the gods for what they had done. For they had, they knew, cut very close to the corner of a tabu—but the provocation had been great and they hoped they would not be punished.

All night the drums would throb.

*

The man tied to the tree struggled with his bonds, but they were strong and his writhings made the knots but tighten.

His eyes became accustomed to the darkness.

He tried to shout, "I am Number One, Lord of—"

And then, because he could not shout and because he could not loosen himself, there came a rift in his madness. He remembered who he was, and all the old hatreds and bitterness welled up in him.

He remembered, too, what had happened in the compound, and wondered why the Venusian natives had not killed him. Why, instead, they had tied him here alone in the darkness of the jungle.

Afar, he heard the throbbing of the drums, and they were like the beating of the heart of night, and there was a louder, nearer sound that was the pulse of blood in his ears as the fear came to him.

The fear that he knew why they had tied him here. The horrible, gibbering fear that, for the last time, an army marched against him.

He had time to savor that fear to the uttermost, to have it become a creeping certainty that crawled into the black corners of his soul as would the soldiers of the coming army crawl into his ears and nostrils while others would eat away his eyelids to get at the eyes behind them.

And then, and only then, did he hear the sound that was like the rustle of dry leaves, in a dank, black jungle where there were no dry leaves to rustle nor breeze to rustle them.

Horribly, Number One, the last of the dictators, did not go mad again; not exactly, but he laughed, and laughed and laughed . . . .

IT'S A SMALL SOLAR SYSTEM

by Allan Howard

Frederik Pohl wrote recently about the time, when he was young, when he spent more time in Barsoom than in Brooklyn. Allan Howard, Director of the Eastern Science Fiction Association in Newark, takes us back to those nostalgic days in this vignette of man's first hours on Mars.

Soon the three representatives of Earth were walking shoulder to shoulder, the Captain first to touch soil.

KNOW HIM?

Well you might say I practically grew up with him. He was my hero in those days. I thought few wiser or greater men ever lived. In my eyes he was greater than Babe Ruth, Lindy, or the President.

Of course, time, and my growing up caused me to bring him into a perspective that I felt to be more consonant with his true position in his field of endeavor. When he died his friends mourned for fond remembrance of things past, but privately many of them felt that he had outlived his best days. Now with this glorious vindication, I wonder how many of them are still alive to feel the twinge of conscience . . . .

Oh, we're delighted of course, but it seems incredible even today to us elated oldsters. Although we were always his staunchest admirers, in retrospect we can see now that no one believed more than we that he did it strictly for the dollar. It is likely there was always a small corps of starry-eyed adolescents who found the whole improbable saga entirely believable, or at least half believed it might be partly true. The attitude of the rest of us ranged from a patronizing disparagement that we thought was expected of us, through grudging admiration, to out-and-out enthusiasm.

Certainly if anybody had taken the trouble to consider it—and why should they have?—the landing of the first manned ship on our satellite seemed to render him as obsolete as a horde of other lesser and even greater lights. At any rate, it was inevitable that the conquest of the moon would be merely a stepping-stone to more distant points.

Oh, no, I had nothing to do with the selection of the Red Planet. Coming in as head of Project P-4 in its latter stages, as I did when Dr. Fredericks died, the selection had already been made. Yes, it's quite likely I may have been plugging for Mars below the conscious level. A combination of chance, expediency and popular demand made Mars the next target, rather than Venus, which was, in some ways, the more logical goal. I would have given anything to have gone, but the metaphorical stout heart that one reporter once credited me with is not the same as an old man's actual fatty heart.

147

And there were heartbreak years ahead before the *Goddard* was finally ready. During this time he slipped further into obscurity while big, important things were happening all around us. You're right, that one really big creation of his *is* bigger than ever. It has passed into the language, and meant employment for thousands of people. Too few of them have even heard of him. Of course, he was still known and welcomed by a small circle of acquaintances, but to the world at large he was truly a "forgotten man."

It is worthy of note that one of the oldest of these acquaintances was present at blast-off time. He happened to be the grandfather of a certain competent young crewman. The old man was a proud figure during the brief ceremonies and his eyes filled with tears as the mighty rocket climbed straight up on its fiery tail. He remained there gazing up at the sky long after it had vanished.

He was heard to murmur, "I am glad the kid could go, but it is just a lark to him. He never had a 'sense of wonder.' How could he—nobody reads anymore."

Afterward, his senile emotions betraying him, he broke down completely and had to be led from the field. It is rumored he did not live long after that.

The *Goddard* drove on until Mars filled the viz-screen. It was planned to make at least a half-dozen braking passes around the planet for observational purposes before the actual business of bringing the ship in for landfall began. As expected the atmosphere proved to be thin. The speculated dead-sea areas, oddly enough, turned out to be just that. To the surprise of some, it was soon evident that Mars possessed, or had possessed, a high civilization. The *canali* of Schiaparelli were indeed broad waterways stretching from pole to pole, too regular to be anything but the work of intelligence. But most wonderful of all were the scattered, but fairly numerous large, walled cities that dotted the world. Everybody was excited, eager to land and start exercising their specialties.

One of the largest of these cities was selected more or less at random. It was decided to set down just outside, yet far enough from the walls to avoid any possibility of damage from the landing jets in the event the city was inhabited. Even if deserted, the entire scientific personnel would have raised a howl that would have been heard back on Earth if just a section of wall was scorched. When planet-fall was completed and observers had time to scan the surroundings it was seen that the city was very much alive.

"What keeps them up!" marvelled Kopchainski, the aeronautics and rocketry authority.

The sky swarmed with ships of strange design. The walls were crowded with inhabitants, too far away for detailed observation. Even as they looked an enormous gate opened and a procession of mounted figures emerged. In the event the place was deserted, the Captain would have had the honor of being the first to touch Martian soil. While atmospheric and other checks were being run, he gave orders for the previously decided alternative. Captain, semanticist and anthropologist would make the First Contact.

With all checks agreeing that it was safe to open locks, soon the three representatives of Earth were walking shoulder to shoulder down the ramp. It was apparent that the two scientists purposely missed stride inches from the end, so that it was the Captain's foot that actually touched ground first.

The cavalcade—though these beasties were certainly not horses—was now near enough to the ship for details to be seen. Surprise and wonderment filled the crew, for while the multi-legged steeds were as alien as anyone might expect to find on an alien world, the riders were very definitely humanoid. Briefly, brightly and barbarically trapped as they were by earthly standards, they seemed to be little distinguishable from homegrown homo saps.

The approaching company appeared to be armed mainly with swords and lances, but also in evidence were some tubular affairs that could very well be some sort of projectile-discharging device. The Captain suddenly felt unaccountably warm. It was a heavy responsibility—he hoped these Martians wouldn't be the type of madmen who believed in the "shoot first, inquire later" theory.

Even as he stood there, outwardly calm but jittering internally, the Martian riders pulled up ten feet from the Earthmen. Their leader, tall, dark-haired, and subtly lighter in hue than his companions, dismounted and approached the Captain. With outstretched hand he took the Captain's in a firm grip.

Let it be recorded here, to the shame of an Earth where reading for pleasure is virtually a lost pastime, that not one man on the *Goddard* realized the significance of what followed.

"How do you do?" he said in perfect English, with an unmistakable trace of Southern accent.

"Welcome to Barsoom! My name is John Carter."

THE VERY BLACK

by Dean Evans

Anders was pretty sure he was going to die. No one had yet flown the new-style jet job and lived to tell the tale. A story both chilling and heart-warming that shows us how bravely the human equation can operate when the chips are stacked against it.

Jet test-pilots and love do not mix too happily as a rule—especially with a ninth-dimensional alter ego messing the whole act.

There was nothing peculiar about that certain night I suppose—except to me personally. A little earlier in the evening I'd walked out on the Doll, Margie Hayman—and a man doesn't do that and cheer over it. Not if he's in love with the Doll he doesn't—not *this* doll. If you've ever seen her you'll give the nod on that.

The trouble had been Air Force's new triangular ship—the new saucer. Not radio controlled, this one—this one was to carry a real live pilot. At least that's what the doll's father, who was Chief Engineer at Airtech, Inc., had in mind when he designed it.

The doll had said to me sort of casually, "Got something, Baby." She called me baby. Me, one eighty-five in goose pimples.

"Toss it over, Doll," I said.

"No strings on you, Baby." She'd grinned that little one-sided grin of hers. "No strings on you. Not even one. You're a flyboy, you are, and you can take off or land any time any place you feel like it."

"Stake your mom's Charleston cup on that," I said.

She nodded. Her one-sided grin seemed to fade slightly but she hooked it up again fast. A doll—like I said. This was the original model, they've never gone into production on girls like her full-time.

She said, "Therefore, I've got no right to go stalking with a salt shaker in one hand and a pair of shears for your tailfeathers in the other."

"You're cute, Doll," I said, still going along with her one hundred percent.

"Nice—we get along nice."

"Somebody oughta set 'em up on that."

"So far."

"Huh?" I blinked. I hate sour notes. That's why I'm not a musician. You never get a sour note in a jet job—or if you do you don't get annoyed. That's the sour note to end all sour notes.

"Brace yourself, Baby," she said.

150

I took a hitch on the highball glass I was holding and let one eye get a serious look in it. "Shoot," I told her.

"This new job—this new saucer the TV newscasts are blatting about. You boys in the Air Force heard about it yet?"

"There's been a rumor," I said. I frowned. Top secret—in a pig's eyelash!

"Uh-huh. Is it true this particular ship is supposed to carry a pilot this time?"

"Where do they dig up all this old stuff?" I growled. "Hell, I knew all about that way way back this afternoon already."

"Uh-huh, Is it also true they've asked a flyboy named Eddie Anders to take it up the first time? This flyboy named Eddie Anders being my Baby?"

I got bored with the highball. I tossed it down the hole in my head and put the glass on a table. "You're psychic," I said.

She shrugged. "Good looking, maybe. Nice shape, maybe. Peachy disposition, maybe. Psychic, unh-unhh. But who else would they ask to do it?"

"A point," I conceded.

"Fork in the road coming up," the Doll said.

"Huh?"

"Fork—look. It'll be voluntary, won't it? You don't have to do it? They won't think the worse of you if you refuse?"

"*Huh?*" I gawked at her.

"I'm scared, Baby."

Her eyes weren't blue anymore. They'd been blue before but not now. Now they were violet balls that were laying me like somebody taking a last long look at the thing down inside the nice white satin before they close the cover on it for the final time.

"Have a drink, Doll," I said. I got up, went to the liquor wagon. "Seltzer? There isn't any mixer left."

"Asked you something, Baby."

I took her glass over. I handed it to her. My own drink I poured down that same hole in my head. I said finally, "Nice smooth bourbon but I like scotch better."

"They've already crashed four of this new type on tests, haven't they?"

I nearly choked. *That* was supposed to be the very pinnacle of the top secret stuff. But she was right of course. Four of the earlier models had cracked up. No pilots in them at the time—radio controlled. But jobs designed to carry pilots nevertheless.

"Some pitchers have great big ugly-looking ears," I said.

She didn't seem to mind. She said, "Or maybe I'm really psychic as you said. Or maybe my Dad's being Chief at Airtech has something to do with it."

"Somebody oughta stitch a zipper across his big fat yap," I said. "And weld the damn thing shut."

"He told only me," she said softly. "And then only because of you. You see, Baby, he isn't like us. He's got old fashioned notions you and I've got strings tied around each other already just because you gave me a ring."

I stared at her.

"Crazy, isn't it? He isn't sensible like us."

"Can the gag lines, Doll," I said sourly. "The old bird's okay."

And that fetched a few moments of silence in the room—thick pervading silence. A silence to be broken at any fractional second and heavy—supercharged—because of it.

I said finally, "Somebody has to take it up. It might as well be me. And they've already asked me."

"You could refuse, Baby."

"Sure I could. It's voluntary. They don't horsewhip a guy into it."

"Uh-huh—voluntary. And you *can* refuse." She stopped, waited, then, "Making me get right down there on the hard bare floor on both knees, Baby? All right. None of us should be proud. None of us has a right to be proud, have we?

"All right, Baby. I'm down there—way, way down there. I'm asking you not to take that ship up. I'm begging you—begging, Baby. Look, on me you've never seen anything like this before. Begging!"

I looked at my empty glass. The taste in my mouth was suddenly bitter. "No strings, we said," I said harshly. "A flyboy, we said. Guy who can take off and land anywhere, anytime he likes. Stuff like that we just got through saying."

She didn't answer that. I waited. She didn't answer. I got up finally, got my lousy new officer's cap off the TV set and went over to the door. I opened the door. I went on through.

But before I closed it I heard her whisper. That's the trouble with whispers, they go incredible distances to get places. The whisper said, "That's right, Baby. Right as rain. No strings—*ever!*"

*

When you don't have any scotch in the house you'd be surprised how well rum will do—even Jamaica rum. I was on my own davenport in my own apartment and there were two shot glasses in front of me. I was taking turns on them so they wouldn't wear out. And what was keeping these glasses busy was me and a fifth of the Jamaica rum in my right hand. And that's when it all began.

Across the room a rather stout woman was needling a classic through the television screen and at the same time needing a shave rather badly. I wasn't paying any attention to her. I was thinking about the Doll. Wondering, worrying a little. And that's when it began.

That's when the voice said, "Mr. Anders, would you do me the goodness to forget that bottle for a moment?"

The voice seemed to be coming from the TV screen although the stout lady hadn't finished her song. The voice was like the disappointed sigh of a poor old bloke down to his last beer dime and having to look up into the bartender's grinning puss as the bartender downs a nice bubbly glass of champagne somebody bought for him. Poor guy, I thought. I downed glass number one. And then glass number two. And then I looked over at the TV screen.

That sent a little shiver up my spine. I dropped my eyes to the glasses, filled them once more. Strong stuff, Jamaica rum. At the first the taste is medicine. A little later the taste is pleasant syrup. And a little later still the taste is delightful. But strong—the whole way strong. I downed glass number one.

I figured I wouldn't touch glass number two yet. I brought up my eyes, let them go over to the TV screen again.

He didn't have any eyes. That was the first thing that struck me. There were other things of course, such as the fact he didn't have any arms or legs. He didn't have any head either, in case he had eyes in the first place. He was a black swirling bioplastic mass of something or other and he was doing a graceful tango directly in front of the TV screen, thereby blocking off from view the stout woman who needed a shave.

He said, "Do you have any idea what I am, Mr. Anders?"

"Sure," I said. "Somebody's blennorrheal nightmare."

"Incorrect, Mr. Anders. This substance is not mucous. Mucous is very seldom black."

"Mucous is very seldom black," I mimicked.

"Correct, Mr. Anders."

So all right. So they were making Jamaica rum a little stronger these days. So *all right*! Next time I wouldn't get rum, I'd get scotch. Hell with rum. I dismissed the thought from my mind. I picked up glass number two, downed it. I wondered if the Doll was feeling sorry for herself.

"Incorrect, Mr. Anders," he said. "The rum is no stronger than usual."

I jerked. I stared at the black sticky-looking thing he was. I shut my eyes tightly, snapped them open again. Then I worked the glasses again with the bottle.

"Don't be shocked, Mr. Anders. I'm not a mind reader. It's just that you discarded the thought of a moment ago. I picked it up, see?"

"Sure," I said. "You picked it out of the junk pile of my mind, where all my little gems go."

"Correct, Mr. Anders."

It was about time to empty the glasses again. I varied the routine this time by picking up number-two glass first.

"Light a cigarette, Mr. Anders."

I'm a guy to go along with a gag. I fished a cigarette out, lit it "Lit," I said. And just at that instant the stout dame without the shave hit a sour one way up around A above high C. My ears cringed. I forgot the cigarette and glared across the room, trying to see through the black swirling mass that stood in front of the TV screen.

"Puff, Mr. Anders."

I puffed. The puff sounded like somebody getting his lips on a very full glass of beer and quickly sucking so that foaming clouds don't go down the sides of the glass and all over the bar. I didn't have any cigarette.

"Ah!"

I blinked. The black swirling mass was going gently to and fro. At about head height on a man my cigarette was sticking out from it and a little curl of smoke was coming from the end. Even as I looked the curl ceased and then a big blue cloud of smoke barreled across the room toward my face.

"Your cigarette, Mr. Anders."

"Nice trick," I said. "Took it out from between my lips and I never felt it. Nice trick."

"Incorrect, Mr. Anders. When the singer flatted that particular note your attention was diverted momentarily. Your senses are exceptional, you see. Your ears register pain at false sounds. Therefore, you discarded the thoughts of your cigarette during the moment you suffered with the singer. Following this reasoning, your cigarette went into abandonment. And I salvaged it. No trick at all, really."

I thought, to hell with the shot glasses. I put the rum bottle to my lips and tilted it up and held it there until it wasn't good for anything anymore. Then I took it down by the neck and heaved it straight at the black mass.

The television screen didn't shatter, which proved something or other. The bottle didn't even reach the screen. It hit the black swirling mass about navel high. It went in, sank in like slamming your fist into a fat man's stomach. And then it rebounded and clattered on the floor.

"Scream!" I said thickly. "You dirty black delusion—scream!"

"I *am* screaming, Mr. Anders. That hurt terribly."

He sort of unfolded then, like unfolding a limp wool sweater in the air. And from this unfolding, something came forth that could have been somebody's old fashioned idea of what a rifle looked like. He held it up in firing position, pointed at my head.

"Don't be alarmed, Mr. Anders. This is to convince you. A gun, yes, a very old gun—a Brown Bess, they used to call it. I just took it from the City Museum, where it was on display."

He had a nice point-blank sight on my forehead. Now he moved the gun, aimed it off me, pointed, it across the room toward the open windows.

"Note the workmanship, Mr. Anders. Note the stock. Someone put a little effort on the carving. Note the sentiment carved here."

The rum was working hard now. I could feel it climbing hand over hand up from my knees.

"Let me read what it says, Mr. Anders—'*Deathe to ye Colonies*'. Note the odd wording, the spelling. And now watch, Mr. Anders."

The gun came up a trifle, stiffened. There was a loud snapping sound, a click of metal on metal—Flintlock. As all the ancient guns were.

And then came the roar. Wood across the room—the window casing—splintered and flew wildly. Smoke and smell filled my senses.

He said, chuckling, "Let's call it the Abandonment Theory for lack of a better name. This old Brown Bess hasn't been thought of acquisitively for some years. It's been in the museum—abandoned. Therefore subject to the discarded junk pile as you yourself so cleverly put it before. Do I make myself clear, Mr. Anders?"

Perfectly—oh, perfectly, Mr. Bioplast. The rum was going around my eyes now. Going up and around and headed like an arrow for the hunk of my brain that can't seem to hide fast enough.

I guess I made it to the bedroom but I wouldn't put any hard cash on it. And I guess I passed out.

*

The morning was a bad one as all bad ones usually are. But no matter how bad they get there's always the consoling thought that in a few hours things will ease up. I hugged this thought through a needle shower, through three cups of coffee in the kitchen. What I was neglecting in this reasoning was the splintered wood in the living room.

I saw it on my way out. It hit me starkly, like the blasted section of a eucalyptus trunk writhing up from the ground. I stopped dead in the doorway and stared at it. Then I got out my knife and got at it.

I probed but it was going to take more than a pocket knife. The ball—and it was just that—was buried a half inch in the soft pine of the casing.

I closed the knife and went to the phone and got Information to ring the museum.

"You people aren't missing a Brown Bess musket," I said. It was a question, of course, but not now—not the way I had said it. "Nobody stole anything out of the museum last night, did they?"

Sweat was oozing over my upper lip. I could feel it. I could feel sweat wetting the phone in my hand. The woman on the other end told me to wait. I said, "Yeah"—not realizing. I waited, not realizing, until a man's voice came on.

"You were saying something about a Brown Bess musket, mister?" A cold sharp voice a gutter voice but with the masking tag of *official* behind it. Like the voice of someone behind a desk writing something on a blotter—a real police voice.

I put the phone down. I pulled all the shades in the living room, went out the door, locked it behind me and drove as fast as you can make a Buick go, out to the field. But *fast!*

The XXE-1 was ready. She'd been ready for weeks. There wasn't a mechanical or electronic flaw in her. We hoped, I hoped, the man who designed her hoped. The Doll's father—he hoped most of all. Even lying quiescent in her hangar, she looked as sleek as a Napoleon hat done in poured monel. When your eyes went over her you knew instinctively they'd thrown the mach numbers out the window when she was done.

I went through a door that had the simple word *Plotting* on it.

The Doll's father was there already behind his desk, studying something as I came in. He looked up, smiled, said, "Hi, guy."

I flipped a finger at him. I wondered if the Doll had told him about last night.

"Wife and I were going to suggest a snack when we got home last night but you had already gone, and Marge was in bed."

I didn't look at him. "Left early, Pop. Growing boy."

"Yeah. You look lousy, guy."

I put my teeth together. I still didn't look at him. "These nights," I said vaguely. "Sure."

I could feel something in his voice. I took a breath and put my eyes on his. He said, "I'm a hell of an old duck."

"Not so old, Pop."

"Sure I am. But not too old to remember back to the days when I wasn't too old." There was a grave look in his eyes.

I didn't have to answer that. The door banged open and Melrose, the LC, came in. He jerked a look at both of us, butted a cigarette he'd just lit—lighted another, butted that. He ran a hand through thick graying hair and frowned.

"Anybody got a cigarette?" he said sourly. "Couldn't sleep last night. This damned responsibility. Worried all night about something we hadn't thought of."

Pop looked up. Melrose went on. "Light—travels in a straight line, no?" He blinked small nervous eyes at us. Then, "Can't go around corners unless it's helped, you see. I mean just this. The XXE-One is expected to hit a significant fraction of the speed of light once it gets beyond the atmosphere. Now here's the point—how in hell do we control it then?"

He waited. I didn't say anything. Pop didn't say anything. Melrose ran a hand through his hair once more, muttered *goddamit* to himself, turned around and went barging out the door.

Pop said wryly, "Another quick memo to the Pentagon. He never heard of the Earth's gravity."

"He's heard," I said. "It's just that it slipped his mind these last few years."

Pop grinned. He handed me a sheaf of typewritten notes. "These'll just about make it. You'll notice the initial flight is charted pretty damn closely."

"Thanks, Pop. I better take these, somewhere else to look 'em over. Melrose might be back."

"Pretty damn closely," he repeated. "Almost as closely as if she was going up under radio control . . . ." He stopped. He looked at me from under his eyebrows.

I studied him. "Already told the brass I'd take her up, Pop." I kept my voice down.

"Sure, guy. Sure. Uh—you mention it to Marge?"

"Last night."

"I see." His eyes got suddenly far away. I left him like that. Hell with him—hell with the whole family!

*

It was in the evening paper, tucked in the second section. They treated it lightly. It seemed the night watchman had opened the rear door of the museum for a breath of air or maybe a smoke. Or maybe to kitchie-koo some babe under the chin in the alley.

That's the only way it could have happened. And he'd discovered the empty exhibit case at 2:10 in the morning. The case still had a little white card on it that told about the Brown Bess musket and the powder horn and the ball shot inside.

But the little white card lied in its teeth. There weren't any such things in the case at all. And he'd notified the curator at once.

There was also mention of a mysterious phone call which couldn't be traced.

Things like this don't happen in 1953. So I didn't get loaded that night. I went home, went to the davenport, sat down and told myself they don't happen. Things like this have never happened, will never happen. What occurred last night was something in the bottom of a bottle of Jamaica rum.

"Thinking, Mr. Anders?"

I took a slow breath. He was swaying gently in the air a foot from my elbow and he was still a black mucous scum, as he had been the night before. I got up.

I said, "I'm not loaded tonight. I haven't had a thing all day." I took two steps toward him.

He wasn't there.

I took another breath—a very very slow breath. I turned around and went back to the davenport.

He was back again.

"They'll find that musket," he said. "I have no use for it now. You see I wanted it only to convince you, Mr. Anders."

I put my hands on my knees and didn't look at him. I was suddenly trying to remember where I'd put that Luger I'd brought home from Germany a couple years back.

"You're not quite convinced yet, Mr. Anders?"

Where in the hell did I put it?

"Very well, Mr. Anders. Now hear this, please. Now watch me." He stirred at about hip height. A shelf-like section of the black mass protruded a little distance from the main part of him. On this shelf suddenly lay a rusted penknife.

"A very little boy, Mr. Anders. And a very long while ago. A talented boy, one of those who has what might be called an exceptional imagination. This boy cherished a penknife when he was quite small. Pick up the knife, Mr. Anders."

The knife was suddenly in my lap. I picked it up. It was rusty. It had a flat bone handle. "Museums again," I whispered to myself.

"So highly did this boy prize his knife that he went to great pains to carve his name very very carefully on one side of the bone handle. Turn the knife over, Mr. Anders."

The name was Edward Anders.

"You lost it when you were eleven. You wouldn't remember though. I found it in an attic where it lay unnoticed. As the years went by you gradually forgot about the knife, you see, and when your mind had completely abandoned the thoughts of it, it was mine—had I wanted it. As a matter of fact I didn't. I retrieved it just today."

I put the knife down. Sweat was coming on my forehead now, I could feel it. I was remembering. I was remembering the knife and what was scaring me even more was I was remembering the very day I had lost it. In the attic.

I said very carefully, "All right. You've made your point. You can take it from there."

"Quite so, Mr. Anders. You now admit I exist, that I have extraordinary powers. I am your own creation, Mr. Anders. As I said before you have exceptional senses, including imagination. And yes, imagination is the greatest of all the senses.

"Some humans with this gift often imagine ludicrous things, exciting things, horrifying things—depending don't you see, on mood, emotion. And the things these mortals imagine become real, are actually, created—only they don't know it, of course."

He stopped. He was probably giving me time to soak that up. Then he went on. "You've forgotten to keep trying to remember where you put that Luger, Mr. Anders. I just picked up the abandoned thought as it left your consciousness just now."

I gulped down something that tried to rise in my throat. I didn't like this guy.

"You created me when you were fourteen, Mr. Anders. You imagined me as a swashbuckling pirate. The only difference between me and the others who have been created in times past is that I have attained the ninth dimension. I am the first to do that. Also the first to capture the secrets of your own third dimension. Naturally then, it would be a pity for me to die."

"Get out," I said.

"Forgive me, Mr. Anders. My time is short. I die tomorrow."

"That's swell. Now get out."

"We're not immortal, you see. When our creators die their imaginations die with them. We too die. It follows. But for some time I've had an idea."

"Out," I said again. "Get the hell out of here!"

"You're going to die tomorrow, Mr. Anders, in that new flying saucer. And I must die with you. Except that I've had this idea."

There are times when you look yourself in the eye and don't like what you see. Or maybe what you see scares the living hell out of you. When those times come along some little something inside tells you you'd better watch out. Then the doubts creep in. After that the melancholy. And from that instant on you aren't very sane anymore.

"*Out!*" I yelled. "Out, *out*, OUT! Get the hell out!"

"One moment, Mr. Anders. Now as to this idea of mine. There's this woman—this Margie Hayman. This woman you call the Doll."

That one jerked me around.

"Exactly. Now listen very carefully. You aren't entirely you anymore, Mr. Anders. I mean, you aren't the complete *whole* individual you as you once were. You love this woman. Something inside you has gone out and is now a part of her."

"Therefore, if you will just discard the thought of her sometime between now and when you take that ship up I can attach myself to her sentient being, don't you see, and thereby exist—at least partly—even though you yourself are dead."

I pushed myself unsteadily to my feet. I stared at the entire black repulsive undulating mass before me. I took a step toward it.

"It isn't much to ask, Mr. Anders. You've quarrelled with her. You want no more of her. You've practically told her that. All I ask is that you finish the job—forget her. Discard her—throw her into the mental junk pile of Abandonment."

I didn't take any more steps. Something inside me was screaming, was ripping at my guts, was roaring with all the cacaphony of all the giant discords of all eternity. Something inside my brain was sucking all my strength in one tremendous, surging power-dive of wish fulfillment. I was willing the black mucous mass of him out of my consciousness.

He was no longer there. The only thing to prove he'd ever been there at all was a very-old, very-rusty penknife over on the table in front of the davenport—the knife with my name carved on the bone handle.

After that I went unsteadily to the dresser in the living room. I got the Doll's picture down off the dresser. I undressed. I took the picture to bed with me. The lights burned in my bedroom the entire night.

*

Lieutenant Colonel Melrose looked weatherbeaten. His graying hair was pulled here and there like a rag mop that's dried dirty—stiff. He had a freshly lit cigarette between his lips. He grinned nervously when he saw me, butted the cigarette, said in a thin voice, "This is it, Anders. Ship goes up in twenty minutes."

"I know," I said.

He poked another cigarette at his lips. He said, "What?" in a startled tone.

"Nothing," I said. "All right, I'll get ready."

He lit the cigarette, took a puff that made the smoke do a frenetic dance around his nostrils. He jabbed it at an ashtray, bobbed his head in a convulsive movement, said, "Righto!"

They strapped me in. Pop came to the open hatch. He stuck his head in, grinned, said, "Hi, guy," softly. There was something in his eyes. The Doll had told him how I hate sour notes.

"How's the Doll, Pop?" I forced myself to say it.

"Swell, Ed. Just got a call from her. On her way out here to see you take off. Looks like she won't make it now though."

I didn't say anything. His eyes went down to the wallet I had propped up on my knees. The wallet was open, celluloid window showing. Inside the window was the Doll's picture.

"Tell her that, Pop," I said.

"Yeah, guy. Luck."

They shut the hatch.

There was no doubt about the takeoff. If one thing was perfected in the XXE-1 it was that. The ship rose like the mercury in a thermometer on a hot day in July. I took it slow to fifty thousand feet.

"Fifty thousand," I said into the throat mike.

"Hear you, Anders." Melrose's voice.

"Smooth," I said. "Radar on me?"

"On you, Anders."

I let the ship have a little head. This job used the clutch of a tax collector's claws for fuel. It just hooked itself on the nothing around us and yanked—and there we were.

One hundred thousand.

"Double that," I said into the mike.

"Yeah, Anders. How is it?"

"Haven't yet begun. Radar still on me?"

I heard a nervous laugh. *He* was nervous. "The General—General Hotchkiss just said something, Anders. He—ha, ha—he said you're on plot like stitches in a fat lady's hip. Ha, ha! He's got *us* all in stitches. Ha, ha!"

Ha, ha!

This was it. I released my grip on the accelerator control, yet it slide up. They say you can't feel speed in the air unless there's something relative within vision to tip you off. They're going to have to revise that. You can not only feel speed you can reach out and break hunks off it—in the XXE-1, that is. I shook my head, took my eyes off the instruments and looked down at the Doll on my lap.

"Melrose?"

"Hear you, Anders."

"This is it. Reaching me on radar still?"

"Naturally."

"All right."

This was it. This was where the other four ships like the XXE-1—the radio controlled models—had disintegrated. This was where it happened, and they didn't come back anymore.

I sucked in oxygen and let the accelerator control go over all the way.

Pulling a ship out of a steep dive, yes. Blackout then, yes. If the wings stay with you everything's fine and you live to mention the incident at the bar a little while later. Blackout accelerating—climbing—is not in the books. But blackout, nevertheless. Not just plain blackout but a thick mucous, slimy undulating blackout—the very black.

The very very black.

*

General Hotchkiss, "What's he saying, Melrose?"

Melrose, "Doesn't answer."

General Eaton, "Try again."

Melrose, "Yes sir."

General Hotchkiss, "What's he saying, Melrose?"

General Eaton, "Still nothing?"

Melrose, "Nothing."

General Hotchkiss, "Dammit, you've still got him on radar, haven't you?"

Melrose, "Yes sir."

General Hotchkiss, "Well, dammit, what's he doing?"

Melrose, "Still going up, sir."

General Eaton, "How far up?"

Melrose, "Signal takes sixty seconds to get back, sir."

General Hotchkiss, "God in heaven! One hundred and twenty thousand miles out! Halfway to the moon. How much more fuel has he?"

Melrose, "Five seconds, sir. Then the auto-switch cuts in. Power will go off until he nears atmosphere again. After that, if he isn't conscious—well, I'm awfully afraid we've lost another ship."

General Eaton, "Cold blooded—"

*

The purple drapes before my eyes were wavering. Hung like rippled steel pieces of a caisson suspended by a perilously thin whisper of thread, they swayed, hesitated, shuddered their entire length, then began to bend in the middle from the combined weights of thirteen galaxies. The bend became a cracking bulge that in another second would explode destruction directly into my face. I screamed.

"Is—is that you, Anders?"

I screamed good this time.

"An—Anders! You all right? What happened? I couldn't get through to you?"

I took my hand from the accelerator control and stared numbly at it. The mark of it was deep in the skin. I sucked in oxygen.

"*Anders!* Your power is off. When you hear the signal you've got just three more seconds. You know what to do then. You've been out of the envelope, Anders! You broke through the atmosphere!"

And then I heard him speak to somebody else—he must have been speaking to somebody else, he couldn't have meant me—"Crissake, give me a cigarette. The guy's still alive."

I suppose I was grinning when they unstrapped me and slid me out of the hatch. They were grinning back at any rate. The ground held me up surprisingly—like it always had all my life before. They'd stopped grinning now, their eyes were eating the inside of the ship. They weren't interested in me anymore—all they wanted was the instruments' readings.

My feet could still move me. Knew where to go. Knew where to find the door that had the simple word *Plotting* on it.

The Doll was there with her father. The two of them didn't say anything, just looked at me—just stared at me. I said, "He tried damned hard. He put everything he had in it. He got me. He had me down and there wasn't any up again for the rest of the world. For me there wasn't."

They stared. Pop stared. The Doll stared.

"Just one thing he forgot," I muttered. "He gave me the tip-off himself and then he forgot it. He told me I wasn't all me anymore, that a part of me had gone out to you since I was supposed to be in love with you. And that's where the tip-off lies. I wasn't all me anymore but I hadn't lost anything. You know why, Doll?"

They stared.

"Simple—any damn fool would tumble. If I wasn't all me, then you weren't all you. Part of you was me—get it? And *you* weren't scheduled to bust out today. Not you—me! And that's what he couldn't work over. That's what brought me down again. He couldn't touch that." I stopped for a moment.

I said suddenly, "What the hell you guys staring at?" I growled.

"That's my Baby," said the Doll.

"No strings," I said.

"Like we said." Her words were soft petals. "Like we said, Baby. Just like we said."

"Sure. Only damn it, I don't like it that way. I *want* strings, see? I want meshes of 'em, balls of 'em, like what comes in yarn—get it?"

The Doll grinned. "Sure, Baby—you're sure you want it that way?"

"Sure I'm sure. I just said it, didn't I? *Didn't* I?"

"You just said it, Baby." She left her father's side, came over to me, put her arm in mine, pulled close. We turned, started to go out the door.

"Where you guys going?" asked Pop. We turned again. He looked like something was skipped somewhere on a sound track he'd been listening to. I grinned.

"Gotta look for a Brown Bess," I said. "Museum just lost one."

THE SECOND VOICE

by Mann Rubin

We proudly enter a new name in the science-fiction sweepstakes. This is Mr. Rubin's initial appearance in the field. His literary efforts to date add up quite handsomely, we think. QUOTE. *I have sold to the TV show,* TALES OF TOMORROW *and two literary quarterlies have published my fiction. Last year I won the Stephen Vincent Benét Award for my one-act plays produced at Stanford University.* UNQUOTE. *The reading pleasure is yours.*

Spud, world-famous dummy, talks to Mars with surprising results.

CRAWFORD COMPLETED the rehearsal in less than an hour. He listened to the orchestra run through its selections, okayed the song the guest vocalist had chosen, then finished up with a long dialogue between Spud and himself. When it was over he checked timing with the program director, made a few script changes and conferred briefly with a Special Service Officer about the number of troops the auditorium could hold. Everything was running smoothly. It was going to be a neat, action-packed show.

Backstage he looked at his watch. He had almost two hours before the regular show began and he was restless. Two hours at Harlow Field could seem like two years. Guards and restrictions all over the place.

Harlow Field was the largest experimental base in the world, a veritable garden of atoms, the proving grounds for every secret weapon ever imagined. The security and the tight regulations gave Crawford the jitters on each of his visits.

He smoked a cigarette and tried making small talk with some of the soldiers on backstage detail. He posed for a picture and gave an interview to a reporter from an army newspaper, then excused himself and went to his dressing room with Spud propped in the crook of his arm.

He was used to it now; the applause, the audiences, the pictures, the autographs, the fuss. Everywhere the response was the same. They had either seen him in the movies or on television or in the nightclubs, where he first broke in his act. Now they wanted to establish an identity with him, to touch the merchandise, to stand close so that they could write home about the visiting celebrity. Crawford was a realist. It was all part of being a name.

It had taken him just five years to make the big time. Five years of road shows, coast-to-coast tours, one-night stands and a dummy named Spud to make him the hottest ventriloquist in the business. His act was tight, well-paced and popular. He had a weekly radio show, a television program and a seven-year contract with a major Hollywood studio. He was riding high.

Still he hadn't forgotten the soldiers. Two months each year he took time off to travel the USO circuit. His agent tore his hair, reminding him of the financial losses, but the USO had given him his first break so he had always answered their call. He liked enthusiastic audiences and the cheering of laugh-hungry men made him happy. Entertainment was his business and he enjoyed exhibiting his talent. The wider the audience the better he liked it.

His dressing room was located back of the auditorium. He closed the door behind him, put Spud on a chair and began getting out of his rehearsal clothes. He lit a cigarette and looked at himself in the mirror. He was tired and needed a shave. In the last week the pace had been fast. The USO tour still had a few days to run, but he was looking forward to its end. A vacation, the luxury of relaxation would all be his then.

He opened a drawer of the dressing table and pulled out a bottle of Scotch. There were two hours to be killed before the show. He drank a shot and thought about it. A shower, a shave, a good dinner and a walk around the base would consume the time. After the show he would drive back to town and check in at a hotel for a good night's sleep.

He was putting the bottle back in the drawer when a knock sounded on the door. He said "Come in," thinking it was one of the cast and didn't turn around. He heard the door open, glanced into the mirror and glimpsed Colonel Meadows, the Commanding Officer of Harlow Field, and a man in civilian clothes he didn't recognize. He turned around, reached for a bathrobe.

"Don't mind us, Robbie," said the Colonel. "Just dropped by to say hello." He was a small, plump man and his face was always red and perspiring. Crawford knew him slightly from the other two times he had played Harlow Field, but this was the first time the Colonel had ever paid him a backstage visit.

"Got a fan here who wants to meet you," continued the Colonel. "Shake hands with Dr. Paul Shalt, one of our base scientists. He and I just caught your rehearsal. Fine, very fine."

The doctor's name struck a chord and Crawford dug deep until it focused. Dr. Paul Shalt was a physicist working with the army. He specialized in the development of radar, was the chief developer of the electrical detonator used in atomic bombs.

"I enjoyed your performance very much," said Dr. Shalt. "Your voice is extraordinary." He had a smooth, angular face, black hair and black, penetrating eyes. "Amazing range."

"Thanks," said Crawford.

"And the clearness of tone is phenomenal," said Dr. Shalt. "Has it always been like that?"

Crawford nodded. "When I was a kid it embarrassed me, my voice," he said, smiling. "A trick voice, everybody called it. But it's a definite asset to a practitioner of the art of ventriloquism."

"You should have seen Dr. Shalt while you were on stage," said Colonel Meadows, beaming at him. "He was running all over the auditorium testing your voice with one of his gadgets."

*

Crawford grinned. "I didn't realize I moved my audience so."

Dr. Shalt laughed. "What Colonel Meadows says is true. I'm *very* interested in your vocal range. While you rehearsed I tested the quality and sound of your tone." He stopped, looked around the room until he discovered Spud where Crawford had put him on the chair. He walked over to the dummy and touched the wooden head with his hand.

"Actually it's a *second voice*, that sound and vibration you use for Spud. It's perfect, perfect for what I need, that second voice."

Dr. Shalt put the dummy back in the position he had found him in, reached into his pocket and brought out a small glass-enclosed instrument which he held in front of him.

"Do you know what this is?" he asked, approaching the dressing table.

"Never saw it before," Crawford said, examining the gadget. A small arrow flickered nervously within a glass cage.

"It's called a Voice Oscillator," explained Dr. Shalt. "It's sensitive to the slightest tonal inflection. We use it to measure the pitch and volume of a human voice."

"What's all this got to do with me?" Crawford asked.

"This—we want to use the voice of Spud for an experiment. A very important experiment. With your permission, we'd like to do it immediately."

"I'm afraid that's impossible," said Crawford. "I have a show in about—"

"Our equipment is all set up," interrupted the doctor. "The entire test will take forty-five minutes. We'll have you back in no time."

Crawford frowned. He was tired and he'd looked forward to relaxing a while before the show. "Couldn't we make it some other time," he said.

*

The Colonel spoke then. "Robbie, do you remember reading four years ago that our radar system was able to beam signals to the moon and have them returned?"

"Sure," said Crawford. "It got a big play in all the newspapers."

"Well, our scientists are now ready to conduct a similar experiment," said Colonel Meadows. "This time to Mars."

"To Mars!" repeated Crawford, wondering what it had to do with him.

"Only this time we plan to send a *voice*, a human voice that can travel through interstellar space," said Dr. Shalt.

"But that's impossible!" Crawford exclaimed.

"With the average voice, yes," said Dr. Shalt. "Cosmic disturbances would drown out a normal voice amplified a thousand times beyond its regular frequency. But a voice in a higher octave—like your second voice . . . Well, we believe there's a certain resonant intonation which can be curved and regulated in any direction, in the voice you use for your dummy."

Crawford nodded.

"Spud's voice contains that quality," continued Dr. Shalt. "I believe it can reach Mars and bounce back. I'm asking you to be the first man ever to throw his voice to another planet."

There was quiet for a moment when he finished. Crawford's cigarette had gone out and he relit it. The smoke steadied him. Outside, in the auditorium the orchestra had begun to rehearse again.

"Where's the station set-up?" asked Crawford finally.

"It's right here on the field, Robbie," Colonel Meadows said quickly. "We've had it under wraps for the last eight months. It'll be a tremendous thing if it works."

Crawford dragged on his cigarette a last time and stamped it out. He walked over to Spud, lifted the dummy into position in the crook of his arm.

"What do you say, Crawford?" asked Dr. Shalt. There was a note of urgency in his voice.

"I don't know," said Crawford slowly. "My crazy voice is my bread and butter. Can't you use somebody else? Somebody whose voice isn't his life?"

"We've wasted weeks testing every man on this field," said Dr. Shalt solemnly. "The average voice becomes static as soon as it gets past Earth's atmosphere. But your voice can break through. I've studied every vibration, every quiver of it. It bends and flexes with each cosmic pressure. You *must* let us try."

Crawford looked at Colonel Meadows.

"Robbie, I promise you there's no danger involved," the Colonel said. "There's been a great deal of time and effort put into this project and we'd like to see it work. This week Mars and Earth are the closest they'll be for the next three years, so it must be done *now*. It's your duty to help in this important project."

Crawford nodded. The matter of patriotism and duty had not occurred to him. "Of course, Colonel, I'll be glad to help."

He looked down at the dummy. "What do you say, Spud? Want to be the first voice to reach Mars?"

"Sounds crazy," came the high, squeaking reply. "But it ought to put us in the history books." Spud's glass eyes shifted to the other two men in the room and one lid winked. "Calling Mars! This is Spud O'Malley, old quiver voice himself, coming in for a landing."

"Good! You'll do it," said Dr. Shalt excitedly. "And if we succeed the publicity will be worldwide."

"Sure," said Crawford. "An actor likes publicity. But are you sure my voice won't be strained?"

"I'm sure," Dr. Shalt said. "You'll be talking into a microphone in the same tone you use for a broadcast. Nothing more."

"How long will it take?" asked Crawford.

Dr. Shalt checked his watch. "Fifteen minutes for the voice to reach Mars and fifteen minutes for its return." He took out a black notebook from his jacket pocket and began to outline the plan while Colonel Meadows put through a call to the laboratory.

Spud's voice was to be relayed directly to a giant amplifying unit which would project it into space. Those regulating the voice in the control room would hear nothing but vibrations because of the high frequency it would immediately attain while passing through. Only on its return from Mars would Spud's voice become audible on Earth. It sounded fantastic but Dr. Shalt spoke of it as if it were a certainty and Crawford knew he was recognized as a great scientist.

A few minutes later Colonel Meadows hung up the phone. He said excitedly, "Everything's set. All the equipment is ready and there's a command car waiting outside."

Crawford caught a quick glimpse of himself in the mirror. No shower, no shave, no quiet dinner, no walk; all that would have to come later. He'd been hooked. "I'm ready any time you are," he said. He folded Spud in his arms and followed the two men to the door.

They did not speak much in the car. The laboratory was on the Northern rim of the field, a ten-minute drive from the auditorium. Approaching the building, Crawford noticed the high radar towers and the steel fences surrounding its frame. They rode past three different guard posts and numerous military policemen before the car halted at the main entrance.

Immediately they were ushered into a small broadcasting studio which was soundproofed and closed off by a heavy metal door. This was Dr. Shalt's home grounds and he took charge.

A microphone had been set up and Dr. Shalt had Crawford test Spud's voice while a technician in the control booth measured it acoustically. After an exact tone had been determined for the amplification unit, Dr. Shalt briefed him on some details, patted him on the back and disappeared into the control booth followed by Colonel Meadows.

Crawford lit another cigarette and smoked nervously while he awaited the go-ahead signal. There was a dry tightness in his throat and he concentrated on relaxing his tension.

High on the studio wall a large clock hacked away at the seconds, and behind the glass façade of the control booth he could see Dr. Shalt and his assistant manipulating dials on an intricate panel. It was almost three minutes before he heard another sound beside the creak of his own impatient footsteps. Then Dr. Shalt's voice came on the feed-back, the speaker system connecting the studio with the booth.

"Crawford, talk into the mike when we flash you the sign. Keep talking for a minute. And remember—it's just another broadcast. Good luck."

Crawford nodded, deposited the cigarette in an ashtray. He moved into position and slid his fingers along the inner wires of Spud's back until they fitted into place. Spud's head came alive.

Dr. Shalt brought his right hand down in a long, sweeping motion. A bright red bulb above the control booth winked into life. Robbie Crawford went into his act.

Inside the booth Dr. Shalt, Colonel Meadows and a technician watched Crawford performing in pantomime and listened to the strange vibrations emanating from the speaker. They could distinguish no understandable sound for the amplifier had lifted the voice beyond human hearing as it released it to the stratosphere. They sat quietly, content to wait for the voice to return from its long, lonely journey.

Crawford spoke until he saw Dr. Shalt signal for a conclusion. A moment later the red bulb blinked out and the broadcast was ended. Crawford felt cold and his hands were perspiring freely. He saw the beaming face of Colonel Meadows motioning him to come inside the booth. He wiped his face, and coughed to relieve the tension in his throat.

The Colonel was the first to greet him as he entered the booth, and his handshake was enthusiastic and firm. Dr. Shalt remained bent over one of the instrument boards rotating a dial, but looked up and nodded excitedly.

"It will be another ten minutes," he said. "Sit down. I've sent out for some supper."

"How did it go?" Crawford asked.

"Good! Good! By now it's half way to its destination."

An orderly came in with a tray of sandwiches and coffee and for the next few minutes they ate and Dr. Shalt described the intricacies of the operation. The technician stayed glued to the receiver, earphones resting lightly across his head.

After ten minutes Dr. Shalt stood up and looked at his watch. "It's time," he said. "Turn up the resonator." He moved closer to the receiving set as the others gathered around him. The low hum of the monitor signal became louder as the technician switched on a new lever. The static emerging from the speaker thickened, obliterating all other noises. Another two minutes went by . . . .

Crawford watched it all, aware of the tension and anxiety on each face, feeling the throbbing excitement himself. So they stood, tensely expectant, awaiting the return of his voice . . . .

Suddenly the technician whispered, "I've got it! It's coming! I hear it returning!" He swung around, offering his earphones to Dr. Shalt, who grabbed for them hurriedly. The scientist raised the cups to his ear and waited. The room fell into deeper silence.

"Yes, yes, it's the voice! Turn up the resonator to full volume! We've got it! The voice is completing the circuit!" Dr. Shalt said tensely.

The technician turned another dial as far as it would go. The sound of the static rose to a roar. Then abruptly the static broke, died out and a strange new sound came in. It was Spud! Spud's voice creeping back from a trip to Mars, thirty-five million miles away!

"*Hello . . . . This is the voice of Spud O'Malley. I speak to you from Harlow Field in the United States of America. My voice is being sent to you by a newly invented Amplification Unit developed by Dr. Paul Shalt at this experimental base. This is the first time such an operation has ever been tried. We extend our heartiest greetings, our deepest felicitations . . .*"

It went on, the high, squeaking voice, friendly, humorous, alive; sending back to them the words that Crawford had spoken into the microphone a few minutes before.

Crawford studied the faces of the other men. They had worked and planned a long time for this single moment, the realization of a long pursued dream. Colonel Meadows was rubbing his hands together gleefully. The voice was reaching its climax. Success was assured. History had been made!

There was a little silence as Spud finished speaking. The technician reached across leisurely to shut off the resonator.

Suddenly the voice started again. The technician's hand froze in mid-air. The same high, squeaking tone, the same inflections, the same pitch. But this time it was commanding, authoritative.

"This is Mars. We have received your voice. We know of you, know your language. We want you to know that we do not like intruders. We want no contact with you. Seek us out no more. The voice was received clearly. It fits our frequency well. We will keep it so that no more communication from you is possible. Let this be a warning. Stay away! We do not want you!"

The voice stopped and there was silence again. Then Colonel Meadows chuckled. "Very clever, Crawford! You really startled me for a moment."

"Yes," said Dr. Shalt, smiling. "So you made a little joke at the end. Very clever."

Crawford's back was to them as he stared at the loudspeaker. His face was contorted in a surprised grimace and the flesh was suddenly white and lifeless. He turned to face them, his body rigid and his mouth trembling as he whispered:

"That voice—that last voice—it wasn't mine! *That wasn't me speaking!*"

Dr. Shalt laughed. "Superb actor. A great performance, Mr. Crawford. We are most grateful to you."

"Robbie's a born comedian," added Colonel Meadows, his eyes sparkling with the humor of the situation. "Never misses a chance to clown."

"Don't you understand—*it wasn't my voice!*" screamed Crawford. He looked from one man to another, his eyes pleading for belief. "The second part was not mine!"

They stared at him, their smiles fading.

Colonel Meadows said, "What do you mean, Robbie?"

"Didn't you hear when I spoke? I never said those last things. Didn't you hear what I said?"

The technician answered him. "We didn't hear a thing, Mr. Crawford. The amplification was too high. It was nothing but mumbling when it passed through this room." He looked at Dr. Shalt for confirmation.

"I explained that to you myself," said the doctor. "You could have recited the Gettysburg Address and we'd never have known until it returned."

Crawford stared down at the limp form of Spud hanging across his arm. He ran a hand across his eyes, dropped the dummy onto the desk. Turning back to Dr. Shalt, he began to speak in a taut, controlled voice.

"Dr. Shalt, I swear to you that was not my voice at the end. I finished with a goodbye. The voice that spoke after that moment of silence was somebody else's voice. It's up to you to find out whose."

"Don't be absurd," said Dr. Shalt, irritably. "That was *your* voice, *your* pitch. The voice of your dummy, Spud." He wasn't going to be taken in by any warped sense of humor. Robbie Crawford was the best ventriloquist in America. He was also noted for his practical jokes. "An experiment of this magnitude shouldn't be treated so lightly," he added acidly.

"You've got to believe me!" screamed Crawford. His voice was choked and his pale face was glistening with perspiration. "It was someone else, imitating my ventriloquist voice! I swear it was not me!"

Colonel Meadows sat down abruptly. The technician ran from the booth and returned a moment later with a glass of water. Colonel Meadows motioned for him to give it to Crawford.

The ventriloquist gulped down the water, then went over and sat down beside the Colonel.

"Look," he said quietly. "I'm not joking and I'm not out of my head. It was a shock to hear a voice so like my own, to hear it threaten us, to know that it's traveling from another world. It's like hearing an echo that shouldn't be."

The Colonel exchanged a puzzled look with Dr. Shalt. After a moment the doctor reached down and picked the dummy up and brought it to Crawford.

"Crawford, listen to me." His voice was gentle, sympathetic. "Perhaps you've been working too hard. These USO trips, the rehearsal, the excitement of the last hour. Maybe you forgot what you said, or said more than you recall."

"I remember everything I said," Crawford said quietly. "I stopped when you gave me the signal. That voice came after I stopped. Can't you check—?"

A phone in the back of the control booth rang sharply and Colonel Meadows answered it. He spoke for a few moments, then hung up. "That was the stage manager calling from the main auditorium. You've got ten minutes before the show. How do you feel?"

Crawford blinked in surprise. He had almost forgotten the program. He tried to rise, found his legs trembling.

"He's in no condition to put on a show," said Dr. Shalt. "Better postpone it."

"No, no, I'm okay," protested Crawford, walking around the small floor, exercising his hands. "It's my show. They're waiting for me. Let's get going."

In the car, during the ride to the auditorium, he did not speak. He sat with Spud resting snugly against his chest, drumming his fingers on an arm rest while Colonel Meadows and Dr. Shalt talked, tried to convince him of the invalidity in his reasoning. There was a simple explanation for the voice; either he had forgotten part of his speech or maybe some amateur radio ham had somehow managed to pick up their signal and was playing a joke. He was too intelligent a man to be frightened by such coincidence. They spoke to him reassuringly all during the ride. At the stage door he thanked them, then went inside the auditorium to give his performance.

The ovation that greeted him was tremendous. The orchestra played his theme and an army announcer introduced him as the Number One ventriloquist in the world. He walked out slowly from the wing, waving and grinning at the audience with Spud sitting erect on his arm.

The soldiers roared and whistled as Spud's head spun, drooped and tilted in the opening routine that he was famous for. Crawford stopped in the middle of the stage, rested his foot on a chair that had been provided, sat Spud on his knee. The applause dwindled gradually and the other members of the cast moved into their positions. The army announcer walked forward to engage Crawford in conversation—to feed him questions that would be answered in Spud's high, squeaky voice.

"Hi, Robbie, Spud," said the announcer. "What took you so long getting here?"

It was Spud's answer. All eyes focused on the dummy's face as it bent forward and its mouth opened slowly. A wooden hand moved up and scratched a wooden head. But only a gurgle came out of the open mouth!

The announcer looked at Crawford, motioned him to speed up. "Speak up, Spud. Can't hear a word you're saying. No time to be bashful."

Again the dummy's mouth opened, the head bobbed and the eyes blinked. The gurgle became a half-strangled gasp. It whined unsteadily a few moments then broke off completely. The cast in the wings began to stir nervously. Crawford was obviously straining. A vein throbbed in the center of his forehead and his lips were tight over his teeth.

"Stage fright," he said in an aside to the audience. Turning his head aside, he coughed and cleared his throat and pretended to whisper with Spud. "Speak up, Pal. This is what we rehearsed for."

The mouth of the dummy flapped up and down without cadence. The soldiers snickered, squirmed restlessly. A sound started, a low, plaintive wail that broke into a dirge and finally into a wild shriek from Crawford's lips. He screamed and kicked over the chair his foot was balanced on. The dummy toppled to the floor.

"I can't! I can't! My voice is gone!" He was screaming and clutching at his throat, trying to loosen his collar. The curtains closed behind him as soldiers leaped to their feet all over the auditorium.

He screamed, "I've lost my second voice! They took it from me! The Martians stole my voice!"

The announcer grabbed his arms then and tried to lead him from the stage. Crawford shoved him away.

"They took it," cried Crawford. "No matter what they tell you, the Martians took Spud's voice. It fitted their frequency. They'll use it to reach Earth! I can't get it back!"

Colonel Meadows and several MPs who were stationed in the wings came out and dragged him from the platform.

The G.I. audience remained silent a moment longer, then broke into loud, nervous rumbling. Seconds later Colonel Meadows returned to the microphone and held up his hand until the confusion died down. He explained briefly about Dr. Shalt's experiment and how Crawford had been asked to participate. He told how a human voice had been sent to Mars for the first time and how Crawford had suffered a temporary shock on hearing his voice return from this journey.

He assured the audience that Crawford would receive the best medical care and would probably be back performing at the field in a few short weeks. He asked the soldiers to remain in their seats and let the show continue out of respect for a great performer.

The orchestra began the refrain of a popular song and the guest vocalist appeared wearing a white strapless evening gown. She blew warm, friendly kisses to the soldiers. The response she received was a healthy one.

And the show went on . . . .

RASTIGNAC THE DEVIL

by Philip José Farmer

Here is high fidelity fiction at Philip José Farmer's story-telling best. It's a vibrant, distractingly different tale of three centuries into the future. And as you read you'll have a vague, uneasy feeling that it's all taking place somewhere in the unexplored parts of the universe, even today.

Enslaved by a triangular powered despotism—one lone man sets his sights to the Six Bright Stars and eventual freedom of his world.

After the Apocalyptic War, the decimated remnants of the French huddled in the Loire Valley were gradually squeezed between two new and growing nations. The Colossus to the north was unfriendly and obviously intended to absorb the little New France. The Colossus to the south was friendly and offered to take the weak state into its confederation of republics as a full partner.

A number of proud and independent French citizens feared that even the latter alternative meant the eventual transmutation of their tongue, religion and nationality into those of their southern neighbor. Seeking a way of salvation, they built six huge space-ships that would hold thirty thousand people, most of whom would be in deep freeze until they reached their destination. The six vessels then set off into interstellar space to find a planet that would be as much like Earth as possible.

That was in the 22nd Century. Over three hundred and fifty years passed before Earth heard of them again. However, we are not here concerned with the home world but with the story of a man of that pioneer group who wanted to leave the New Gaul and sail again to the stars . . . .

*

Rastignac had no Skin. He was, nevertheless, happier than he had been since the age of five.

He was as happy as a man can be who lives deep under the ground. Underground organizations are often under the ground. They are formed into cells. Cell Number One usually contains the leader of the underground.

Jean-Jacques Rastignac, chief of the Legal Underground of the Kingdom of L'Bawpfey, was literally in a cell beneath the surface of the earth. He was in jail.

For a dungeon, it wasn't bad. He had two cells. One was deep inside the building proper, built into the wall so that he could sit in it when he wanted to retreat from the sun or the rain. The adjoining cell was at the bottom of a well whose top was covered with a grille of thin steel bars. Here he spent most of his waking hours. Forced to look upwards if he wanted to see the sky or the stars, Rastignac suffered from a chronic stiff neck.

Several times during the day he had visitors. They were allowed to bend over the grille and talk down to him. A guard, one of the King's mucketeers,(Mucketeer is the best translation of the 26th century French noun *foutriquet*, pronounced *vfeutwikey*.) stood by as a censor.

When night came, Rastignac ate the meal let down by ropes on a platform. Then another of the King's mucketeers stood by with drawn épée until he had finished eating. When the tray was pulled back up and the grille lowered and locked, the mucketeer marched off with the turnkey.

Rastignac sharpened his wit by calling a few choice insults to the night guard, then went into the cell inside the wall and lay down to take a nap. Later, he would rise and pace back and forth like a caged tiger. Now and then he would stop and look upwards, scan the stars, hunch his shoulders and resume his savage circuit of the cell. But the time would come when he would stand statue-still. Nothing moved except his head, which turned slowly.

"Some day I'll ride to the stars with you."

He said it as he watched the Six Flying Stars speed across the night sky—six glowing stars that moved in a direction opposite to the march of the other stars. Bright as Sirius seen from Earth, strung out one behind the other like jewels on a velvet string, they hurtled across the heavens.

They were the six ships on which the original Loire Valley Frenchmen had sailed out into space, seeking a home on a new planet. They had been put into an orbit around New Gaul and left there while their thirty thousand passengers had descended to the surface in chemical-fuel rockets. Mankind, once on the fair and fresh earth of the new planet, had never again ascended to re-visit the great ships.

For three hundred years the six ships had circled the planet known as New Gaul, nightly beacons and glowing reminders to Man that he was a stranger on this planet.

When the Earthmen landed on the new planet they had called the new land *Le Beau Pays*, or, as it was now pronounced, *L'Bawpfey*—The Beautiful Country. They had been delighted, entranced with the fresh new land. After the burned, war-racked Earth they had just left, it was like coming to Heaven.

They found two intelligent species living on the planet, and they found that the species lived in peace and that they had no conception of war or of poverty. And they were quite willing to receive the Terrans into their society.

Provided, that is, they became integrated, or—as they phrased it—natural. The Frenchmen from Earth had been given their choice. They were told:

"You can live with the people of the Beautiful Land on our terms—war with us, or leave to seek another planet."

The Terrans conferred. Half of them decided to stay; the other half decided to remain only long enough to mine uranium and other chemicals. Then they would voyage onwards.

But nobody from that group of Earthmen ever again stepped into the ferry-rockets and soared up to the six ion-beam ships circling about Le Beau Pays. All succumbed to the Philosophy of the Natural. Within a few generations a stranger landing upon the planet would not have known without previous information that the Terrans were not aboriginal.

He would have found three species. Two were warm-blooded egglayers who had evolved directly from reptiles without becoming mammals—the Ssassarors and the Amphibs. Somewhere in their dim past—like all happy nations, they had no history—they had set up their society and been very satisfied with it since.

It was a peaceful quiet world, largely peasant, where nobody had to scratch for a living and where a superb manipulation of biological forces ensured very long lives, no disease, and a social lubrication that left little to desire—from their viewpoint, anyway.

The government was, nominally, a monarchy. The Kings were elected by the people and were a different species than the group each ruled. Ssassaror ruled Human, and vice versa, each assisted by foster-brothers and sisters of the race over which they reigned. These were the so-called Dukes and Duchesses.

The Chamber of Deputies—*L'Syawp t' Tapfuti*—was half Human and half Ssassaror. The so-called Kings took turns presiding over the Chamber for forty day intervals. The Deputies were elected for ten-year terms by constituents who could not be deceived about their representatives' purposes because of the sensitive Skins which allowed them to determine their true feelings and worth.

In one custom alone did the ex-Terrans differ from their neighbors. This was in carrying arms. In the beginning, the Ssassaror had allowed the Men to wear their short rapiers, so they would feel safe even though in the midst of aliens.

As time went on, only the King's mucketeers—and members of the official underground—were allowed to carry épées. These men, it might be noticed, were the congenital adventurers, men who needed to swashbuckle and revel in the name of individualist.

Like the egg-stealers, they needed an institution in which they could work off anti-social steam.

From the beginning the Amphibians had been a little separate from the Ssassaror and when the Earthmen came they did not get any more neighborly. Nevertheless, they preserved excellent relations and they, too, participated in the Changeling-custom.

This Changeling-custom was another social device set up millennia ago to keep a mutual understanding between all species on the planet. It was a peculiar institution, one that the Earthmen had found hard to understand and ever more difficult to adopt. Nevertheless, once the Skins had been accepted they had changed their attitude, forgot their speculations about its origin and threw themselves into the custom of stealing babies—or eggs—from another race and raising the children as their own.

You rob my cradle; I'll rob yours. Such was their motto, and it worked.

A Guild of Egg Stealers was formed. The Human branch of it guaranteed, for a price, to bring you a Ssassaror child to replace the one that had been stolen from you. Or, if you lived on the sea-shore, and an Amphibian had crept into your nursery and taken your baby—always under two years old, according to the rules—then the Guildsman would bring you an Amphib or, perhaps, the child of a Human Changeling reared by the Seafolk.

You raised it and loved it as your own. How could you help loving it?

Your Skin told you that it was small and helpless and needed you and was, despite appearances, as Human as any of your babies. Nor did you need to worry about the one that had been abducted. It was getting just as good care as you were giving this one.

It had never occurred to anyone to quit the stealing and voluntary exchange of babies. Perhaps that was because it would strain even the loving nature of the Skin-wearers to give away their own flesh and blood. But once the transfer had taken place, they could adapt.

Or perhaps the custom was kept because tradition is stronger than law in a peasant-monarchy society and also because egg-and-baby stealing gave the more naturally aggressive and daring citizens a chance to work off anti-social behavior.

Nobody but a historian would have known, and there were no historians in The Beautiful Land.

Long ago the Ssassaror had discovered that if they lived meatless, they had a much easier time curbing their belligerency, obeying the Skins and remaining cooperative. So they induced the Earthmen to put a taboo on eating flesh. The only drawback to the meatless diet was that both Ssassaror and Man became as stunted in stature as they did in aggressiveness, the former so much so that they barely came to the chins of the Humans. These, in turn, would have seemed short to a Western European.

But Rastignac, an Earthman, and his good friend, Mapfarity, the Ssassaror Giant, became taboo-breakers when they were children and played together on the beach where they first ate seafood out of curiosity, then continued because they liked it. And due to their protein diet the Terran had grown well over six feet in height and the Ssassaror seemed to have touched off a rocket of expansion in his body with his protein-eating. Those Ssassarors who shared his guilt—became meat-eaters—became ostracized and eventually moved off to live by themselves. They were called Ssassaror-Giants and were pointed to as an object lesson to the young of the normal Ssassarors and Humans on the land.

*

If a stranger had landed shortly before Rastignac was born, however, he would have noticed that all was not as serene as it was supposed to be among the different species. The cause for the flaw in the former Eden might have puzzled him if he had not known the previous history of L'Bawfey and the fact that the situation had not changed for the worst until the introduction of Human Changelings among the Amphibians.

Then it had been that blood-drinking began among them, that Amphibians began seducing Humans to come live with them by their tales of easy immortality, and that they started the system of leaving savage little carnivores in the Human nurseries.

When the Land-dwellers protested, the Amphibs replied that these things were carried out by unnaturals or outlaws, and that the Sea-King could not be held responsible. Permission was given to Chalice those caught in such behavior.

Nevertheless, the suspicion remained that the Amphib monarch had, in accordance with age-old procedure, given his unofficial official blessing and that he was preparing even more disgusting and outrageous and unnatural moves. Through his control of the populace by the Master Skin, he would be able to do as he pleased with their minds.

It was the Skins that had made the universal peace possible on the planet of New Gaul. And it would be the custom of the Skins that would make possible the change from peace to conflict among the populace.

Through the artificial Skins that were put on all babies at birth—and which grew with them, attached to their body, feeding from their bloodstreams, their nervous systems—the Skins, controlled by a huge Master Skin that floated in a chemical vat in the palace of the rulers, fed, indoctrinated and attended day and night by a crew of the most brilliant scientists of the planet, gave the Kings complete control of the minds and emotions of the inhabitants of the planet.

Originally the rulers of New Gaul had desired only that the populace live in peace and enjoy the good things of their planet equally. But the change that had been coming gradually—the growth of conflict between the Kings of the different species for control of the whole populace—was beginning to be generally felt. Uneasiness, distrust of each other was growing among the people. Hence the legalizing of the Underground, the Philosophy of Violence by the government, an effort to control the revolt that was brewing.

Yet, the Land-dwellers had managed to take no action at all and to ignore the growing number of vicious acts.

But not all were content to drowse. One man was aroused. He was Rastignac.

They were Rastignac's hope, those Six Stars, the gods to which he prayed. When they passed quickly out of his sight he would continue his pacing, meditating for the twenty-thousandth time on a means for reaching one of those ships and using it to visit the stars. The end of his fantasies was always a curse because of the futility of such hopes. He was doomed! Mankind was doomed!

*

And it was all the more maddening because Man would not admit that he was through. Ended, that is, as a human being.

Man was changing into something not quite *homo sapiens*. It might be a desirable change, but it would mean the finish of his climb upwards. So it seemed to Rastignac. And he, being the man he was, had decided to do something about it even if it meant violence.

That was why he was now in the well-dungeon. He was an advocator of violence against the status quo.

II

There was another cell next to his. It was also at the bottom of a well and was separated from his by a thin wall of cement. A window had been set into it so that the prisoners could talk to each other. Rastignac did not care for the woman who had been let down into the adjoining cell, but she was somebody to talk to.

"Amphib-changelings" was the name given to those human beings who had been stolen from their cradles and raised among the non-humanoid Amphibians as their own. The girl in the adjoining cell, Lusine, was such a person. It was not her fault that she was a blood-drinking Amphib. Yet he could not help disliking her for what she had done and for the things she stood for.

She was in prison because she had been caught in the act of stealing a Man child from its cradle. This was no crime, but she had left in the cradle, under the covers, a savage and blood-thirsty little monster that had leaped up and slashed the throat of the unsuspecting baby's mother.

Her cell was lit by a cageful of glowworms. Rastignac, peering through the grille, could see her shadowy shape in the inner cell inside the wall. She rose langorously and stepped into the circle of dim orange light cast by the insects.

"*B'zhu, m'fweh,*" she greeted him.

It annoyed him that she called him her brother, and it annoyed him even more to know that she knew it. It was true that she had some excuse for thus addressing him.

She did resemble him. Like him, she had straight glossy blue-black hair, thick bracket-shaped eyebrows, brown eyes, a straight nose and a prominent chin. And where his build was superbly masculine, hers was magnificently feminine.

Nevertheless, this was not her reason for so speaking to him. She knew the disgust the Land-walker had for the Amphib-changeling, and she took a perverted delight in baiting him.

He was proud that he seldom allowed her to see that she annoyed him. "*B'zhu, fam tey zafeep,*" he said. "Good evening, woman of the Amphibians."

Mockingly she said, "Have you been watching the Six Flying Stars, Jean-Jacques?"

"*Vi.* I do so every time they come over."

"Why do you eat your heart out because you cannot fly up to them and then voyage among the stars on one of them?"

He refused to give her the satisfaction of knowing his real reason. He did not want her to realize how little he thought of Mankind and its chances for surviving—as humanity—upon the face of this planet, L'Bawpfey.

"I look at them because they remind me that Man was once captain of his soul."

"Then you admit that the Land-walker is weak?"

"I think he is on the way to becoming non-human, which is to say that he is weak, yes. But what I say about Landman goes for Seaman, too. You Changelings are becoming more Amphibian every day and less Human. Through the Skins the Amphibs are gradually changing you completely. Soon you will be completely sea-people."

She laughed scornfully, exposing perfect white teeth as she did so.

"The Sea will win out against the Land. It launches itself against the shore and shakes it with the crash of its body. It eats away the rock and the dirt and absorbs it into its own self. It can't be worn away nor caught and held in a net. It is elusive and all-powerful and never-tiring."

Lusine paused for breath. He said, "That is a very pretty analogy, but it doesn't apply. You Seafolk are as much flesh and blood as we Landfolk. What hurts us hurts you."

She put a hand around one bar. The glow-light fell upon it in such a way that it showed plainly the webbing of skin between her fingers. He glanced at it with a faint repulsion under which was a counter-current of attraction. This was the hand that had, indirectly, shed blood.

She glanced at him sidewise, challenged him in trembling tones. "You are not one to throw stones, Jean-Jacques. I have heard that you eat meat."

"Fish, not meat. That is part of my Philosophy of Violence," he retorted. "I maintain that one of the reasons man is losing his power and strength is that he has so long been upon a vegetable diet. He is as cowed and submissive as the grass-eating beast of the fields."

Lusine put her face against the bars.

"That is interesting," she said. "But how did you happen to begin eating fish? I thought we Amphibs alone did that."

What Lusine had just said angered him. He had no reply.

Rastignac knew he should not be talking to a Sea-changeling. They were glib and seductive and always searching for ways to twist your thoughts. But being Rastignac, he had to talk. Moreover, it was so difficult to find anybody who would listen to his ideas that he could not resist the temptation.

"I was given fish by the Ssassaror, Mapfarity, when I was a child. We lived along the sea-shore. Mapfarity was a child, too, and we played together. Don't eat fish!' my parents said. To me that meant 'Eat it!' So, despite my distaste at the idea, and my squeamish stomach, I did eat fish. And I liked it. And as I grew to manhood I adopted the Philosophy of Violence and I continued to eat fish although I am not a Changeling."

"What did your Skin do when it detected you?" Lusine asked. Her eyes were wide and luminous with wonder and a sort of glee as if she relished the confession of his sins. Also, he knew, she was taunting him about the futility of his ideas of violence so long as he was a prisoner of the Skin.

He frowned in annoyance at the reminder of the Skin. Much thought had he given, in a weak way, to the possibility of life without the Skin.

Ashamed now of his weak resistance to the Skin, he blustered a bit in front of the teasing Amphib girl.

"Mapfarity and I discovered something that most people don't know," he answered boastfully. "We found that if you can stand the shocks your Skin gives you when you do something wrong, the Skin gets tired and quits after a while. Of course your Skin recharges itself and the next time you eat fish it shocks you again. But after very many shocks it becomes accustomed, forgets its conditioning, and leaves you alone."

Lusine laughed and said in a low conspirational tone, "So your Ssassaror pal and you adopted the Philosophy of Violence because you remained fish and meat eaters?"

"Yes, we did. When Mapfarity reached puberty he became a Giant and went off to live in a castle in the forest. But we have remained friends through our connection in the underground."

"Your parents must have suspected that you were a fish eater when you first proposed your Philosophy of Violence?" she said.

"Suspicion isn't proof," he answered. "But I shouldn't be telling you all this, Lusine. I feel it is safe for me to do so only because you will never have a chance to tell on me. You will soon be taken to Chalice and there you will stay until you have been cured."

She shivered and said, "This Chalice? What is it?"

"It is a place far to the north where both Terrans and Ssassarors send their incorrigibles. It is an extinct volcano whose steep-sided interior makes an inescapable prison. There those who have persisted in unnatural behavior are given special treatment."

"They are bled?" she asked, her eyes widening as her tongue flicked over her lips again hungrily.

"No. A special breed of Skin is given them to wear. These Skins shock them more powerfully than the ordinary ones, and the shocks are associated with the habit they are trying to cure. The shocks effect a cure. Also, these special Skins are used to detect hidden unnatural emotions. They re-condition the deviate. The result is that when the Chaliced Man is judged able to go out and take his place in society again, he is thoroughly re-conditioned. Then his regular Skin is given back to him and it has no trouble keeping him in line from then on. The Chaliced Man is a very good citizen."

"And what if a revolter doesn't become Chaliced?"

"Then he stays in Chalice until he decides to become so."

Her voice rose sharply as she said, "But if I go there, and I am not fed the diet of the Amphibs, I will grow old and die!"

"No. The government will feed you the diet you need until you are re-conditioned. Except . . . ." He paused.

"Except I won't get blood," she wailed. Then, realizing she was acting undignified before a Landman, she firmed her voice.

"The King of the Amphibians will not allow them to do this to me," she said. "When he hears of it he will demand my return. And if the King of Men refuses, my King will use violence to get me back."

Rastignac smiled and said, "I hope he does. Then perhaps my people will wake up and get rid of their Skins and make war upon your people."

"So that is what you Philosophers of Violence want, is it? Well, you will not get it. My father, the Amphib King, will not be so stupid as to declare a war."

"I suppose not," replied Rastignac. "He will send a band to rescue you. If they're caught they'll claim to be criminals and say they are *not* under the King's orders."

Lusine looked upwards to see if a guard was hanging over the well's mouth listening. Perceiving no one, she nodded and said, "You have guessed it correctly. And that is why we laugh so much at you stupid Humans. You know as well as we do what's going on, but you are afraid to tell us so. You keep clinging to the idea that your turn-the-other-cheek policy will soften us and insure peace."

"Not I," said Rastignac. "I know perfectly well there is only one solution to man's problems. That is—"

"That is Violence," she finished for him. "That is what you have been preaching. And that is why you are in this cell, waiting for trial."

"You don't understand," he said. "Men are not put into the Chalice for *proposing* new philosophies. As long as they behave naturally they may say what they wish. They may even petition the King that the new philosophy be made a law. The King passes it on to the Chamber of Deputies. They consider it and put it up to the people. If the people like it, it becomes a law. The only trouble with that procedure is that it may take ten years before the law is considered by the Chamber of Deputies."

"And in those ten years," she mocked him, "the Amphibs and the Amphibian-changelings will have won the planet."

"That is true," he said.

"The King of the Humans is a Ssassaror and the King of the Ssassaror is a Man," said Lusine. "Our King can't see any reason for changing the status quo. After all, it is the Ssassaror who are responsible for the Skins and for Man's position in the sentient society of this planet. Why should he be favorable to a policy of Violence? The Ssassarors loathe violence."

"And so you have preached Violence without waiting for it to become a law? And for that you are now in this cell?"

"Not exactly. The Ssassarors have long known that to suppress too much of Man's naturally belligerent nature only results in an explosion. So they have legalized illegality—up to a point. Thus the King officially made me the Chief of the Underground and gave me a state license to preach—but not practice—Violence. I am even allowed to advocate overthrow of the present system of government—as long as I take no action that is too productive of results.

"I am in jail now because the Minister of Ill-Will put me here. He had my Skin examined, and it was found to be 'unhealthy.' He thought I'd be better off locked up until I became 'healthy' again. But the King . . . ."

III

Lusine's laughter was like the call of a silverbell bird. Whatever her unhuman appetites, she had a beautiful voice. She said, "How comical! And how do you, with your brave ideas, like being regarded as a harmless figure of fun, or as a sick man?"

"I like it as well as you would," he growled.

She gripped the bars of her window until the tendons on the back of her long thin hands stood out and the membranes between her fingers stretched like wind-blown tents. Face twisted, she spat at him, "Coward! Why don't you kill somebody and break out of this ridiculous mold—that Skin that the Ssassarors have poured you into?"

Rastignac was silent. That was a good question. Why didn't he? Killing was the logical result of his philosophy. But the Skin kept him docile. Yes, he could vaguely see that he had purposely shut his eyes to the destination towards which his ideas were slowly but inevitably traveling.

And there was another facet to the answer to her question—if he had to kill, he would not kill a Man. His philosophy was directed towards the Amphibians and the Sea-changelings.

He said, "Violence doesn't necessarily mean the shedding of blood, Lusine. My philosophy urges that we take a more vigorous action, that we overthrow some of the bio-social institutions which have imprisoned Man and stripped him of his dignity as an individual."

"Yes, I have heard that you want Man to stop wearing the Skin. That is what has horrified your people, isn't it?"

"Yes," he said. "And I understand it has had the same effect among the Amphibians."

She bridled, her brown eyes flashing in the feeble glowworms' light. "Why shouldn't it? What would we be without our Skins?"

"What, indeed?" he said, laughing derisively afterwards.

Earnestly she said, "You don't understand. We Amphibians—our Skins are not like yours. We do not wear them for the same reason you do. You are imprisoned by your Skins—they tell you how to feel, what to think. Above all, they keep you from getting ideas about non-cooperation or non-integration with Nature as a whole.

"That, to us individualistic Amphibians, is false. The purpose of our Skins is to make sure that our King's subjects understand what he wants so that we may all act as one unit and thus further the progress of the Seafolk."

The first time Rastignac had heard this statement he had howled with laughter. Now, however, knowing that she could not see the fallacy, he did not try to argue the point. The Amphibs were, in their way, as hidebound—no pun intended—as the Land-walkers.

"Look, Lusine," he said, "there are only three places where a Man may take off his Skin. One is in his own home, when he may hang it upon the halltree. Two is when he is, like us, in jail and therefore may not harm anybody. The third is when a man is King. Now you and I have been without our Skins for a week. We have gone longer without them than anybody, except the King. Tell me true, don't you feel free for the first time in your life?

"Don't you feel as if you belong to nobody but yourself, that you are accountable to no one but yourself, and that you love that feeling? And don't you dread the day we will be let out of prison and made to wear our Skins again? That day which, curiously enough, will be the very day that we will lose our freedom."

Lusine looked as if she didn't know what he was talking about.

"You'll see what I mean when we are freed and the Skins are put back upon us," he said. Immediately after, he was embarrassed. He remembered that she would go to the Chalice where one of the heavy and powerful Skins used for unnaturals would be fastened to her shoulders.

Lusine did not notice. She was considering the last but most telling point in her argument "You cannot win against us," she said, watching him narrowly for the effect of her words. "We have a weapon that is irresistible. We have immortality."

His face did not lose its imperturbability.

She continued, "And what is more, we can give immortality to anyone who casts off his Skin and adopts ours. Don't think that your people don't know this. For instance, during the last year more than two thousand Humans living along the beaches deserted and went over to us, the Amphibs."

He was a little shocked to hear this, but he did not doubt her. He remembered the mysterious case of the schooner *Le Pauvre Pierre* which had been found drifting and crewless, and he remembered a conversation he had had with a fisherman in his home port of Marrec.

He put his hands behind his back and began pacing. Lusine continued staring at him through the bars. Despite the fact that her face was in the shadows, he could see—or feel—her smile. He had humiliated her, but she had won in the end.

Rastignac quit his limited roving and called up to the guard.

"Shoo l'footyay, kal u ay tee?"

The guard leaned over the grille. His large hat with its tall wings sticking from the peak was green in the daytime. But now, illuminated only by a far off torchlight and by a glowworm coiled around the band, it was black.

"Ah, *shoo Zhaw-Zhawk W'stenyek*," he said, loudly. "What time is it? What do you care what time it is?" And he concluded with the stock phrase of the jailer, unchanged through millenia and over light-years. "You're not going any place, are you?"

Rastignac threw his head back to howl at the guard but stopped to wince at the sudden pain in his neck. After uttering, "*Sek Ploo!*" and "*S'pweestee!*" both of which were close enough to the old Terran French so that a language specialist might have recognized them, he said, more calmly, "If you would let me out on the ground, *monsieur le foutriquet*, and give me a good épée, I would show you where I am going. Or, at least, where my sword is going. I am thinking of a nice sheath for it."

Tonight he had a special reason for keeping the attention of the King's mucketeer directed towards himself. So, when the guard grew tired of returning insults—mainly because his limited imagination could invent no new ones—Rastignac began telling jokes. They were broad and aimed at the mucketeer's narrow intellect.

"Then," said Rastignac, "there was the itinerant salesman whose *s'fel* threw a shoe. He knocked on the door of the hut of the nearest peasant and said . . . ." What was said by the salesman was never known.

A strangled gasp had come from above.

IV

Rastignac saw something enormous blot out the smaller shadow of the guard. Then both figures disappeared. A moment later a silhouette cut across the lines of the grille. Unoiled hinges screeched; the bars lifted. A rope uncoiled from above to fall at Rastignac's feet. He seized it and felt himself being drawn powerfully upwards.

When he came over the edge of the well, he saw that his rescuer was a giant Ssassaror. The light from the glowworm on the guard's hat lit up feebly his face, which was orthagnathous and had quite humanoid eyes and lips. Large canine teeth stuck out from the mouth, and its huge ears were tipped with feathery tufts. The forehead down to the eyebrows looked as if it needed a shave, but Rastignac knew that more light would show the blue-black shade came from many small feathers, not stubbled hair.

"Mapfarity!" Rastignac said. "It's good to see you after all these years!"

The Ssassaror giant put his hand on his friend's shoulder. Clenched, it was almost as big as Rastignac's head. He spoke with a voice like a lion coughing at the bottom of a deep well.

"It is good to see you again, my friend."

"What are you doing here?" said Rastignac, tears running down his face as he stroked the great fingers on his shoulder.

Mapfarity's huge ears quivered like the wings of a bat tied to a rock and unable to fly off. The tufts of feathers at their ends grew stiff and suddenly crackled with tiny sparks.

The electrical display was his equivalent of the human's weeping. Both creatures discharged emotion; their bodies chose different avenues and manifestations. Nevertheless, the sight of the other's joy affected each deeply.

"I have come to rescue you," said Mapfarity. "I caught Archambaud here,"—he indicated the other man—"stealing eggs from my golden goose. And . . . ."

Raoul Archambaud—pronounced Wawl Shebvo—interrupted excitedly, "I showed him my license to steal eggs from Giants who were raising counterfeit geese, but he was going to lock me up anyway. He was going to take my Skin off and feed me on meat . . . ."

"Meat!" said Rastignac, astonished and revolted despite himself. "Mapfarity, what have you been doing in that castle of yours?"

Mapfarity lowered his voice to match the distant roar of a cataract. "I haven't been very active these last few years," he said, "because I am so big that it hurts my feet if I walk very much. So I've had much time to think. And I, being logical, decided that the next step after eating fish was eating meat. It couldn't make me any larger. So, I ate meat. And while doing so, I came to the same conclusion that you, apparently, have done independently. That is, the Philosophy of . . . ."

"Of Violence," interrupted Archambaud. "Ah, Jean-Jacques, there must be some mystic bond that brings two Humans of such different backgrounds as yours and the Ssassaror together, giving you both the same philosophy. When I explained what you had been doing and that you were in jail because you had advocated getting rid of the Skins, Mapfarity petitioned . . . ."

"The King to make an official jail-break," said Mapfarity with an impatient glance at the rolypoly egg-stealer. "And . . . ."

"The King agreed," broke in Archambaud, "provided Mapfarity would turn in his counterfeit goose and provided you would agree to say no more about abandoning Skins, but . . . ."

The Giant's basso profundo-redundo pushed the egg-stealer's high pitch aside. "If this squeaker will quit interrupting, perhaps we can get on with the rescue. We'll talk later, if you don't mind."

At that moment Lusine's voice floated up from the bottom of her cell. "Jean-Jacques, my love, my brave, my own, would you abandon me to the Chalice? Please take me with you! You will need somebody to hide you when the Minister of Ill-Will sends his muckveteers after you. I can hide you where no one will ever find you." Her voice was mocking, but there was an undercurrent of anxiety to it.

Mapfarity muttered, "She will hide us, yes, at the bottom of a sea-cave where we will eat strange food and suffer a change. Never . . . ."

"Trust an Amphib," finished Archambaud for him.

Mapfarity forgot to whisper. "*Bey-t'cul, vu nu fez yey! Fe'm sa!*" he roared.

A shocked hush covered the courtyard. Only Mapfarity's wrathful breathing could be heard. Then, disembodied, Lusine's voice floated from the well.

"Jean-Jacques, do not forget that I am the foster-daughter of the King of the Amphibians! If you were to take me with you, I could assure you of safety and a warm welcome in the halls of the Sea-King's Palace!"

"Pah!" said Mapfarity. "That web-footed witch!"

Rastignac did not reply to her. He took the broad silk belt and the sheathed épée from Archambaud and buckled them around his waist. Mapfarity handed him a mucketeer's hat; he clapped that on firmly. Last of all, he took the Skin that the fat egg-stealer had been holding out to him.

For the first time he hesitated. It was his Skin, the one he had been wearing since he was six. It had grown with him, fed off his blood for twenty-two years, clung to him as clothing, censor, and castigator, and parted from him only when he was inside the walls of his own house, went swimming, or, as during the last seven days, when he laid in jail.

A week ago, after they had removed his second Skin, he had felt naked and helpless and cut off from his fellow creatures. But that was a week ago. Since then, as he had remarked to Lusine, he had experienced the birth of a strange feeling. It was, at first, frightening. It made him cling to the bars as if they were the only stable thing in the center of a whirling universe.

Later, when that first giddiness had passed, it was succeeded by another intoxication—the joy of being an individual, the knowledge that he was separate, not a part of a multitude. Without the Skin he could think as he pleased. He did not have a censor.

Now, he was on level ground again, out of the cell. But as soon as he had put that prison-shaft behind him he was faced with the old second Skin.

Archambaud held it out like a cloak in his hands. It looked much like a ragged garment. It was pale and limp and roughly rectangular with four extensions at each corner. When Rastignac put it on his back, it would sink four tiny hollow teeth into his veins and the suckers on the inner surface of its flat body would cling to him. Its long upper extensions would wrap themselves around his shoulders and over his chest;

the lower, around his loins and thighs. Soon it would lose its paleness and flaccidity, become pink and slightly convex, pulsing with Rastignac's blood.

V

Rastignac hesitated for a few seconds. Then he allowed the habit of a lifetime to take over. Sighing, he turned his back. In a moment he felt the cold flesh descend over his shoulders and the little bite of the four teeth as they attached the Skin to his shoulders. Then, as his blood poured into the creature he felt it grow warm and strong. It spread out and followed the passages it had long ago been conditioned to follow, wrapped him warmly and lovingly and comfortably. And he knew, though he couldn't feel it, that it was pushing nerves into the grooves along the teeth. Nerves to connect with his.

A minute later he experienced the first of the expected *rapport*. It was nothing that you could put a mental finger on. It was just a diffused tingling and then the sudden consciousness of how the others around him *felt*.

They were ghosts in the background of his mind. Yet, pale and ectoplasmic as they were, they were easily identifiable. Mapfarity loomed above the others, a transparent Colossus radiating streamers of confidence in his clumsy strength. A meat-eater, uncertain about the future, with a hope and trust in Rastignac to show him the right way. And with a strong current of anger against the conqueror who had inflicted the Skin upon him.

Archambaud was a shorter phantom, rolypoly even in his psychic manifestations, emitting bursts of impatience because other people did not talk fast enough to suit him, his mind leaping on ahead of their tongues, his fingers wriggling to wrap themselves around something valuable—preferably the eggs of the golden goose—and a general eagerness to be up and about and onwards. He was one round fidget on two legs, yet a good man for any project requiring action.

Faintly, Rastignac detected the slumbering guard as if he were the tendrils of some plant at the sea-bottom, floating in the green twilight, at peace and unconscious.

And even more faintly he felt Lusine's presence, shielded by the walls of the shaft. Hers was a pale and light hand, one whose fingers tapped a barely heard code of impotent rage and voiceless screaming fear. Yet beneath that anguish was a base of confidence and mockery at others. She might be temporarily upset, but when the chance came for her to do something she would seize it with every ability at her command.

Another radiation dipped into the general picture and out. A wild glowworm had swooped over them and disturbed the smooth reflection built up by the Skins.

This was the way the Skins worked. They penetrated into you and found out what you were feeling and emoting, and then they broadcast it to other closeby Skins, which then projected their hosts' psychosomatic responses. The whole was then integrated so that each Skin-wearer could detect the group-feeling and at the same time, though in a much duller manner, the feeling of the individuals of the *gestalt*.

That wasn't the only function of the Skin. The parasite, created in the bio-factories, had several other social and biological uses.

Rastignac almost fell into a reverie at that point. It was nothing unusual. The effect of the Skins was a slowing-down one. The wearer thought more slowly, acted more leisurely, and was much more contented.

But now, by a deliberate wrenching of himself from the feeling-pattern, Rastignac woke up. There were things to do, and standing around and drinking in the lotus of the group-rapport was not one of them.

He gestured at the prostrate form of the mucketeer. "You didn't hurt him?"

The Ssassaror rumbled, "No. I scratched him with a little venom of the dream-snake. He will sleep for an hour or so. Besides, I would not be allowed to hurt him. You forget that all this is carefully staged by the King's Official Jail-breaker."

"*Me'dt!*" swore Rastignac.

Alarmed, Archambaud said, "What's the matter, Jean-Jacques?"

"Can't we do anything on our own? Must the King meddle in everything?"

"You wouldn't want us to take a chance and have to shed *blood*, would you?" breathed Archambaud.

"What are you carrying those swords for? As a decoration?" Rastignac snarled.

"*Seelahs, m'fweh,*" warned Mapfarity. "If you alarm the other guards, you will embarrass them. They will be forced to do their duty and recapture you. And the Jail-breaker would be reprimanded because he had fallen down on his job. He might even get a demotion."

Rastignac was so upset that his Skin, reacting to the negative fields racing over the Skin and the hormone imbalance of his blood, writhed away from his back.

"What are we, a bunch children playing war?"

Mapfarity growled, "We are all God's children, and we mustn't hurt anyone if we can help it."

"Mapfarity, you eat meat!"

"*Voo zavf w'zaw m'fweh,*" admitted the Giant. "But it is the flesh of unintelligent creatures. I have not yet shed the blood of any being that can talk with the tongue of Man."

Rastignac snorted and said, "If you stick with me you will some day do that, *m'fweh* Mapfarity. There is no other course. It is inevitable."

"Nature spare me the day! But if it comes it will find Mapfarity unafraid. They do not call me Giant for nothing."

Rastignac sighed and walked ahead. Sometimes he wondered if the members of his underground—or anybody else for that matter—ever realized the grim conclusions formed by the Philosophy of Violence.

The Amphibians, he was sure, did. And they were doing something positive about it. But it was the Amphibians who had driven Rastignac to adopt a Philosophy of Violence.

"*Law*," he said again. "Let's go."

The three of them walked out of the huge courtyard and through the open gate. Nearby stood a short man whose Skin gleamed black-red in the light shed by the two glowworms attached to his shoulders. The Skin was oversized and hung to the ground.

The King's man, however, did not think he was a comic figure. He sputtered, and the red of his face matched the color of the skin on his back.

"You took long enough," he said accusingly and then, when Rastignac opened his mouth to protest, the Jail-breaker said, "Never mind, never mind. *Sa n'apawt*. The thing is that we get you away fast. The Minister of Ill-Will has doubtless by now received word that an official jail-break is planned for tonight. He will send a company of his mucketeers to intercept you. By coming in advance of the appointed time we shall have time to escape before the official rescue party arrives."

"How much time do we have?" asked Rastignac.

The King's man said, "Let's see. After I escort you through the rooms of the Duke, the King's foster-brother—he is most favorable to the Violent Philosophy, you know, and has petitioned the King to become your official patron, which petition will be considered at the next meeting of the Chamber of Deputies in three months—let's see, where was I? Ah, yes, I escort you through the rooms of the King's brother. You will be disguised as His Majesty's mucketeers, ostensibly looking for the escaped prisoners. From the rooms of the Duke you will be let out through a small door in the wall of the palace itself. A car will be waiting.

"From then on it will be up to you. I suggest, however, that you make a dash for Mapfarity's castle. Follow the *Rue des Nues*; that is your best chance. The mucketeers have been pulled off that boulevard. However, it is possible that Auverpin, the Ill-Will Minister, may see that order and will rescind it, realizing what it means. If he does, I suppose I will see you back in your cell, Rastignac."

He bowed to the Ssassaror and Archambaud and said, "And you two gentlemen will then be with him."

"And then what?" rumbled Mapfarity.

"According to the law, you will be allowed one more jail-break. Any more after that will, of course, be illegal. That is, unthinkable."

Rastignac unsheathed his épée and slashed it at the air. "Let the mucketeers stand in my way," he said fiercely. "I will cut them down with this!"

The Jail-breaker staggered back, hands outthrust.

"Please, Monsieur Rastignac! Please! Don't even talk about it! You know that your philosophy is, as yet, illegal. The shedding of blood is an act that will be regarded with horror throughout the sentient planet. People would think you are an Amphibian!"

"The Amphibians know what they're doing far better than we do," answered Rastignac. "Why do you think they're winning against us Humans?"

Suddenly, before anybody could answer, the sound of blaring horns came from somewhere on the ramparts. Shouts went up; drums began to beat, calling the mucketeers to alert.

And above it all came the roar of a giant Ssassaror voice: "*An Earthship has landed in the sea! And the pilot of the ship is in the hands of the Amphibians!*"

As the meaning of the words seeped into Rastignac's consciousness he made a sudden violent movement—and began to tear the Skin from his body!

VI

Rastignac ran down the steps, out into the courtyard. He seized the Jail-breaker's arm and demanded the key to the grilles. Dazed, the white-faced official meekly and silently handed it to him. Without his Skin Rastignac was no longer fearfully inhibited. If you were forceful enough and did not behave according to the normal pattern you could get just about anything you wanted. The average Man or Ssassaror did not know how to react to his violence. By the time they had recovered from their confusion he could be miles away.

Such a thought flashed through his head as he ran towards the prison wells. At the same time he heard the horn-blasts of the king's mucketeers and knew that he shortly would have a different type of Man to deal with. The mucketeers, closest approach to soldiers in this pacifistic land, wore Skins that conditioned them to be more belligerent than the common citizen. They carried épées and, while it was true that their points were dull and their wielders had never engaged in serious swordsmanship, the mucketeers could be dangerous from a viewpoint of numbers alone.

Mapfarity bellowed, "Jean-Jacques, what are you doing?"

He called back over his shoulder, "I'm taking Lusine with us! She can help us get the Earthman from the Amphibians!"

The Giant lumbered up behind him, threw a rope down to the eager hands of Lusine and pulled her up without effort to the top of the well. A second later, Rastignac leaped upon Mapfarity's back, dug his hands under the upper fringe of the huge Skin and, ignoring its electrical blasts, ripped downwards.

Mapfarity cried out with shock and surprise as his skin flopped on the stones like a devilfish on dry land.

Archambaud ran up then and, without bothering to explain, the Ssassaror and the Man seized him and peeled off *his* artificial hide.

"Now we're all free men!" panted Rastignac. "And the mucketeers have no way of locating us if we hide, nor can they punish us with shocks."

He put the Giant on his right side, Lusine on his left, and the egg-stealer behind him. He removed the Jail-breaker's rapier from his sheath. The official was too astonished to protest.

"*Law, m'zawfa!*" cried Rastignac, parodying in his grotesque French the old Gallic war cry of "*Allons, mes enfants!*"

The King's official came to life and screamed orders at the group of mucketeers who had poured into the courtyard. They halted in confusion. They could not hear him above the roar of horns and thunder of drums and the people sticking their heads out of windows and shouting.

Rastignac scooped up with his épée one of the abandoned Skins flopping on the floor and threw it at the foremost guard. It descended upon the man's head, knocking off his hat and wrapping itself around the head and shoulders. The guard dropped his sword and staggered backwards into the group. At the same time the escapees charged and bowled over their feeble opposition.

It was here that Rastignac drew first blood. The tip of his épée drove past a bewildered mucketeer's blade and entered the fellow's throat just below the chin. It did not penetrate very far because of the dullness of the point. Nevertheless, when Rastignac withdrew his sword he saw blood spurt.

It was the first flower of violence, this scarlet blossom set against the whiteness of a Man's skin.

It would, if he had worn his Skin, have sickened him. Now, he exulted with a shout of triumph.

Lusine swooped up from behind him, bent over the fallen man. Her fingers dipped into the blood and went to her mouth. Greedily, she sucked her fingers.

Rastignac struck her cheek hard with the flat of his hand. She staggered back, her eyes narrow, but she laughed.

The next moments were busy as they entered the castle, knocked down two mucketeers who tried to prevent their passage to the Duke's rooms, then filed across the long suite.

The Duke rose from his writing-desk to greet them. Rastignac, determined to sever all ties and impress the government with the fact that he meant a real violence, snarled at his benefactor, *"Va t'feh fout!"*

The Duke was disconcerted at this harsh command, so obviously impossible to carry out. He blinked and said nothing. The escapees hurried past him to the door that gave exit to the outside. They pushed it open and stepped out into the car that waited for them. A chauffeur leaned against its thin wooden body.

Mapfarity pushed him aside and climbed in. The others followed. Rastignac was the last to get in. He examined in a glance the vehicle they were supposed to make their flight in.

It was as good a car as you could find in the realm. A Renault of the large class, it had a long boat-shaped scarlet body. There wasn't a scratch on it. It had seats for six. And that it had the power to outrun most anything was indicated by the two extra pairs of legs sticking out from the bottom. There were twelve pairs of legs, equine in form and shod with the best steel. It was the kind of vehicle you wanted when you might have to take off across the country. Wheeled cars could go faster on the highway, but this Renault would not be daunted by water, plowed fields, or steep hillsides.

Rastignac climbed into the driver's seat, seized the wheel and pressed his foot down on the accelerator. The nerve-spot beneath the pedal sent a message to the muscles hidden beneath the hood and the legs projecting from the body. The Renault lurched forward, steadied, and began to pick up speed. It entered a broad paved highway. Hooves drummed; sparks shot out from the steel shoes.

Rastignac guided the brainless, blind creature concealed within the body. He was helped by the somatically-generated radar it employed to steer it past obstacles. When he came to the *Rue des Nues*, he slowed it down to a trot. There was no use tiring it out. Halfway up the gentle slope of the boulevard, however, a Ford galloped out from a side-street. Its seats bristled with tall peaked hats with outspread glowworm wings and with drawn épées.

Rastignac shoved the accelerator to the floor. The Renault broke into a gallop. The Ford turned so that it would present its broad side. As there was a fencework of tall shrubbery growing along the boulevard, the Ford was thus able to block most of the passage.

But, just before his vehicle reached the Ford, Rastignac pressed the Jump button. Few cars had this; only sportsmen or the royalty could afford to have such a neural circuit installed. And it did not allow for gradations in leaping. It was an all-or-none reaction; the legs spurned the ground in perfect unison and with every bit of the power in them. There was no holding back.

The nose lifted, the Renault soared into the air. There was a shout, a slight swaying as the trailing hooves struck the heads of mucketeers who had been stupid enough not to duck, and the vehicle landed with a screeching lurch, upright, on the other side of the Ford. Nor did it pause.

Half an hour later Rastignac reined in the car under a large tree whose shadow protected them. "We're well out in the country," he said.

"What do we do now?" asked impatient Archambaud.

"First we must know more about this Earthman," Rastignac answered. "Then we can decide."

VII

Dawn broke through night's guard and spilled a crimson swath on the hills to the East, and the Six Flying Stars faded from sight like a necklace of glowing jewels dipped into an ink bottle.

Rastignac halted the weary Renault on the top of a hill, looked down over the landscape spread out for miles below him. Mapfarity's castle—a tall rose-colored tower of flying buttresses—flashed in the rising sun. It stood on another hill by the sea shore. The country around was a madman's dream of color. Yet to Rastignac every hue sickened the eye. That bright green, for instance, was poisonous; that flaming scarlet was bloody; that pale yellow, rheumy; that velvet black, funeral; that pure white, maggotty.

"Rastignac!" It was Mapfarity's bass, strumming irritation deep in his chest.

"What?"

"What do we do now?"

Jean-Jacques was silent. Archambaud spoke plaintively.

"I'm not used to going without my Skin. There are things I miss. For one thing, I don't know what you're thinking, Jean-Jacques. I don't know whether you're angry at me or love me or are indifferent to me. I don't know where other people *are*. I don't feel the joy of the little animals playing, the freedom of the flight of birds, the ghostly plucking of the growing grass, the sweet stab of the mating lust of the wild-horned apigator, the humming of bees working to build a hive, and the sleepy stupid arrogance

197

of the giant cabbage-eating *deuxnez*. I can feel nothing without the Skin I have worn so long. I feel alone."

Rastignac replied, "You are not alone. I am with you."

Lusine spoke in a low voice, her large brown eyes upon his.

"I, too, feel alone. My Skin is gone, the Skin by which I knew how to act according to the wisdom of my father, the Amphib King. Now that it is gone and I cannot hear his voice through the vibrating tympanum, I do not know what to do."

"At present," replied Rastignac, "you will do as I tell you."

Mapfarity repeated, "What now?"

Rastignac became brisk. He said, "We go to your castle, Giant. We use your smithy to put sharp points on our swords, points to slide through a man's body from front to back. Don't pale! That is what we must do. And then we pick up your goose that lays the golden eggs, for we must have money if we are to act efficiently. After that, we buy—or steal—a boat and we go to wherever the Earthman is held captive. And we rescue him."

"And then?" said Lusine, her eyes shining with emotion.

"What you do then will be up to you. But I am going to leave this planet and voyage with the Earthman to other worlds."

Silence. Then Mapfarity said, "Why leave here?"

"Because there is no hope for this land. Nobody will give up his Skin. *Le Beau Pays* is doomed to a lotus-life. And that is not for me."

Archambaud jerked a thumb at the Amphib girl. "What about her people?"

"They may win, the water-people. What's the difference? It will be just the exchange of one Skin for another. Before I heard of the landing of the Earthman I was going to fight no matter what the cost to me or inevitable defeat. But not now."

Mapfarity's rumble was angry. "Ah, Jean-Jacques, this is not my comrade talking. Are you sure you haven't swallowed your Skin? You talk as if you were inside-out. What is the matter with your brain? Can't you see that it will indeed make a difference if the Amphibs get the upper hand? Can't you see *who* is making the Amphibs behave the way they have been?"

Rastignac urged the Renault towards the rose-colored lacy castle high upon a hill. The vehicle trotted tiredly along the rough and narrow forest path.

"What do you mean?" he said.

"I mean the Amphibs got along fine with the Ssassaror until a new element entered their lives—the Earthmen. Then the antagonising began. What is this new element? It's the Changelings—the mixture of Earthmen and Amphibs or Ssassaror and Terran.

Add it up. Turn it around. Look at it from any angle. It is the Changelings who are behind this restlessness—the Human element.

"Another thing. The Amphibs have always had Skins different from ours. Our factories create our Skins to set up an affinity and communication between their wearers and all of Nature. They are designed to make it easier for every Man to love his neighbor.

"Now, the strange thing about the Amphibs' Skin is that they, too, were once designed to do such things. But in the past thirty or forty years new Skins have been created for one primary purpose—to establish a communication between the Sea-King and his subjects. Not only that, the Skins can be operated at long distances so that the King may punish any disobedient subject. And they are set so that they establish affinity only among the Waterfolk, not between them and all of Nature."

"I had gathered some of that during my conversations with Lusine," said Rastignac. "But I did not know it had gone to such lengths."

"Yes, and you may safely bet that the Changelings are behind it."

"Then it is the human element that is corrupting?"

"What else?"

Rastignac said, "Lusine, what do you say to this?"

"I think it is best that you leave this world. Or else turn Changeling-Amphib."

"Why should I join you Amphibians?"

"A man like you could become a Sea-King."

"And drink blood?"

"I would rather drink blood than mate with a Man. Almost, that is. But I would make an exception with you, Jean-Jacques."

If it had been a Land-woman who made such a blunt proposal he would have listened with equanimity. There was no modesty, false or otherwise in the country of the Skin-wearers. But to hear such a thing from a woman whose mouth had drunk the blood of a living man filled him with disgust.

Yet, he had to admit Lusine was beautiful. If she had not been a blood-drinker . . . .

Though he lacked his receptive Skin, Mapfarity seemed to sense Rastignac's emotions. He said, "You must not blame her too much, Jean-Jacques. Sea-changelings are conditioned from babyhood to love blood. And for a very definite purpose, too, unnatural though it is. When the time comes for hordes of Changelings to sweep out of the sea and overwhelm the Landfolk, they will have no compunctions about cutting the throats of their fellow-creatures."

Lusine laughed. The rest of them shifted uneasily but did not comment. Rastignac changed the subject.

"How did you find out about the Earthman, Mapfarity?" he said.

The Ssassaror smiled. Two long yellow canines shone wetly; the nose, which had nostrils set in the sides, gaped open; blue sparks shot out from it; at the same time the feathered tufts on the ends of the elephantine ears stiffened and crackled with red-and-blue sparks.

"I have been doing something besides breeding geese to lay golden eggs," he said. "I have set traps for Waterfolk, and I have caught two. These I caged in a dungeon in my castle, and I experimented with them. I removed their Skins and put them on me, and I found out many interesting facts."

He leered at Lusine, who was no longer laughing, and he said, "For instance, I discovered that the Sea-King can locate, talk to, and punish any of his subjects anywhere in the sea or along the coast. He has booster Skins planted all over his realm so that any message he sends will reach the receiver, no matter how far away he is. Moreover, he has conditioned each and every Skin so that, by uttering a certain code-word to which only one particular Skin will respond, he may stimulate it to shock or even to kill its carrier."

Mapfarity continued, "I analyzed those two Skins in my lab and then, using them as models, made a number of duplicates in my fleshforge. They lacked only the nerves that would enable the Sea-King to shock us."

Rastignac smiled his appreciation of this coup. Mapfarity's ears crackled blue sparks of joy, his equivalent of blushing.

"Ah, then you have doubtless listened in to many broadcasts. And you know where the Earthman is located?"

"Yes," said the Giant. "He is in the palace of the Amphib King, upon the island of Kataproimnoin. That is only thirty miles out to the sea."

Rastignac did not know what he would do, but he had two advantages in the Amphibs' Skins and in Lusine. And he burned to get off this doomed planet, this land of men too sunk in false happiness, sloth, and stupidity to see that soon death would come from the water.

He had two possible avenues of escape. One was to use the newly arrived Earthman's knowledge so that the fuels necessary to propel the ferry-rockets could be manufactured. The rockets themselves still stood in a museum. Rastignac had not planned to use them because neither he nor any one else on this planet knew how to make fuel for them. Such secrets had long ago been forgotten.

But now that science was available through the newcomer from Earth, the rockets could be equipped and taken up to one of the Six Flying Stars. The Earthman could study the rocket, determine what was needed in the way of supplies, then it could be outfitted for the long voyage.

An alternative was the Terran's vessel. Perhaps he might invite him to come along in it . . . .

The huge gateway to Mapfarity's castle interrupted his thoughts.

VIII

He halted the Renault, told Archambaud to find the Giant's servant and have him feed their vehicle, rub its legs down with liniment, and examine the hooves for defective shoes.

Archambaud was glad to look up Mapfabvisheen, the Giant's servant, because he had not seen him for a long time. The little Ssassaror had been an active member of the Egg-stealer's Guild until the night three years ago when he had tried to creep into Mapfarity's strongroom. The crafty guildsman had avoided the Giant's traps and there found the two geese squatting upon their bed of minerals.

These fabulous geese made no sound when he picked them up with lead-lined gloves and put them in his bag, also lined with lead-leaf. They were not even aware of him. Laboratory-bred, retort-shaped, their protoplasm a blend of silicon-carbon, unconscious even that they lived, they munched upon lead and other elements, ruminated, gestated, transmuted, and every month, regular as the clockwork march of stars or whirl of electrons, each laid an octagonal egg of pure gold.

Mapfabvisheen had trodden softly from the strongroom and thought himself safe. And then, amazingly, frighteningly, and totally unethically, from his viewpoint, the geese had begun honking loudly!

He had run, but not fast enough. The Giant had come stumbling from his bed in response to the wild clamor and had caught him. And, according to the contract drawn up between the Guild of Egg-stealers and the League of Giants, a guildsman seized within the precincts of a castle must serve the goose's owner for two years. Mapfabvisheen had been greedy; he had tried to take both geese. Therefore, he must wait upon the Giant for a double term.

Afterwards, he found out how he'd been trapped. The egglayers themselves hadn't been honking. Mouthless, they were utterly incapable of that. Mapfarity had fastened a so-called "goose-tracker" to the strong-room's doorway. This device clicked loudly whenever a goose was nearby. It could smell out one even through a lead-leaf-lined bag. When Mapfabvisheen passed underneath it, its clicks woke up a small Skin beside it. The Skin, mostly lung-sac and voice organs, honked its warning. And the dwarf, Mapfabvisheen, began his servitude to the Giant, Mapfarity.

Rastignac knew the story. He also knew that Mapfarity had infected the fellow with the philosophy of Violence and that he was now a good member of his Underground. He was eager to tell him his servitor days were over, that he could now take his place in their band as an equal. Subject, of course, to Rastignac's order.

Mapfabvisheen was stretched out upon the floor and snoring a sour breath. A grey-haired man was slumped on a nearby table. His head, turned to one side, exhibited the same slack-jawed look that the Ssassaror's had, and he flung the ill-smelling gauntlet of his breath at the visitors. He held an empty bottle in one loose hand. Two other bottles lay on the stone floor, one shattered.

Besides the bottles lay the men's Skins. Rastignac wondered why they had not crawled to the halltree and hung themselves up.

"What ails them? What is that smell?" said Mapfarity.

"I don't know," replied Archambaud, "but I know the visitor. He is Father Jules, priest of the Guild of Egg-stealers."

Rastignac raised his queer, bracket-shaped eyebrows, picked up a bottle in which there remained a slight residue, and drank.

"Mon Dieu, it is the sacrament wine!" he cried.

Mapfarity said, "Why would they be drinking that?"

"I don't know. Wake Mapfabvisheen up, but let the good father sleep. He seems tired after his spiritual labors and doubtless deserves a rest."

Doused with a bucket of cold water the little Ssassaror staggered to his feet. Seeing Archambaud, he embraced him. "Ah, Archambaud, old baby-abductor, my sweet goose-bagger, my ears tingle to see you again!"

They did. Red and blue sparks flew off his ear-feathers.

"What is the meaning of this?" sternly interrupted Mapfarity. He pointed at the dirt swept into the corners.

Mapfabvisheen drew himself up to his full dignity, which wasn't much. "Good Father Jules was making his circuits," he said. "You know he travels around the country and hears confession and sings Mass for us poor egg-stealers who have been unlucky enough to fall into the clutches of some rich and greedy and anti-social Giant who is too stingy to hire servants, but captures them instead, and who won't allow us to leave the premises until our servitude is over . . . ."

"Cut it!" thundered Mapfarity. "I can't stand around all day, listening to the likes of you. My feet hurt too much. Anyway, you know I've allowed you to go into town every week-end. Why don't you see a priest then?"

Mapfabvisheen said, "You know very well the closest town is ten kilometers away and it's full of Pantheists. There's not a priest to be found there."

Rastignac groaned inwardly. Always it was thus. You could never hurry these people or get them to regard anything seriously.

Take the case they were wasting their breath on now. Everybody knew the Church had been outlawed a long time ago because it opposed the use of the Skins and certain other practices that went along with it. So, no sooner had that been done than the Ssassarors, anxious to establish their check-and-balance system, had made arrangements through the Minister of Ill-Will to give the Church unofficial legal recognizance.

Then, though the aborigines had belonged to that pantheistical organization known as the Sons of Good And Old Mother Nature, they had all joined the Church of the Terrans. They operated under the theory that the best way to make an institution innocuous was for everybody to sign up for it. Never persecute. That makes it thrive.

*

Much to the Church's chagrin, the theory worked. How can you fight an enemy who insists on joining you and who will also agree to everything you teach him and then still worship at the other service? Supposedly driven underground, the Church counted almost every Landsman among its supporters from the Kings down.

Every now and then a priest would forget to wear his Skin out-of-doors and be arrested, then released later in an official jail-break. Those who refused to cooperate were forcibly kidnapped, taken to another town and there let loose. Nor did it do the priest any good to proclaim boldly who he was. Everybody pretended not to know he was a fugitive from justice. They insisted on calling him by his official pseudonym.

However, few priests were such martyrs. Generations of Skin-wearing had sapped the ecclesiastical vigor.

The thing that puzzled Rastignac about Father Jules was the sacrament wine. Neither he nor anybody else in L'Bawpfey, as far as he knew, had ever tasted the liquid outside of the ceremony. Indeed, except for certain of the priests, nobody even knew how to make wine.

He shook the priest awake, said, "What's the matter, Father?"

Father Jules burst into tears. "Ah, my boy, you have caught me in my sin. I am a drunkard."

Everybody looked blank. "What does that word *drunkard* mean?"

"It means a man who's damned enough to fill his Skin with alcohol, my boy, fill it until he's no longer a man but a beast."

"Alcohol? What is that?"

"The stuff that's in the wine, my boy. You don't know what I'm talking about because the knowledge was long ago forbidden except to us of the cloth. Cloth, he says! Bah! We go around like everybody, naked except for these extradermal monstrosities which reveal rather than conceal, which not only serve us as clothing but as mentors, parents, censors, interpreters, and, yes, even as priests. Where's a bottle that's not empty? I'm thirsty."

Rastignac stuck to the subject "Why was the making of this alcohol forbidden?"

"How should I know?" said Father Jules. "I'm old, but not so ancient that I came with the Six Flying Stars . . . . Where is that bottle?"

Rastignac was not offended by his crossness. Priests were notorious for being the most ill-tempered, obstreperous, and unstable of men. They were not at all like the clerics of Earth, whom everybody knew from legend had been sweet-tempered, meek, humble, and obedient to authority. But on L'Bawpfey these men of the Church had reason to be out of sorts. Everybody attended Mass, paid their tithes, went to confession, and did not fall asleep during sermons. Everybody believed what the priests told them and were as good as it was possible for human beings to be. So, the priests had no real incentive to work, no evil to fight.

Then why the prohibition against alcohol?

"*Sacre Bleu!*" groaned Father Jules. "Drink as much as I did last night and you'll find out. Never again, I say. Ah, there's another bottle, hidden by a providential fate under my traveling robe. Where's that corkscrew?"

Father Jules swallowed half of the bottle, smacked his lips, picked up his Skin from the floor, brushed off the dirt and said, "I must be going, my sons. I've a noon appointment with the bishop, and I've a good twelve kilometers to travel. Perhaps one of you gentlemen has a car?"

Rastignac shook his head and said he was sorry but their car was tired and had, besides, thrown a shoe. Father Jules shrugged philosophically, put on his Skin and reached out again for the bottle.

Rastignac said, "Sorry, Father. I'm keeping this bottle."

"For what?" asked father Jules.

"Never mind. Say I'm keeping you from temptation."

"Bless you, my son, and may you have a big enough hangover to show you the wickedness of your ways."

Smiling, Rastignac watched the Father walk out. He was not disappointed. The priest had no sooner reached the huge door than his Skin fell off and lay motionless upon the stone.

"Ah," breathed Rastignac. "The same thing happened to Mapfabvisheen when he put his on. There must be something about the wine that deadens the Skins, makes them fall off."

After the padre had left, Rastignac handed the bottle to Mapfarity. "We're dedicated to breaking the law most illegally, brother. So I'm asking you to analyze this wine and find out how to make it."

"Why not ask Father Jules?"

"Because priests are pledged never to reveal the secret. That was one of the original agreements whereby the Church was allowed to remain on L'Bawpfey. Or, at least that's what my parish priest told me. He said it was a good thing, as it removed an evil from man's temptation. He never did say why it was so evil. Maybe he didn't know.

"That doesn't matter. What does matter is that the Church has inadvertently given us a weapon whereby we may free Man from his bondage to the Skins and it has also given itself once again a chance to be really persecuted and to flourish on the blood of its martyrs."

"Blood?" said Lusine, licking her lips. "The Churchmen drink blood?"

Rastignac did not explain. He could be wrong. If so, he'd feel less like a fool if they didn't know what he thought.

Meanwhile, there were the first steps to be taken for the unskinning of an entire planet.

IX

Later that day the mucketeers surrounded the castle but they made no effort to storm it. The following day one of them knocked on the huge front door and presented Mapfarity with a summons requiring them to surrender. The Giant laughed, put the document in his mouth and ate it. The server fainted and had to be revived with a bucket of cold water before he could stagger back to report this tradition-shattering reception.

Rastignac set up his underground so it could be expanded in a hurry. He didn't worry about the blockade because, as was well known, Giants' castles had all sorts of subterranean tunnels and secret exits. He contacted a small number of priests who were willing to work for him. These were congenital rebels who became quite enthusiastic when he told them their activities would result in a fierce persecution of the Church.

The majority, however, clung to their Skins and said they would have nothing to do with this extradermal-less devil. They took pride and comfort in that term. The vulgar phrase for the man who refused to wear his Skin was "devil," and, by law and logic, the Church could not be associated with a devil. As everybody knew, the priests have always been on the side of the angels.

Meanwhile, the Devil's band slipped out of the tunnels and made raids. Their targets were Giants' castles and government treasuries; their loot, the geese. So many raids did they make that the president of the League of Giants and the Business Agent for the Guild of Egg-stealers came to plead with them. And remained to denounce. Rastignac was delighted with their complaints, and, after listening for a while, threw them out.

Rastignac had, like all other Skin-wearers, always accepted the monetary system as a thing of reason and steady balance. But, without his Skin he was able to think objectively and saw its weaknesses.

For some cause buried far in history, the Giants had always had control of the means for making the hexagonal golden coins called *oeufs*. But the Kings, wishing to get control of the golden eggs, had set up that élite branch of the Guild which specialized in abducting the half-living 'geese.' Whenever a thief was successful he turned the goose over to his King. The monarch, in turn, sent a note to the robbed Giant informing him that the government intended to keep the goose to make its own currency. But even though the Giant was making counterfeit geese, the King, in his generosity, would ship to the Giant one out of every thirty eggs laid by the kidnappee.

The note was a polite and well-recognized lie. The Giants made the only genuine gold-egg-laying geese on the planet because the Giants' League alone knew the secret. And the King gave back one-thirtieth of his loot so the Giant could accumulate enough money to buy the materials to create another goose. Which would, possibly, be stolen later on.

Rastignac, by his illegal rape of geese, was making money scarce. Peasants were hanging on to their produce and waiting to sell until prices were at their highest. The government, merchants, the league, the guild, all saw themselves impoverished.

Furthermore, the Amphibs, taking note of the situation, were making raids of their own and blaming them on Rastignac.

He did not care. He was intent on trying to find a way to reach Kataproimnoin and rescue the Earthman so he could take off in the spaceship floating in the harbor. But he knew that he would have to take things slowly, to scout out the land and plan accordingly.

Furthermore, Mapfarity had made him promise he would do his best to set up the Landsmen so they would be able to resist the Waterfolk when the day for war came.

Rastignac made his biggest raid when he and his band stole one moonless night into the capital itself to rob the big Goose House, only an egg's throw away from the Palace and the Ministry of Ill-Will. They put the Goose House guards to sleep with little arrows smeared with dream-snake venom, filled their lead-leaf-lined bags with gold eggs, and sneaked out the back door.

As they left, Rastignac saw a cloaked figure slinking from the back door of the Ministry. Seized with intuition, he tackled the figure. It was an Amphib-changeling. Rastignac struck the Amphib with a venomous arrow before the Water-human could cry out or stab back.

Mapfarity grabbed up the limp Amphib and they raced for the safety of the castle.

They questioned the Amphib, Pierre Pusipremnoos, in the castle. At first silent, he later began talking freely when Mapfarity got a heavy Skin from his fleshforge and put it on the fellow. It was a Skin modeled after those worn by the Water-people, but it differed in that the Giant could control, through another Skin, the powerful neural shocks.

After a few shocks Pierre admitted he was the foster-son of the Amphibian King and that, incidentally, Lusine was his foster-sister. He further stated he was a messenger between the Amphib King and the Ssarraror's Ill-Will Minister.

More shocks extracted the fact that the Minister of Ill-Will, Auverpin, was an Amphib-changeling who was passing himself off as a born Landsman. Not only that, the Human hostages among the Amphibs were about to stage a carefully planned revolt against the born Amphibs. It would kill off about half of them. The rest would then be brought under control of the Master Skin.

When the two stepped from the lab they were attacked by Lusine, knife in hand. She gashed Rastignac in the arm before he knocked her out with an upper-cut. Later, while Mapfarity applied a little jelly-like creature called a *scar-jester* to the wound, Rastignac complained:

"I don't know if I can endure much more of this. I thought the way of Violence would not be hard to follow because I hated the Skins and the Amphibs so much. But it is easier to attack a faceless, hypothetical enemy, or torture him, than the individual enemy. Much easier."

"My brother," boomed the Giant, "if you continue to dwell upon the philosophical implications of your actions you will end up as helpless and confused as the leg-counting centipede. Better not think. Warriors are not supposed to. They lose their keen fighting edge when they think. And you need all of that now."

"I would suppose that thought would sharpen them."

"When issues are simple, yes. But you must remember that the system on this planet is anything but uncomplicated. It was set up to confuse, to keep one always off balance. Just try to keep one thing in mind—the Skins are far more of an impediment to Man than they are a help. Also, that if the Skins don't come off the Amphibs will soon be cutting our throats. The only way to save ourselves is to kill them first. Right?"

"I suppose so," said Rastignac. He stooped and put his hands under the unconscious Lusine's armpits. "Help me put her in a room. We'll keep her locked up until she cools off. Then we'll use her to guide us when we get to Kataproimnoin. Which reminds me—how many gallons of the wine have you made so far?"

X

A week later Rastignac summoned Lusine. She came in frowning, and with her lower lip protruding in a pretty pout.

He said, "Day after tomorrow is the day on which the new Kings are crowned, isn't it?"

Tonelessly she said, "Supposedly. Actually, the present Kings will be crowned again."

Rastignac smiled. "I know. Peculiar, isn't it, how the 'people' always vote the same Kings back into power? However, that isn't what I'm getting at. If I remember correctly, the Amphibs give their King exotic and amusing gifts on coronation day. What do you think would happen if I took a big shipload of bottles of wine and passed it out among the population just before the Amphibs begin their surprise massacre?"

Lusine had seen Mapfarity and Rastignac experimenting with the wine and she had been frightened by the results. Nevertheless, she made a brave attempt to hide her fear now. She spit at him and said, "You mud-footed fool! There are priests who will know what it is! They will be in the coronation crowd."

"Ah, not so! In the first place, you Amphibs are almost entirely Aggressive Pantheists. You have only a few priests, and you will now pay for that omission of wine-tasters. Second, Mapfarity's concoction tastes not at all vinous and is twice as strong."

She spat at him again and spun on her heel and walked out.

That night Rastignac's band and Lusine went through a tunnel which brought them up through a hollow tree about two miles west of the castle. There they hopped into the Renault, which had been kept in a camouflaged garage, and drove to the little port of Marrec. Archambaud had paved their way here with golden eggs and a sloop was waiting for them.

Rastignac took the boat's wheel. Lusine stood beside him, ready to answer the challenge of any Amphib patrol that tried to stop them. As the Amphib-King's foster-daughter, she could get the boat through to the Amphib island without any trouble at all.

Archambaud stood behind her, a knife under his cloak, to make sure she did not try to betray them. Lusine had sworn she could be trusted. Rastignac had answered that he was sure she could be, too, as long as the knife point pricked her back to remind her.

Nobody stopped them. An hour before dawn they anchored in the harbor of Kataproimnoin. Lusine was tied hand and foot inside the cabin. Before Rastignac could scratch her with dream-snake venom, she pleaded, "You could not do this to me, Jean-Jacques, if you loved me."

"Who said anything about loving you?"

"Well, I like that! You said so, you cheat!"

"Oh, *then*! Well, Lusine, you've had enough experience to know that such protestations of tenderness and affection are only inevitable accompaniments of the moment's passion."

For the first time since he had known her he saw Lusine's lower lip tremble and tears come in her eyes. "Do you mean you were only using me?" she sobbed.

"You forget I had good reason to think you were just using *me*. Remember, you're an Amphib, Lusine. Your people can't be trusted. You blood-drinkers are as savage as the little sea-monsters you leave in Human cradles."

"Jean-Jacques, take me with you! I'll do anything you say! I'll even cut my foster-father's throat for you!"

He laughed. Unheeding, she swept on. "I want to be with you, Jean-Jacques! Look, with me to guide you in, my homeland—with my prestige as the Amphib-King's daughter—you can become King yourself after the rebellion. I'd get rid of the Amphib-King for you so there'll be nobody in your way!"

She felt no more guilt than a tigress. She was naive and terrible, innocent and disgusting.

"No, thanks, Lusine." He scratched her with the dream-snake needle. As her eyes closed he said, "You don't understand. All I want to do is voyage to the stars. Being King means nothing to me. The only person I'd trade places with would be the Earthman the Amphibs hold prisoner."

He left her sleeping in the locked cabin.

Noon found them loafing on the great square in front of the Palace of the Two Kings of the Sea and the Islands. All were disguised as Waterfolk. Before they'd left the castle, they had grafted webs between their fingers and toes—just as Amphib-changelings who weren't born with them, did—and they wore the special Amphib Skins that Mapfarity had grown in his fleshforge. These were able to tune in on the Amphibs' wavelengths, but they lacked their shock mechanism.

Rastignac had to locate the Earthman, rescue him, and get him to the spaceship that lay anchored between two wharfs, its sharp nose pointing outwards. A wooden bridge had been built from one of the wharfs to a place halfway up its towering side.

Rastignac could not make out any breaks in the smooth metal that would indicate a port, but reason told him there must be some sort of entrance to the ship at that point.

A guard of twenty Amphibs repulsed any attempt on the crowd's part to get on the bridge.

Rastignac had contacted the harbor-master and made arrangements for workmen to unload his cargo of wine. His freehandedness with the gold eggs got him immediate service even on this general holiday. Once in the square, he and his men uncrated the wine but left the two heavy chests on the wagon which was hitched to a powerful little six-legged Jeep.

They stacked the bottles of wine in a huge pile while the curious crowd in the square encircled them to watch. Rastignac then stood on a chest to survey the scene, so that he could best judge the time to start. There were perhaps seven or eight thousand of all three races there—the Ssassarors, the Amphibs, the Humans—with an unequal portioning of each.

Rastignac, looking for just such a thing, noticed that every non-human Amphib had at least two Humans tagging at his heels.

It would take two Humans to handle an Amphib or a Ssassaror. The Amphibs stood upon their seal-like hind flippers at least six and a half feet tall and weighed about three hundred pounds. The Giant Ssassarors, being fisheaters, had reached the same enormous height as Mapfarity. The Giants were in the minority, as the Amphibs had always preferred stealing Human babies from the Terrans. These were marked for death as much as the Amphibs.

Rastignac watched for signs of uneasiness or hostility between the three groups. Soon he saw the signs. They were not plentiful, but they were enough to indicate an uneasy undercurrent. Three times the guards had to intervene to break up quarrels. The Humans eyed the non-human quarrelers, but made no move to help their Amphib fellows against the Giants. Not only that, they took them aside afterwards and seemed to be reprimanding them. Evidently the order was that everyone was to be on his behavior until the time to revolt. Rastignac glanced at the great tower-clock. "It's an hour before the ceremonies begin," he said to his men. "Let's go."

XI

Mapfarity, who had been loitering in the crowd some distance away, caught Archambaud's signal and slowly, as befit a Giant whose feet hurt, limped towards them. He stopped, scrutinized the pile of bottles, then, in his lion's-roar-at-the-bottom-of-a-well voice said, "Say, what's in these bottles?"

Rastignac shouted back, "A drink which the new Kings will enjoy very much."

"What's that?" replied Mapfarity. "Sea-water?"

The crowd laughed.

"No, it's not water," Rastignac said, "as anybody but a lumbering Giant should know. It is a delicious drink that brings a rare ecstacy upon the drinker. I got the formula for it from an old witch who lives on the shores of far off Apfelabvidanahyew. He told me it had been in his family since the coming of Man to L'Bawpfey. He parted with the formula on condition I make it only for the Kings."

"Will only Their Majesties get to taste this exquisite drink?" bellowed Mapfarity.

"That depends upon whether it pleases Their Majesties to give some to their subjects to celebrate the result of the elections."

Archambaud, also planted in the crowd, shrilled, "I suppose if they do, the big-paunched Amphibs and Giants will get twice as much as us Humans. They always do, it seems."

There was a mutter from the crowd; approbation from the Amphibs, protest from the others.

"That will make no difference," said Rastignac, smiling. "The fascinating thing about this is that an Amphib can drink no more than a Human. That may be why the old man who revealed his secret to me called the drink Old Equalizer."

"Ah, you're skinless," scoffed Mapfarity, throwing the most deadly insult known. "I can out-drink, out-eat, and out-swim any Human here. Here, Amphib, give me a bottle, and we'll see if I'm bragging."

An Amphib captain pushed himself through the throng, waddling clumsily on his flippers like an upright seal.

"No, you don't!" he barked. "Those bottles are intended for the Kings. No commoner touches them, least of all a Human and a Giant."

Rastignac mentally hugged himself. He couldn't have planned a better intervention himself! "Why can't I?" he replied. "Until I make an official presentation, these bottles are mine, not the Kings'. I'll do what I want with them."

"Yeah," said the Amphibs. "That's telling him!"

The Amphib's big brown eyes narrowed and his animal-like face wrinkled, but he couldn't think of a retort. Rastignac at once handed a bottle apiece to each of his comrades. They uncorked and drank and then assumed an ecstatic expression which was a tribute to their acting, for these three bottles held only fruit juice.

"Look here, captain," said Rastignac, "why don't you try a swig yourself? Go ahead. There's plenty. And I'm sure Their Majesties would be pleased to contribute some of it on this joyous occasion. Besides, I can always make more for the Kings."

"As a matter of fact," he added, winking, "I expect to get a pension from the courts as the Kings' Old Equalizer-maker."

The crowd laughed. The Amphib, afraid of losing face, took the bottle—which contained wine rather than fruit juice. After a few long swallows the Amphib's eyes became red and a silly grin curved his thin, black-edged lips. Finally, in a thickening voice, he asked for another bottle.

Rastignac, in a sudden burst of generosity, not only gave him one, but began passing out bottles to the many eager reaching hands. Mapfarity and the two egg-thieves helped him. In a short time, the pile of bottles had dwindled to a fourth of its former height. When a mixed group of guards strode up and demanded to know what the commotion was about, Rastignac gave them some of the bottles.

Meanwhile, Archambaud slipped off into the mob. He lurched into an Amphib, said something nasty about his ancestors, and pulled his knife. When the Amphib lunged for the little man, Archambaud jumped back and shoved a Human-Amphib into the giant flipper-like arms.

Within a minute the square had erupted into a fighting mob. Staggering, red-eyed, slur-tongued, their long-repressed hostility against each other, released by the liquor which their bodies were unaccustomed to, Human, Ssassaror and Amphib fell to with the utmost will, slashing, slugging, fighting with everything they had.

None of them noticed that every one who had drunk from the bottles had lost his Skin. The Skins had fallen off one by one and lay motionless on the pavement where they were kicked or stepped upon. Not one Skin tried to crawl back to its owner because they were all nerve-numbed by the wine.

Rastignac, seated behind the wheel of the Jeep, began driving as best he could through the battling mob. After frequent stops he halted before the broad marble steps that ran like a stairway to heaven, up and up before it ended on the Porpoise Porch of the Palace. He and his gang were about to take the two heavy chests off the wagon when they were transfixed by a scene before them.

A score of dead Humans and Amphibs lay on the steps, evidence of the fierce struggle that had taken place between the guards of the two monarchs. Evidently the King had heard of the riot and hastened outside. There the Amphib-changeling King had apparently realized that the rebellion was way ahead of schedule, but he had attacked the Amphib King anyway.

And he had won, for his guardsmen held the struggling flipper-footed Amphib ruler down while two others bent his head back over a step. The Changeling-King himself, still clad in the coronation robes, was about to draw his long ceremonial knife across the exposed and palpitating throat of the Amphib King.

This in itself was enough to freeze the onlookers. But the sight of Lusine running up the stairway towards the rulers added to their paralysis. She had a knife in her hand and was holding it high as she ran toward her foster-father, the Amphib King.

Mapfarity groaned, but Rastignac said, "It doesn't matter that she has escaped. We'll go ahead with our original plan."

They began unloading the chests while Rastignac kept an eye on Lusine. He saw her run up, stop, say a few words to the Amphib King, then kneel and stab him, burying the knife in his jugular vein. Then, before anybody could stop her she had applied her mouth to the cut in his neck.

The Human-King kicked her in the ribs and sent her rolling down the steps. Rastignac saw correctly that it was not her murderous deed that caused his reaction. It was because she had dared to commit it without his permission and had also drunk the royal blood first.

He further noted with grim satisfaction that when Lusine recovered from the blow and ran back up to talk to the King, he ignored her. She pointed at the group around the wagon but he dismissed her with a wave of his hand. He was too busy gloating over his vanquished rival lying at his feet.

The plotters hoisted the two chests and staggered up the steps. The King passed them as he went down with no more than a curious glance. Gifts had been coming up those steps all day for the King, so he undoubtedly thought of them only as more gifts. So Rastignac and his men walked past the knives of the guards as if they had nothing to fear.

Lusine stood alone at the top of the steps. She was in a half-crouch, knife ready. "I'll kill the King and I'll drink from his throat!" she cried hoarsely. "No man kicks me except for love. Has he forgotten that I am the foster-daughter of the Amphib King?"

Rastignac felt revulsion but he had learned by now that those who deal in violence and rebellion must march with strange steppers.

"Bear a hand here," he said, ignoring her threat.

Meekly she grabbed hold of a chest's corner. To his further questioning, she replied that the Earthman who had landed in the ship was held in a suite of rooms in the west wing. Their trip thereafter was fast and direct. Unopposed, they carted the chests to the huge room where the Master Skin was kept.

There they found ten frantic bio-technicians excitedly trying to determine why the great extraderm—the Master Skin through which all individual Skins were controlled—was not broadcasting properly. They had no way as yet of knowing that it was operating perfectly but that the little Skins upon the Amphibs and their hostage Humans were not shocking them into submission because they were lying in a wine-stupor on the ground. No one had told them that the Skins, which fed off the bloodstream of their hosts, had become anesthetized from the alcohol and failed any longer to react to their Master Skin.

That, of course, applied only to those Skins in the square that were drunk from the wine. Elsewhere all over the kingdom, Amphibs writhed in agony and Ssassarors and Terrans were taking advantage of their helplessness to cut their throats. But not here, where the crux of the matter was.

XII

The Landsmen rushed the techs and pushed them into the great chemical vat in which the twenty-five hundred foot square Master Skin floated. Then they uncrated the lead-leaf-lined bags filled with stolen geese and emptied them into the nutrient fluid. According to Mapfarity's calculations, the radio-activity from the silicon-carbon geese should kill the big Skin within a few days. When a new one was grown, that, too, would die. Unless the Amphib guessed what was wrong and located the geese on the bottom of the ten-foot deep tank, they would not be able to stop the process. That did not seem likely.

In either case, it was necessary that the Master Skin be put out of temporary commission, at least, so the Amphibs over the Kingdom could have a fighting chance. Mapfarity plunged a hollow harpoon into the isle of floating protoplasm and through a tube connected to that poured into the Skin three gallons of the dream-snake venom. That was enough to knock it out for an hour or two. Meanwhile, if the Amphibs had any sense at all, they'd have rid themselves of their extraderms.

They left the lab and entered the west wing. As they trotted up the long winding corridors Lusine said, "Jean-Jacques, what do you plan on doing now? Will you try to make yourself King of the Terrans and fight us Amphibs?" When he said nothing she went on. "Why don't you kill the Amphib-changeling King and take over here? I could help you do that. You could then have all of L'Bawpfey in your power."

He shot her a look of contempt and cried, "Lusine, can't you get it through that thick little head of yours that everything I've done has been done so that I can win one goal: reach the Flying Stars? If I can get the Earthman to his ship I'll leave with him and not set foot again for years on this planet. Maybe never again."

She looked stricken. "But what about the war here?" she asked.

"There are a few men among the Landfolk who are capable of leading in wartime. It will take strong men, and there are very few like me, I admit, but—oh, oh, opposition!" He broke off at sight of the six guards who stood before the Earthman's suite.

Lusine helped, and within a minute they had slain three and chased away the others. Then they burst through the door—and Rastignac received another shock.

The occupant of the apartment was a tiny and exquisitely formed redhead with large blue eyes and very unmasculine curves!

"I thought you said Earth*man*?" protested Rastignac to the Giant who came lumbering along behind them.

"Oh, I used that in the generic sense," Mapfarity replied. "You didn't expect me to pay any attention to sex, did you? I'm not interested in the gender of you Humans, you know."

There was no time for reproach. Rastignac tried to explain to the Earthwoman who he was, but she did not understand him. However, she did seem to catch on to what he wanted and seemed reassured by his gestures. She picked up a large book from a table and, hugging it to her small, high and rounded bosom, went with him out the door.

They raced from the palace and descended onto the square. Here they found the surviving Amphibs clustered into a solid phalanx and fighting, bloody step by step, towards the street that led to the harbor.

Rastignac's little group skirted the battle and started down the steep avenue toward the harbor. Halfway down he glanced back and saw that nobody as yet was paying any attention to them. Nor was there anybody on the street to bother them, though the pavement was strewn with Skins and bodies. Apparently, those who'd lived through the first savage mêlée had gone to the square.

They ran onto the wharf. The Earthwoman motioned to Rastignac that she knew how to open the spaceship, but the Amphibs didn't. Moreover, if they did get in, they wouldn't know how to operate it. She had the directions for so doing in the book hugged so desperately to her chest. Rastignac surmised she hadn't told the Amphibs about that. Apparently they hadn't, as yet, tried to torture the information from her.

Therefore, her telling him about the book indicated she trusted him.

Lusine said, "Now what, Jean-Jacques? Are you still going to abandon this planet?"

"Of course," he snapped.

"Will you take me with you?"

He had spent most of his life under the tutelage of his Skin, which ensured that others would know when he was lying. It did not come easy to hide his true feelings. So a habit of a lifetime won out.

"I will not take you," he said. "In the first place, though you may have some admirable virtues, I've failed to detect one. In the second place, I could not stand your blood-drinking nor your murderous and totally immoral ways."

"But, Jean-Jacques, I will give them up for you!"

"Can the shark stop eating fish?"

"You would leave Lusine, who loves you as no Earthwoman could, and go with that—that pale little doll I could break with my hands?"

"Be quiet," he said. "I have dreamed of this moment all my life. Nothing can stop me now."

They were on the wharf beside the bridge that ran up the smooth side of the starship. The guard was no longer there, though bodies showed that there had been reluctance on the part of some to leave.

They let the Earthwoman precede them up the bridge.

Lusine suddenly ran ahead of him, crying, "If you won't have me, you won't have her, either! Nor the stars!"

Her knife sank twice into the Earthwoman's back. Then, before anybody could reach her, she had leaped off the bridge and into the harbor.

Rastignac knelt beside the Earthwoman. She held out the book to him, then she died. He caught the volume before it struck the wharf.

"My God! My God!" moaned Rastignac, stunned with grief and shock and sorrow. Sorrow for the woman and shock at the loss of the ship and the end of his plans for freedom.

Mapfarity ran up then and took the book from his nerveless hand. "She indicated that this is a manual for running the ship," he said. "All is not lost."

"It will be in a language we don't know," Rastignac whispered.

Archambaud came running up, shrilled, "The Amphibs have broken through and are coming down the street! Let's get to our boat before the whole blood-thirsty mob gets here!"

Mapfarity paid him no attention. He thumbed through the book, then reached down and lifted Rastignac from his crouching position by the corpse.

"There's hope yet, Jean-Jacques," he growled. "This book is printed with the same characters as those I saw in a book owned by a priest I knew. He said it was in Hebrew, and that it was the Holy Book in the original Earth language. This woman must be a citizen of the Republic of Israeli, which I understand was rising to be a great power on Earth at the time you French left.

"Perhaps the language of this woman has changed somewhat from the original tongue, but I don't think the alphabet has. I'll bet that if we get this to a priest who can read it—there are only a few left—he can translate it well enough for us to figure out everything."

They walked to the wharf's end and climbed down a ladder to a platform where a dory was tied up. As they rowed out to their sloop Mapfarity said:

"Look, Rastignac, things aren't as bad as they seem. If you haven't the ship nobody else has, either. And you alone have the key to its entrance and operation. For that you can thank the Church, which has preserved the ancient wisdom for emergencies which it couldn't forsee, such as this. Just as it kept the secret of wine, which will eventually be the greatest means for delivering our people from their bondage to the Skins and, thus enable them to fight the Amphibs back instead of being slaughtered.

"Meanwhile, we've a battle to wage. You will have to lead it. Nobody else but the Skinless Devil has the prestige to make the people gather around him. Once we accuse the Minister of Ill-Will of treason and jail him, without an official Breaker to release him, we'll demand a general election. You'll be made King of the Ssassaror; I, of the Terrans. That is inevitable, for we are the only skinless men and, therefore, irresistible. After the war is won, we'll leave for the stars. How do you like that?"

Rastignac smiled. It was weak, but it was a smile. His bracket-shaped eyebrows bent into their old sign of determination.

"You are right," he replied. "I have given it much thought. A man has no right to leave his native land until he's settled his problems here. Even if Lusine hadn't killed the Earthwoman and I had sailed away, my conscience wouldn't have given me any rest. I would have known I had abandoned the fight in the middle of it. But now that I have stripped myself of my Skin—which was a substitute for a conscience—and now that I am being forced to develop my own inward conscience, I must admit that immediate flight to the stars would have been the wrong thing."

The pleased and happy Mapfarity said, "And you must also admit, Rastignac, that things so far have had a way of working out for the best. Even Lusine, evil as she was, has helped towards the general good by keeping you on this planet. And the Church, though it has released once again the old evil of alcohol, has done more good by so doing than . . . ."

But here Rastignac interrupted to say he did not believe in this particular school of thought, and so, while the howls of savage warriors drifted from the wharfs, while the structure of their world crashed around them, they plunged into that most violent and circular of all whirlpools—the Discussion Philosophical.

TEXAS WEEK

by Albert Hernhuter

One of the chief purposes of psychiatry is to separate fantasy from reality. It is reasonable to expect that future psychiatrists will know more about this borderline than the most learned doctors of today. Yet now and again even the best of them may encounter situations that defy all logic.

Meeting the little man who isn't there is rated an horrendous experience. But discovery that the man is there may be even worse.

THE SLICK black car sped along the wide and straight street. It came to a smooth stop in front of a clean white house. A man got out of the car and walked briskly to the door. Reaching out with a pink hand, he pressed the doorbell with one well-manicured finger.

The door was answered by a housewife. She was wearing a white blouse, a green skirt and a green apron trimmed with white. Her feet were tucked into orange slippers, her blonde hair was done up in a neat bun. She was dressed as the government had ordered for that week.

The man said, "You are Mrs. Christopher Nest?"

There was a trace of anxiety in her voice as she answered. "Yes. And you are . . . ? . . . ?"

"My name is Maxwell Hanstark. As you may already know, I am the official psychiatrist for this district. My appointment will last until the end of this year."

Mrs. Nest invited him in. They stepped into a clean living-room. At one end was the television set, at the other end were several chairs. There was nothing between the set and the chairs except a large grey rug which stretched from wall to wall. They walked to the chairs and sat down.

"Now, just what is the matter with your husband, Mrs. Nest?"

Mrs. Nest reached into a large bowl and absently picked up a piece of stale popcorn. She daintily placed it in her mouth and chewed thoughtfully before she answered.

"I wish I knew. All he does all day long is sit in the backyard and stare at the grass. He insists that he is standing on top of a cliff."

Hanstark took out a small pad and a short ball-point pen. He wrote something down before he spoke again. "Is he violent? Did he get angry when you told him there was no cliff?"

Mrs. Nest was silent for a moment. A second piece of popcorn joined the first. Hanstark's pen was poised above the pad. "No. He didn't get violent."

Hanstark wrote as he asked the next question. "Just what *was* his reaction?"

"He said *I* must be crazy."

"Were those his exact words?"

"No. He said that I was"— She thought for a moment—"loco. Yes, that was the word."

"Loco?"

"Yes. He said it just like those cowboys on the television."

Hanstark looked puzzled. "Perhaps you had better tell me more about this. When did he first start acting this way?"

Mrs. Nest glanced up at the television set, then back at Hanstark. "It was right after Texas Week. You remember—they showed all of those old cowboy pictures."

Hanstark nodded.

"Well, he stayed up every night watching them. Some nights he didn't even go to sleep. Even after the set was off, he sat in one of the chairs, just staring at the screen. This morning, when I got up, he wasn't in the house. I looked all over but I couldn't find him. I was just about ready to phone the police when I glanced out the window into the backyard. And I saw him."

"What was he doing?"

"He was just sitting there in the middle of the yard, staring. I went out and tried to bring him into the house. He told me he had to watch for someone. When I asked him what he was talking about he told me that I was crazy. That was when I phoned you, Mr. Hanstark."

"A very wise move, Mrs. Nest. And would you show me where your husband is right now?"

She nodded her head and they both got up from the chairs. They walked through the dining-room and kitchen. On the back porch Hanstark came to a halt.

"You'd better stay here, Mrs. Nest." He walked to the door and opened it.

"Mr. Hanstark," Mrs. Nest called.

Hanstark turned and saw her standing next to the automatic washing machine. "Yes?"

"Please be careful."

Hanstark smiled. "I shall be, Mrs. Nest."

He walked out the door and down three concrete steps. Looking a little to his right, he saw a man squatted on his heels. He walked up to the man. "You are Mr. Christopher Nest?"

The man looked up and stared for a moment at Hanstark. "Yep," he answered. Then he turned and stared at the grass again.

"And may I ask you what you are doing?"

219

Nest answered without looking up. "Guardin' the pass."

Hanstark scribbled something in his notebook. "And why are you guarding the pass?"

Nest rose to his feet and stared down at Hanstark. "Just what are you askin' all of these questions for, stranger?"

Hanstark saw Nest was bigger than he and decided to play along for a while. After all, strategy . . .

"I'm just interested in your welfare, Mr. Nest."

Nest shrugged his shoulders. He reached into his shirt pocket and pulled out a sack of tobacco and some paper. Holding a piece of paper in one hand, he carefully poured a little tobacco onto it. In one quick movement he rolled the paper and tobacco into a perfect cylinder.

He put the sack of tobacco and paper back into his pocket and took out a wooden kitchen match. He scraped it to life on the sole of his shoe and applied the flame to the tip of the cigarette. He puffed it into life and threw the match away. It burned for a few moments in the moist grass, then went out. A thin trail of smoke rose from it, and then was gone.

"Why are you guarding the pass?" Hanstark asked again.

Nest resumed his crouch on the grass. "News is around that Dirty Dan the cattle rustler is gonna try to steal some of my cattle." He patted an imaginary holster at his side. "And I aim to stop him."

Hanstark thought for a moment. Strategy—he must use strategy . . . "Mr. Nest." He waited until Nest had turned to him. "Mr. Nest. What would you say if I told you that there was no pass down there?"

"Why shucks, pardner. I'd say you'd been chewin' some loco weed."

"And if I could prove it?"

Nest answered after a moment's pause. "Why then, I guess *I'd* be loco."

Hanstark thought it was going to be easy. "Mr. Nest, it is a well known fact that no one can walk in mid-air. Is that not true?"

Nest took a deep drag on his cigarette and blew the smoke out of his nostrils. "Shore."

"Then if I were to walk out above your pass you'd have to admit there is no pass."

"Reckon so."

Hanstark began to walk in the direction of Nest's "cliff." Nest jumped to his feet and grabbed the official psychiatrist by the arm.

"What're you tryin' to do," Nest said angrily, "kill yourself?"

Hanstark shook free of his grasp. "Mr. Nest, I am not going to kill myself. I am merely going to walk in that direction." He pointed to where the cliff was supposed to be. "To you it will look as if I were walking in mid-air."

Nest dropped his hands to his sides. "Shucks, I don't care if you kill yourself. It's just that it's liable to make the cattle nervous."

Hanstark gave him a cold glare and began to walk. He took three paces and stopped. "You see, Mr. Nest. There is no cliff."

Nest looked at him and laughed. "You just take one more step and you'll find there *is* a cliff!"

Hanstark took another step—a long one. His face bore a surprised look as he disappeared beneath the grass. His screams could be heard for a moment before he landed on the rocks below.

Nest walked to the edge of the cliff and looked down at the mangled body. He took off his hat in respect. "Little feller had a lotta guts." Then he added, "Poor little feller."

He put his hat back on and looked down at the entrance to the valley. A horse and rider appeared from behind several rocks.

"Dirty Dan!" Nest exclaimed. He reached down and picked up his rifle.

THE HOUSE FROM NOWHERE

by Arthur G. Stangland

Time-travel continues to exercise its mesmeric fascination upon writers, readers and editors of science fiction alike. Probably because almost all of us, at one time or another, have longed greatly to visit either the future or the past. Perhaps, in view of the dangerous paradoxes such travel must involve, it is a good thing that such horological journeys have to date been confined to the printed page.

New neighbors are always exciting. But the anachronistic MacDonalds offered a bit too much.

*

The morning paper lay unread before Philon Miller on the breakfast table and even the prospects of steaming coffee, ham, eggs and orange juice could not make him forget his last night's visitors.

On the closed-circuit Industrial TV screen glowed the words, *Food Preparation Center breakfast menu for July 24, 2052. No. 1, orange juice, coffee, ham and eggs. No. 2, waffle, coffee . . . .*

Automatically he punched the button for *No. 1.* Oh, his visitors had made matters appear justifiable. The presidential election campaign was going badly, Rakoff the chairman said, and his poll-quota for the election had been upped from twenty-five grand to fifty.

A stainless-steel capsule popped into the transparent wall dock. Of course the party quota system was taken for granted, he mused, removing the capsule, but it was an obligation you didn't welsh on. The muscle boys in the party organization saw to that. But still, fifty thousand . . . .

Across the table John, his sixteen-year-old adopted son, stirred. "I guess you aren't as hungry as I am, Phil."

"What? Oh, sorry." John—down here for breakfast? What was the matter? The kid sick or something? Every morning he took his meal to his room to eat in solitude. Funny kid.

Philon removed the food capsule from the wall dock, stopping the soft gushing of air in the suction tube. Setting it on the table he snapped it open and removed the individual thermocels of food.

Philon poured coffee from the thermos and absently stirred in cream and sugar. Fifty thousand . . . .

John was well into his breakfast already. "Phil, I was down to visit those people on the corner—you know, the house that appeared there over-night."

"Um."

"Their name is MacDonald," John said. "And they have a son, Jimmie, just my age, and a younger girl, Jean. Gosh, you ought to see the inside of their house, Phil. Old-fashioned! At the windows they got something called venetian blinds instead of our variable mirror thermopanes. And you know what? They don't even have an FP connection. They prepare all their meals in the house!"

John's excitement finally aroused Philon's attention. "No Food Preparation service? But that's unheard of!"

"They're sure swell people though."

"Where in the world did they come from?" Philon poured more coffee.

"Some place out West—Oregon, I think. Lived in a small town."

"How come their house appeared over-night?"

"Yeah, I asked them about that," John said. "They said their house is a prefab and it was cheaper to move it from Oregon than to buy one here. So they moved in one night—lock, stock and barrel."

John looked at Philon with a tentative air. "And another thing—Jimmie and Jean are their real children."

Philon began to frown in disgust. "Real children—how vulgar! No one does that anymore. That custom went out years ago with the Eugenic Act of two thousand twenty-nine. Breeding perfect children is the job of selected specimens. Why, I remember the day we passed our check over to Maternity Clinic! You were the best specimen in the place—and you carried the highest price tag too—ten thousand dollars!"

At that moment Ursula, his wife, her green rinse tumbling in stringy tufts over her forehead pattered into the breakfast room. Her right eye was closed in a tight squint against her cigarette smoke.

"Well, do I get my share of breakfast," she muttered, "or do I have to scrabble at the trough like the rest of the hogs around here?"

Philon nodded at a third thermocel in the capsule. "That's yours, Ursula." He fixed her with a cocked eye. "What time did that gigolo get you home this morning?"

Ursula blew the hair out of her eyes, then took a good look at her husband. "Why all the sudden concern about my affairs? I feel like going to the Cairo I call up Francois. He dances divinely. I feel like making love I call up Jose . . . ." She shrugged. "So, I say, why the sudden concern? All these years you say nothing. Every minute away from home you're involved in big deals to make money, steal money—maybe even eat it."

He looked at her cryptically. "I've got to raise a fifty-grand quota."

Without even looking up from her breakfast Ursula said absently, "Oh, that. It *is* election year again, isn't it?"

"And I'll have to ask you to cancel all unnecessary expenditures for the time being."

She shook her head. "Can't—I've already reserved *Love's Passion* for this afternoon and a whole block of titles for three months."

Philon compressed his mouth, then practically blew the words at her. "Damn it, Ursula, you're spending too much time psycho-dreaming these cheap plays. You know the psychiatrist has warned you to lay off them. Stimulates your endocrine system too much. No wonder you live on sleeping pills."

"Oh, shut up!" She stared at him, the anger in her tugging at her loose mouth. "If I feel like a psychoplay I'm going to have me a psychoplay. It's the only stimulation I get any more."

Muttering, "T'hell with it!" Philon got up from the table and walked into the living room. Slipping into his gray top coat and hat he ascended to the copter roofport.

Before stepping into the copter seat he paused to study the MacDonald house on the corner. Odd-looking house at that. Mid-twentieth century, yet it looked brand new.

Then, putting the house out of mind, Philon shot his copter skyward and joined Skyway No. 7 traffic into town.

Descending on his office building he left the ship in care of the parking attendant and by elevator dropped to his floor. At a door marked *Miller Electronic Manufacturing Co.* he walked in.

In his office he slouched into his chair and stared at the small calendar on his desk. Rakoff wanted the fifty-thousand before Royal Pastel Mink Monday. One week—that wasn't very much time.

Flinching from the unpleasant problem, he stared at the city skyline, his mind drifting lazily. He thought about Royal Pastel Mink Monday. Some said it was just another Day dreamed up by furriers to make people fur-conscious. Others said it commemorated a period of great public indifference which cost large numbers their freedom to vote.

Of course the other party had their symbology too—like the Teapot Celebration. No one seemed to know for sure what it meant. Anyway, why worry how they started? Why did people knock on wood for luck—or throw salt over their left shoulder?

But then once in awhile there arose some who spelled out a strange lonely cry, calling themselves the conscience of the people. They spoke sternly of the thin moral fiber of the country, berating the people for what they called their amoral evolution brought on by indifference and negligence until they no longer could hear the still guiding voice of their conscience. But they were scornfully laughed down and it seemed to Philon he heard less and less of these men.

In the late afternoon a whip from party headquarters dropped in. "Hello, Feisel," Philon said with little enthusiasm for the swarthy-faced man.

Without even the formality of a greeting Feisel smiled down at Philon in a half-sneer. "Well, Philon, how we doin' with the fifty grand, eh?"

Philon tossed a sheaf of papers on the desk with a gesture of impatience. "Now look, I'll raise the fifty G's by the end of the week."

Feisel lifted a thin black eyebrow and shrugged elaborately. "Just inquiring, my friend, just inquiring. You know—just showing friendly interest."

"Well, go peddle your papers to somebody else. You make me nervous."

Feisel sniffed with injured pride. "That's gratitude for you. And just when I was going to put a little bee in your bonnet. I thought you'd like to know what happened to another guy just like you. You see, he got ideas, instead of digging to get his quota. He tried to lam out and you know where they found him? On the sidewalk below his twenty-third-floor window."

As Feisel went out, Philon swore softly at his retreating back. But Feisel's little story sent a chill through him.

That evening when he descended from his copter port and stepped into his living room he was surprised to hear young voices upstairs. Deciding to investigate he stepped on the escalator. At John's door he poked his head in.

"Hello."

A young blond-headed boy with bright clear eyes turned to look at him and a younger girl with short curly hair smiled back.

John said, "Phil, this is Jimmie, and Jean, his sister. They don't have a home-school teleclass rig yet, so they're attending with me."

"I see." Philon nodded to the children. "And how did you like your first day at school?"

"Fine," Jean said, beaming until her eyes almost disappeared. "It was fun. The teacher was talking about the history of atomic energy and when I told her we had one of the first editions of the famous Smyth report on *Atomic Energy* she was surprised."

"A first edition of the *Smyth Report*? No wonder your teacher was surprised." Through Philon's mind ran the recollection that first editions of the Smyth Report brought as high as seventy thousand dollars.

The children's excited chatter was suddenly interrupted by the front door chimes. Stepping to the wall televiewer, Philon pressed a button and said, "Who is it?"

A pleasant-faced man with a startled look said, "Oh—sorry. This gadget on the door-casing surprised me. Ah—I think my children, Jimmie and Jean, are here. I'm Bill MacDonald."

Behind him Philon heard Jean suppress a dismayed cry. "Gosh, Jimmie, it's late. Daddy's had to come for us!"

Philon said, "And I'm Phil Miller, MacDonald. Come in. We'll be down in a moment."

The MacDonald children and John headed for the stairs in a happy rush, ignoring the descending escalator, two steps at a time. Philon followed at a meditative pace, his thoughts trooping stealthily abreast. Seventy thousand dollars. Now, if he were to . . . .

"Beautiful home you've got here, Miller."

Philon came out of his daydreaming to see MacDonald coming into view around the corner of a living room ell.

Philon took his extended hand. "Thanks. Glad you like it."

Jean broke in breathlessly. "Oh, Daddy, you ought to see how they conduct classes—by school TV. You write on a glass square and it appears immediately at the teacher's roll-board. And when you—"

Jimmie interrupted. "Aw, lemme tell 'im something too, Jean. Dad, John used a spare TV for Jean's freshman class while we 'showed' for junior class on his. Gosh, in history, Dad, their old newsreels go back to World War Two. I even saw your Marine unit—"

MacDonald cut his son short. "That's enough, Jimmie. You can tell us about it later." He herded his children toward the front door. "Thanks, Miller, for letting the kids use the school TV. I'm having one installed tomorrow."

After they left John said with a sparkle Philon had never seen before, "You know, Phil, those are the most interesting kids I've ever met. All the others I know are bored stiff. They've been everyplace and they've done everything.

"But Jimmie and Jean ask more questions about things than anybody I know. They're really interested. Every time I drop in on them they're studying history beginning with the middle of the Twentieth Century. They're absolutely fascinated and read it like fiction."

With more on his mind than his neighbors' unusual behavior Philon said, "Mmm." He stood looking at the boy for a long moment until John finally shifted self-consciously.

"What's the matter, Phil?"

Philon ended his musing. "Tomorrow night we're all going to call on the MacDonalds. And while we're there I want you to slip that copy of the *Smyth Report* out of their library."

For a moment the young boy's smooth face was a blank mask. Then it filled in with shocked surprise, then resentment and finally anger. "You mean—steal?"

"Of course. If they're too innocent to realize the value of the book that's their hard luck."

"But, Phil, I can't imagine myself stealing from . . . ."

Impatiently, Philon said, "Since when did you suddenly get so holier-than-thou? Life is harsh, life is iron-fisted and if you don't keep your guard up you're going to get socked in the kisser."

John said slowly with a certain tone of shame, "Yes, I know. As far back as I can remember you've told me that. But in spite of it I can't help feeling it isn't right to treat the MacDonalds that way. They're too nice, too good."

"Look, John. You might as well learn the hard facts of life. All the high-sounding arguments for a moral world and all the laws on the books implementing those arguments are just eyewash. Sure, the President swears that he will uphold the constitution and enforce all the laws.

"Then we carefully surround him with counterspies—wire his rooms with dictaphones, slit his mail, install secret informers on his staff. All because no matter who the party is able to elect we don't trust him—because the society he represents does not trust itself."

"Is that why we have more and bigger jails than ever?"

Philon shrugged. "All I'm trying to tell you is don't go soft-headed or the world will take your shirt."

The next day before leaving for the office Philon said to his wife, "Call up the MacDonalds and if they're going to be home tonight tell them we'll be over for a visit."

Ursula made a face. "Do we *have* to call on those people? They'll bore me stiff."

"For heaven's sake, Ursula! It's a matter of vital importance to me—and you also, if I have to appeal to your wide streak of selfishness."

"I can't see it."

"I'll explain later. I've got to go."

During the day Ursula called him. "Well, Phil, I called as you said and I've committed us for dinner tonight."

"Dinner! Hmm, they *are* convivial people."

"Yes and the dinner is going to be cooked right there in their house. How vulgar can some people get?"

That evening while dressing Ursula said, "Phil, John spends a lot of time at the MacDonalds'. What do you suppose he sees in them? It gets me the way he quotes them all the time and reports their least doings. Today he came tearing into the house and said, 'Ursula, it's wonderful!' I said, 'What's wonderful?' And John said, 'The dinner they're cooking at MacDonalds'. I've never smelled anything like it in all my life. Why don't we cook in our house like they do? Mrs. MacDonald was baking cookies and let me have one right out of the oven. Mmmm, boy was it *good*!'"

Ursula finished, "Now, I ask you, did you ever hear anything so barbaric—cooking in the house and having all the odors permeate the whole place?"

"Well, we'll see."

Later when they arrived at the MacDonalds' they were welcomed with a quiet warmth and friendliness that Philon cynically assumed to be a new and different front.

As they sat down to dinner Mrs. MacDonald, a rosy-cheeked woman with a quick and ready smile, said, "I'm sorry we aren't able to get a connection yet. So everything we're eating tonight is right out of our deep-freeze."

John Miller said, "Gosh, Mrs. MacDonald, as far as I'm concerned, I'd rather eat from your deep-freeze anytime than from the FP!"

Bill MacDonald looked across the table at Jean and said, "All right, Jean."

Jean and all the MacDonalds bent their heads and the girl began, "We thank Thee for our daily bread as by Thy hands . . . ."

As the girl spoke Phil's gaze drifted around to his wife, who lifted her shoulders in mystified amazement. But it was a bigger surprise to see John's bent head. For the moment John was a part of this family—part of a wholeness tied together by an invisible bond. The utter strangeness of it shocked Philon into rare clarity of insight.

He saw himself wrapped up in his business with little regard for Ursula or John, letting them exist under his roof without making them a part of his life. Ursula with her succession of gigolos and her psycho-plays and John withdrawn into his upstairs room with his books. Then he closed his mind again as if the insight were too blinding.

What strange customs these MacDonalds had! Yet he had to admit the meal looked more appetizing than anything he had ever seen. It gave an impression of sumptuous plenty to see the food for everybody in one place instead of individually packaged under glistening thermocel. And instead of throwaway dishes they used chinaware that could have come right out of a museum.

Ursula asked, "What kind of fish is this?"

Bill MacDonald answered with a big grin. "It's Royal Chinook salmon that I caught in the fish derby on the Columbia River only last—"

Mrs. MacDonald colored suddenly. "You'll have to forgive Bill. He gets himself so wrapped up in his fishing."

Glancing at MacDonald Philon was surprised to see the same confusion and embarrassment on his host's face.

It was after dinner when Mrs. MacDonald and Jean were clearing the table that Philon looked over the library shelves. MacDonald himself appeared uneasy and hovered in the background.

"You'll have to excuse my selections. They're all pretty old. I—er—inherited most of them from a grandfather."

In a few minutes Philon spotted the *Smyth Report*. Fixing its position well in mind he turned away. MacDonald was saying, "Come down in the basement and I'll show you my hobby room."

"Glad to." As MacDonald led the way Philon whispered to John, "You'll find the book on the second shelf from the bottom on the right side."

John returned him a stony stare of belligerence and Philon clamped his jaw. The boy dropped his glance and gave a reluctant nod of acquiescence.

Upstairs a half hour later Ursula, who had filled her small ashtray with a mound of stubs, suddenly told Philon she was going home.

"But, Ursula, I thought that—"

With thin-lipped impatience she snapped, "I just remembered I had another engagement at eight."

Mrs. MacDonald was genuinely sorry. "Oh, that's too bad, I thought we could have the whole evening together."

Casting a meaningful glance at John and getting a confirming cold-eyed nod in return, Philon got on his feet. "Sorry, folks. Maybe we'll get together another time."

"I hope so," MacDonald said.

In angry silence Philon walked home. Not until they were all in the house and Ursula was hastening toward her second-floor room did he say a word. "I suppose your 'other engagement' means the Cairo again tonight?"

Ascending on the escalator Ursula turned to look scornfully over her shoulder. "Yes! Anything to escape from boredom. All that woman talked about while you were in the basement was redecorating the house or about cooking and asking my opinions. *Ugh!*"

Philon laughed mirthlessly. "Yeah, I guess she picked a flat number to discuss those things with. Anything you might have learned about them you must have got out of a psychoplay."

Stepping off the escalator at the top Ursula spit a nasty epithet his way, then disappeared into the upstairs hall.

John stood at the foot of the escalator, a reluctant witness to the bickering. Divining his attitude Philon mentally shrugged it off. The kid might as well learn what married life was like in these modern days.

"You got the book, eh?"

John pulled a book from his suit coat and laid it on a small table. "Yes, there's the book—and I never felt so rotten about anything in all my life!"

Philon said, "Kid, you've got a lot to learn about getting along in this world."

"All right—so I've got a lot to learn," John cried bitterly. "But there must be more to life than trying to stop the other guy from stripping the shirt off your back while you succeed in stripping off his!"

With that he took the escalator to the upper hall while Philon watched him disappear.

Left alone now, Philon settled into a chair by a window and stared down the street at the MacDonald house. Odd people—it almost seemed they didn't belong in this time and period, considering their queer ways of thinking and looking at things. MacDonald himself in particular had some odd personal attitudes.

Like that incident in his basement—Philon had curiously pulled open a heavy steel door to a small cubicle filled with a most complex arrangement of large coils and heavy insulators and glassed-in filaments. MacDonald was almost rude in closing the door when he found Philon opening it. He had fumbled and stuttered around, explaining the room was a niche where he did a little experimenting on his own. Yes, strange people.

The next day Philon eagerly hastened to a bookstore dealing in antique editions. Hugging the book closely Philon told himself his troubles were all over. The book would surely bring between fifty and a hundred grand.

A clerk approached. "Can I help you?"

"I want to talk to Mr. Norton himself."

The clerk spoke into a wrist transmitter. "Mr. Norton, a man to see you."

In a few moments a bulbous man came heavily down the aisle, peering through dark tinted glasses at Philon. "Yes?"

"I have a very rare first edition of Smyth's *Atomic Energy*," said Philon, showing the book.

Norton adjusted his glasses, then took the book. He carefully handled it, looking over the outside of the covers, then thumbed the pages. After a long frowning moment, he said, "Publication date is nineteen forty-six but the book's fairly new. Must have been kept hermetically sealed in helium for a good many years."

"Yeah, yeah, it was," Philon said matter-of-factly. "Came from my paternal grandfather's side of the family. A book like this ought to be worth at the very least seventy-five thousand."

But the bulbous Mr. Norton was not impressed. He shrugged vaguely. "Well—it's just possible—" He looked up at Philon suddenly. "Before I make any offer to you I shall have to radiocarbon date the book. Are you willing to sacrifice a back flyleaf in the process?"

"Why a flyleaf?"

"We have to convert a sample of the book into carbon dioxide to geigercount the radioactivity in the carbon. You see, all living things like the cotton in the rags the paper is made of absorb the radioactive carbon fourteen that is formed in the upper atmosphere by cosmic radiation. Then it begins to decay and we can measure very accurately the amount, which gives us an absolute time span."

With a frustrated feeling Philon agreed. "Well okay then. It's a waste of time I think. The book is obviously a first edition."

"It will take the technician about two hours to complete the analysis. We'll have an answer for you—say after lunch."

The two hours dragged by and Philon eagerly hastened to the store.

When Mr. Norton appeared he wore the grim look of a righteously angry man. He thrust the book at Philon. "Here, sir, is your book. The next time you try to foist one over on a book trader remember science is a shrewd detective and you'll have to be cleverer than you've been this time. This book is, I'll admit, a clever job, but nevertheless a forgery. It was not printed in nineteen forty-six. The radiocarbon analysis fixes its age at a mere five or six years. Good day, sir!"

Philon's mouth fell open. "But—but the MacDonalds have had it for . . . ." He caught himself, and stammered, "There must be some mistake because I . . . ."

Norton said firmly, "I bid you good day, sir!"

With a sense of the sky falling in on him, Philon found himself out on the street. No one could be trusted nowadays and he shouldn't have been surprised at the MacDonalds. Everyone had a little sideline, a gimmick, to put one over on whoever was gullible enough to swallow it.

Why should he assume a hillbilly family from way out in Oregon was any different? This was probably Bill MacDonald's little racket and it was just Philon's bad luck to stumble on it. MacDonald probably peddled his spurious first editions down on Front Street for a few hundred dollars to old bookstores unable to afford radiocarbon dating.

For awhile he stared out his office window, brooding. The fifty grand just wasn't to be had—legally or illegally. And when he recalled Feisel's little gem about the man falling out his office window Philon was definitely ill.

Then the cunning that comes to the rescue of all scheming gentry who depend on their wits emerged from perverse hiding. An ingenious idea to solve the nagging problem of the fifty thousand arrived full-blown. Grinning secretively to himself, he walked into the telecommunications room.

He got the Technical Reference Room at the Public Library and asked for the detailed plans of the big electronic National Vote Tabulating machine in Washington. At the other end a microfilm reel clicked into place, ready to obey his finger-tip control.

For two hours he read and read, making notes and studying the circuits of the complicated machine. Then, satisfied with his information, he returned the microfilm.

Leaving the office he descended to the streets and set out for the party headquarters. Now if only he could sell the neat little idea to the hierarchy . . . .

At the luxurious marbled headquarters he asked to be let into the general chairman's office. The receptionist announced him and Philon walked in to find Rakoff awaiting him behind his beautiful carved desk.

Rakoff's dead-white cheeks never stirred and his stiff blond hair stood up in a rigid crew cut. He rolled his cigar in his big mouth. "Hello, Miller. What's on your mind?"

Philon took a breath and it seemed to him now that this idea was a crazy one. "I came to tell you I'm unable to raise my fifty grand quota, Rakoff."

The man's brows moved slightly and his eyes narrowed significantly. With a rasp in his voice he said deliberately, "That's too bad, Mr. Miller—for you."

The rasping tongue put a faint quaver in Philon's voice but he went on. "However, I've brought you an idea that's worth more than fifty grand. It's worth millions."

Rakoff's eyes hardly blinked. "I'm listening—you're talking."

And Philon talked, talked rapidly and convincingly. When he finished Rakoff slapped his fat thigh in excitement.

That evening Philon dropped in on Bill MacDonald, who was sitting in his slippers smoking an old fashioned wood pipe.

"Come in, come in." MacDonald greeted him with a friendly smile. "I was just doing a little reading."

Philon held out the book. "I'm returning your masterpiece," he said with a sardonic smile.

MacDonald received it, glancing at the title. "Oh, Smyth's *Atomic Energy*. Good book—did you find it interesting?"

*

Philon began to laugh. "Well, I'll tell you, Bill, your little racket of having spurious first editions printed some place and then peddling them sure caught up with me."

The good-natured smile on MacDonald's face faded in a look of incredulity. He took the pipe from his mouth. "Spurious first editions?"

"Yeah, I sure took a beating today but I couldn't help laughing over it afterwards. Here I've been thinking of you folks as simon-pure numbers. But I got to hand it to you. You sure took me in with Smyth's *Atomic Energy* as being a genuine first edition." Philon went on to explain the radiocarbon dating of the book.

MacDonald finally broke in to protest, "But that book really *is* over a hundred years old." Then he looked up at his wife. "Of course, Carol, that's the explanation. The radiocarbon wouldn't decay a full hundred years any more than we . . . ." Suddenly, he seemed to catch himself, as his wife raised a hand in apparent agitation.

"But why did you want to sell my book to a dealer?" MacDonald continued.

Philon went on to explain the system of the poll quota. He told him a lot of other things too about the election of a President and the organized political machines that levied upon all registered voters what amounted to a checkoff of their incomes.

Carol MacDonald said, "You mean that not everyone can vote?"

Philon looked at her in surprise. "Well, of course not. Only people of means vote—and why shouldn't they? They take the most interest in the elections and all the candidates come from the higher-middle-class of income. Anyway why should the people squawk? They took less and less interest in the elections.

"When the proportion of voters turning out for elections got down to thirty percent those that did turn out passed laws disenfranchising those who hadn't voted for two Presidential elections. So if things aren't being run to suit those who lost their rights to vote they've got no one to thank but themselves."

Bill MacDonald looked at his wife and said in a voice filled with incredulity, "My lord, Carol, if the people back there only knew what their careless and negligent disinterest would one day do to their country!"

Philon looked from one to the other, saying, "You sound as if you were talking about the past."

MacDonald said hurriedly, "I—er—was referring to the history books."

That night Philon did not sleep well for the morrow would be a day he'd never forget. Even to his calloused mind the dangers involved in the exploit were considerable.

In the morning he went into John's room and stood looking down at the boy, who sleepily opened his eyes.

Philon said, "I'm going to be gone from my office all day. And if anyone calls or comes to see me here at the house tell him I'm sick. If necessary I'm ordering you to swear in court that I was here all day and night. Ursula's gone for the weekend to the seashore, so I'm depending on you. Do you understand?"

John frowned in confusion. "You say you're sick and staying home all day?"

Impatience edging his words Philon went over the explanation again.

"What d'you mean 'swear in court?' What are you planning to do, Phil?" John's eyes were wide open now and full of apprehension.

"Never mind what I'm doing. Just tell anybody inquiring that I'm sick at home."

"You mean *lie*, eh?"

Phil lifted his hand, then swung, leaving the imprint of his four fingers on the boy's left cheek. "Now do you understand?"

The boy blinked back a tear and nodded wordlessly.

*

In the late afternoon Philon landed at Washington and under an assumed name made his way to the government building housing the big Election Tabulator. At the technical maintenance offices Philon asked, "Is Al Brant around?"

"Nope. He doesn't come on duty until tomorrow."

At Brant's address Philon knocked on an apartment door. Footsteps approached inside and the door was opened by a medium-sized man with black tousled hair. He appeared less than happy to see Philon.

"Hello, Phil. What's on your mind?"

Philon stuck out his hand. "Al, glad to see you again. I know you're not pleased to see me but let's let bygones be bygones. Can we talk?"

Al Brant stepped back reluctantly. "Well, I guess so. I thought we'd said everything we had to say the last time."

Philon walked in and settled himself on the davenport. "Yeah, I know, Al, we had some pretty harsh words. But at least I got you out of the mess."

Brant said bitterly, "Yeah, got me out of a mess I got into helping you on one of your shady deals when I worked for you. Well, as I said before, what's on your mind?"

Philon patted his right chest saying, "Got a hundred thousand here for you, Al."

Brant's brows lifted in amazement. "A hundred thousand! What's the catch, Phil?"

Philon's voice dropped to a confidential tone. "You always were a clever man with electronics, Al, and I've got something here that's just your meat. I've been studying the design of the Election Tabulator, and I've discovered a wonderful opportunity for you and me.

"Now listen—it's possible to replace two transmitters on the main teletype trunk so that a winning percentage of the incoming votes will be totaled up for my party. Simple little job, isn't it? Worth a hundred thousand!"

For a long moment Al Brant sat and stared at Philon in cold silence. Finally, he said, "Do you know what the penalty is for jimmying the Tabulator to influence voting?"

"No."

"It's life imprisonment!" Brant got up slowly and started across the room to Philon. "I fell for your line once and got burned—and here you come again. You must think I'm a born sucker. This time I'm doing the talking. Give me the hundred grand or I'll kill you with my bare hands!"

Philon watched him coming as if he were witness to a nightmare. He was trapped. And in this moment of snowballing fear he ceased to think. The gun in his pocket went off without conscious effort. Brant stopped, then collapsed to the floor. Panic took over Philon's mind and he fled the apartment building as rapidly as was safe.

He was almost back in the city when he tuned in a news broadcast As he listened, he sat in stunned silence. Brant had roused himself enough before he died to talk to the man who found him in his apartment. Brant had named his killer as Philon Miller. Miller felt as if he had turned to ice.

Then his mind thawed out with a rush of reassuring words. After all, why should he be worrying? He had John's word in court as a perfect alibi. Yes, everything would be all right. Everything *had* to be all right.

In the late evening Philon arrived at his house with a consuming sense of great relief, as if the very act of entering his home would protect him from anything. There was a sense of safety in the mere familiarity of the environment.

On the mail table he found a note from Ursula saying she had gone for the weekend. Philon shrugged indifferently. He was glad to have her out of the way anyhow. But John—there was the best ten thousand dollars he had ever spent. A sound investment, about to pay its first real dividend.

"*John!*" His voice echoed in the house with a disturbing hollow sound. He wet his dry lips and shouted again, "*John—where* are *you?*"

Only his echoing voice answered him. In growing fright he pounded up the escalator and rushed into John's room. It was empty. On a desk he found a message in John's neat hand—

Phil and Ursula,

For a long time I have been very unhappy living with you. I'm grateful for the food and shelter and education you've provided. But you have never given me the love and warmth that

I seem to crave. The funny part of it is that I never understood my craving and what it meant until I saw how love and affection bound the MacDonald kids and their folks.

This afternoon Jimmie and Jean came over to say good-by because they said their father told them they didn't belong here—that he was taking his family back where they belonged, atomic bomb threat and all—whatever he meant by that. After they left I got to thinking how much I'd like to go with them. So I'm leaving. Somehow I'm going to talk them into taking me with them wherever they are going. So this will have to be good-by.

John.

Philon lifted his eyes from the note and his glance strayed to the window. Dreading to look he took two slow steps and peered down the street. The sight of the empty lot on the corner paralyzed him in his tracks.

John gone! The MacDonald house gone! Gone was his perfect alibi! In Washington a dying man's words had spelled out his own death sentence.

A step at the door roused him from his horror-stricken trance. He looked up to see a detective and a policeman regarding him with cold calculation.

"What's the matter, Miller?" asked the detective. "We've punched your announcer button half a dozen times. You deaf? You better come along to Headquarters to answer some questions about your movements today."

A WORLD APART

by Sam Merwin, Jr.

For obvious reasons, since time-travel has yet to be invented as far as we know, science fiction authors usually attribute it to the future. Yet there is always the possibility that somewhere, somehow, somewhen, it has already been put to use. A possibility which Sammy Merwin here considers in highly intriguing and human terms. Let's go back with Coulter . . . .

Most men of middle age would welcome a chance to live their lives a second time. But Coulter did not.

IT WASN'T MUCH of a bump. The shock absorbers of the liquid-smooth convertible neutralized all but a tiny percent of the jarring impact before it could reach the imported English flannel seat of Coulter's expensively-tailored pants. But it was sufficient to jolt him out of his reverie, trebly induced by a four-course luncheon with cocktails and liqueur, the nostalgia of returning to a hometown unvisited in twenty years and the fact that he was driving westward into an afternoon sun.

Coulter grunted mild resentment at being thus disturbed. Then, as he quickly, incredulously scanned the road ahead and the car whose wheel was gripped by his gloved hands, he narrowed his eyes and muttered to himself, "Wake up! For God's sake snap out of it!"

The road itself had changed. From a twin-laned ten-car highway, carefully graded and landscaped and clover-leafed, it had become a single-laned three-car thoroughfare, paved with tar instead of concrete and high-crowned along its center. He swung the wheel quickly to avoid running onto a dirt shoulder hardened with ice.

Its curves were no longer graded for high-speed cars but were scarcely tilted at all, when they didn't slant the wrong way. Its crossings were blind, level and unprotected by traffic lights. Neat unattractive clusters of mass-built houses interspersed with occasional clumps of woodland had been replaced with long stretches of pine woods, only occasionally relieved by houses and barns of obviously antique manufacture. Some of these looked disturbingly familiar.

And the roadside signs—all at once they were everywhere. Here a weathered but still-legible little Burma-Shave series, a wooden Horlick's contented cow, Socony, That Good Gulf Gasoline, the black cat-face bespeaking Catspaw Rubber Heels. Here were the coal-black Gold Dust twins, Kelly Springfield's Lotta Miles peering through a large rubber tire, a cocked-hatted boniface advertising New York's Prince George Hotel, the sleepy Fisk Tire boy in his pajamas and carrying a candle.

And then a huge opened book with a quill pen stuck in an inkwell alongside. On the right-hand page it said, *United States Tires Are Good Tires* and on the left, *You are*

3½ miles from Lincolnville. In 1778 General O'Hara, leading a British raiding party inland, was ambushed on this spot by Colonel Amos Coulter and his militia and forced to retreat with heavy loss.

Slowing down because the high-crowned road was slippery with sun-melted ice, Coulter noted that the steering wheel responded heavily. Then he saw suddenly that it was smaller than he'd remembered and made of black rubber instead of the almond-hued plastic of his new convertible. And his light costly fabric gloves had become black leather, lined with fur!

A gong rang in his memory. He had driven this road many times in years gone by, he had known all these signs as quasi-landmarks, he had worn such gloves one winter. There had been a little triangular tear in the heel of the left one, where he had snagged it on a nail sticking out of the garage wall. But that had been many years ago . . . .

He looked and found the tear and felt cold sweat bathe his body under his clothes. And he was suddenly, mightily, afraid . . . .

He hit another bump and this time the springs did not take up the shock. He felt briefly like a rodeo cowboy riding a bucking mustang. The car in which he rode had changed. It was no longer the sleek convertible of the mid-1950's. It was his old Pontiac sedan, the car he had driven for two years before leaving Lincolnville behind him twenty years ago!

Nor was he wearing the dark-blue vicuna topcoat he had reclaimed an hour before from the checkroom girl in the restaurant back in the city. His sleeves now were of well-worn camel's hair. He didn't dare pull the rear-view mirror around so he could see his face. He said again, fiercely, "Snap out of it! For God's sake wake up before you hit something!"

He didn't hit anything. Road, signs, car, clothing, all stayed the same. Fields abridged by wooded low hills fell away on either side of the road. The snow had been heavier away from the city and covered tillage, trees and stone walls alike with a tracked and sullen late-winter dark-white blanket.

He came to a hill and the obsolete engine knocked and panted. Once over the top of the hill, he thought with a sudden encouraging flash, he could prove that whatever was happening to him was illusion. At its foot on the other side had lain the Brigham Farm, a two-century-old house and barn converted into a restaurant by a pair of energetic spinsters. A restaurant where Coulter and his parents had habitually dined out on Thursday, the servants' night off.

He had heard a long while ago that the Brigham Farm had been struck by lightning and burned during August of 1939. If it were still there . . .

He breasted the hill and there it was, ancient timbers painted a neat dark red with white door and window-frames and shutters. He held his eyes carefully away from it after the one look, held them on the road, which was now paved with a hard-packed layer of snow.

He passed an ear-flapped and baa-baa-coated farmer who sat atop a pung drawn by a patient percheron whose nostrils emitted twin plumes of steam. A pung! How many times had he and the other boys of Lincolnville ridden the runners of such utility sleighs on hitch-hiked rides through the by-ways of the lovely surrounding countryside!

Coulter maneuvered in his seat to take a quick look at this relic from the past—and caught a glimpse of his face in the mirror above the windshield. He said just one word—"*Jesus!*" Nor was he blasphemous in saying it.

He thought of Jurgen, of Faust—for in some miraculous way he had reclaimed his youth or been reclaimed by it. The face that looked back at him was fresh-skinned, unlined, unweathered by life. He saw with surprise, from the detachment of almost two decades, that he had been better looking than he remembered.

He looked down, saw that his body, beneath the camel's hair coat, was thin. The fat and fatigue of too many years of rich eating and drinking, of sedentary work, of immense nervous pressures, had been swept away without diet, without tiresome exercise. He was young again—and he almost ran the Pontiac into a ditch at the side of the road . . . .

If it was a dream, he decided, it was a dream he was going to enjoy. He recalled what Shaw had said about youth being such a wonderful thing it was a pity to waste it on children. And he knew that he, at any rate, was no child, whatever the body that had so miraculously been restored to him.

The unhappy Pontiac cleared another hilltop and Lincolnville lay stretched out before Coulter, naked and exposed, stripped of its summer foliage. He had forgotten how dominated it was by the five church steeples—Unitarian, Episcopal, Trinitarian, Roman Catholic and Swedish Reform. There was no spire atop the concrete-and-stucco pillared building in which the Christian Scientists held their Sunday readings.

Half-consciously he dug for a cigar in his breast pocket, looked with mild surprise on the straight-stemmed pipe he found there. He had forgotten that he once smoked a pipe as completely as he had forgotten the churchly domination of his home town.

Even though Lincolnville remained fixed in his memory as it had looked twenty years ago—as it looked now awaiting his belated return—he was aware of many anachronisms while tooling the Pontiac slowly along Clinton Street. He had become used to the many outer changes of the past two decades, was unable completely to suppress surprise at not finding them present on his return.

For one thing there was the vast amount of overhead wiring. Coulter had forgotten how its lacework of insulation and poles took up space even in a comparatively small community. He had long since forgotten the English sparrows, erstwhile avian pest of America, that were to vanish so swiftly with the final abolition of the horse.

There were more horses than he recalled, parked here and there among the shoppers' automobiles. And the cars themselves looked like refugees from a well-aged television movie, all straight-up-and-down windshields and unbuilt-in fenders and wooden spoked or wire wheels. He suspected the Pontiac he was driving would look as odd to him once he got out and examined it.

A dark-overcoated policeman, lounging against the front of the Rexall store at the main intersection, lifted a mittened hand in casual salute. Coulter replied in kind, drove on through the Center, took the fork past the old library with the skeleton of its summer coat of ivy looking bare and chilly against the sunset breeze. The bit of sky he could see through the houses and leafless trees was grey and yellow and cold.

The house was there, just as he had left it. It was still a good-sized mansion in comfortable ugly space-wasting Reign-of-Terror Tuscan, standing ornate and towered and turreted behind a fence of granite posts connected by long iron pipes that sagged in the middle as the result of children walking them on their way to and from the public schools around the corner on Sheldon Street.

Coulter turned left and felt the crunch of ashes under his tires as he drove across the sidewalk, through the fence opening, into the driveway to the open-doored garage awaiting him. He reminded himself to be careful of the jutting nail that had torn his glove.

The concrete floor of the garage felt cold against the soles of his shoes. Coulter stamped his feet as he turned on the heater and moved toward the door. It stuck—he had forgotten about that—and he swore lustily as he exerted strength he had forgotten ever possessing to yank it clear of the snag and across the front of the building.

He didn't want the Pontiac to freeze. Not when he had a date with Eve Lawton . . . . A date with Eve Lawton . . . . He hadn't thought of Eve in years, except on those occasional sleepless nights when he amused himself with seeking to visualize the women he had known in a Biblical sense of the word.

Most of them were faceless units in a faceless and somewhat undignified parade. But not Eve. She wasn't pretty—not in the sense of the doll-faced creatures that adorned the movie magazines or even the healthy maidens with whom he occasionally rollicked since coming home from college.

Eve had a sensitivity of feature that was a sounding board for her emotions. Coulter paused against the garage door and thought about her. With the knowledge of twenty years he knew now that what Eve had, or had had twenty years ago, was the basis of beauty, the inner intangible which stamps a woman a woman above other women . . . .

What in hell has happened to me, is happening to me? Coulter felt the chill of the evening wind stab deep into his bones. Then he looked down at his vanished embonpoint and patted with his gloves the flat hardness that had replaced it. It was all right with him as long as he didn't wake up too soon—before his date with Eve anyway.

Coulter walked around the house and in through the front with its extra winter doorway. There was the big square sapphire-blue carpet with the worn spot at the foot of the stairs. There was the antique cherry card table which, to his definite knowledge, should be standing in the front hall of his own house in Scarborough, more than two hundred miles and twenty years away.

His mother appeared in the door of the library, edged with light from the cannel-coal fire in the grate behind her. She said, "Oh, there you are, Banny. I'm glad you're back in time for . . . Heaven's sake, Banny! What's all this for?"

Coulter felt himself grow hot with embarrassment. He and his mother had never been much given to outward show of affection. Yet, knowing she would be dead within the year, he had been unable to resist the urge to embrace her. He was going to have to watch his step. He said, fumbling a little, "I don't know, mother. I guess I just felt like it, that's all."

"Well—all right." She was mollified, patted the blue-white hair above delicately handsome features to make certain no strand had been disarranged. Then, "Did you remember to stop at MacAuliffe's and pick up my lighter?"

Feeling lost, Coulter felt in the pockets of his polo coat. To his relief he found a small package in one of them, pulled it out. It was wrapped with the city jeweler's tartan paper and he handed it to his mother. She said, "Thanks—I've missed it this last week."

He had forgotten his mother was a smoker. Coulter took off his coat and hat and hung them up, trying to remember details of a life he had long since allowed to blur into soft focus. She had taken up the habit about a year after his father died of a ruptured appendix while on a hunting trip down in the Maine woods.

He noticed the skis and ski-boots and ski-poles standing at attention in the back of the closet, wondered if he could still execute a decent Christie. Then, emerging, he said, "Just us for dinner tonight, mother?"

"Just us," she said, regarding him with a faint frown from over a fresh-lit cigarette.

"Good!" he said. "How about a drink?"

"Banny," said his mother with patient sternness, "you know as well as I that you're the family liquor-provider since your father died. I'm not going to deal with bootleggers. And there's nothing but a little vermouth in the pantry."

"Snooping again," he said, carefully unsmiling. Good God, it was still Prohibition! Memory stabbed at him, bringing what had so recently emerged from past into present clearly into focus, technicolored focus. "I've got a little surprise upstairs in my closet."

He found himself taking the stairs two at a time without effort. Shaw had definitely been right, he decided when he discovered the exertion had not winded him in the slightest. He went into the big room overlooking the front lawn, now covered with much-trodden snow, that he had fallen heir to after his father died.

Karen, the Swedish-born second maid, was opening the bed. He had completely forgotten Karen, had to battle against staring at her. She was a perfect incipient human brood-mare—lush not-yet-fat figure, broad pelvis, meaningless pretty-enough face. Now what the devil had been his relations with *her?*

Since he couldn't remember, he decided they must have been innocuous. He said, "Hi, Karen, broken up any new homes lately?"

She said, "Oh—*you,* Mr. Coulter!" She giggled and fled, stumbling over the threshold in her hurry.

Coulter looked after her, his eyebrows high. Well, he thought, here was something he had evidently missed entirely. Karen's crush was painfully apparent, viewed from a vantage of two decades of added experience. Or perhaps he had been smarter than he remembered.

The gallon of home-made gin was stuck behind the textbook-filled carton on the back floor of his closet, where somehow he had known it must be. It was between a third and half full of colorless liquid. He uncorked it, sniffed and shuddered. Prohibition was going to take a bit of getting used to after two decades of Repeal.

Half an hour later he sipped his rather dire martini and listened to his mother talk. Not to the words especially, for she was one of those nearly-extinct well-bred women, brought up in the horsehair amenities of the late Victorian era, who could talk charmingly and vivaciously and at considerable length without saying anything. It was pleasant merely to sit and sip and let the words flow over him.

She looked remarkably well, he thought, for a woman who was to die within a year of galloping cancer. She seemed to have recovered entirely from the emotional aftermath of his father's death. So much so that he found himself wondering how deeply she had loved the man with whom she had spent some thirty-eight years of her life.

She was slim and quick and sure in her movements and her figure, of which she was inordinately proud, resembled that of a girl rather than the body of a woman nibbling late middle-age. Slowly he realized she had stopped talking, had asked him a question and was awaiting his answer. He smiled apologetically and said, "Sorry, mother, I must have been wool-gathering."

"You're tired, lamb." No one had called him that in twenty years. "And no wonder, with all that *run*ning around for Mr. Simms on the *news*paper."

Mr. Simms—that would be Patrick "Paddy" Simms, his managing editor, the old-school city-room tyrant who had taught him his job so well that he had gone on to make a successful career of public relations and the organization of facts into words—at rates far more imposing than those paid a junior reporter during the Great Depression.

In his swell of memories Coulter almost lost his mother's question a second time, barely managed to catch its meaning. He sipped his drink and said, "I agree, mother, the burning of the books in Germany *is* a threat to freedom. But I don't think you'll have to worry about Adolph Hitler very long."

She misread his meaning, of course, frowned charmingly and said, "I *do* hope you're right, Banny. Nellie Maynard had a few of us for tea this afternoon and Margot Henson, she's tre*men*dously chic and her husband knows *all* those big men in the New Deal in Washington—not that he a*grees* with them, thank goodness—well, *she* says the big men in the State Department are really *wor*ried about Hitler. They think he may try to make Germany strong enough to start an*oth*er war."

"It could happen, of course," Coulter told her. He had forgotten his mother's trick of stressing one syllable of a word. Funny, Connie, his wife—if she was still his wife after whatever had happened—had the same trick. With an upper-class Manhattan dry soda-cracker drawl added.

He wondered if he were going to have to live through it all again—the NRA, the Roosevelt boomlet, the Recession, the string of Hitler triumphs in Europe, the war, Pearl Harbor and all that followed—Truman, the Cold War, Korea, McCarthy . . .

Seated across from her at the gleaming Sheraton dining table, which should by rights be in his own dining room in Scarborough overlooking the majestic Hudson, he wondered how he could put his foreknowledge to use. There was the market, of course. And he could recall the upset football win of Yale over Princeton in 1934, the Notre Dame last-minute triumph over Ohio State a year later, most of the World Series winners. On the Derby winners he was lost . . . .

When the meal was over and they were returning to the library with its snug insulating bookshelves and warm cannel-coal fire, his mother said, "Banny, it's been so nicehaving this talk with you. We haven't had *many* lately. I *wish* you'd stay home tonight with me. You really *do* look tired, you know."

"Sorry, mother," he replied. "I've got a date."

"With the *Law*ton girl, I suppose," she said without affection. Then, accepting a cigarette and holding it before lighting it, "I do wish you *wouldn't* see quite so much of her. I'll admit she's a perfectly nice girl, of course. But she *is* strange and people are beginning to talk. I hope you're not going to be *foolish* about her."

"Don't worry," Coulter replied. Since when, he wondered, had wanting a girl as he wanted Eve Lawton been foolish. He added, "What's wrong with Eve anyway?"

His mother lit a cigarette. "Lamb, it's not that there's anything *really* wrong with Eve. As a matter of fact I believe her family is quite distinguished—good old Lincolnville stock."

"I'm aware of that," he replied drily. "I believe her great, great, great grandfather was a brigadier while mine was only a colonel in the Revolution."

His mother dismissed the distant past with a gesture. "But the Lawtons haven't managed to keep up," she stated. "Think of your schooling, dear—you've had the *very* best. While Eve . . . " With a shrug.

"Went to grammar and high-school right here in Lincolnville," Coulter finished for her. "Mother, Eve has more brains and character than any of the debs I know." Then, collecting himself, "But don't worry, mother—I'm not going to let it upset my life."

"I'm *very* glad to hear it," Mrs. Coulter said simply. "Remember, Banny, you and your Eve are a world apart. Besides, we're going to take a trip *abroad* this summer. There'sso much I want us to see together. It would be a shame to . . . " She let it hang.

Coulter looked at his mother, remembering hard. He had been able to stymie that trip on the excuse that he'd almost certainly lose his job and that new jobs were too hard to get in a depression era. He thought that his surviving parent was, beneath her well-mannered surface, a shallow, domineering, snobbish empress. Granted his new vista of vision, he realized for the first time how she had dominated both his father and himself.

*

He thought, *I hate this woman. No, not hate, just loathe.*

He glanced at the watch on his wrist, a Waltham he had long since lost or broken or given away—he couldn't recall which. He said, "All the same, mother, a date's a date. I'm a little late now. Don't wait up for me."

"I shan't," she replied, looking after him with a frown of pale concern as he headed for the hall closet.

It took a few minutes to get the Pontiac warmed up but once out of the driveway Coulter knew the way to Eve Lawton's house as if he had been there last night, not two decades earlier. The small cold winter moon cast its frigid light over an intimate little group of apple tapioca clouds and made the snow-clad fields a dark grey beneath the black evergreens that backed the fields beside the road.

As he slowed to a stop in front of the old white-frame house with its graceful utilitarian lines of roof and gable, he found himself wondering whether this were the dream or the other—the twenty years that had found him an orphan. That had given him enough inherited money to strike out for himself in New York. That had seen him win success as a highly-paid publicist. That had seen him married to wealthy Connie Marlin and a way of life as far from that of Lincolnville as he himself now was from Scarborough and Connie.

*

Eve opened the door before he reached it. She was as willowy and alive as he remembered her, and a great deal more vital and beautiful. She put up her face to be kissed as soon as he was inside and his arms went around her soft angora sweater and he wondered a little at what he had so cavalierly dismissed and left behind him.

She said, "You're late, Banning. I thought you'd forgotten."

He kept one arm around her as they walked into the living room with its blazing fire. He said, "Sorry. Mother wanted to talk."

"Is she terribly worried about me?" Eve asked. Her face, in inquiry, was like a half-opened rose.

Coulter hesitated, then replied, "I think so, darling. She was afraid your stock had gone to seed. I had to remind her that your great, great, great grandfather outranked mine."

The odd, in her case beautiful, blankness of fear smoothed Eve's forehead. She said, her voice low, her eyes not meeting his, "Yesterday you'd never have noticed what she was thinking."

"Yesterday?" He forced her to look at him. "Yesterday I was another man—a whole twenty-four hours younger." He added the last hastily, so as not to rouse suspicion. Eve, he both knew at once and remembered, was highly sensitive, intuitively brilliant.

"I know," she said simply, and for the second time since the amazing transformation of the afternoon he felt the tight grip of terror. Watching her as she turned from him and began to stoke the fire, he wondered just what she did know.

The album rested on the table against the back of the sofa in front of the fireplace. It was a massive leather-and-parchment tome, with imitation medieval brass clasps and hinges. He opened it carelessly, seeking reassurance in idle action.

He flipped the pages idly, in bunches. There was Eve, a lacy little moppet, held in the arms of her drunkard farming father. A sort of local mad-Edison whose inventions never worked or, if they did, were promptly stolen from him by more profit-minded promoters. Her brother Jim, sturdy, cowlicked, squinting into the sun, stood at his father's knee. He wondered what had happened to Jim but didn't dare ask. Presumably he should know since Jim shared the house with his sister and an ancient housekeeper, doubtless long since asleep.

He flipped more pages, came to a snapshot of Eve in a bathing suit at Lake Tahoe. Bill Something-or-other, Lincolnville High School football hero of five years before, had an arm around Eve's slim, wool-covered waist. Two-piece suits and bikinis were still a long way in the future. He said, "What's become of Bill?"

She said, "Don't you remember? He was killed in that auto crash coming home from the city last year." There was an odd questing flatness in her voice.

Coulter remembered the incident now, of course. There had been a girl in the car, who had been disfigured for life. Plastic surgery, like bikinis, still lay well ahead. He and Eve had begun going together right after that accident . . . .

Something about Eve's tone, some urgency, disturbed him. He looked at her quickly. She was standing by the fireplace, watching him, watching him as if he were doing something important. The fright within him renewed itself. Quickly he turned back to the album, flipped further pages.

He was close to the end of the album. What he saw was a newspaper clipping, a clipping showing himself and Harvey MacIlwaine of Consolidated Motors shaking hands at a banquet table. The headline above the picture read, AUTHOR AND AUTO MAGNATE CELEBRATE BIOGRAPHY.

Above the headline was the date: *January 16, 1947.*

With hard-forced deliberation, because every nerve in his body was singing its song of fear like a banjo string, Coulter closed the album. The honeymoon, if that was the right term for it, was over. He knew now which was the dream, which the reality.

He said, "All of this is your doing, Eve." It was not a question.

She said quietly, "That's right, Banning, it's my doing." She looked at him with a cool detachment that added to his bewilderment—and to his fright.

He said, "Why, Eve? *Why* have you done this?"

She said, "Banning, do you know what a Jane Austen villain is?"

He shook his head. "Hardly my pitch, is it?"

"Hardly." There was a trace of sadness in her voice. Then, "A Jane Austen villain is an attractive, powerful, good-natured male who rides through life roughshod, interested only in himself, completely unaware of his effect on those unlucky souls whose existences become entangled in his."

"And I am a Jane Austen villain?" He was puzzled, disturbed that anyone—Eve or anyone—should think of him as a villain. Mentally he began to search for kindnesses, for unselfishnesses. He found generosities, yes, but these, he supposed with sudden dreadful clarity, had been little more than balm to his ego.

"You are perhaps a classic example, Banning," she told him. Her face, in shadow, was exquisitely beautiful. "When you left Lincolnville twenty years ago, without seeing me, without letting me see you, you destroyed me."

"Good God!" Coulter exclaimed. "But how? I know it was rude, but I did mean to come back. And when things moved differently it seemed better to keep a clean break clean." He hesitated, added, "I'm sorry."

"Sorry that you destroyed me?" Her tone was acid-etched.

"Dammit, do you want me down on my knees?" he countered. "How the devil did my leaving destroy *you?*" Anger, prodded by fear, was warming his blood.

"I was sensitive—aware of the collapse of my family, of my own shortcomings, of my lack of opportunity," she said, staring with immense grey eyes at the wall behind him. "I was just beginning to feel I could be somebody, could mean something to someone I—liked—when you dropped me and never looked back.

"I took a job at the bank. For twenty years I've sat in a cage, counting out money and putting little legends in bank-books. I've felt myself drying up day by day, week by week, year by year. When I've sought love I've merely defiled myself. You taught me passion, Banning, then destroyed my capacity to enjoy it with anyone but you. You destroyed me and never even knew it."

"You could have gone out into the world," he said with a trace of contempt. "Other girls have."

"Other girls are not me," Eve replied steadily. "Other girls don't give themselves to a man as completely as I gave myself to you."

"What can I do now?" Coulter asked, running a hand through his newly crew-cut hair. Recalling Eve at dinner, seeing her in the doorway, holding her briefly in his arms—he had almost decided that in this new life she was the partner he would carry with him.

Now, however, he was afraid of her. It was Eve who had, in some strange way, brought him back twenty years for purposes she had yet to divulge. One thing he knew, logically and intuitively—he could never endure life with anyone of whom he was frightened.

She was no longer looking at the wall—she was looking directly at him and with curious intensity. She said, "Do you have to ask?"

She was testing him, of course. Sensitive, brilliant, she might be—yet she was a fool not to have judged the effect of his fear of her. He walked around the table, took hold of her shoulders, turned her to face him, said, "What has this particular evening to do with bringing me—us—back?"

"Everything!" she said, her eyes suddenly ablaze. "*Everything*, Banning! Can't you understand?"

He released her, lit himself a cigarette, seeking the calmness he knew he must have to keep his thinking clear. He said, "Perhaps I understand why—a little. But how, Eve, *how*?"

She got up and walked across the wide hearth, kicked a fallen log back into place. Its glowing red scales burst into yellow flame. She turned and said, "Remember my father's last work? His efforts to discover the secrets of Time?"

"I remember he threw away what should have been your inheritance on a flock of crackpot ideas," he told her.

"This wasn't a crackpot idea," she said, eyeing him as if he were another log for the fire. "His basic premise that Time is all-existent was sound. Time is past, present and future."

"I might have argued that with you—before today," he replied.

"It was like everything else he tried." She made an odd little gesture of helplessness. "He went at it wrong-end-to, of course. Not until after he died and Jim got back from M.I.T. did we get to work on it. I was merely the helper who held the tools for Jim. And when we completed it *he* lacked the courage to try it out." There was the acid of contempt in her voice at her brother's poltroonery.

"I don't blame him," said Coulter. "After all . . . " He changed the subject, asked, "Where *is* Jim?"

"He was killed at Iwo Jima," she told him.

"What's to keep him from walking in here tonight—or to keep *you* from walking in on us?" he asked.

"Jim's in Cambridge, studying for exams," she replied. "As for my meeting myself, it's impossible. It's hard to explain but in coming back here I became reintegrated with the past me. Just as you are both a present and a past you. You must have noticed a certain duplication of memories, an overlapping? *I* have."

"I've noticed," he said. "But *why* only we two?"

"I'll show you," she said. "Come." She led him down rough wooden cellar stairs to a basement, unfastened with pale and dexterous fingers a padlocked wooden door behind the big old-fashioned furnace with its up-curving stovepipe arms, under which he had to stoop to avoid bumping his head.

The sharp sting of dead furnace-ashes was in his nostrils as he looked at the strange device. The strange cage-like device, the strange jerry-built apparatus was centered in a bizarre instrument panel that seemed to hang from nothing at all. He said, eyeing a bucket-seat for the operator, "It looks like Red Barber's cat-bird seat, Eve."

"And we're sitting in it, just you and I, darling," she replied. "Just you and I out of all the people who ever lived. Think of what we can do with our lives now, the mistakes we can avoid!"

"I'm thinking of them," said Coulter. Then, after a brief pause, "But how in hell did you manage to get *me* into the act?"

She stepped inside the odd cage, plucked things from a cup-like receptacle that hung from the instrument panel, showed them to him. There were a lock of hair, a scarf, what looked like fingernail parings. At his bewilderment her face lighted briefly with the shadow of a smile.

She said, "These are *you*, darling. Oh, you *still* don't understand! Lacking the *person* or *thing* to be sent back in Time, something that is part of the person or thing will work. It keys directly to individual patterns."

"And you've kept those things—those pieces of me—in there all this time?" He shuddered. "It looks like voodoo to me."

She put back the mementos, stepped out of the cage, put her arms fiercely around him. "Banning, darling, after you left me I *did* try voodoo. I wanted you to suffer as I suffered. But then, when the Time machine was finished and Jim was afraid to use it, I put the things in it—and waited. It's been a long wait."

"How did it reach me while I was still miles away?" he asked.

"Jim always said its working radius was about five miles," she said. "When you drove within range, it took over . . . . But let's go back upstairs, darling—we have our lives to plan."

To change the subject Coulter said, when they emerged from the basement, "You must have had a time picking the right moment for this little reunion—or was it hit or miss?"

"The machine is completely accurate," she said firmly. She stood there, the firelight making a halo of her dark hair. There was urgency in her, an expectation that the remark would mean something to him. It didn't.

Finally she burst out with, "Banning, are you really so forgetful? Don't you remember what tonight was . . . *don't* you?"

Coulter did some hasty mental kangaroo-hopping. He knew it was important to Eve and, because of the incredible thing she had accomplished, he felt a new wave of fright. From some recess of his memory he got a flash—Jim was in Cambridge, the housekeeper asleep in the rear ell of the old farmhouse, he and Eve were alone.

He drew her gently close to him and kissed her soft waiting lips as he had kissed them twenty years before, felt the quiver of her slim body against him as he had felt it twenty years before. He should have known—Eve had selected for their reunion the anniversary of the first time they had truly given themselves to each other.

He said, "Of course I remember, darling. If I'm a little slow on the uptake it's because I've had a lot of things happen to me all at once."

"The old Banning Coulter would never have understood," she said, giving him a quick hug before standing clear of him. Her eyes were shining like star sapphires. "Banning, you've grown up!"

"People do," he said drily. There was an odd sort of tension between them as they stood there, knowing what was to happen between them. Eve took a deep unsteady breath and the rise and fall of her angora sweater made his arms itch to pull her close.

She said, before he could translate desire into action, "Oh, I've been so *wrong* about so many things, darling. But I was so *right* to bring you back. Think of what we're going to be able to do, you and I together, now that we have this second chance. We'll know just what's going to happen. We'll be rich and free and lord it over ordinary mortals. I'll have furs and you'll have yachts and we'll . . . "

"I'm a lousy sailor," said Coulter. "No, I don't want a yacht."

"Nonsense, we'll have a yacht and cruise wherever we want to go. Think of how easy it will be for us to make money." Her eyes were shining more brightly still. "No more standing in a teller's cage for me. No more feeling the life-sap dry up inside me, handling thousands of dollars a day and none of it mine."

She stepped to him, gripped him tightly, her fingernails making themselves felt even through the heavy material of his jacket. She kissed him fiercely and said in a throaty whisper, "Darling, I'm going upstairs. Come up in ten minutes—and be young again with me."

She left him standing alone in front of the fire . . . .

Coulter filled his pipe and lit it. His mother had said *we* when she talked of her plans, as if her son were merely an object to be moved about at her whim. *Pick up my lighter at MacAuliffe's . . . going to take a trip abroad this summer . . . not going to be foolish about her . . . .* He could see the phrases as vividly as if they were written on a video teleprompter.

And then he saw another set of phrases—different in content, yet strangely alike in meaning. *Nonsense, we'll have a yacht . . . lord it over ordinary mortals . . . a long wait.* He thought of the voodoo and the fingernail parings, of the savage materialism of the woman who was even now preparing herself to receive him upstairs, who was planning to relive his life with him in *her* image.

He thought of his wife, foolish perhaps, but true to him and never domineering. He thought of the Scarborough house and the good friends he had there, hundreds of miles and twenty years away. He wondered if he could go back if he got beyond the five-mile radius of the strange machine in the basement.

He looked down with regret at his slim young body, so unexpectedly regained—and thought of the heavier, older less vibrant body that lay waiting for him five miles away. Then swiftly, silently, he tiptoed into the hall, donned coat and hat and gloves, slipped through the front door and bolted for the Pontiac.

He drove like a madman over the icy roads through the dark. Somehow he sensed he would have to get beyond the reach of the machine before Eve grew impatient and came downstairs and found him gone. She might, in her anger, send him back to some other Time—or perhaps the machine worked both ways. He didn't know. He could only flee in fear . . . and hope . . . .

At times, in the years that had passed since his abrupt breaking-off of his romance with Eve Lawton, he had wondered a little about why he had dropped her so quickly, just when his mother's death seemed to open the path for their marriage.

Now he knew that youthful instinct had served him better than he knew. Somehow, beneath the charm and wit and beauty of the girl, he had sensed the domineering woman. Perhaps a lifetime with his mother had made him extra-aware of Eve's desire to dominate without its reaching his conscious mind.

But to have exchanged the velvet glove of his mother for the velvet glove of Eve would have meant a lifetime of bondage. He would never have been his own man, never . . . .

He could feel cold sweat bathe his body once more as he sped past the Brigham Farm. According to his wristwatch just eight and a quarter minutes had elapsed since Eve had left him and gone upstairs. He felt a sudden urge to turn around and go back to her—he knew she would forgive his attempt to run away. After all, he couldn't even guess at what would happen when he reached the outer limit of the machine's influence. Would he be in 1934 or 1954—or irretrievably lost in some timeless nowhere at all?

He thought again of what Eve had said about yachts and world traveling and wondered how she could hope to do so if the radius of influence was only five miles.

Eve might be passionate, headstrong and neurotic, but she was not a fool. If she had planned travel on a world of two decades past she must have found a way of making his and her stay in that past permanent, without trammels.

If she had altered the machine . . . But she wouldn't have until he was caught in her trap when, inevitably, he returned to look at the scenes of his childhood. He tried to recall what she had done, what gestures she had made, when she demonstrated the machine. As nearly as he could remember, all Eve had done was to pluck out his nail parings, the bit of hair and scarf, then return them to their receptacle.

Voodoo . . . . She was close to mad. Or perhaps he was mad himself. He wiped his streaming forehead with a sleeve, barely avoided overturning as he rounded a curve flanked by signboards . . . .

He felt a bump . . . .

And suddenly he was in the big convertible again, guiding it over to one of the parking lanes at the side of the magnificent two-laned highway. He looked down at his sleek dark vicuna coat, visualized the rise of plump stomach beneath it, reached in his breast pocket for a panatella.

*

He noticed the tremble in his hand. *No, no cigars now*, he thought. *Not with the old pump acting up like this. Too much excitement.* He reached for the little box of nitroglycerin tablets in his watch-pocket, got it out, took one, waited.

Maybe his life wasn't perfect, maybe there wasn't much of it left to live—but what there was was his, not his mother's, not Eve's. The unsteadiness in his chest was fading. He turned on the ignition, drove slowly back through the housing developments, the neon signs and clover-leaf turns and graded crossings toward the city . . . .

When he got back to the hotel he would call Connie in Scarborough. It would be heavenly, the sound of her high, silly little voice . . . .

BEAR TRAP

by Alan E. Nourse

Dr. Alan E. Nourse, who when last heard of was vacationing in Alaska—and probably gathering material for SF or Mystery stories set against this background—is the author of many mystery and science fiction stories including MARTYR, the lead novel in our January 1957 issue.

The man's meteoric rise as a peacemaker in a nation tired by the long years of war made the truth even more shocking.

THE HUGE troop transport plane eased down through the rainy drizzle enshrouding New York International Airport at about five o'clock in the evening. Tom Shandor glanced sourly through the port at the wet landing strip, saw the dim landing lights reflected in the steaming puddles. On an adjacent field he could see the rows and rows of jet fighters, wings up in the foggy rain, poised like ridiculous birds in the darkness. With a sigh he ripped the sheet of paper from the small, battered portable typewriter on his lap, and zipped the machine up in its slicker case.

Across the troop hold the soldiers were beginning to stir, yawning, shifting their packs, collecting their gear. Occasionally they stared at Shandor as if he were totally alien to their midst, and he shivered a little as he collected the sheets of paper scattered on the deck around him, checked the date, 27 September, 1982, and rolled them up to fit in the slim round mailing container. Ten minutes later he was shouldering his way through the crowd of khaki-clad men, scowling up at the sky, his nondescript fedora jammed down over his eyes to keep out the rain, slicker collar pulled up about his ears. At the gangway he stopped before a tired-looking lieutenant and flashed the small fluorescent card in his palm. "Public Information Board."

The officer nodded wearily and gave his coat and typewriter a cursory check, then motioned him on. He strode across the wet field, scowling at the fog, toward the dimmed-out waiting rooms.

He found a mailing chute, and popped the mailing tube down the slot as if he were glad to be rid of it. Into the speaker he said: "Special Delivery. PIB business. It goes to press tonight."

The female voice from the speaker said something, and the red "clear" signal blinked. Shandor slipped off his hat and shook it, then stopped at a coffee machine and extracted a cup of steaming stuff from the bottom after trying the coin three times. Finally he walked across the room to an empty video booth, and sank down into the chair with an exhausted sigh. Flipping a switch, he waited several minutes for an operator to appear. He gave her a number, and then said, "Let's scramble it, please."

"Official?"

He showed her the card, and settled back, his whole body tired. He was a tall man, rather slender, with flat, bland features punctuated only by blond caret-shaped eyebrows. His grey eyes were heavy-lidded now, his mouth an expressionless line as he waited, sunk back into his coat with a long-cultivated air of lifeless boredom. He watched the screen without interest as it bleeped a time or two, then shifted into the familiar scrambled-image pattern. After a moment he muttered the Public Information Board audio-code words, and saw the screen even out into the clear image of a large, heavyset man at a desk.

"Hart," said Shandor. "Story's on its way. I just dropped it from the Airport a minute ago, with a rush tag on it. You should have it for the morning editions."

The big man in the screen blinked, and his heavy face lit up. "The story on the Rocket Project?"

Shandor nodded. "The whole scoop. I'm going home now." He started his hand for the cutoff switch.

"Wait a minute—" Hart picked up a pencil and fiddled with it for a moment. He glanced over his shoulder, and his voice dropped a little. "Is the line scrambled?"

Shandor nodded.

"What's the scoop, boy? How's the Rocket Project coming?"

Shandor grinned wryly. "Read the report, daddy. Everything's just ducky, of course—it's all ready for press. You've got the story, why should I repeat it?"

Hart scowled impatiently. "No, no— I mean the *scoop*. The real stuff. How's the Project going?"

"Not so hot." Shandor's face was weary. "Material cutoff is holding them up something awful. Among other things. The sabotage has really fouled up the west coast trains, and shipments haven't been coming through on schedule. You know—they ask for one thing, and get the wrong weight, or their supplier is out of material, or something goes wrong. And there's personnel trouble, too—too much direction and too little work. It's beginning to look as if they'll never get going. And now it looks like there's going to be another administration shakeup, and you know what that means—"

Hart nodded thoughtfully. "They'd better get hopping," he muttered. "The conference in Berlin is on the skids—it could be hours now." He looked up. "But you got the story rigged all right?"

Shandor's face flattened in distaste. "Sure, sure. You know me, Hart. Anything to keep the people happy. Everything's running as smooth as satin, work going fine, expect a test run in a month, and we should be on the moon in half a year, more or less, maybe, we hope—the usual swill. I'll be in to work out the war stories in the morning. Right now I'm for bed."

He snapped off the video before Hart could interrupt, and started for the door. The rain hit him, as he stepped out, with a wave of cold wet depression, but a cab slid up to the curb before him and he stepped in. Sinking back he tried to relax, to get his stomach to stop complaining, but he couldn't fight the feeling of almost physical illness sweeping over him. He closed his eyes and sank back, trying to drive the ever-plaguing thoughts from his mind, trying to focus on something pleasant, almost hoping that his long-starved conscience might give a final gasp or two and die altogether. But deep in his mind he knew that his screaming conscience was almost the only thing that held him together.

Lies, he thought to himself bitterly. White lies, black lies, whoppers—you could take your choice. There should be a flaming neon sign flashing across the sky, telling all people: "Public Information Board, Fabrication Corporation, fabricating of all lies neatly and expeditiously done." He squirmed, feeling the rebellion grow in his mind. Propaganda, they called it. A nice word, such a very handy word, covering a multitude of seething pots. PIB was the grand clearing house, the last censor of censors, and he, Tom Shandor, was the Chief Fabricator and Purveyor of Lies.

He shook his head, trying to get a breath of clean air in the damp cab. Sometimes he wondered where it was leading, where it would finally end up, what would happen if the people ever really learned, or ever listened to the clever ones who tried to sneak the truth into print somewhere. But people couldn't be told the truth, they had to be coddled, urged, pushed along. They had to be kept somehow happy, somehow hopeful, they had to be kept whipped up to fever pitch, because the long, long years of war and near war had exhausted them, wearied them beyond natural resiliency. No, they had to be spiked, urged and goaded—what would happen if they learned?

He sighed. No one, it seemed, could do it as well as he. No one could take a story of bitter diplomatic fighting in Berlin and simmer it down to a public-palatable "peaceful and progressive meeting;" no one could quite so skillfully reduce the bloody fighting in India to a mild "enemy losses topping American losses twenty to one, and our boys are fighting staunchly, bravely,"— No one could write out the lies quite so neatly, so smoothly as Tom Shandor—

The cab swung in to his house, and he stepped out, tipped the driver, and walked up the walk, eager for the warm dry room. Coffee helped sometimes when he felt this way, but other things helped even more. He didn't even take his coat off before mixing and downing a stiff rye-and-ginger, and he was almost forgetting his unhappy conscience by the time the video began blinking.

He flipped the receiver switch and sat down groggily, blinked at John Hart's heavy face as it materialized on the screen. Hart's eyes were wide, his voice tight and nervous as he leaned forward. "You'd better get into the office pronto," he said, his eyes bright. "You've *really* got a story to work on now—"

Shandor blinked. "The War—"

Hart took a deep breath. "Worse," he said. "David Ingersoll is dead."

*

Tom Shandor shouldered his way through the crowd of men in the anteroom, and went into the inner office. Closing the door behind him coolly, he faced the man at the desk, and threw a thumb over his shoulder. "Who're the goons?" he growled. "You haven't released a story yet—?"

John Hart sighed, his pinkish face drawn. "The press. I don't know how they got the word—there hasn't been a word released, but—" He shrugged and motioned Shandor to a seat. "You know how it goes."

Shandor sat down, his face blank, eyeing the Information chief woodenly. The room was silent for a moment, a tense, anticipatory silence. Then Hart said: "The Rocket story was great, Tommy. A real writing job. You've got the touch, when it comes to a ticklish news release—"

Shandor allowed an expression of distaste to cross his face. He looked at the chubby man across the desk and felt the distaste deepen and crystallize. John Hart's face was round, with little lines going up from the eyes, an almost grotesque, burlesque-comic face that belied the icy practical nature of the man behind it. A thoroughly distasteful face, Shandor thought. Finally he said, "The story, John. On Ingersoll. Let's have it, straight out."

Hart shrugged his stocky shoulders, spreading his hands. "Ingersoll's dead," he said. "That's all there is to it. He's stone-cold dead."

"But he can't be dead!" roared Shandor, his face flushed. "We just can't *afford* to have him dead—"

Hart looked up wearily. "Look, I didn't kill him. He went home from the White House this evening, apparently sound enough, after a long, stiff, nasty conference with the President. Ingersoll wanted to go to Berlin and call a showdown at the International conference there, and he had a policy brawl with the President, and the President wouldn't let him go, sent an undersecretary instead, and threatened to kick Ingersoll out of the cabinet unless he quieted down. Ingersoll got home at 4:30, collapsed at 5:00, and he was dead before the doctor arrived. Cerebral hemorrhage, pretty straightforward. Ingersoll's been killing himself for years—he knew it, and everyone else in Washington knew it. It was bound to happen sooner or later."

"He was trying to prevent a war," said Shandor dully, "and he was all by himself. Nobody else wanted to stop it, nobody that mattered, at any rate. Only the people didn't want war, and who ever listens to them? Ingersoll got the people behind him, so they gave him a couple of Nobel Peace Prizes, and made him Secretary of State, and then cut his throat every time he tried to do anything. No wonder he's dead—"

Hart shrugged again, eloquently indifferent. "So he was a nice guy, he wanted to prevent a war. As far as I'm concerned, he was a pain in the neck, the way he was forever jumping down Information's throat, but he's dead now, he isn't around any more—" His eyes narrowed sharply. "The important thing, Tommy, is that the people won't like it that he's dead. They trusted him. He's been the people's Golden Boy, their last-ditch hope for peace. If they think their last chance is gone with his death, they're going to be mad. They won't like it, and there'll be hell to pay—"

Shandor lit a smoke with trembling fingers, his eyes smouldering. "So the people have to be eased out of the picture," he said flatly. "They've got to get the story so they won't be so angry—"

Hart nodded, grinning. "They've got to have a real story, Tommy. Big, blown up, what a great guy he was, defender of the peace, greatest, most influential man America has turned out since the half-century—you know what they lap up, the usual garbage, only on a slightly higher plane. They've got to think that he's really saved them, that he's turned over the reins to other hands just as trustworthy as his—you can give the president a big hand there—they've got to think his work is the basis of our present foreign policy—can't you see the implications? It's got to be spread on with a trowel, laid on skillfully—"

Shandor's face flushed deep red, and he ground the stub of his smoke out viciously. "I'm sick of this stuff, Hart," he exploded. "I'm sick of you, and I'm sick of this whole rotten setup, this business of writing reams and reams of lies just to keep things under control. Ingersoll was a great man, a *really* great man, and he was *wasted*, thrown away. He worked to make peace, and he got laughed at. He hasn't done a thing—because he couldn't. Everything he has tried has been useless, wasted. *That's* the truth—why not tell that to the people?"

Hart stared. "Get hold of yourself," he snapped. "You know your job. There's a story to write. The life of David Ingersoll. It has to go down smooth." His dark eyes shifted to his hands, and back sharply to Shandor. "A propagandist has to write it, Tommy—an ace propagandist. You're the only one I know that could do the job."

"Not me," said Shandor flatly, standing up. "Count me out. I'm through with this, as of now. Get yourself some other whipping boy. Ingersoll was one man the people could trust. And he was one man I could never face. I'm not good enough for him to spit on, and I'm not going to sell him down the river now that he's dead."

With a little sigh John Hart reached into the desk. "That's very odd," he said softly. "Because Ingersoll left a message for you—"

Shandor snapped about, eyes wide. "Message—?"

The chubby man handed him a small envelope. "Apparently he wrote that a long time ago. Told his daughter to send it to Public Information Board immediately in event of his death. Read it."

Shandor unfolded the thin paper, and blinked unbelieving:

In event of my death during the next few months, a certain amount of biographical writing will be inevitable. It is my express wish that this writing, in whatever form it may take, be done by Mr. Thomas L. Shandor, staff writer of the Federal Public Information Board.

I believe that man alone is qualified to handle this assignment.

(Signed) David P. Ingersoll
Secretary of State,
United States of America.

4 June, 1981

Shandor read the message a second time, then folded it carefully and placed it in his pocket, his forehead creased. "I suppose you want the story to be big," he said dully.

Hart's eyes gleamed a moment of triumph. "As big as you can make it," he said eagerly. "Don't spare time or effort, Tommy. You'll be relieved of all assignments until you have it done—if you'll take it."

"Oh, yes," said Shandor softly. "I'll take it."

*

He landed the small PIB 'copter on an airstrip in the outskirts of Georgetown, haggled with Security officials for a few moments, and grabbed an old weatherbeaten cab, giving the address of the Ingersoll estate as he settled back in the cushions. A small radio was set inside the door; he snapped it on, fiddled with the dial until he found a PIB news report. And as he listened he felt his heart sink lower and lower, and the old familiar feeling of dirtiness swept over him, the feeling of being a part in an enormous, overpowering scheme of corruption and degradation. The Berlin conference was reaching a common meeting ground, the report said, with Russian, Chinese, and American officials making the first real progress in the week of talks. Hope rising for an early armistice on the Indian front. Suddenly he hunched forward, blinking in surprise as the announcer continued the broadcast: "The Secretary of State, David Ingersoll, was stricken with a slight head cold this evening on the eve of his departure for the Berlin Conference, and was advised to postpone the trip temporarily. John

Harris Darby, first undersecretary, was dispatched in his place. Mr. Ingersoll expressed confidence that Mr. Darby would be able to handle the talks as well as himself, in view of the optimistic trend in Berlin last night—"

Shandor snapped the radio off viciously, a roar of disgust rising in his throat, cut off just in time. Lies, lies, lies. Some people *knew* they were lies—what could they really think? People like David Ingersoll's wife—

Carefully he reined in his thoughts, channelled them. He had called the Ingersoll home the night before, announcing his arrival this morning—

The taxi ground up a gravelled driveway, stopped before an Army jeep at the iron-grilled gateway. A Security Officer flipped a cigarette onto the ground, shaking his head. "Can't go in, Secretary's orders."

Shandor stepped from the cab, briefcase under his arm. He showed his card, scowled when the officer continued shaking his head. "Orders say *nobody*—"

"Look, blockhead," Shandor grated. "If you want to hang by your toes, I can put through a special check-line to Washington to confirm my appointment here. I'll also recommend you for the salt mines."

The officer growled, "Wise guy," and shuffled into the guard shack. Minutes later he appeared again, jerked his thumb toward the estate. "Take off," he said. "See that you check here at the gate before you leave."

He was admitted to the huge house by a stone-faced butler, who led him through a maze of corridors into a huge dining room. Morning sunlight gleamed through a glassed-in wall, and Shandor stopped at the door, almost speechless.

He knew he'd seen the girl somewhere. At one of the Washington parties, or in the newspapers. Her face was unmistakable; it was the sort of face that a man never forgets once he glimpses it—thin, puckish, with wide-set grey eyes that seemed both somber and secretly amused, a full, sensitive mouth, and blonde hair, exceedingly fine, cropped close about her ears. She was eating her breakfast, a rolled up newspaper by her plate, and as she looked up, her eyes were not warm. She just stared at Shandor angrily for a moment, then set down her coffee cup and threw the paper to the floor with a slam. "You're Shandor, I suppose."

Shandor looked at the paper, then back at her. "Yes, I'm Tom Shandor. But you're not Mrs. Ingersoll—"

"A profound observation. Mother isn't interested in seeing anyone this morning, particularly you." She motioned to a chair. "You can talk to me if you want to."

Shandor sank down in the proffered seat, struggling to readjust his thinking. "Well," he said finally. "I—I wasn't expecting you—" he broke into a grin—"but I should think you could help. You know what I'm trying to do—I mean, about your father. I want to write a story, and the logical place to start would be with his family—"

The girl blinked wide eyes innocently. "Why don't you start with the newspaper files?" she asked, her voice silky. "You'd find all sorts of information about daddy there. Pages and pages—"

"No, no—I don't want that kind of information. You're his daughter, Miss Ingersoll, you could tell me about him as a man. Something about his personal life, what sort of man he was—"

She shrugged indifferently, buttered a piece of toast, as Shandor felt most acutely the pangs of his own missed breakfast. "He got up at seven every morning," she said. "He brushed his teeth and ate breakfast. At nine o'clock the State Department called for him—"

Shandor shook his head unhappily. "No, no, that's not what I mean."

"Then perhaps you'd tell me precisely what you *do* mean?" Her voice was clipped and hard.

Shandor sighed in exasperation. "The personal angle. His likes and dislikes, how he came to formulate his views, his relationship with his wife, with you—"

"He was a kind and loving father," she said, her voice mocking. "He loved to read, he loved music—oh, yes, put that down, he was a *great* lover of music. His wife was the apple of his eye, and he tried, for all the duties of his position, to provide us with a happy home life—"

"Miss Ingersoll."

She stopped in mid-sentence, her grey eyes veiled, and shook her head slightly. "That's not what you want, either?"

Shandor stood up and walked to a window, looking out over the wide veranda. Carefully he snubbed his cigarette in an ashtray, then turned sharply to the girl. "Look. If you want to play games, I can play games too. Either you're going to help me, or you're not—it's up to you. But you forget one thing. I'm a propagandist. I might say I'm a very expert propagandist. I can tell a true story from a false one. You won't get anywhere lying to me, or evading me, and if you choose to try, we can call it off right now. You know exactly the type of information I need from you. Your father was a great man, and he rates a fair shake in the write-ups. I'm asking you to help me."

Her lips formed a sneer. "And *you're* going to give him a fair shake, I'm supposed to believe." She pointed to the newspaper. "With garbage like that? Head cold!" Her face flushed, and she turned her back angrily. "I know your writing, Mr. Shandor. I've been exposed to it for years. You've never written an honest, true story in your life, but you always want the truth to start with, don't you? I'm to give you the truth, and let you do what you want with it, is that the idea? No dice, Mr. Shandor. And you even have the gall to brag about it!"

Shandor flushed angrily. "You're not being fair. This story is going to press straight and true, every word of it. This is one story that won't be altered."

And then she was laughing, choking, holding her sides, as the tears streamed down her cheeks. Shandor watched her, reddening, anger growing up to choke him. "I'm not joking," he snapped. "I'm breaking with the routine, do you understand? I'm through with the lies now, I'm writing this one straight."

She wiped her eyes and looked at him, bitter lines under her smile. "You couldn't do it," she said, still laughing. "You're a fool to think so. You could write it, and you'd be out of a job so fast you wouldn't know what hit you. But you'd never get it into print. And you know it. You'd never even get the story to the inside offices."

Shandor stared at her. "That's what you think," he said slowly. "This story will get to the press if it kills me."

The girl looked up at him, eyes wide, incredulous. "You *mean* that, don't you?"

"I never meant anything more in my life."

She looked at him, wonderingly, motioned him to the table, a faraway look in her eyes. "Have some coffee," she said, and then turned to him, her eyes wide with excitement. The sneer was gone from her face, the coldness and hostility, and her eyes were pleading. "If there were some way to do it, if you really meant what you said, if you'd really *do* it—give people a true story—"

Shandor's voice was low. "I told you, I'm sick of this mill. There's something wrong with this country, something wrong with the world. There's a rottenness in it, and your father was fighting to cut out the rottenness. This story is going to be straight, and it's going to be printed if I get shot for treason. And it could split things wide open at the seams."

She sat down at the table. Her lower lip trembled, and her voice was tense with excitement. "Let's get out of here," she said. "Let's go someplace where we can talk—"

*

They found a quiet place off the business section in Washington, one of the newer places with the small closed booths, catering to people weary of eavesdropping and overheard conversations. Shandor ordered beers, then lit a smoke and leaned back facing Ann Ingersoll. It occurred to him that she was exceptionally lovely, but he was almost frightened by the look on her face, the suppressed excitement, the cold, bitter lines about her mouth. Incongruously, the thought crossed his mind that he'd hate to have this woman against him. She looked as though she would be capable of more than he'd care to tangle with. For all her lovely face there was an edge of thin ice to her smile, a razor-sharp, dangerous quality that made him curiously uncomfortable. But now she was nervous, withdrawing a cigarette from his pack with trembling fingers, fumbling with his lighter until he struck a match for her. "Now," he said. "Why the secrecy?"

She glanced at the closed door to the booth. "Mother would kill me if she knew I was helping you. She hates you, and she hates the Public Information Board. I think dad hated you, too."

Shandor took the folded letter from his pocket. "Then what do you think of this?" he asked softly. "Doesn't this strike you a little odd?"

She read Ingersoll's letter carefully, then looked up at Tom, her eyes wide with surprise. "So this is what that note was. This doesn't wash, Tom."

"You're telling me it doesn't wash. Notice the wording. 'I believe that man alone is qualified to handle this assignment.' Why me? And of all things, why me *alone*? He knew my job, and he fought me and the PIB every step of his career. Why a note like this?"

She looked up at him. "Do you have any idea?"

"Sure, I've got an idea. A crazy one, but an idea. I don't think he wanted me because of the writing. I think he wanted me because I'm a propagandist."

She scowled. "It still doesn't wash. There are lots of propagandists—and why would he want a propagandist?"

Shandor's eyes narrowed. "Let's let it ride for a moment. How about his files?"

"In his office in the State Department."

"He didn't keep anything personal at home?"

Her eyes grew wide. "Oh, no, he wouldn't have dared. Not the sort of work he was doing. With his files under lock and key in the State Department nothing could be touched without his knowledge, but at home anybody might have walked in."

"Of course. How about enemies? Did he have any particular enemies?"

She laughed humorlessly. "Name anybody in the current administration. I think he had more enemies than anybody else in the cabinet." Her mouth turned down bitterly. "He was a stumbling block. He got in people's way, and they hated him for it. They killed him for it."

Shandor's eyes widened. "You mean you think he was murdered?"

"Oh, no, nothing so crude. They didn't have to be crude. They just let him butt his head against a stone wall. Everything he tried was blocked, or else it didn't lead anywhere. Like this Berlin Conference. It's a powder keg. Dad gambled everything on going there, forcing the delegates to face facts, to really put their cards on the table. Ever since the United Nations fell apart in '72 dad had been trying to get America and

Russia to sit at the same table. But the President cut him out at the last minute. It was planned that way, to let him get up to the very brink of it, and then slap him down hard. They did it all along. This was just the last he could take."

Shandor was silent for a moment. "Any particular thorns in his side?"

Ann shrugged. "Munitions people, mostly. Dartmouth Bearing had a pressure lobby that was trying to throw him out of the cabinet. The President sided with them, but he didn't dare do it for fear the people would squawk. He was planning to blame the failure of the Berlin Conference on dad and get him ousted that way."

Shandor stared. "But if that conference fails, *we're in full-scale war!*"

"Of course. That's the whole point." She scowled at her glass, blinking back tears. "Dad could have stopped it, but they wouldn't let him. *It killed him*, Tom!"

Shandor watched the smoke curling up from his cigarette. "Look," he said. "I've got an idea, and it's going to take some fast work. That conference could blow up any minute, and then I think we're going to be in real trouble. I want you to go to your father's office and get the contents of his personal file. Not the business files, his personal files. Put them in a briefcase and subway-express them to your home. If you have any trouble, have them check with PIB—we have full authority, and I'm it right now. I'll call them and give them the word. Then meet me here again, with the files, at 7:30 this evening."

She looked up, her eyes wide. "What—what are you going to do?"

Shandor snubbed out his smoke, his eyes bright. "I've got an idea that we may be onto something—just something I want to check. But I think if we work it right, we can lay these boys that fought your father out by the toes—"

*

The Library of Congress had been moved when the threat of bombing in Washington had become acute. Shandor took a cab to the Georgetown airstrip, checked the fuel in the 'copter. Ten minutes later he started the motor, and headed upwind into the haze over the hills. In less than half an hour he settled to the Library landing field in western Maryland, and strode across to the rear entrance.

The electronic cross-index had been the last improvement in the Library since the war with China had started in 1958. Shandor found a reading booth in one of the alcoves on the second floor, and plugged in the index. The cold, metallic voice of the automatic chirped twice and said, "Your reference, pleeyuz."

Shandor thought a moment. "Give me your newspaper files on David Ingersoll, Secretary of State."

"Through which dates, pleeyuz."

"Start with the earliest reference, and carry through to current." The speaker burped, and he sat back, waiting. A small grate in the panel before him popped open, and a small spool plopped out onto a spindle. Another followed, and another. He turned to the reader, and reeled the first spool into the intake slot. The light snapped on, and he began reading.

Spools continued to plop down. He read for several hours, taking a dozen pages of notes. The references commenced in June, 1961, with a small notice that David Ingersoll, Republican from New Jersey, had been nominated to run for state senator. Before that date, nothing. Shandor scowled, searching for some item predating that one. He found nothing.

Scratching his head, he continued reading, outlining chronologically. Ingersoll's election to state senate, then to United States Senate. His rise to national prominence as economist for the post-war Administrator of President Drayton in 1966. His meteoric rise as a peacemaker in a nation tired from endless dreary years of fighting in China and India. His tremendous popularity as he tried to stall the re-intensifying cold-war with Russia. The first Nobel Peace Prize, in 1969, for the ill-fated Ingersoll Plan for World Sovereignty. Pages and pages and pages of newsprint. Shandor growled angrily, surveying the pile of notes with a sinking feeling of incredulity. The articles, the writing, the tone—it was all too familiar. Carefully he checked the newspaper sources. Some of the dispatches were Associated Press; many came direct desk from Public Information Board in New York; two other networks sponsored some of the wordage. But the tone was all the same.

Finally, disgusted, Tom stuffed the notes into his briefcase, and flipped down the librarian lever. "Sources, please."

A light blinked, and in a moment a buzzer sounded at his elbow. A female voice, quite human, spoke as he lifted the receiver. "Can I help you on sources?"

"Yes. I've been reading the newspaper files on David Ingersoll. I'd like the by-lines on this copy."

There was a moment of silence. "Which dates, please?"

Shandor read off his list, giving dates. The silence continued for several minutes as he waited impatiently. He was about to hang up and leave when the voice spoke up again. "I'm sorry, sir. Most of that material has no by-line. Except for one or two items it's all staff-written."

"By whom?"

"I'm sorry, no source is available. Perhaps the PIB offices could help you—"

"All right, ring them for me, please." He waited another five minutes, saw the PIB cross-index clerk appear on the video screen. "Hello, Mr. Shandor. Can I help you?"

"I'm trying to trace down the names of the Associated Press and PIB writers who covered stories on David Ingersoll over a period from June 1961 to the present date—"

The girl disappeared for several moments. When she reappeared, her face was puzzled. "Why, Mr. Shandor, you've been doing the work on Ingersoll from August, 1978 to Sept. 1982. We haven't closed the files on this last month yet—"

He scowled in annoyance. "Yes, yes, I know that. I want the writers before I came."

The clerk paused. "Until you started your work there was no definite assignment. The information just isn't here. But the man you replaced in PIB was named Frank Mariel."

Shandor turned the name over in his mind, decided that it was familiar, but that he couldn't quite place it. "What's this man doing now?"

The girl shrugged. "I don't know, just now, and have no sources. But according to our files he left Public Information Board to go to work in some capacity for Dartmouth Bearing Corporation."

Shandor flipped the switch, and settled back in the reading chair. Once again he fingered through his notes, frowning, a doubt gnawing through his mind into certainty. He took up a dozen of the stories, analyzed them carefully, word for word, sentence by sentence. Then he sat back, his body tired, eyes closed in concentration, an incredible idea twisting and writhing and solidifying in his mind.

It takes one to catch one. That was his job—telling lies. Writing stories that weren't true, and making them believable. Making people think one thing when the truth was something else. It wasn't so strange that he could detect exactly the same sort of thing when he ran into it. He thought it through again and again, and every time he came up with the same answer. There was no doubt.

Reading the newspaper files had accomplished only one thing. He had spent the afternoon reading a voluminous, neat, smoothly written, extremely convincing batch of bold-faced lies. Lies about David Ingersoll. Somewhere, at the bottom of those lies was a shred or two of truth, a shred hard to analyze, impossible to segregate from the garbage surrounding it. But somebody had written the lies. That meant that somebody knew the truths behind them.

Suddenly he galvanized into action. The video blinked protestingly at his urgent summons, and the Washington visiphone operator answered. "Somewhere in those listings of yours," Shandor said, "you've got a man named Frank Mariel. I want his number."

*

He reached the downtown restaurant half an hour early, and ducked into a nearby visiphone station to ring Hart. The PIB director's chubby face materialized on the

265

screen after a moment's confusion, and Shandor said: "John—what are your plans for releasing the Ingersoll story? The morning papers left him with a slight head cold, if I remember right—" Try as he would, he couldn't conceal the edge of sarcasm in his voice.

Hart scowled. "How's the biography coming?"

"The biography's coming along fine. I want to know what kind of quicksand I'm wading through, that's all."

Hart shrugged and spread his hands. "We can't break the story proper until you're ready with your buffer story. Current plans say that he gets pneumonia tomorrow, and goes to Walter Reed tomorrow night. We're giving it as little emphasis as possible, running the Berlin Conference stories for right-hand column stuff. That'll give you all day tomorrow and half the next day for the preliminary stories on his death. Okay?"

"That's not enough time." Shandor's voice was tight.

"It's enough for a buffer-release." Hart scowled at him, his round face red and annoyed. "Look, Tom, you get that story in, and never mind what you like or don't like. This is dynamite you're playing with—the Conference is going to be on the rocks in a matter of hours—that's straight from the Undersecretary—and on top of it all, there's trouble down in Arizona—"

Shandor's eyes widened. "The Rocket Project—?"

Hart's mouth twisted. "Sabotage. They picked up a whole ring that's been operating for over a year. Caught them red-handed, but not before they burnt out half a calculator wing. They'll have to move in new machines now before they can go on—set the Project back another week, and that could lose the war for us right there. Now *get that story in*." He snapped the switch down, leaving Shandor blinking at the darkened screen.

Ten minutes later Ann Ingersoll joined him in the restaurant booth. She was wearing a chic white linen outfit, with her hair fresh, like a blonde halo around her head in the fading evening light. Her freshness contrasted painfully with Tom's curling collar and dirty tie, and he suddenly wished he'd picked up a shave. He looked up and grunted when he saw the fat briefcase under the girl's arm, and she dropped it on the table between them and sank down opposite him, studying his face. "The reading didn't go so well," she said.

"The reading went lousy," he admitted sheepishly. "This the personal file?"

She nodded shortly and lit a cigarette. "The works. They didn't even bother me. But I can't see why all the precaution— I mean, the express and all that—"

Shandor looked at her sharply. "If what you said this morning was true, that file is a gold mine, for us, but more particularly, for your father's enemies. I'll go over it closely when I get out of here. Meantime, there are one or two other things I want to talk over with you."

She settled herself, and grinned. "Okay, boss. Fire away."

He took a deep breath, and tiredness lined his face. "First off: what did your father do before he went into politics?"

Her eyes widened, and she arrested the cigarette halfway to her mouth, put it back on the ashtray, with a puzzled frown on her face. "That's funny," she said softly. "I thought I knew, but I guess I don't. He was an industrialist—way, far back, years and years ago, when I was just a little brat—and then we got into the war with China, and I don't know what he did. He was always making business trips; I can remember going to the airport with mother to meet him, but I don't know what he did. Mother always avoided talking about him, and I never got to see him enough to talk—"

Shandor sat forward, his eyes bright. "Did he ever entertain any business friends during that time—any that you can remember?"

She shook her head. "I can't remember. Seems to me a man or two came home with him on a couple of occasions, but I don't know who. I don't remember much before the night he came home and said he was going to run for Congress. Then there were people galore—have been ever since."

"And what about his work at the end of the China war? After he was elected, while he was doing all that work to try to smooth things out with Russia—can you remember him saying anything, to you, or to your mother, about *what* he was doing, and how?"

She shook her head again. "Oh, yes, he'd talk—he and mother would talk—sometimes argue. I had the feeling that things weren't too well with mother and dad many times. But I can't remember anything specific, except that he used to say over and over how he hated the thought of another war. He was afraid it was going to come—"

Shandor looked up sharply. "But he hated it—"

"Yes." Her eyes widened. "Oh, yes, he hated it. Dad was a good man, Tom. He believed with all his heart that the people of the world wanted peace, and that they were being dragged to war because they couldn't find any purpose to keep them from it. He believed that if the people of the world had a cause, a purpose, a driving force, that there wouldn't be any more wars. Some men fought him for preaching peace, but he wouldn't be swayed. Especially he hated the pure-profit lobbies, the patriotic drumbeaters who stood to get rich in a war. But dad had to die, and there aren't many men like him left now, I guess."

"I know." Shandor fell silent, stirring his coffee glumly. "Tell me," he said, "did your father have anything to do with a man named Mariel?"

Ann's eyes narrowed. "Frank Mariel? He was the newspaper man. Yes, dad had plenty to do with him. He hated dad's guts, because dad fought his writing so much. Mariel was one of the 'fight now and get rich' school that were continually plaguing dad."

"Would you say that they were enemies?"

She bit her lip, wrinkling her brow in thought. "Not at first. More like a big dog with a little flea, at first. Mariel pestered dad, and dad tried to scratch him away. But Mariel got into PIB, and then I suppose you could call them enemies—"

Shandor sat back, frowning, his face dark with fatigue. He stared at the table top for a long moment, and when he looked up at the girl his eyes were troubled. "There's something wrong with this," he said softly. "I can't quite make it out, but it just doesn't look right. Those newspaper stories I read—pure bushwa, from beginning to end. I'm dead certain of it. And yet—" he paused, searching for words. "Look. It's like I'm looking at a jigsaw puzzle that *looks* like it's all completed and lying out on the table. But there's something that tells me I'm being foxed, that it isn't a complete puzzle at all, just an illusion, yet somehow I can't even tell for sure where pieces are missing—"

The girl leaned over the table, her grey eyes deep with concern. "Tom," she said, almost in a whisper. "Suppose there *is* something, Tom. Something big, what's it going to do to *you*, Tom? You can't fight anything as powerful as PIB, and these men that hated dad could break you."

Tom grinned tiredly, his eyes far away. "I know," he said softly. "But a man can only swallow so much. Somewhere, I guess, I've still got a conscience—it's a nuisance, but it's still there." He looked closely at the lovely girl across from him. "Maybe it's just that I'm tired of being sick of myself. I'd like to *like* myself for a change. I haven't liked myself for years." He looked straight at her, his voice very small in the still booth. "I'd like some other people to like me, too. So I've got to keep going—"

Her hand was in his, then, grasping his fingers tightly, and her voice was trembling. "I didn't think there was anybody left like that," she said. "Tom, you aren't by yourself—remember that. No matter what happens, I'm with you all the way. I'm—I'm afraid, but I'm with you."

He looked up at her then, and his voice was tight. "Listen, Ann. Your father planned to go to Berlin before he died. What was he going to *do* if he went to the Berlin Conference?"

She shrugged helplessly. "The usual diplomatic fol-de-rol, I suppose. He always—"

"No, no—that's not right. He wanted to go so badly that he died when he wasn't allowed to, Ann. He must have had something in mind, something concrete, something tremendous. Something that would have changed the picture a great deal."

And then she was staring at Shandor, her face white, grey eyes wide. "Of course he had something," she exclaimed. "He *must* have—oh, I don't know what, he wouldn't say what was in his mind, but when he came home after that meeting with the President he was furious— I've never seen him so furious, Tom, he was almost out of his mind with anger, and he paced the floor, and, swore and nearly tore the room apart. He wouldn't speak to anyone, just stamped around and threw things. And then we heard him cry out, and when we got to him he was unconscious on the floor, and he was dead when the doctor came—" She set her glass down with trembling fingers. "He had something big, Tom, I'm sure of it. He had some information that he planned to drop on the conference table with such a bang it would stop the whole world cold. *He knew something* that the conference doesn't know—"

Tom Shandor stood up, trembling, and took the briefcase. "It should be here," he said. "If not the whole story, at least the missing pieces." He started for the booth door. "Go home," he said. "I'm going where I can examine these files without any interference. Then I'll call you." And then he was out the door, shouldering his way through the crowded restaurant, frantically weaving his way to the street. He didn't hear Ann's voice as she called after him to stop, didn't see her stop at the booth door, watch in a confusion of fear and tenderness, and collapse into the booth, sobbing as if her heart would break. Because a crazy, twisted, impossible idea was in his mind, an idea that had plagued him since he had started reading that morning, an idea with an answer, an acid test, folded in the briefcase under his arm. He bumped into a fat man at the bar, grunted angrily, and finally reached the street, whistled at the cab that lingered nearby.

The car swung up before him, the door springing open automatically. He had one foot on the running board before he saw the trap, saw the tight yellowish face and the glittering eyes inside the cab. Suddenly there was an explosion of bright purple brilliance, and he was screaming, twisting and screaming and reeling backward onto the sidewalk, doubled over with the agonizing fire that burned through his side and down one leg, forcing scream after scream from his throat as he blindly staggered to the wall of the building, pounded it with his fists for relief from the searing pain. And then he was on his side on the sidewalk, sobbing, blubbering incoherently to the uniformed policeman who was dragging him gently to his feet, seeing through burning eyes the group of curious people gathering around. Suddenly realization dawned through the pain, and he let out a cry of anger and bolted for the curb, knocking the policeman aside, his eyes wild, searching the receding stream of traffic for the cab, a picture of the occupant burned indelibly into his mind, a face he had seen, recognized. The cab was gone, he knew, gone like a breath of wind. The briefcase was also gone—

*

He gave the address of the Essex University Hospital to the cabby, and settled back in the seat, gripping the hand-guard tightly to fight down the returning pain in his side and leg. His mind was whirling, fighting in a welter of confusion, trying to find some avenue of approach, some way to make sense of the mess. The face in the cab recurred again and again before his eyes, the gaunt, putty-colored cheeks, the sharp glittering eyes. His acquaintance with Frank Mariel had been brief and unpleasant, in the past, but that was a face he would never forget. But how could Mariel have known where he would be, and when? There was precision in that attack, far too smooth precision ever to have been left to chance, or even to independent planning. His mind skirted the obvious a dozen times, and each time rejected it angrily. Finally he knew he could no longer reject the thought, the only possible answer. Mariel had known where he would be, and at what time. Therefore, someone must have told him.

He stiffened in the seat, the pain momentarily forgotten. Only one person could have told Mariel. Only one person knew where the file was, and where it would be after he left the restaurant—he felt cold bitterness creep down his spine. She had known, and sat there making eyes at him, and telling him how wonderful he was, how she was with him no matter what happened—and she'd already sold him down the river. He shook his head angrily, trying to keep his thoughts on a rational plane. *Why?* Why had she strung him along, why had she even started to help him? And why, above all, turn against her own father?

The Hospital driveway crunched under the cab, and he hopped out, wincing with every step, and walked into a phone booth off the lobby. He gave a name, and in a moment heard the P.A. system echoing it: "Dr. Prex; calling Dr. Prex." In a moment he heard a receiver click off, and a familiar voice said, "Prex speaking."

"Prex, this is Shandor. Got a minute?"

The voice was cordial. "Dozens of them. Where are you?"

"I'll be up in your quarters." Shandor slammed down the receiver and started for the elevator to the Resident Physicians' wing.

He let himself in by a key, and settled down in the darkened room to wait an eternity before a tall, gaunt man walked in, snapped on a light, and loosened the white jacket at his neck. He was a young man, no more than thirty, with a tired, sober face and jet black hair falling over his forehead. His eyes lighted as he saw Shandor, and he grinned. "You look like you've been through the mill. What happened?"

Shandor stripped off his clothes, exposing the angry red of the seared skin. The tall man whistled softly, the smile fading. Carefully he examined the burned area, his fingers gentle on the tender surface, then he turned troubled eyes to Shandor. "You've been messing around with dirty guys, Tom. Nobody but a real dog would turn a scalder on a man." He went to a cupboard, returned with a jar of salve and bandages.

"Is it serious?" Shandor's face was deathly white. "I've been fighting shock with thiamin for the last hour, but I don't think I can hold out much longer."

Prex shrugged. "You didn't get enough to do any permanent damage, if that's what you mean. Just fried the pain-receptors in your skin to a crisp, is all. A little dose is so painful you can't do anything but holler for a while, but it won't hurt you permanently unless you get it all over you. Enough can kill you." He dressed the burned areas carefully, then bared Shandor's arm and used a pressure syringe for a moment. "Who's using one of those things?"

Shandor was silent for a moment. Then he said, "Look, Prex. I need some help, badly." His eyes looked up in dull anger. "I'm going to see a man tonight, and I want him to talk, hard and fast. I don't care right now if he nearly dies from pain, but I want him to talk. I need somebody along who knows how to make things painful."

Prex scowled, and pointed to the burn. "This the man?"

"That's the man."

Prex put away the salve. "I suppose I'll help you, then. Is this official, or grudge?"

"A little of both. Look, Prex, I know this is a big favor to ask, but it's on the level. Believe me, it's square, nothing shady about it. The method may not be legal, but the means are justified. I can't tell you what's up, but I'm asking you to trust me."

Prex grinned. "You say it's all right, it's all right. When?"

Shandor glanced at his watch. "About 3:00 this morning, I think. We can take your car."

They talked for a while, and a call took the doctor away. Shandor slept a little, then made some black coffee. Shortly before three the two men left the Hospital by the Physicians' entrance, and Prex's little beat-up Dartmouth slid smoothly into the desultory traffic for the suburbs.

*

The apartment was small and neatly furnished. Shandor and the Doctor had been admitted by a sleepy doorman who had been jolted to sudden attention by Tom's PIB card, and after five minutes pounding on the apartment door, a sleepy-eyed man opened the door a crack. "Say, what's the idea pounding on a man's door at this time of night? Haven't you—"

Shandor gave the door a shove with his shoulder, driving it open into the room. "Shut up," he said bluntly. He turned so the light struck his face, and the little man's jaw dropped in astonishment. "Shandor!" he whispered.

Frank Mariel looked like a weasel—sallow, sunken-cheeked, with a yellowish cast to his skin that contrasted unpleasantly with the coal black hair. "That's right," said Shandor. "We've come for a little talk. Meet the doctor."

Mariel's eyes shifted momentarily to Prex's stoney face, then back to Shandor, ghosts of fear creeping across his face. "What do you want?"

"I've come for the files."

The little man scowled. "You've come to the wrong man. I don't have any files."

Prex carefully took a small black case from his pocket, unsnapped a hinge, and a small, shiny instrument fell out in his hand. "The files," said Shandor. "Who has them?"

"I—I don't know—"

Shandor smashed a fist into the man's face, viciously, knocking him reeling to the floor. "You tried to kill me tonight," he snarled. "You should have done it up right. You should stick to magazine editing and keep your nose out of dirty games, Mariel. Who has the files?"

Mariel picked himself up, trembling, met Shandor's fist, and sprawled again, a trickle of blood appearing at his mouth. "Harry Dartmouth has the files," he groaned. "They're probably in Chicago now."

"What do you know about Harry Dartmouth?"

Mariel gained a chair this time before Shandor hit him. "I've only met him a couple of times. He's the president of Dartmouth Bearing Corporation and he's my boss—Dartmouth Bearing publishes 'Fighting World.' I do what he tells me."

Shandor's eyes flared. "Including murder, is that right?" Mariel's eyes were sullen. "Come on, talk! Why did Dartmouth want Ingersoll's personal files?"

The man just stared sullenly at the floor. Prex pressed a stud on the side of the shiny instrument, and a purple flash caught Mariel's little finger. Mariel jerked and squealed with pain. "Speak up," said Shandor. "I didn't hear you."

"Probably about the bonds," Mariel whimpered. His face was ashen, and he eyed Prex with undisguised pleading. "Look, tell him to put that thing away—"

Shandor grinned without humor. "You don't like scalders, eh? Get a big enough dose, and you're dead, Mariel—but I guess you know that, don't you? Think about it. But don't think too long. What about the bonds?"

"Ingersoll has been trying to get Dartmouth Bearing Corporation on legal grounds for years. Something about the government bonds they held, bought during the China wars. You know, surplus profits—Dartmouth Bearing could beat the taxes by buying bonds. Harry Dartmouth thought Ingersoll's files had some legal dope against them—he was afraid you'd try to make trouble for the company—"

"So he hired his little pixie, eh? Seems to me you'd have enough on your hands editing that rag—"

Mariel shot him an injured look. "'*Fighting World*' has the second largest magazine circulation in the country. It's a good magazine."

"It's a warmonger propaganda rag," snapped Shandor. He glared at the little man. "What's your relation to Ingersoll?"

"I hated his guts. He was carrying his lily-livered pacifism right to the White House, and I couldn't see it. So I fought him every inch of the way. I'll fight what he stands for now he's dead—"

Shandor's eyes narrowed. "That was a mistake, Mariel. You weren't supposed to know he is dead." He walked over to the little man, whose face was a shade whiter yet. "Funny," said Shandor quietly. "You say you hated him, but I didn't get that impression at all."

Mariel's eyes opened wide. "What do you mean?"

"Everything you wrote for PIB seems to have treated him kindly."

A shadow of deep concern crossed Mariel's face, as though for the first time he found himself in deep water. "PIB told me what to write, and I wrote it. You know how they work."

"Yes, I know how they work. I also know that most of your writing, while you were doing Public Information Board work, was never ordered by PIB. Ever hear of Ben Chamberlain, Mariel? Or Frank Eberhardt? Or Jon Harding? Ever hear of them, Mariel?" Shandor's voice cut sharply through the room. "Ben Chamberlain wrote for every large circulation magazine in the country, after the Chinese war. Frank Eberhardt was the man behind Associated Press during those years. Jon Harding was the silent publisher of three newspapers in Washington, two in New York, and one in Chicago. Ever hear of those men, Mariel?"

"No, no—"

"You know damned well you've heard of them. Because *those men were all you*. Every single one of them—" Shandor was standing close to him, now, and Mariel sat like he had seen a ghost, his lower lip quivering, forehead wet. "No, no, you're wrong—"

"No, no, I'm right," mocked Shandor. "I've been in the newspaper racket for a long time, Mariel. I've got friends in PIB—real friends, not the shamus crowd you're acquainted with that'll take you for your last nickel and then leave you to starve. Never mind how I found out. You hated Ingersoll so much you handed him bouquets all the time. How about it, Mariel? All that writing—you couldn't praise him enough. Boosting him, beating the drum for him and his policies—every trick and gimmick known in the propaganda game to give him a boost, make him the people's darling—how about it?"

Mariel was shaking his head, his little eyes nearly popping with fright. "It wasn't him," he choked. "Ingersoll had nothing to do with it. It was Dartmouth Bearing. They bought me into the spots. Got me the newspapers, supported me. Dartmouth Bearing ran the whole works, and they told me what to write—"

"Garbage! Dartmouth Bearing—the biggest munitions people in America, and I'm supposed to believe that they told you to go to bat for the country's strongest pacifist! What kind of sap do you take me for?"

"It's true! Ingersoll had nothing to do with it, nothing at all." Mariel's voice was almost pleading. "Look, I don't know what Dartmouth Bearing had in mind. Who was I to ask questions? You don't realize their power, Shandor. Those bonds I spoke of—they hold millions of dollars worth of bonds! They hold enough bonds to topple the economy of the nation, they've got bonds in the names of ten thousand subsidiary companies. They've been telling Federal Economics Commission what to do for the past ten years! And they're getting us into this war, Shandor—lock, stock and barrel. They pushed for everything they could get, and they had the money, the power, the men to do whatever they wanted. You couldn't fight them, because they had everything sewed up so tight nobody could approach them—"

Shandor's mind was racing, the missing pieces beginning, suddenly, to come out of the haze. The incredible, twisted idea broke through again, staggering him, driving through his mind like icy steel. "Listen, Mariel. I swear I'll kill you if you lie to me, so you'd better tell the truth. Who put you on my trail? Who told you Ingersoll was dead, and that I was scraping up Ingersoll's past?"

The little man twisted his hands, almost in tears. "Harry Dartmouth told me—"

"And who told Harry Dartmouth?"

Mariel's voice was so weak it could hardly be heard. "The girl," he said.

Shandor felt the chill deepen. "And where are the files now?"

"Dartmouth has them. Probably in Chicago—I expressed them. The girl didn't dare send them direct, for fear you would check, or that she was being watched. I was supposed to pick them up from you, and see to it that you didn't remember—"

Shandor clenched his fist. "Where are Dartmouth's plants located?"

"The main plants are in Chicago and Newark. They've got a smaller one in Nevada."

"And what do they make?"

"In peacetime—cars. In wartime they make tanks and shells."

"And their records? Inventories? Shipping orders, and files? Where do they keep them?"

"I—I don't know. You aren't thinking of—"

"Never mind what I'm thinking of, just answer up. Where are they?"

"All the administration offices are in Chicago. But they'd kill you, Shandor—you wouldn't stand a chance. They can't be fought, I tell you."

Shandor nodded to Prex, and started for the door. "Keep him here until dawn, then go on home, and forget what you heard. If anything happens, give me a ring at my home." He glared at Mariel. "Don't worry about me, bud—they won't be doing anything to me when I get through with them. They just won't be doing anything at all."

*

The idea had crystallized as he talked to Mariel. Shandor's mind was whirling as he walked down toward the thoroughfare. Incredulously, he tried to piece the picture together. He had known Dartmouth Bearing was big—but that big? Mariel might have been talking nonsense, or he might have been reading the Gospel. Shandor hailed a cab, sat back in the seat scratching his head. How big could Dartmouth Bearing be? Could *any* corporation be that big? He thought back, remembering the rash of post-war scandals and profit-gouging trials, the anti-trust trials. In wartime, bars are let down, *no one* can look with disfavor on the factories making the weapons. And if one corporation could buy, and expand, and buy some more—it might be too powerful to be prosecuted after the war—

Shandor shook his head, realizing that he was skirting the big issue. Dartmouth Bearing connected up, in some absurd fashion, but there was a missing link. Mariel fit into one side of the puzzle, interlocking with Dartmouth. The stolen files might even fit, for that matter. But the idea grew stronger. A great, jagged piece in the middle of the puzzle was missing—the key piece which would tie everything together. He felt his skin prickle as he thought. An impossible idea—and yet, he realized, if it were true, everything else would fall clearly into place—

He sat bolt upright. It *had* to be true—

He leaned forward and gave the cabby the landing field address, then sat back, feeling his pulse pounding through his arms and legs. Nervously he switched on the radio. The dial fell to some jazz music, which he tolerated for a moment or two, then flipped to a news broadcast. Not that news broadcasts really meant much, but he wanted to hear the Ingersoll story release for the day. He listened impatiently to a roundup of local news: David Ingersoll stricken with pneumonia, three Senators protesting the current tax bill—he brought his attention around sharply at the sound of a familiar name—

"—disappeared from his Chicago home early this morning. Mr. Dartmouth is president of Dartmouth Bearing Corporation, currently engaged in the manufacture of munitions for Defense, and producing much of the machinery being used in the Moon-rocket in Arizona. Police are following all possible leads, and are confident that there has been no foul play.

"On the international scene, the Kremlin is still blocking—" Shandor snapped off the radio abruptly, his forehead damp. Dartmouth disappeared, and with him the files—why? And where to go now to find them? If the idea that was plaguing him was true, sound, valid—he'd *have* to have the files. His whole body was wet with perspiration as he reached the landing field.

The trip to the Library of Congress seemed endless, yet he knew that the Library wouldn't be open until 8:00 anyway. Suddenly he felt a wave of extreme weariness sweep over him—when had he last slept? Bored, he snapped the telephone switch and rang PIB offices for his mail. To his surprise, John Hart took the wire, and exploded in his ear, "Where in hell have you been? I've been trying to get you all night. Listen, Tom, drop the Ingersoll story cold, and get in here. The faster the better."

Shandor blinked. "Drop the story? You're crazy!"

"*Get in here!*" roared Hart. "From now on you've *really* got a job. The Berlin Conference blew up tonight, Tom—high as a kite. *We're at war with Russia—*"

Carefully, Shandor plopped the receiver down on its hook, his hands like ice. Just one item first, he thought, just one thing I've got to know. *Then* back to PIB, maybe.

He found a booth in the Library, and began hunting, time pressing him into frantic speed. The idea was incredible, but it *had* to be true. He searched the micro-film files for three hours before he found it, in a "Who's Who" dating back to 1958, three years before the war with China. A simple, innocuous listing, which froze him to his seat. He read it, unbelievingly, yet knowing that it was the only possible link. Finally he read it again.

David P. Ingersoll. Born 1922, married 1947. Educated at Rutgers University and MIT. Worked as administrator for International Harvester until 1955. Taught Harvard University from 1955 to 1957.

David P. Ingersoll, becoming, in 1958, the executive president of Dartmouth Bearing Corporation . . . .

*

He found a small, wooded glade not far from the Library, and set the 'copter down skillfully, his mind numbed, fighting to see through the haze to the core of incredible truth he had uncovered. The great, jagged piece, so long missing, was suddenly plopped right down into the middle of the puzzle, and now it didn't fit. There were still holes, holes that obscured the picture and twisted it into a nightmarish impossibility. He snapped the telephone switch, tried three numbers without any success, and finally reached the fourth. He heard Dr. Prex's sharp voice on the wire.

"Anything happen since I left, Prex?"

"Nothing remarkable." The doctor's voice sounded tired. "Somebody tried to call Mariel on the visiphone about an hour after you had gone, and then signed off in a hurry when he saw somebody else around. Don't know who it was, but he sounded mighty agitated." The doctor's voice paused. "Anything new, Tom?"

"Plenty," growled Shandor bitterly. "But you'll have to read it in the newspapers." He flipped off the connection before Prex could reply.

Then Shandor sank back and slept, the sleep of total exhaustion, hoping that a rest would make the shimmering, indefinite picture hold still long enough for him to study it. And as he drifted into troubled sleep a greater and more pressing question wormed upward into his mind.

He woke with a jolt, just as the sun was going down, and he knew then with perfect clarity what he had to do. He checked quickly to see that he had been undisturbed, and then manipulated the controls of the 'copter. Easing the ship into the sky toward Washington, he searched out a news report on the radio, listened with a dull feeling in the pit of his stomach as the story came through about the breakdown of the Berlin Conference, the declaration of war, the President's meeting with Congress that morning, his formal request for full wartime power, the granting of permission by a wide-eyed, frightened legislature. Shandor settled back, staring dully at the ground moving below him, the whisps of evening haze rising over the darkening land. There was only one thing to do. He had to have Ingersoll's files. He knew only one way to get them.

Half an hour later he was settling the ship down, under cover of darkness, on the vast grounds behind the Ingersoll estate, cutting the motors to effect a quiet landing. Tramping down the ravine toward the huge house, he saw it was dark; down by the gate he could see the Security Guard, standing in a haze of blue cigarette smoke under the dim-out lights. Cautiously he slipped across the back terrace, crossing behind the house, and jangled a bell on a side porch.

Ann Ingersoll opened the door, and gasped as Shandor forced his way in. "Keep quiet," he hissed, slipping the door shut behind him. Then he sighed, and walked through the entrance into the large front room.

"Tom! Oh, Tom, I was afraid— Oh, *Tom!*" Suddenly she was in his arms sobbing, pressing her face against his shirt front. "Oh, I'm so glad to see you, Tom—"

He disengaged her, turning from her and walking across the room. "Let's turn it off, Ann," he said disgustedly. "It's not very impressive."

"Tom—I—I *wanted* to tell you. I just didn't know what to do. I didn't believe them when they said you wouldn't be harmed, I was afraid. Oh, Tom, I wanted to tell you, believe me—"

"You didn't tell me," he snapped. "They were nervous, they slipped up. That's the only reason I'm alive. They planned to kill me."

She stared at him tearfully, shaking her head from side to side, searching for words. "I—I didn't want that—"

He whirled, his eyes blazing. "You silly fool, what do you think you're doing when you play games with a mob like this? Do you think they're going to play fair? You're no clod, you know better than that—" He leaned over her, trembling with anger. "You set me up for a sucker, but the plan fell through. And now I'm running around loose, and if you thought I was dangerous before, you haven't seen anything like how dangerous I am now. You're going to tell me some things, now, and you're going to tell them straight. You're going to tell me where Harry Dartmouth went with those files, where they are right now. Understand that? *I want those files.* Because when I have them I'm going to do exactly what I started out to do. I'm going to write a story, the whole rotten story about your precious father and his two-faced life. I'm going to write about Dartmouth Bearing Corporation and all its flunky outfits, and tell what they've done to this country and the people of this country." He paused, breathing heavily, and sank down on a chair, staring at her. "I've learned things in the past twenty-four hours I never dreamed could be true. I should be able to believe anything, I suppose, but these things knocked my stilts out from under me. This country has been had—right straight down the line, for a dozen years. We've been sold down the river like a pack of slaves, and now we're going to get a look at the cold ugly truth, for once."

She stared at him. "What do you mean—about my precious father—?"

"Your precious father was at the bottom of the whole slimy mess."

"No, no—not dad." She shook her head, her face chalky. "Harry Dartmouth, maybe, but not dad. Listen a minute. I didn't set you up for anything. I didn't know what Dartmouth and Mariel were up to. Dad left instructions for me to contact Harry Dartmouth immediately, in case he died. He told me that—oh, a year ago. Told me that before I did anything else, I should contact Dartmouth, and do as he said. So when he died, I contacted Harry, and kept in contact with him. He told me you were out to burn my father, to heap garbage on him after he was dead before the people who loved him, and he said the first thing you would want would be his personal files. Tom, I didn't know you, then—I knew Harry, and knew that dad trusted him, for some reason, so I believed him. But I began to realize that what he said wasn't true. I got the files, and he said to give them to you, to string you along, and he'd pick them up from you before you had a chance to do any harm with them. He said he wouldn't hurt you, but I—I didn't believe him, Tom. I believed you, that you wanted to give dad a fair shake—"

Shandor was on his feet, his eyes blazing. "So you turned them over to Dartmouth anyway? And what do you think he's done with them? Can you tell me that? Where has he gone? Has he burnt them? If not, what's he going to do with them?"

Her voice was weak, and she looked as if she were about to faint. "That's what I'm trying to tell you," she said, shakily. "He doesn't have them. I have them."

Shandor's jaw dropped. "Now, wait a minute," he said softly. "You gave me the briefcase, Mariel snatched it and nearly killed me—"

"A dummy, Tom. I didn't know who to trust, but I knew I believed you more than I believed Harry. Things happened so fast, and I was so confused—" She looked straight at him. "I gave you a dummy, Tom."

His knees walked out from under him, then, and he sank into a chair. "You've got them here, then," he said weakly.

"Yes. I have them here."

*

The room was in the back of the house, a small, crowded study, with a green-shaded desk lamp. Shandor dumped the contents of the briefcase onto the desk, and settled down, his heart pounding in his throat. He started at the top of the pile, sifting, ripping out huge sheafs of papers, receipts, notes, journals, clippings. He hardly noticed when the girl slipped out of the room, and he was deep in study when she returned half an hour later with steaming black coffee. With a grunt of thanks he drank it, never shifting his attention from the scatter of papers, papers from the personal file of a dead man. And slowly, the picture unfolded.

An ugly picture. A picture of deceit, a picture full of lies, full of secret promises, a picture of scheming, of plotting, planning, influencing, coercing, cheating, propagandizing—all with one single-minded aim, with a single terrible goal.

Shandor read, numbly, his mind twisting in protest as the picture unfolded. David Ingersoll's control of Dartmouth Bearing Corporation and its growing horde of subsidiaries under the figurehead of his protege, Harry Dartmouth. The huge profits from the Chinese war, the relaxation of control laws, the millions of war-won dollars ploughed back into government bonds, in a thousand different names, all controlled by Dartmouth Bearing Corporation—

And Ingersoll's own work in the diplomatic field—an incredibly skillful, incredibly evil channeling of power and pressure toward the inevitable goal, hidden under the cloak of peaceful respectability and popular support. The careful treaties, quietly disorganizing a dozen national economics, antagonizing the great nation to the East under the all too acceptable guise of "peace through strength." Reciprocal trade agreements bitterly antagonistic to Russian economic development. The continual bickering, the skillful manipulation hidden under the powerful propaganda cloak of a hundred publications, all coursing to one ultimate, terrible goal, all with one purpose, one aim—

War. War with anybody, war in the field and war on the diplomatic front. Traces even remained of the work done within the enemy nations, bitter anti-Ingersoll propaganda from within the ranks of Russia herself, manipulated to strengthen Ingersoll in America, to build him up, to drive the nations farther apart, while presenting Ingersoll as the pathetic prince of world peace, fighting desperately to stop the ponderous wheels of the irresistible juggernaut—

And in America, the constant, unremitting literary and editorial drumbeating, pressuring greater war preparation, distilling hatreds in a thousand circles, focussing them into a single channel. Tremendous propaganda pressure to build armies, to build weapons, to get the Moon-rocket project underway—

Shandor sat back, eyes drooping, fighting to keep his eyes open. His mind was numb, his body trembling. A sheaf of papers in a separate folder caught his eye, production records of the Dartmouth Bearing Corporation, almost up to the date of Ingersoll's death. Shandor frowned, a snag in the chain drawing his attention. He peered at the papers, vaguely puzzled. Invoices from the Chicago plant, materials for tanks, and guns, and shells. Steel, chemicals. The same for the New Jersey plant, the same with a dozen subsidiary plants. Shipments of magnesium and silver wire to the Rocket Project in Arizona, carried through several subsidiary offices. The construction of a huge calculator for the Project in Arizona. Motors and materials, all for Arizona—something caught his mind, brought a frown to his large bland face, some off-key note in the monstrous symphony of production and intrigue that threw up a red flag in his mind, screamed for attention—

And then he sipped the fresh coffee at his elbow and sighed, and looked up at the girl standing there, saw her hand tremble as she steadied herself against the desk, and sat down beside him. He felt a great confusion, suddenly, a vast sympathy for this girl, and he wanted to take her in his arms, hold her close, *protect* her, somehow. She didn't know, she *couldn't* know about this horrible thing. She couldn't have been a party to it, a part of it. He knew the evidence said yes, she knows the whole story, she *helped*them, but he also knew that the evidence, somehow, was wrong, that somehow, he still didn't have the whole picture—

She looked at him, her voice trembling. "You're wrong, Tom," she said.

He shook his head, helplessly. "I'm sorry. It's horrible, I know. But I'm not wrong. This war was planned. We've been puppets on strings, and one man engineered it, from the very start. Your father."

Her eyes were filled with tears, and she shook her head, running a tired hand across her forehead. "You didn't know him, Tom. If you did, you'd know how wrong you are. He was a great man, fine man, but above all he was a *good* man. Only a monster could have done what you're thinking. Dad hated war, he fought it all his life. He couldn't be the monster you think."

Tom's voice was soft in the darkened room, his eyes catching the downcast face of the trembling girl, fighting to believe in a phantom, and his hatred for the power that could trample a faith like that suddenly swelled up in bitter hopeless rage. "It's here, on paper, it can't be denied. It's hateful, but it's here, it's what I set out to learn. It's not a lie this time, Ann, it's the truth, and this time it's *got to be told*. I've written my last false story. This one is going to the people the way it is. This one is going to be the truth."

He stopped, staring at her. The puzzling, twisted hole in the puzzle was suddenly there, staring him in the face, falling down into place in his mind with blazing clarity. Staring, he dived into the pile of papers again, searching, frantically searching for the missing piece, something he had seen, and passed over, the one single piece in the story that didn't make sense. And he found it, on the lists of materials shipped to the Nevada plant. Pig Iron. Raw magnesium. Raw copper. Steel, electron tubes, plastics, from all parts of the country, all being shipped to the Dartmouth Plant in Nevada—

Where they made only shells—

At first he thought it was only a rumble in his mind, the shocking realization storming through. Then he saw Ann jump up suddenly, white-faced and race to the window, and he heard the small scream in her throat. And then the rumbling grew louder, stronger, and the house trembled. He heard the whine of jet planes scream over the house as he joined her at the window, heard the screaming whines mingled with the rumbling thunder. And far away, on the horizon, the red glare was glowing, rising, burning up to a roaring conflagration in the black night sky—

"Washington!" Her voice was small, infinitely frightened.

"Yes. That's Washington."

"Then it really *has* started." She turned to him with eyes wide with horror, and snuggled up to his chest like a frightened child. "Oh, Tom—"

"It's here. What we've been waiting for. What your father started could never be stopped any other way than this—"

The roar was louder now, rising to a whining scream as another squad of dark ships roared overhead, moving East and South, jets whistling in the night. "This is what your father wanted."

She was crying, great sobs shaking her shoulders. "You're wrong, you're wrong—oh, Tom, you must be wrong—"

His voice was low, almost inaudible in the thundering roar of the bombardment. "Ann, I've got to go ahead. I've got to go tonight. To Nevada, to the Dartmouth plant there. I know I'm right, but I have to go, to check something—to make sure of something." He paused, looking down at her. "I'll be back, Ann. But I'm afraid of what I'll find out there. I need you behind me. Especially with what I have to do, I need you. You've got to decide. Are you for me? Or against me?"

She shook her head sadly, and sank into a chair, gently removing his hands from her waist. "I loved my father, Tom," she said in a beaten voice. "I can't help what he's done—I loved him. I—I can't be with you, Tom."

*

Far below him he could see the cars jamming the roads leaving Washington. He could almost hear the noise, the screeching of brakes, the fistfights, the shouts, the blatting of horns. He moved south over open country, hoping to avoid the places where the 'copter might be spotted and stopped for questioning. He knew that Hart would have an alarm out for him by now, and he didn't dare risk being stopped until he reached his destination, the place where the last piece to the puzzle could be found, the answer to the question that was burning through his mind. Shells were made of steel and chemicals. The tools that made them were also made of steel. Not manganese. Not copper. Not electron relays, nor plastic, nor liquid oxygen. Just steel.

The 'copter relayed south and then turned west over Kentucky. Shandor checked the auxiliary tanks which he had filled at the Library landing field that morning; then he turned the ship to robot controls and sank back in the seat to rest. His whole body clamored for sleep, but he knew he dare not sleep. Any slip, any contact with Army aircraft or Security patrol could throw everything into the fire— For hours he sat, gazing hypnotically at the black expanse of land below, flying high over the pitch-black countryside. Not a light showed, not a sign of life.

Bored, he flipped the radio button, located a news broadcast. "—the bombed area did not extend west of the Appalachians. Washington DC was badly hit, as were New

York and Philadelphia, and further raids are expected to originate from Siberia, coming across the great circle to the West coast or the Middle west. So far the Enemy appears to have lived up to its agreement in the Ingersoll pact to outlaw use of atomic bombs, for no atomic weapons have been used so far, but the damage with block-busters has been heavy. All citizens are urged to maintain strictest blackout regulations, and to report as called upon in local work and civil defense pools as they are set up. The attack began—"

Shandor sighed, checked his instrument readings. Far in the East the horizon was beginning to lighten, a healthy, white-grey light. His calculations placed him over Eastern Nebraska, and a few moments later he nosed down cautiously and verified his location. Lincoln Airbase was in a flurry of activity; the field was alive with men, like little black ants, preparing the reserve fighters and pursuits for use in a fever of urgent speed. Suddenly the 'copter radio bleeped, and Tom threw the switch. "Over."

An angry voice snarled, "You up there, whoever you are, where'd you leave your brains? No civilian craft are allowed in the air, and that's orders straight from Washington. Don't you know there's a war on? Now get down here, before you're shot down—"

Shandor thought quickly. "This is a Federal Security ship," he snapped. "I'm just on a reconnaissance—"

The voice was cautious. "Security? What's your corroboration number?"

Shandor cursed. "JF223R-864. Name is Jerry Chandler. Give it a check if you want to." He flipped the switch, and accelerated for the ridge of hills that marked the Colorado border as the radio signal continued to bleep angrily, and a trio of pursuit planes on the ground began warming up. Shandor sighed, hoping they would check before they sent ships after him. It might at least delay them until he reached his destination.

Another hour carried him to the heart of the Rockies, and across the great salt fields of Utah. His fuel tanks were low, being emptied one by one as the tiny ship sped through the bright morning sky, and Tom was growing uneasy, until suddenly, far to the west and slightly to the north he spotted the plant, nestling in the mountain foothills. It lay far below, sprawling like some sort of giant spider across the rugged terrain. Several hundred cars spread out to the south of the plant, and he could see others speeding in from the temporary village across the ridge. Everything was quiet, orderly. He could see the shipments, crated, sitting in freight cars to the north. And then he saw the drill line running over to the right of the plant. He followed it, quickly checking a topographical map in the cockpit, and his heart started pounding. The railroad branch ran between two low peaks and curved out toward the desert.

Moving over it, he saw the curve, saw it as it cut off to the left—and seemed to stop dead in the middle of the desert sand—

Shandor circled even lower, keeping one ear cocked on the radio, and settled the ship on the railroad line. And just as he cut the motors, he heard the shrill whine of three pursuit ships screaming in from the Eastern horizon—

He was out of the 'copter almost as soon as it had touched, throwing a jacket over his arm, and racing for the place where the drill line ended. Because he had seen as he slid in for a landing, just what he had suspected from the topographical map. The drill didn't end in the middle of a desert at all. It went right on into the mountainside.

The excavation was quite large, the entrance covered and camouflaged neatly to give the very impression that he had gotten from the air. Under the camouflage the space was crowded, stacked with crates, boxes, materials, stacked all along the walls of the tunnel. He followed the rails in, lighting his way with a small pocket flashlight when the tunnel turned a corner, cutting off the daylight. Suddenly the tunnel widened, opening out into a much wider room. He sensed, rather than saw, the immense size of the vault, smelt the odd, bitter odor in the air. With the flashlight he probed the darkness, spotting the high, vaulted ceiling above him. And below him—

At first he couldn't see, probing the vast excavation before him, and then, strangely, he saw but couldn't realize what he saw. He stared for a solid minute, uncomprehending, then, stifling a gasp, he *knew what he was looking at*—

Lights. He had to have lights, to see clearly what he couldn't believe. Frantically, he spun the flashlight, seeking a light panel, and then, fascinated, he turned the little oval of light back to the pit. And then he heard the barest whisper of sound, the faintest intake of breath, and he ducked, frozen, as a blow whistled past his ear. A second blow from the side caught him solidly in the blackness, grunting, flailing out into a tangle of legs and arms, cursing, catching a foot in his face, striking up into soft, yielding flesh—

And his head suddenly exploded into a million dazzling lights as he sank unconscious to the ground—

*

It was a tiny room, completely without windows, the artificial light filtering through from ventilation slits near the top. Shandor sat up, shaking as the chill in the room became painfully evident. A small electric heater sat in the corner beaming valiantly, but the heat hardly reached his numbed toes. He stood up, shaking himself, slapping his arms against his sides to drive off the coldness—and he heard a noise through the door as soon as he had made a sound.

Muted footsteps stopped outside the door, and a huge man stepped inside. He looked at Shandor carefully, then closed the door behind him, without locking it. "I'm Baker," he rasped cheerfully. "How are you feeling?"

Shandor rubbed his head, suddenly and acutely aware of a very sore nose and a bruised rib cage. "Not so hot," he muttered. "How long have I been out?"

"Long enough." The man pulled out a plug of tobacco, ripped off a chunk with his teeth. "Chew?"

"I smoke." Shandor fished for cigarettes in an empty pocket.

"Not in here you don't," said Baker. He shrugged his huge shoulders and settled affably down on a bench near the wall. "You feel like talking?"

Shandor eyed the unlocked door, and turned his eyes to the huge man. "Sure," he said. "What do you want to talk about?"

"I don't want to talk about nothin'," the big man replied, indifferently. "Thought you might, though."

"Are you the one that roughed me up?"

"Yuh." Baker grinned. "Hope I didn't hurt you much. Boss said to keep you in one piece, but we had to hurry up, and take care of those Army guys you brought in on your tail. That was dumb. You almost upset everything."

Memory flooded back, and Shandor's eyes widened. "Yes—they followed me all the way from Lincoln—what happened to them?"

Baker grinned and chomped his tobacco. "They're a long way away now. Don't worry about them."

Shandor eyed the door uneasily. The latch hadn't caught, and the door had swung open an inch or two. "Where am I?" he asked, inching toward the door. "What—what are you planning to do to me?"

Baker watched him edging away. "You're safe," he said. "The boss'll talk to you pretty soon if you feel like it—" He squinted at Tom in surprise, pointing an indolent thumb toward the door. "You planning to go out or something?"

Tom stopped short, his face red. The big man shrugged. "Go ahead. I ain't going to stop you." He grinned. "Go as far as you can."

Without a word Shandor threw open the door, looked out into the concrete corridor. At the end was a large, bright room. Cautiously he started down, then suddenly let out a cry and broke into a run, his eyes wide—

He reached the room, a large room, with heavy plastic windows. He ran to one of the windows, pulse pounding, and stared, a cry choking in his throat. The blackness of the crags contrasted dimly with the inky blackness of the sky beyond. Mile upon mile of jagged, rocky crags, black rock, ageless, unaged rock. And it struck him with a jolt how easily he had been able to run, how lightning-swift his movements. He stared again, and then he saw what he had seen in the pit, standing high outside the building on a rocky flat, standing bright and silvery, like a phantom finger pointing to the inky heavens, sleek, smooth, resting on polished tailfins, like an other-worldly bird poised for flight—

A voice behind him said, "You aren't really going anyplace, you know. Why run?" It was a soft voice, a kindly voice, cultured, not rough and biting like Baker's voice. It came from directly behind Shandor, and he felt his skin crawl. He had heard that voice before—many times before. Even in his dreams he had heard that voice. "You see, it's pretty cold out there. And there isn't any air. You're on the Moon, Mr. Shandor—"

He whirled, his face twisted and white. And he stared at the small figure standing at the door, a stoop-shouldered man, white hair slightly untidy, crow's-feet about his tired eyes. An old man, with eyes that carried a sparkle of youth and kindliness. The eyes of David P. Ingersoll.

*

Shandor stared for a long moment, shaking his head like a man seeing a phantom. When he found words, his voice was choked, the words wrenched out as if by force. "You're—you're alive."

"Yes. I'm alive."

"Then—" Shandor shook his head violently, turning to the window, and back to the small, white-haired man. "Then your death was just a fake."

The old man nodded tiredly. "That's right. Just a fake."

Shandor stumbled to a chair, sat down woodenly. "I don't get it," he said dully. "I just don't get it. The war—that—that I can see. I can see how you worked it, how you engineered it, but this—" he gestured feebly at the window, at the black, impossible landscape outside. "This I can't see. They're bombing us to pieces, they're bombing out Washington, probably your own home, your own family—last night—" he stopped, frowning in confusion—"no, it couldn't have been last night—two days ago?—well, whatever day it was, they were bombing us to pieces, and you're up here—*why*? What's it going to get you? This war, this whole rotten intrigue mess, and then *this*?"

The old man walked across the room and stared for a moment at the silent ship outside. "I hope I can make you understand. We had to come here. We had no choice. We couldn't do what we wanted any other way than to come here—*first*. Before anybody else."

"But why *here*? They're building a rocket there in Arizona. They'll be up here in a few days, maybe a few weeks—"

"Approximately forty-eight hours," corrected Ingersoll quietly. "Within forty-eight hours the Arizona rocket will be here. If the Russian rocket doesn't get here first."

"It doesn't make sense. It won't do you any good to be here if the Earth is blasted to bits. Why come here? And why bring *me* here, of all people? What do you want with me?"

Ingersoll smiled and sat down opposite Shandor. "Take it easy," he said gently. "You're here, you're safe, and you're going to get the whole story. I realize that this is a bit of a jolt—but you had to be jolted. With you I think the jolt will be very beneficial, since we want you with us. That's why we brought you here. We need your help, and we need it very badly. It's as simple as that."

Shandor was on his feet, his eyes blazing. "No dice. This is your game, not mine. I don't want anything to do with it—"

"But you don't know the game—"

"I know plenty of the game. I followed the trail, right from the start. I know the whole rotten mess. The trail led me all the way around Robin Hood's barn, but it told me things—oh, it told me plenty! It told me about you, and this war. And now you want me to help you! What do you want me to do? Go down and tell the people it isn't really so bad being pounded to shreds? Should I tell them they aren't really being bombed, it's all in their minds? Shall I tell them this is a war to defend their freedoms, that it's a great crusade against the evil forces of the world? What kind of a sap do you think I am?" He walked to the window, his whole body trembling with anger. "I followed this trail down to the end, I scraped my way down into the dirtiest, slimiest depths of the barrel, and I've found you down there, and your rotten corporations, and your crowd of heelers. And on the other side are three hundred million people taking the lash end of the whip on Earth, helping to feed you. And you ask me to help you!"

"Once upon a time," Ingersoll interrupted quietly, "there was a fox."

Shandor stopped and stared at him.

"—and the fox got caught in a trap. A big bear trap, with steel jaws, that clamped down on him and held him fast by the leg. He wrenched and he pulled, but he couldn't break that trap open, no matter what he did. And the fox knew that the farmer would come along almost any time to open that bear trap, and the fox knew the farmer would kill him. He knew that if he didn't get out of that trap, he'd be finished, sure as sin. But he was a clever fox, and he found a way to get out of the bear trap." Ingersoll's voice was low, tense in the still room. "Do you know what he did?"

Shandor shook his head silently.

"It was a very simple solution," said Ingersoll. "Drastic, but simple. *He gnawed off his leg.*"

Another man had entered the room, a small, weasel-faced man with sallow cheeks and slick black hair. Ingersoll looked up with a smile, but Mariel waved him on, and took a seat nearby.

"So he chewed off his leg," Shandor repeated dully. "I don't get it."

"The world is in a trap," said Ingersoll, watching Shandor with quiet eyes. "A great big bear trap. It's been in that trap for decades—ever since the first World War. The world has come to a wall it can't climb, a trap it can't get out of, a vicious, painful, torturous trap, and the world has been struggling for seven decades to get out. It hasn't succeeded. And the time is drawing rapidly nigh for the farmer to come. Something had to be done, and done fast, before it was too late. The fox had to chew off its leg. And I had to bring the world to the brink of a major war."

Shandor shook his head, his mind buzzing. "I don't see what you mean. We never had a chance for peace, we never had a chance to get our feet on the ground from one round to the next. No time to do anything worthwhile in the past seventy years—I don't see what you mean about a trap."

Ingersoll settled back in his chair, the light catching his face in sharp profile. "It's been a century of almost continuous war," he said. "You've pointed out the whole trouble. We haven't had time to catch our breath, to make a real peace. The first World War was a sorry affair, by our standards—almost a relic of earlier European wars. Trench fighting, poor rifles, soap-box aircraft—nothing to distinguish it from earlier wars but its scope. But twenty uneasy years went by, and another war began, a very different sort of war. This one had fast aircraft, fast mechanized forces, heavy bombing, and finally, to cap the climax, atomics. That second World War could hold up its head as a real, strapping, fighting war in any society of wars. It was a stiff war, and a terrible one. Quite a bit of progress, for twenty years. But essentially, it was a war of ideologies, just as the previous one had been. A war of intolerance, of unmixable ideas—"

The old man paused, and drew a sip of water from the canister in the corner. "Somewhere, somehow, the world had missed the boat. Those wars didn't solve anything, they didn't even make a very strong pretense. They just made things worse. Somewhere, human society had gotten into a trap, a vicious circle. It had reached the end of its progressive tether, it had no place to go, no place to expand, to great common goal. So ideologies arose to try to solve the dilemma of a basically static society, and they fought wars. And they reached a point, finally, where they could destroy themselves unless they broke the vicious circle, somehow."

Shandor looked up, a deep frown on his face. "You're trying to say that they needed a new frontier."

"Exactly! They desperately needed it. There was only one more frontier they could reach for. A frontier which, once attained, has no real end." He gestured toward the black landscape outside. "There's the frontier. Space. The one thing that could bring human wars to an end. A vast, limitless frontier which could drive men's spirits upward and outward for the rest of time. And that frontier seemed unattainable. It was blocked off by a wall, by the jaws of a trap. Oh, they tried. After the first war the work began. The second war contributed unimaginably to the technical knowledge. But after the second war, they could go no further. Because it cost money, it required a tremendous effort on the part of the people of a great nation to do it, and they couldn't see why they should spend the money to get to space. After all, they had to work up the atomics and new weapons for the next war—it was a trap, as strong and treacherous as any the people of the world had ever encountered.

"The answer, of course, was obvious. Each war brought a great surge of technological development, to build better weapons, to fight bigger wars. Some developments led to extremely beneficial ends, too—if it hadn't been for the second war, a certain British biologist might still be piddling around his understaffed, underpaid laboratory, wishing he had more money, and wondering why it was that that dirty patch of mold on his petri dish seemed to keep bacteria from growing—but the second war created a sudden, frantic, urgent demand for something, anything, that would *stop infection—fast.* And in no time, penicillin was in mass production, saving untold thousands of lives. There was no question of money. Look at the Manhattan project. How many millions went into that? It gave us atomic power, for war, and for peace. For peaceful purposes, the money would never have been spent. But if it was for the sake of war—"

Ingersoll smiled tiredly. "Sounds insane, doesn't it? But look at the record. I looked at the record, way back at the end of the war with China. Other men looked at the record, too. We got together, and talked. We knew that the military advantage of a rocket base on the moon could be a deciding factor in another major war. Military experts had recognized that fact back in the 1950's. Another war could give men the technological kick they needed to get them to space—possibly *in time.* If men got to space before they destroyed themselves, the trap would be broken, the frontier would be opened, and men could turn their energies away from destruction toward something infinitely greater and more important. With space on his hands men could get along without wars. But if we waited for peacetime to go to space, we might never make it. It might be too late.

"It was a dreadful undertaking. I saw the wealth in the company I directed and controlled at the end of the Chinese war, and the idea grew strong. I saw that a huge industrial amalgamation could be undertaken, and succeed. We had a weapon in our favor, the most dangerous weapon ever devised, a thousand times more potent than atomics. Hitler used it, with terrible success. Stalin used it. Haro-Tsing used it. Why couldn't Ingersoll use it? Propaganda—a terrible weapon. It could make people think the right way—it could make them think almost *any* way. It made them think war. From the end of the last war we started, with propaganda, with politics, with money. The group grew stronger as our power became more clearly understood. Mariel handled propaganda through the newspapers, and PIB, and magazines—a clever man—and Harry Dartmouth handled production. I handled the politics and diplomacy. We had but one aim in mind—to bring about a threat of major war that would drive men to space. To the moon, to a man-made satellite, *somewhere or anywhere* to break through the Earth's gravity and get to space. And we aimed at a controlled war. We had the power to do it, we had the money and the plants. We just had to be certain it wasn't the *ultimate* war. It wasn't easy to make sure that atomic weapons wouldn't be used this time—but they will not. Both nations are too much afraid, thanks to our propaganda program. They both leaped at a chance to make a face-saving agreement. And we hoped that the war could be held off until we got to the moon, and until the Arizona rocket project could get a ship launched for the moon. The wheels we had started just moved too fast. I saw at the beginning of the Berlin Conference that it would explode into war, so I decided the time for my 'death' had arrived. I had to come here, to make sure the war doesn't go on any longer than necessary."

Shandor looked up at the old man, his eyes tired. "I still don't see where I'm supposed to fit in. I don't see why you came here at all. Was that a wild-goose chase I ran down there, learning about this?"

"Not a wild goose chase. The important work can't start, you see, until the rocket gets here. It wouldn't do much good if the Arizona rocket got here, to fight the war. It may come for war, but it must go back for peace. We built this rocket to get us here first—built it from government specifications, though they didn't know it. We had the plant to build it in, and we were able to hire technologists *not* to find the right answers in Arizona until we were finished. Because the whole value of the war-threat depended solely and completely upon our getting here *first*. When the Arizona rocket gets to the moon, the war must be stopped. Only then can we start the real 'operation Bear Trap.' That ship, whether American or Russian, will meet with a great surprise when it reaches the Moon. We haven't been spotted here. We left in darkness and solitude, and if we were seen, it was chalked off as a guided missile. We're well camouflaged, and although we don't have any sort of elaborate base—just a couple of sealed rooms—we have a ship and we have weapons. When the first ship comes up here, the control of the situation will be in our hands. Because when it comes, it will be sent back with an ultimatum to *all* nations—to cease warfare, or suffer the most terrible, nonpartisan bombardment the world has ever seen. A pinpoint bombardment, from our ship, here on the Moon. There won't be too much bickering I think. The war will stop. All eyes will turn to us. And then the big work begins."

He smiled, his thin face showing tired lines in the bright light. "I may die before the work is done. I don't know, nor care. I have no successor, nor have we any plans to perpetuate our power once the work is done. As soon as the people themselves will take over the work, the job is theirs, because no group can hope to ultimately control space. But first people must be sold on space, from the bottom up. They must be forced to realize the implications of a ship on the moon. They must realize that the first ship was the hardest, that the trap is sprung. The amputation is a painful one, there wasn't any known anaesthetic, but it will heal, and from here there is no further need for war. But the people must see that, understand its importance. They've got to have the whole story, in terms that they can't mistake. And that means a propagandist—"

"You have Mariel," said Shandor. "He's had the work, the experience—"

"He's getting tired. He'll tell you himself his ideas are slow, he isn't on his toes any longer. He needs a new man, a helper, to take his place. When the first ship comes, his job is done." The old man smiled. "I've watched you, of course, for years. Mariel saw that you were given his job when he left PIB to edit 'Fighting World.' He didn't think you were the man, he didn't trust you—thought you had been raised too strongly on the sort of gibberish you were writing. I thought you were the only man we could use. So we let you follow the trail, and watched to see how you'd handle it. And when you came to the Nevada plant, we *knew* you were the man we had to have—"

Shandor scowled, looking first at Ingersoll, then at Mariel's impassive face. "What about Ann?" he asked, and his voice was unsteady. "She knew about it all the time?"

"No. She didn't know anything about it. We were afraid she had upset things when she didn't turn my files over to Dartmouth as he'd told her. We were afraid you'd go ahead and write the story as you saw it then, which would have wrecked our plan completely. As it was, she helped us sidestep the danger in the long run, but she didn't know what she was really doing." He grinned. "The error was ours, of course. We simply underestimated our man. We didn't know you were that tenacious."

Shandor's face was haggard. "Look. I—I don't know what to think. This ship in Arizona—how long? When will it come? How do you know it'll ever come?"

"We waited until our agents there gave us a final report. The ship may be leaving at any time. But there's no doubt that it'll come. If it doesn't, one from Russia will. It won't be long." He looked at Shandor closely. "You'll have to decide by then, Tom."

"And if I don't go along with you?"

"We could lose. It's as simple as that. Without a spokesman, the plan could fall through completely. There's only one thing you need to make your decision, Tom—faith in men, and a sure conviction that man was made for the stars, and not for an endless circle of useless wars. Think of it, Tom. That's what your decision means."

Shandor walked to the window, stared out at the bleak landscape, watched the great bluish globe of earth, hanging like a huge balloon in the black sky. He saw the myriad pinpoints of light in the blackness on all sides of it, and shook his head, trying to think. So many things to think of, so very many things—

"I don't know," he muttered. "I just don't know—"

*

It was a long night. Ideas are cruel, they become a part of a man's brain, an inner part of his chemistry, they carve grooves deep in his mind which aren't easily wiped away. He knew he'd been living a lie, a bitter, hopeless, endless lie, all his life, but a liar grows to believe his own lies. Even to the point of destruction, he believes them. It was so hard to see the picture, now that he had the last piece in place.

A fox, and a bear trap. Such a simple analogy. War was a hellish proposition, it was cruel, it was evil. It could be lost, so very easily. And it seemed so completely, utterly senseless to cut off one's own leg—

And then he thought, somewhere, sometime, he'd see her again. Perhaps they'd be old by then, but perhaps not—perhaps they'd still be young, and perhaps she wouldn't know the true story yet. Perhaps he could be the first to tell her, to let her know that he had been wrong— Maybe there could be a chance to be happy, on Earth, sometime. They might marry, even, there might be children. To be raised for what? Wars and wars and more wars? Or was there another alternative? Perhaps the stars were winking brighter—

*

A hoarse shout rang through the quiet rooms. Ingersoll sat bolt upright, turned his bright eyes to Mariel, and looked down the passageway. And then they were crowding to the window as one of the men snapped off the lights in the room, and they were staring up at the pale bluish globe that hung in the sky, squinting, breathless—

And they saw the tiny, tiny burst of brightness on one side of that globe, saw a tiny whisp of yellow, cutting an arc from the edge, moving farther and farther into the black circle of space around the Earth, slicing like a thin scimitar, moving higher and higher, and then, magically, winking out, leaving a tiny, evaporating trail behind it.

"You saw it?" whispered Mariel in the darkness. "You saw it, David?"

"Yes. I saw it." Ingersoll breathed deeply, staring into the blackness, searching for a glimmer, a glint, some faint reassurance that it had not been a mirage they had seen. And then Ingersoll felt a hand in his, Tom Shandor's hand, gripping his tightly, wringing it, and when the lights snapped on again, he was staring at Shandor, tears of happiness streaming from his pale, tired eyes. "You saw it?" he whispered.

Shandor nodded, his heart suddenly too large for his chest, a peace settling down on him greater than any he had ever known in his life.

"They're coming," he said.

NOW WE ARE THREE

by Joe L. Hensley

Where are we going? What will the world be like in the days—perhaps not too distant—when we have tested and tested the bombs to the finite degree? Joe L. Hensley, attorney in Madison, Indiana, and increasingly well known in SF, returns with this challenging story of that Tomorrow.

It didn't matter that he had quit. He was still one of the guilty. He had seen it in her eyes and in the eyes of others.

JOHN RUSH smoothed the covers over his wife, tucking them in where her restless moving had pulled them away from the mattress. The twins moved beside him, their smooth hands following his in the task, their blind eyes intent on nothingness.

"Thank you," he said softly to them, knowing they could not hear him. But it made him feel better to talk.

His wife, Mary, was quiet. Her breathing was smooth, easy—almost as if she were sleeping.

The long sleep.

He touched her forehead, but it was cool. The doctor had said it was a miracle she had lived this long. He stood away from the bed for a moment watching before he went on out to the porch. The twins moved back into what had become a normal position for them in the past months: One on each side of the bed, their thin hands holding Mary's tightly, the milky blind eyes surveying something that could not be seen by his eyes. Sometimes they would stand like this for hours.

Outside the evening was cool, the light not quite gone. He sat in the rocking chair and waited for the doctor who had promised to come—and yet might not come. The bitterness came back, the self-hate. He remembered a young man and promises made, but not kept; a girl who had believed and never lost faith even when he had retreated back to the land away from everything. Long sullen silences, self-pity, brooding over the news stories that got worse and worse. And the children—one born dead—two born deaf and dumb and blind.

Worse than dead.

You helped, he accused himself. You worked for those who set off the bombs and tested and tested while the cycle went up and up beyond human tolerance—not the death level, but the level where nothing was sure again, the level that made cancer a thing of epidemic proportions, replacing statistically all of the insane multitude of things that man could do to kill himself. Even the good things that the atom had brought were destroyed in the panic that ensued. No matter that you quit. You are still

294

one of the guilty. You have seen it hidden in her eyes and you have seen it in the milky eyes of the twins.

Worse than dead.

Dusk became night and finally the doctor came. It had begun to lightning and a few large drops of rain stroked Rush's cheek. Not a good year for the farming he had retreated to. Not a good year for anything. He stood to greet the doctor and the other man with him.

"Good evening, doctor," he said.

"Mr. Rush—" the doctor shook hands gingerly, "I hope you don't mind me bringing someone along—this is Mr. North. He is with the County Juvenile Office." The young doctor smiled. "How is the patient this evening?"

"She is the same," John Rush said to the doctor. He turned to the other man, keeping his face emotionless, hands at his side. He had expected this for some time. "I think you will be wanting to look at the twins. They are by her bed." He opened the door and motioned them in and then followed.

He heard the Juvenile man catch his breath a little. The twins were playing again. They had left their vigil at the bedside and they were moving swiftly around the small living room, their hands and arms and legs moving in some synchronized game that had no meaning—their movements quick and sure—their faces showing some intensity, some purpose. They moved with grace, avoiding obstructions.

"I thought these children were blind," Mr. North said.

John smiled a little. "It is unnerving. I have seen them play like this before—though they have not done so for a long time—since my wife has been ill." He lowered his head. "They are blind, deaf, and dumb."

"How old are they?"

"Twelve."

"They do not seem to be more than eight—nine at the most."

"They have been well fed," John said softly.

"How about schooling, Mr. Rush? The teaching of handicapped children is not something that can be done by a person untrained in the field."

"I have three degrees, Mr. North. When my wife became ill and I began to care for them I taught them to read braille. They picked it up very quickly, though they showed little continued interest in it. I read a number of books in the field of teaching handicapped children . . . " He let it trail off.

"Your degrees were in physics, were they not, Mr. Rush?" Now the touch of malice came.

"That is correct." He sat down in one of the wooden chairs. "I quit working long before the witch hunts came. I was never indicted."

"Nevertheless your degrees are no longer bona fide. All such degrees have been stricken from the records." He looked down and John saw that his eyes no longer hid the hate. "If your wife dies I doubt that any court would allow you to keep custody of these children."

A year before—even six months and John would not have protested. Now he had to make the effort. "They are my children—such as they are—and I will fight any attempt to take them from me."

The Juvenile Man smiled without humor. "My wife and I had a child last year, Mr. Rush. Or perhaps I should say that a child was born to us. I am glad that child was born dead—I think my wife is even glad. Perhaps we should try again—I understand that you and your kind have left us an even chance on a normal birth." He paused for a moment. "I shall file a petition with the circuit court asking that the Juvenile Office be appointed guardians of your children, Mr. Rush. I hope you do not choose to resist that petition—feeling would run pretty high against an ex-physicist who tried to prove he *deserved* children." He turned away stiffly and went out the front door. In a little while Rush heard the car door slam decisively.

The doctor was replacing things in the black bag. "I'm sorry, John. He said he was going to come out here anyway so I invited him to come with me."

John nodded. "My wife?"

"There is no change."

"And no chance."

"There never has been one. The brain tumor is too large and too inaccessible for treatment or surgery. It will be soon now. I am surprised that she has lasted this long. I am prolonging a sure process." He turned away. "That's all I can do."

"Thank you for coming, doctor—I appreciate that." Rush smiled bitterly, unable to stop himself. "But aren't you afraid that your other patients will find out?"

The doctor stopped, his face paling slightly. "I took an oath when I graduated from medical school. Sometimes I want to break that oath, but I have not so far." He paused. "Try as I may I cannot blame them for hating you. You know why."

Rush wanted to laugh and cry at the same time. "Don't you realize that the government that punished the men I worked with for their 'criminal negligence' is the same government that commissioned them to do that work—that officials were warned and rewarned of the things that small increases in radiation might do and that such things might not show up immediately—and yet they ordered us ahead?" He stopped for a moment and put his head down, touching his work-roughened hands to his eyes.

"They put us in prison for refusing to do a job or investigated us until no one could or would trust us in civilian jobs—then when it was done they put us in prison or worse because the very things we warned them of came true."

"Perhaps that is true," the doctor said stiffly, "but the choice of refusing was still possible."

"Some of us did refuse to work," Rush said softly. "I did, for one. Perhaps you think that we alone will bear the blame. You are wrong. Sooner or later the stigma will spread to all of the sciences—and to you, doctor. Too many now that you can't save; in a little while the hate will surround you also. When we are gone and they must find something new to hate they will blame you for every malformed baby and every death. You think that one of you will find a cure for this thing. Perhaps you would if you had a hundred years or a thousand years, but you haven't. They killed a man on the street in New York the other day because he was wearing a white laboratory smock. What do you wear in your office, doctor? Hate-blind eyes can't tell the difference: Physicist, chemist, doctor . . . . We all look the same to a fool. Even if there were a cancer cure that is only a part of the problem. There are the babies. Your science cannot cope with the cause—only mine can do that."

The doctor lowered his head and turned away toward the door.

There was another thing left to say: "If the plumbing went bad in your home, doctor, you would call a plumber, for he would be the one competent to fix it." Rush shook his head slowly. "But what happens when there are no plumbers left?"

*

The children were by the bed, their hands holding those of the mother. Gently John Rush tugged those hands away and led them toward their own bed. The small hands were cold in his own and he felt a tiny feeling of revulsion as they tightened. Then the feeling slipped away and was replaced—as if a current had crossed from their hands to his. It was a warm feeling—one that he had known before when they touched him, but for which he had never been able to find mental words to express the sensation.

Slowly he helped them undress. When they were in the single bed he covered them with the top sheet. Their milky eyes surveyed him, unseeing, somehow withdrawn.

"I have not known you well," he said. "I left that to her. I have sat and brooded and buried myself in the earth until it is too late for much else." He touched the small heads. "I wish you could hear me. I wish . . . "

Outside on the road a truck roared past. Instinctively he set to hear it. The faces below him did not change.

He turned away quickly then and went back out on the porch. He filled his pipe and sat down in the old, creaky rocker. A tiny rain had begun to fall hesitantly—as if afraid of striking the sun-hardened ground.

Somewhere out there, somewhere hunted, but not found, the plumbers gathered. There had been a man—what was his name? Masser—that was it. He had been working on a way to inhibit radioactivity—speed up the half-life until they had taken the grant away. If a man can do whatever he thinks of—can he undo that which he has done?

Masser was the theoreticist—I was the applier, the one who translated equations into cold blueprints. And I was good until they . . .

They had hounded him back to the land when he quit. Others had not been so lucky. When a whole people panic then an object for their hate must be found. A naming. An immediate object. He remembered the newspaper story that began: "They lynched twelve men, twelve ex-men, in New Mexico last night . . . "

Have I been wrong? Have I done the right thing? He remembered the tiny hands in his own, the blind eyes.

Those hands. Why do they make me feel like . . .

He let his head slide back against the padded top of the rocking chair and fell into a light, uneasy sleep.

The dreams came as they had before. Tiny, inhumanly capable hands clutched at him and the sun was hot above. There was a background sound of hydrogen bombs, heard mutely. He looked down at the hands that touched and asked something of his own. The eyes were not milky now. They stared up at him, alert and questioning. *What is it you want?*

The wind tore holes in tiny voices and there was the sound of laughter and his wife's eyes were looking into his own, sorry only for him, at peace with the rest. And they formed a ring around him, those three, hands caught together, enclosing him. *What is it you are saying?*

It seemed to him that the words would come clear, but the rain came then, great torrents of it, washing all away, all sight and sound . . . .

*

He awoke and only the rain was true. The tiny rain had increased to a wind-driven downpour and he was soaked where it had blown under the eaves onto the porch.

From inside the house he heard a cry.

She was sitting upright in bed. Her eyes were open and full of pain. He went quickly to her and touched her pulse. It was faint and reedy.

"I hurt," she whispered.

Quickly, as the doctor had taught him, he made up a shot of morphine, a full quarter grain, and gave it to her. Her eyes glazed down, but did not close.

"John," she said softly, "the children . . . they . . . talk to . . . " She twisted on the bed and he held her with strong arms until the eyes closed again and her breathing became easy. He pushed the ruffled hair back from her eyes and straightened the awry sheets.

The vibration of his walking might have wakened the twins. He tiptoed to *their* bed—for they refused to be parted even in sleep.

For a second he thought that the small night-light had tricked him by shadows on shadows. He reached down to touch . . .

They were gone.

He fought down sudden panic. Where can two children, deaf and dumb and blind go in the middle of the night?

Not far.

He opened the door to the kitchen, hand-hunted for the hanging light. They were not there—nor were they on the small back porch. The panic passed critical mass, exploded out of control. He lurched back into the combination living room, bed room. He looked under all of the beds and into the small closet—everywhere that two children might conceal themselves.

Outside the rain had increased. He peered out into the lightning night. A truck horn blew ominously far down the road.

The road?

He slogged through the mud, instantly soaking as soon as he was out of shelter, not knowing or caring. Through the front yard, out to the road. He could see the lights of the truck coming from far away, two tiny points in the darkness. But no twins.

He waited helplessly while the truck rushed past, its headlights cutting holes in the darkness—fearing those lights would outline something that he had not seen. But there was nothing.

For another eternity he hunted the muddy fields, the small barn and outbuildings. The clutch of fear made him shout their names, though he knew they could not hear.

And then, suddenly, all fear was gone—like a summer squall near the sea, with the sun close behind. It was as if their hands had reached out and touched him and brought the strange feeling again.

"They are in the house," he said aloud and knew he was right.

He took time to discard muddy shoes on the porch before he opened the door. And they were there—by the mother's bed, hands clasped over hers.

He felt a tiny chill. Their eyes were watching the door as he opened it, their faces set to receive some stimuli—already set—as if they had known he was coming.

Mary was breathing softly. On her face all trace of pain had disappeared and now there was the tiny smile that had been hers long ago. Her breathing was even, but light as forgotten conversation.

Gently he tried to pry their resisting hands away from hers. The hands fought back with a terrible strength beyond normality. By sheer greater force he tore one of the twins away.

It was like releasing a bomb. Sudden pain stabbed through his body. The twin struggled in his arms, the small hands reaching blindly out for the thing they had lost. And Mary's eyes opened and all of the uncontrolled pain came back into those eyes. Her body writhed on the bed, tearing the coverings away. The twin squirmed away from his slackening hold and once again caught at the hands of the mother.

All struggle ceased. Mary's eyes shut again, the pain lines smoothed themselves, the tiny smile flowered.

He reached out and touched the small hands on each side of the mother and the feeling for which there were no words came through more strongly than ever before. Tiny voices tried to whisper within the corners of his mind, partially blotted, sometimes heard. The *real* things, the things of hate and fear and despair retreated beyond the bugle call that sounded somewhere.

"She will die," the voice said; one voice for two. "This part of her will die."

And then *her* voice came—as it had been once before when all of the world was young. "You must not be afraid, John. I have known for a long time—for they were a part of me. And you could not know for your mind was hiding and alone. I have seen . . . "

He cried out and pulled his hands away. Sound died, the room was normal again. The milky, white eyes surveyed him, the hands remained locked securely over those of the mother. The thin carven features of the children were emotionless, waiting.

He strove for rational meaning within his brain. *These are my sons—they can not see or hear or speak. They are identical twins—born with those defects.*

Take two children, blind them, make them deaf to all sound, cut away their voices. They are identical twins, facing the same environment, sharing the same heredity of blasted chromosomes. They will have intelligence and curiosity that increases as they mature. They will not be blinded by the senses—the easy way. The first thing they will discover is each other.

What else might they then discover?

It has been said that when sight is lost the sense of touch and hearing increase to almost unbelievable acuteness—Rush knew that. The blind often also develop a sense almost like radar which allows them to perceive an object ahead of them and gives them the ability to follow twisting paths.

Take one child and put him under the disability that the twins were born with. As intelligence grows so does single bewilderment. The world is a puzzling and bewildering place. Braille is a great discovery—a way to communicate with the unknown that lies beyond.

But the twins had shown almost no interest in Braille.

He reached back down for the tiny hands.

*

"Yes, we can communicate," the single voice that spoke for two said. "We have tried with you before, but we could not break through. Your mind speaks in a language we do not understand, in figures and equations that are not real to us. Those things lie all through your mind—on the surface we have sensed only your pity for us and your hate for the shadowy ones around you, the ones we do not know. It was a wall we could not climb. She is different.

"A part of her will go with us," the voice said. "There is another place that touches this one which we perceive and know more fully than this one."

The voice died away and brief pictures of a land of other dimensions beyond sight flashed in his brain. He had seen them before imperfectly in the disquieting dreams. "She must go with us for she can no longer exist here," the voice said softly. "Perhaps there are others like us to come—we do not yet know what we are or whether there will be others like us. But we must go now, before we were ready, because of her."

The mother's voice came. "You must go too. There is nothing here for you but sorrow. They will take you, John." A softness touched at him. "Please, John."

The longing was a thing of fire. To cast off the world that had already given him all of the hate and fear that he could stand, that had made him worse than a coward. To go with her.

But she no longer needed him. She was complete—as they were, only necessary to themselves.

He could not go.

During the long night he kept the vigil by the bedside; long after any need to keep it.

The twins were gone and she with them.

He could not cry for all tears seemed useless. He said a small prayer, something he had not done in years, over the cold thing left behind.

The rain had ceased outside. Somewhere out there in his world there were men trying to undo the harm that had been done, harm that he had helped to do, then retreated from. He had no right to retreat further.

Something spoke a requiem sentence in his consciousness, light as late sunset, only vaguely there. "*We are* here—we will wait for you . . . come to us . . . come . . . "

He wrote a short note for the doctor and the others who would come and hunt and go through the motions that men must live by. Perhaps the doctor might even understand.

"I have gone plumbing," the note said.

ONE OUT OF TEN

by J. Anthony Ferlaine

Television quiz programs with an aspect of having just staged a raid on Fort Knox are very much in the news these days. Certainly the prizes to be won are astronomical and the contestants scarcely less so. Step right up, little lady and tell us why your eyes look so strange! What's that? You want us to read this astounding science fantasy documentary by J. Anthony Ferlaine first? Well—perhaps we should play it safe while the flying saucer folk are watching us!

There may be a town called Mars in Montana. But little Mrs. Freda Dunny didn't come from there!

I WATCHED Don Phillips, the commercial announcer, out of the corner of my eye. The camera in front of me swung around and lined up on my set.

"... And now, on with the show," Phillips was saying. "And here, ready to test your wits, is your quizzing quiz master, Smiling Jim Parsons."

I smiled into the camera and waited while the audience applauded. The camera tally light went on and the stage manager brought his arm down and pointed at me.

"Good afternoon," I said into the camera, "here we go again with another half hour of fun and prizes on television's newest, most exciting, game, 'Parlor Quiz.' In a moment I'll introduce you to our first contestant. But first here is a special message to you mothers . . . "

The baby powder commercial appeared on the monitor and I walked over to the next set. They had the first contestant lined up for me. I smiled and took her card from the floor man. She was a middle-aged woman with a faded print dress and old-style shoes. I never saw the contestants until we were on the air. They were screened before the show by the staff. They usually tried to pick contestants who would make good show material—an odd name or occupation—or somebody with twenty kids. Something of that nature.

I looked at the card for the tip off. "Mrs. Freda Dunny," the card said. "Ask her where she comes from."

I smiled at the contestant again and took her by the hand. The tally light went on again and I grinned into the camera.

"Well, now, we're all set to go . . . and our first contestant today is this charming little lady right here beside me. Mrs. Freda Dunny." I looked at the card. "How are you, Mrs. Dunny?"

"Fine! Just fine."

"All set to answer a lot of questions and win a lot of prizes?"

"Oh, I'll win all right," said Mrs. Dunny, smiling around at the audience.

The audience tittered a bit at the remark. I looked at the card again.

"Where are you from, Mrs. Dunny?"

"Mars!" said Mrs. Dunny.

"Mars!" I laughed, anticipating the answer. "Mars, Montana? Mars, Peru?"

"No, *Mars*! Up there," she said, pointing up in the air. "The planet Mars. The fourth planet out from the sun."

My assistant looked unhappy.

I smiled again, wondering what the gag was. I decided to play along.

"Well, well," I said, "all the way from Mars, eh? And how long have you been on Earth, Mrs. Dunny?"

"Oh, about thirty or forty years. I've been here nearly all my life. Came here when I was a wee bit of a girl."

"Well," I said, "you're practically an Earthwoman by now, aren't you?" The audience laughed. "Do you plan on going back someday or have you made up your mind to stay here on Earth for the rest of your days?"

"Oh, I'm just here for the invasion," said Mrs. Dunny. "When that's over I'll probably go back home again."

"The invasion?"

"Yes, the invasion of Earth. As soon as enough of us are here we'll get started."

"You mean there are others here, too?"

"Oh, yes, there are several million of us here in the United States already—and more are on the way."

"There are only about a hundred and seventy million people in the United States, Mrs. Dunny," I said. "If there are several million Martians among us, one out of every hundred would have to be a Martian."

"One out of every ten!" said Mrs. Dunny. "That's what the boss said just the other day. 'We're getting pretty close to the number we need to take over Earth.'"

"What do you need?" I asked. "One to one? One Martian for every Earthman?"

"Oh, no," said Mrs. Dunny, "one Martian is worth ten Earthmen. The only reason we're waiting is we don't want any trouble."

"You don't look any different from us Earth people, Mrs. Dunny. How does one tell the difference between a Martian and an Earthman when one sees one?"

"Oh, we don't *look* any different," said Mrs. Dunny. "Some of the kids don't even know they're Martians. Most mothers don't tell their children until they're grown-up. And there are other children who are never told because they just don't develop their full powers."

"What powers?"

"Oh, telepathy, thought control—that sort of thing."

"You mean that Martians can read people's thoughts?"

"Sure! It's no trouble at all. It's very easy really, once you get the hang of it."

"Can you read my mind?" I asked, smiling.

"Sure!" said Mrs. Dunny, smiling up at me. "That's why I said that I'd know the answers. I'll be able to read the answers from your mind when you look at that sheet of paper."

"Now, that's hardly sporting, is it, Mrs. Dunny?" I said, turning to the camera. The audience laughed. "Everybody else has to do it the hard way and here you are reading it from my mind."

"All's fair in love and war," said Mrs. Dunny.

"Tell me, Mrs. Dunny. Why are you telling me about all this? Isn't it supposed to be a secret?"

"I have my reasons," said Mrs. Dunny. "Nobody believes me anyhow."

"Oh, I believe you, Mrs. Dunny," I said gravely. "And now, let's see how you do on the questions. Are you ready?"

She nodded.

"Name the one and only mammal that has the ability to fly," I asked, reading from the script.

"A bat," she said.

"Right! Did you read that from my mind?"

"Oh, yes, you're coming over very clear!" said Mrs. Dunny.

"Try this one," I said. "A princess is any daughter of a sovereign. What is a princess royal?"

"The eldest daughter of a sovereign," she said.

"Correct! How about this one? Is a Kodiak a kind of simple box camera; a type of double-bowed boat; or a type of Alaskan bear?"

"A bear," said Mrs. Dunny.

"Very good," I said. "That was a hard one." I asked her seven more questions and she got them all right. None of the other contestants even came close to her score, so I wound up giving her the gas range and a lot of other smaller prizes.

After we were off the air I followed the audience out into the hall. Mrs. Dunny was walking towards the lobby with an old paper shopping bag under her arm. An attendant was following her with an armful of prizes.

I caught up with her before she reached the door.

"Mrs. Dunny," I said, and she turned around. "I want to talk to you."

"When do I get the gas stove?" she said.

"Your local dealer will send it to you in a few days. Did you give them your address?"

"Yes, I gave it to them. My Philadelphia address, that is. I don't even remember my address at home any more."

"Come, now, Mrs. Dunny. You don't have to keep up that Mars business now that we're off the air."

"It's the truth and I didn't come here just by accident," said Mrs. Dunny, looking over her shoulder toward the attendant who was still holding the prizes. "I came here to see you."

"Me?"

Mrs. Dunny set the paper bag down on the floor and dug down into her pocketbook. She took out a dog-eared piece of white paper and bent it up in her hand.

"Yes," she said finally. "I came to see you. And you didn't follow me out here because you wanted to. I commanded you to come."

"Commanded me to come!" I spluttered. "What for?"

"To prove something to you. Do you see this piece of paper?" She held out the paper in her hand with the blank side toward me. "My address is on this paper. I am reading the address. Concentrate on what I'm reading."

I looked at her.

I concentrated.

Suddenly, I knew.

"Two fifty-one South Eighth Street, Philadelphia, Pennsylvania," I said aloud.

"You see, it's very easy once you get the hang of it," she said.

I nodded and smiled down at her. Now I understood. I picked up her bag and put my hand on her shoulder.

"Let's go," I said. "We have a lot to talk about."

THE CALM MAN

by Frank Belknap Long

Dip the pen of a Frank Belknap Long into a bottle of ink and the result is always bound to be a scintillating piece of brilliant imaginative science fiction. And he's done it again in the tortured story of Sally.

Sally watched the molten gold glow in the sky. Then knew she would not see her son and her husband ever again on Earth.

SALLY ANDERS had never really thought of herself as a wallflower. A girl could be shy, couldn't she, and still be pretty enough to attract and hold men?

Only this morning she had drawn an admiring look from the milkman and a wolf cry from Jimmy on the corner, with his newspapers and shiny new bike. What if the milkman was crowding sixty and wore thick-lensed glasses? What if Jimmy was only seventeen?

A male was a male, and a glance was a glance. Why, if I just primp a little more, Sally told herself, I'll be irresistible.

Hair ribbons and perfume, a mirror tilted at just the right angle, an invitation to a party on the dresser—what more did a girl need?

"Dinner, Sally!" came echoing up from the kitchen. "Do you want to be late, child?"

Sally had no intention of being late. Tonight she'd see him across a crowded room and her heart would skip a beat. He'd look at her and smile, and come straight toward her with his shoulders squared.

There was always one night in a girl's life that stands above all other nights. One night when the moon shone bright and clear and the clock on the wall went *tick tock, tick tock, tick tock*. One night when each tick said, "You're beautiful! Really beautiful!"

Giving her hair a final pat Sally smiled at herself in the mirror.

In the bathroom the water was still running and the perfumed bath soap still spread its aromatic sweet odor through the room. Sally went into the bathroom and turned off the tap before going downstairs to the kitchen.

"My girl looks radiant tonight!" Uncle Ben said, smiling at her over his corned beef and cabbage.

Sally blushed and lowered her eyes.

"Ben, you're making her nervous," Sally's mother said, laughing.

Sally looked up and met her uncle's stare, her eyes defiant. "I'm not bad-looking whatever you may think," she said.

"Oh, now, Sally," Uncle Ben protested. "No sense in getting on a high horse. Tonight you may find a man who just won't be able to resist you."

"Maybe I will and maybe I won't," Sally said. "You'd be surprised if I did, wouldn't you?"

It was Uncle Ben's turn to lower his eyes.

"I'll tell the world you've inherited your mother's looks, Sally," he said. "But a man has to pride himself on something. My defects of character are pretty bad. But no one has ever accused me of dishonesty."

Sally folded her napkin and rose stiffly from the table.

"Good night, Uncle," she said.

When Sally arrived at the party every foot of floor space was taken up by dancing couples and the reception room was so crowded that, as each new guest was announced, a little ripple of displeasure went through the men in midnight blue and the women in Nile green and lavender.

For a moment Sally did not move, just stood staring at the dancing couples, half-hidden by one of the potted palms that framed the sides of the long room.

Moonlight silvered her hair and touched her white throat and arms with a caress so gentle that simply by closing her eyes she could fancy herself already in his arms.

Moonlight from tall windows flooding down, turning the dancing guests into pirouetting ghosts in diaphanous blue and green, scarlet and gold.

Close your eyes, Sally, close them tight! Now open them! That's it . . . Slowly, slowly . . .

He came out of nothingness into the light and was right beside her suddenly.

He was tall, but not too tall. His face was tanned mahogany brown, and his eyes were clear and very bright. And he stood there looking at her steadily until her mouth opened and a little gasp flew out.

He took her into his arms without a word and they started to dance . . .

They were still dancing when he asked her to be his wife.

"You'll marry me, of course," he said. "We haven't too much time. The years go by so swiftly, like great white birds at sea."

They were very close when he asked her, but he made no attempt to kiss her. They went right on dancing and while he waited for her answer he talked about the moon . . .

"When the lights go out and the music stops the moon will remain," he said. "It raises tides on the Earth, it inflames the minds and hearts of men. There are cyclic rhythms which would set a stone to dreaming and desiring on such a night as this."

He stopped dancing abruptly and looked at her with calm assurance.

"You *will* marry me, won't you?" he asked. "Allowing for a reasonable margin of error I seriously doubt if I could be happy with any of these other women. I was attracted to you the instant I saw you."

A girl who has never been asked before, who has drawn only one lone wolf cry from a newsboy could hardly be expected to resist such an offer.

Don't resist, Sally. He's strong and tall and extremely good-looking. He knows what he wants and makes up his mind quickly. Surely a man so resolute must make enough money to support a wife.

"Yes," Sally breathed, snuggling close to him. "Oh, yes!"

She paused a moment, then said, "You may kiss me now if you wish, my darling."

He straightened and frowned a little, and looked away quickly. "That can wait," he said.

*

They were married a week later and went to live on an elm-shaded street just five blocks from where Sally was born. The cottage was small, white and attractively decorated inside and out. But Sally changed the curtains, as all women must, and bought some new furniture on the installment plan.

The neighbors were friendly folk who knew her husband as Mr. James Rand, an energetic young insurance broker who would certainly carve a wider swath for himself in his chosen profession now that he had so charming a wife.

Ten months later the first baby came.

Lying beneath cool white sheets in the hospital Sally looked at the other women and felt so deliriously happy she wanted to cry. It was a beautiful baby and it cuddled close to her heart, its smallness a miracle in itself.

The other husbands came in and sat beside their wives, holding on tight to their happiness. There were flowers and smiles, whispers that explored bright new worlds of tenderness and rejoicing.

Out in the corridor the husbands congratulated one another and came in smelling of cigar smoke.

"Have a cigar! That's right. Eight pounds at birth. That's unusual, isn't it? Brightest kid you ever saw. Knew his old man right off."

He was beside her suddenly, standing straight and still in shadows.

"Oh, darling," she whispered. "Why did you wait? It's been three whole days."

"Three days?" he asked, leaning forward to stare down at his son. "Really! It didn't seem that long."

"Where were you? You didn't even phone!"

"Sometimes it's difficult to phone," he said slowly, as if measuring his words. "You have given me a son. That pleases me very much."

A coldness touched her heart and a despair took hold of her. "It pleases you! Is that all you can say? You stand there looking at me as if I were a—a patient . . . "

"A patient?" His expression grew quizzical. "Just what do you mean, Sally?"

"You said you were pleased. If a patient is ill her doctor hopes that she will get well. He is pleased when she does. If a woman has a baby a doctor will say, 'I'm so pleased. The baby is doing fine. You don't have to worry about him. I've put him on the scales and he's a bouncing, healthy boy.'"

"Medicine is a sane and wise profession," Sally's husband said. "When I look at my son that is exactly what I would say to the mother of my son. He is healthy and strong. You have pleased me, Sally."

He bent as he spoke and picked Sally's son up. He held the infant in the crook of his arm, smiling down at it.

"A healthy male child," he said. "His hair will come in thick and black. Soon he will speak, will know that I am his father."

He ran his palm over the baby's smooth head, opened its mouth gently with his forefinger and looked inside.

Sally rose on one elbow, her tormented eyes searching his face.

"He's your child, your son!" she sobbed. "A woman has a child and her husband comes and puts his arms around her. He holds her close. If they love each other they are so happy, so very happy, they break down and cry."

"I am too pleased to do anything so fantastic, Sally," he said. "When a child is born no tears should be shed by its parents. I have examined the child and I am pleased with it. Does not that content you?"

"No, it doesn't!" Sally almost shrieked. "Why do you stare at your own son as if you'd never seen a baby before? He isn't a mechanical toy. He's our own darling, adorable little baby. *Our child!* How can you be so *inhumanly* calm?"

He frowned, put the baby down.

"There is a time for love-making and a time for parenthood," he said. "Parenthood is a serious responsibility. That is where medicine comes in, surgery. If a child is not perfect there are emergency measures which can be taken to correct the defect."

Sally's mouth went suddenly dry. "Perfect! What do you mean, Jim? Is there something *wrong* with Tommy?"

"I don't think so," her husband said. "His grasp is firm and strong. He has good hearing and his eyesight appears to be all that could be desired. Did you notice how his eyes followed me every moment?"

"I wasn't looking at his eyes!" Sally whispered, her voice tight with alarm. "Why are you trying to frighten me, Jim? If Tommy wasn't a normal, healthy baby do you imagine for one instant they would have placed him in my arms?"

"That is a very sound observation," Sally's husband said. "Truth is truth, but to alarm you at a time like this would be unnecessarily cruel."

"Where does that put you?"

"I simply spoke my mind as the child's father. I had to speak as I did because of my natural concern for the health of our child. Do you want me to stay and talk to you, Sally?"

Sally shook her head. "No, Jim. I won't let you torture me any more."

Sally drew the baby into her arms again and held it tightly. "I'll scream if you stay!" she warned. "I'll become hysterical unless you leave."

"Very well," her husband said. "I'll come back tomorrow."

He bent as he spoke and kissed her on the forehead. His lips were ice cold.

For eight years Sally sat across the table from her husband at breakfast, her eyes fixed upon a nothingness on the green-blue wall at his back. Calm he remained even while eating. The eggs she placed before him he cracked methodically with a knife and consumed behind a tilted newspaper, taking now an assured sip of coffee, now a measured glance at the clock.

The presence of his young son bothered him not at all. Tommy could be quiet or noisy, in trouble at school, or with an A for good conduct tucked with his report card in his soiled leather zipper jacket. It was always: "Eat slowly, my son. Never gulp your food. Be sure to take plenty of exercise today. Stay in the sun as much as possible."

Often Sally wanted to shriek: "Be a father to him! A real father! Get down on the floor and play with him. Shoot marbles with him, spin one of his tops. Remember the toy locomotive you gave him for Christmas after I got hysterical and screamed at you? Remember the beautiful little train? Get it out of the closet and wreck it accidentally. He'll warm up to you then. He'll be broken-hearted, but he'll feel close to you, then you'll know what it means to have a son!"

Often Sally wanted to fly at him, beat with her fists on his chest. But she never did.

You can't warm a stone by slapping it, Sally. You'd only bruise yourself. A stone is neither cruel nor tender. You've married a man of stone, Sally.

He hasn't missed a day at the office in eight years. She'd never visited the office but he was always there to answer when she phoned. "I'm very busy, Sally. What did you say? You've bought a new hat? I'm sure it will look well on you, Sally. What did you say? Tommy got into a fight with a new boy in the neighborhood? You must take better care of him, Sally."

There are patterns in every marriage. When once the mold has set, a few strange behavior patterns must be accepted as a matter of course.

"I'll drop in at the office tomorrow, darling!" Sally had promised right after the breakfast pattern had become firmly established. The desire to see where her husband worked had been from the start a strong, bright flame in her. But he asked her to wait a while before visiting his office.

A strong will can dampen the brightest flame, and when months passed and he kept saying 'no,' Sally found herself agreeing with her husband's suggestion that the visit be put off indefinitely.

Snuff a candle and it stays snuffed. A marriage pattern once established requires a very special kind of re-kindling. Sally's husband refused to supply the needed spark.

Whenever Sally had an impulse to turn her steps in the direction of the office a voice deep in her mind seemed to whisper: "No sense in it, Sally. Stay away. He's been mean and spiteful about it all these years. Don't give in to him now by going."

Besides, Tommy took up so much of her time. A growing boy was always a problem and Tommy seemed to have a special gift for getting into things because he was so active. And he went through his clothes, wore out his shoes almost faster than she could replace them.

Right now Tommy was playing in the yard. Sally's eyes came to a focus upon him, crouching by a hole in the fence which kindly old Mrs. Wallingford had erected as a protection against the prying inquisitiveness of an eight-year-old determined to make life miserable for her.

A thrice-widowed neighbor of seventy without a spiteful hair in her head could put up with a boy who rollicked and yelled perhaps. But peep-hole spying was another matter.

Sally muttered: "Enough of that!" and started for the kitchen door. Just as she reached it the telephone rang.

Sally went quickly to the phone and lifted the receiver. The instant she pressed it to her ear she recognized her husband's voice—or thought she did.

"Sally, come to the office!" came the voice, speaking in a hoarse whisper. "Hurry—or it will be too late! Hurry, Sally!"

Sally turned with a startled gasp, looked out through the kitchen window at the autumn leaves blowing crisp and dry across the lawn. As she looked the scattered leaves whirled into a flurry around Tommy, then lifted and went spinning over the fence and out of sight.

The dread in her heart gave way to a sudden, bleak despair. As she turned from the phone something within her withered, became as dead as the drifting leaves with their dark autumnal mottlings.

She did not even pause to call Tommy in from the yard. She rushed upstairs, then down again, gathering up her hat, gloves and purse, making sure she had enough change to pay for the taxi.

The ride to the office was a nightmare . . . Tall buildings swept past, facades of granite as gray as the leaden skies of mid-winter, beehives of commerce where men and women brushed shoulders without touching hands.

Autumnal leaves blowing, and the gray buildings sweeping past. Despite Tommy, despite everything there was no shining vision to warm Sally from within. A cottage must be lived in to become a home and Sally had never really had a home.

One-night stand! It wasn't an expression she'd have used by choice, but it came unbidden into her mind. If you live for nine years with a man who can't relax and be human, who can't be warm and loving you'll begin eventually to feel you might as well live alone. Each day had been like a lonely sentinel outpost in a desert waste for Sally.

She thought about Tommy . . . Tommy wasn't in the least like his father when he came racing home from school, hair tousled, books dangling from a strap. Tommy would raid the pantry with unthinking zest, invite other boys in to look at the Westerns on TV, and trade black eyes for marbles with a healthy pugnacity.

Up to a point Tommy *was* normal, *was* healthy.

But she had seen mirrored in Tommy's pale blue eyes the same abnormal calmness that was always in his father's, and the look of derisive withdrawal which made him seem always to be staring down at her from a height. And it filled her with terror to see that Tommy's mood could change as abruptly and terrifyingly cold . . .

Tommy, her son. Tommy, no longer boisterous and eager, but sitting in a corner with his legs drawn up, a faraway look in his eyes. Tommy seeming to look right through her, into space. Tommy and Jim exchanging silent understanding glances. Tommy roaming through the cottage, staring at his toys with frowning disapproval. Tommy drawing back when she tried to touch him.

Tommy, Tommy, come back to me! How often she had cried out in her heart when that coldness came between them.

Tommy drawing strange figures on the floor with a piece of colored chalk, then erasing them quickly before she could see them, refusing to let her enter his secret child's world.

Tommy picking up the cat and stroking its fur mechanically, while he stared out through the kitchen window at rusty blackbirds on the wing . . .

"This is the address you gave me, lady. Sixty-seven Vine Street," the cab driver was saying.

Sally shivered, remembering her husband's voice on the phone, remembering where she was . . . "*Come to the office, Sally! Hurry, hurry—or it will be too late!*"

Too late for what? Too late to recapture a happiness she had never possessed?

"This is it, lady!" the cab driver insisted. "Do you want me to wait?"

"No," Sally said, fumbling for her change purse. She descended from the taxi, paid the driver and hurried across the pavement to the big office building with its mirroring frontage of plate glass and black onyx tiles.

The firm's name was on the directory board in the lobby, white on black in beautifully embossed lettering. White for hope, and black for despair, mourning . . .

The elevator opened and closed and Sally was whisked up eight stories behind a man in a checkered suit.

"Eighth floor!" Sally whispered, in sudden alarm. The elevator jolted to an abrupt halt and the operator swung about to glare at her.

"You should have told me when you got on, Miss!" he complained.

"Sorry," Sally muttered, stumbling out into the corridor. How horrible it must be to go to business every day, she thought wildly. To sit in an office, to thumb through papers, to bark orders, to be a machine.

Sally stood very still for an instant, startled, feeling her sanity threatened by the very absurdity of the thought. People who worked in offices could turn for escape to a cottage in the sunset's glow, when they were set free by the moving hands of a clock. There could be a fierce joy at the thought of deliverance, at the prospect of going home at five o'clock.

But for Sally was the brightness, the deliverance withheld. The corridor was wide and deserted and the black tiles with their gold borders seemed to converge upon her, hemming her into a cool magnificence as structurally somber as the architectural embellishments of a costly mausoleum.

She found the office with her surface mind, working at cross-purposes with the confusion and swiftly mounting dread which made her footsteps falter, her mouth go dry.

Steady, Sally! Here's the office, here's the door. Turn the knob and get it over with . . .

Sally opened the door and stepped into a small, deserted reception room. Beyond the reception desk was a gate, and beyond the gate a large central office branched off into several smaller offices.

Sally paused only an instant. It seemed quite natural to her that a business office should be deserted so late in the afternoon.

She crossed the reception room to the gate, passed through it, utter desperation giving her courage.

Something within her whispered that she had only to walk across the central office, open the first door she came to to find her husband . . .

The first door combined privacy with easy accessibility. The instant she opened the door she knew that she had been right to trust her instincts. This was his office . . .

He was sitting at a desk by the window, a patch of sunset sky visible over his right shoulder. His elbows rested on the desk and his hands were tightly locked as if he had just stopped wringing them.

He was looking straight at her, his eyes wide and staring.

"Jim!" Sally breathed. "Jim, what's wrong?"

He did not answer, did not move or attempt to greet her in any way. There was no color at all in his face. His lips were parted, his white teeth gleamed. And he was more stiffly controlled than usual—a control so intense that for once Sally felt more alarm than bitterness.

There was a rising terror in her now. And a slowly dawning horror. The sunlight streamed in, gleaming redly on his hair, his shoulders. He seemed to be the center of a flaming red ball . . .

He sent for you, Sally. Why doesn't he get up and speak to you, if only to pour salt on the wounds you've borne for eight long years?

Poor Sally! You wanted a strong, protective, old-fashioned husband. What have you got instead?

Sally went up to the desk and looked steadily into eyes so calm and blank that they seemed like the eyes of a child lost in some dreamy wonderland barred forever to adult understanding.

For an instant her terror ebbed and she felt almost reassured. Then she made the mistake of bending more closely above him, brushing his right elbow with her sleeve.

*

That single light woman's touch unsettled him. He started to fall, sideways and very fast. Topple a dead weight and it crashes with a swiftness no opposing force can counter-balance.

It did Sally no good to clutch frantically at his arm as he fell, to tug and jerk at the slackening folds of his suit. The heaviness of his descending bulk dragged him down and away from her, the awful inertia of lifeless flesh.

He thudded to the floor and rolled over on his back, seeming to shrink as Sally widened her eyes upon him. He lay in a grotesque sprawl at her feet, his jaw hanging open on the gaping black orifice of his mouth . . .

Sally might have screamed and gone right on screaming—if she had been a different kind of woman. On seeing her husband lying dead her impulse might have been to throw herself down beside him, give way to her grief in a wild fit of sobbing.

But where there was no grief there could be no sobbing . . .

One thing only she did before she left. She unloosed the collar of the unmoving form on the floor and looked for the small brown mole she did not really expect to find. The mole she knew to be on her husband's shoulder, high up on the left side.

She had noticed things that made her doubt her sanity; she needed to see the little black mole to reassure her . . .

She had noticed the difference in the hair-line, the strange slant of the eyebrows, the crinkly texture of the skin where it should have been smooth . . .

Something was wrong . . . horribly, weirdly wrong . . .

Even the hands of the sprawled form seemed larger and hairier than the hands of her husband. Nevertheless it was important to be sure . . .

The absence of the mole clinched it.

Sally crouched beside the body, carefully readjusting the collar. Then she got up and walked out of the office.

Some homecomings are joyful, others cruel. Sitting in the taxi, clenching and unclenching her hands, Sally had no plan that could be called a plan, no hope that was more than a dim flickering in a vast wasteland, bleak and unexplored.

But it was strange how one light burning brightly in a cottage window could make even a wasteland seem small, could shrink and diminish it until it became no more than a patch of darkness that anyone with courage might cross.

The light was in Tommy's room and there was a whispering behind the door. Sally could hear the whispering as she tiptoed upstairs, could see the light streaming out into the hall.

She paused for an instant at the head of the stairs, listening. There were two voices in the room, and they were talking back and forth.

Sally tiptoed down the hall, stood with wildly beating heart just outside the door.

"She knows now, Tommy," the deepest of the two voices said. "We are very close, your mother and I. She knows now that I sent her to the office to find my 'stand in.' Oh, it's an amusing term, Tommy—an Earth term we'd hardly use on Mars. But it's a term your mother would understand."

A pause, then the voice went on, "You see, my son, it has taken me eight years to repair the ship. And in eight years a man can wither up and die by inches if he does not have a growing son to go adventuring with him in the end."

"Adventuring, father?"

"You have read a good many Earth books, my son, written especially for boys. *Treasure Island, Robinson Crusoe, Twenty Thousand Leagues Under The Sea.* What paltry books they are! But in them there is a little of the fire, a little of the glow of *our* world."

"No, father. I started them but I threw them away for I did not like them."

"As you and I must throw away all Earth things, my son. I tried to be kind to your mother, to be a good husband as husbands go on Earth. But how could I feel proud and strong and reckless by her side? How could I share her paltry joys and sorrows, chirp with delight as a sparrow might chirp hopping about in the grass? Can an eagle pretend to be a sparrow? Can the thunder muffle its voice when two white-crested clouds collide in the shining depths of the night sky?"

"You tried, father. You did your best."

"Yes, my son, I did try. But if I had attempted to feign emotions I did not feel your mother would have seen through the pretense. She would then have turned from me completely. Without her I could not have had you, my son."

"And now, father, what will we do?"

"Now the ship has been repaired and is waiting for us. Every day for eight years I went to the hill and worked on the ship. It was badly wrecked, my son, but now my patience has been rewarded, and every damaged astronavigation instrument has been replaced."

"You never went to the office, father? You never went at all?"

"No, my son. My stand-in worked at the office in my place. I instilled in your mother's mind an intense dislike and fear of the office to keep her from ever coming face to face with the stand-in. She might have noticed the difference. But I had to have a stand-in, as a safeguard. Your mother *might* have gone to the office despite the mental block."

"She's gone now, father. Why did you send for her?"

"To avoid what she would call a scene, my son. That I could not endure. I had the stand-in summon her on the office telephone, then I withdrew all vitality from it. She will find it quite lifeless. But it does not matter now. When she returns we will be gone."

"Was constructing the stand-in difficult, father?"

"Not for me, my son. On Mars we have many androids, each constructed to perform a specific task. Some are ingenious beyond belief—or would seem so to Earthmen."

There was a pause, then the weaker of the two voices said, "I will miss my mother. She tried to make me happy. She tried very hard."

"You must be brave and strong, my son. We are eagles, you and I. Your mother is a sparrow, gentle and dun-colored. I shall always remember her with tenderness. You want to go with me, don't you?"

"Yes, father. Oh, yes!"

"Then come, my son. We must hurry. Your mother will be returning any minute now."

Sally stood motionless, listening to the voices like a spectator sitting before a television screen. A spectator can see as well as hear, and Sally could visualize her son's pale, eager face so clearly there was no need for her to move forward into the room.

She could not move. And nothing on Earth could have wrenched a tortured cry from her. Grief and shock may paralyze the mind and will, but Sally's will was not paralyzed.

It was as if the thread of her life had been cut, with only one light left burning. Tommy was that light. He would never change. He would go from her forever. But he would always be her son.

The door of Tommy's room opened and Tommy and his father came out into the hall. Sally stepped back into shadows and watched them walk quickly down the hall to the stairs, their voices low, hushed. She heard them descend the stairs, their footsteps dwindle, die away into silence . . .

You'll see a light, Sally, a great glow lighting up the sky. The ship must be very beautiful. For eight years he labored over it, restoring it with all the shining gifts of skill and feeling at his command. He was calm toward you, but not toward the ship, Sally—the ship which will take him back to Mars!

How is it on Mars, she wondered. My son, Tommy, will become a strong, proud adventurer daring the farthest planet of the farthest star?

You can't stop a boy from adventuring. Surprise him at his books and you'll see tropical seas in his eyes, a pearly nautilus, Hong Kong and Valparaiso resplendent in the dawn.

There is no strength quite like the strength of a mother, Sally. Endure it, be brave . . .

Sally was at the window when it came. A dazzling burst of radiance, starting from the horizon's rim and spreading across the entire sky. It lit up the cottage and flickered over the lawn, turning rooftops to molten gold and gilding the long line of rolling hills which hemmed in the town.

Brighter it grew and brighter, gilding for a moment even Sally's bowed head and her image mirrored on the pane. Then, abruptly, it was gone . . .

FOUNDLING ON VENUS

by John & Dorothy de Courcy

Venus was the most miserable planet in the system, peopled by miserable excuses for human beings. And somewhere among this conglomeration of boiling protoplasm there was a being unlike the others, a being who walked and talked like the others but who was different—and afraid the difference would be discovered. You'll remember this short story.

The foundling could not have been more than three years old. Yet he held a secret that was destined to bring joy to many unhappy people.

UNLIKE GAUL, the north continent of Venus is divided into *four* parts. No Caesar has set foot here either, nor shall one—for the dank, stinging, caustic air swallows up the lives of men and only Venus may say, *I conquered.*

This is colonized Venus, where one may walk without the threat of sudden death—except from other men—the most bitterly fought for, the dearest, bloodiest, most worthless land in the solar system.

Separated by men into East and West at the center of the Twilight Zone, the division across the continent is the irregular, jagged line of Mud River, springing from the Great Serpent Range.

The African Republic holds one quarter which the Negroes exploit as best they can, encumbered by filter masks and protective clothing.

The Asians still actually try to colonize their quarter, while the Venusian primitives neither help nor hinder the bitter game of power-politics, secret murder, and misery—most of all, misery.

The men from Mars understand this better, for their quarter is a penal colony. Sleepy-eyed, phlegmatic Martians, self-condemned for minute violations of their incredible and complex mores—without guards save themselves—will return to the subterranean cities, complex philosophies, and cool, dry air of Mars when they have declared their own sentences to be at an end.

Meanwhile, they labor to extract the wealth of Venus without the bitterness and hate, without the savagery and fear of their neighbors. Hence, they are regarded by all with the greatest suspicion.

The Federated States, after their fashion, plunder the land and send screaming ships to North America laden with booty and with men grown suddenly rich—and with men who will never care for riches or anything else again. These are the fortunate dead. The rest are received into the sloppy breast of Venus where even a tombstone or marker is swallowed in a few, short weeks. And they die quickly on Venus, and often.

319

From the arbitrary point where the four territories met, New Reno flung its sprawling, dirty carcass over the muddy soil and roared and hooted endlessly, laughed with the rough boisterousness of miners and spacemen, rang with the brittle, brassy laughter of women following a trade older than New Reno. It clanged and shouted and bellowed so loudly that quiet sobbing was never heard.

But a strange sound hung in the air, the crying of a child. A tiny child, a boy, he sat begrimed by mud at the edge of the street where an occasional ground car flung fresh contamination on his small form until he became almost indistinguishable from the muddy street. His whimpering changed to prolonged wailing sobs. He didn't turn to look at any of the giant passers-by nor did they even notice him.

But finally one passer-by stopped. She was young and probably from the Federated States. She was not painted nor was she well-dressed. She had nothing to distinguish her, except that she stopped.

"Oh, my!" she breathed, bending over the tiny form. "You poor thing. Where's your mama?"

The little figure rubbed its face, looked at her blankly and heaved a long, shuddering sigh.

"I can't leave you sitting here in the mud!" She pulled out a handkerchief and tried to wipe away some of the mud and then helped him up. His clothes were rags, his feet bare. She took him by the hand and as they walked along she talked to him. But he seemed not to hear.

Soon they reached the dirty, plastic front of the Elite Cafe. Once through the double portals, she pulled the respirator from her face. The air inside was dirty and smelly but it was breathable. People were eating noisily, boisterously, with all the lusty, unclean young life that was Venus. They clamored, banged and threw things for no reason other than to throw them.

She guided the little one past the tables filled with people and into the kitchen. The door closed with a bang, shutting out much of the noise from the big room. Gingerly she sat him down on a stool, and with detergent and water she began removing the mud. His eyes were horribly red-rimmed.

"It's a wonder you didn't die out there," she murmured. "Poor little thing!"

"Hey! Are you going to work or aren't you, Jane?" a voice boomed.

A large ruddy man in white had entered the kitchen and he stood frowning at the girl. Women weren't rare on Venus, and she was only a waitress . . .

"What in the blue blazes is that!" He pointed to the child.

"He was outside," the girl explained, "sitting in the street. He didn't have a respirator."

The ruddy man scowled at the boy speculatively. "His lungs all right?"

"He isn't coughing much," she replied.

"But what are you going to do with him?" the man asked Jane.

"I don't know," she said. "Something. Tell the Patrol about him, I guess."

The beefy man hesitated. "It's been a long time since I've seen a kid this young on Venus. They always ship 'em home. Could have been dumped. Maybe his parents left him on purpose."

The girl flinched.

He grunted disgustedly, his face mirroring his thoughts. *Stringy hair . . . plain face . . . and soft as Venus slime clear through!* He shrugged. "Anyway, he's got to eat." He looked at the small figure. "Want to eat, kid? Would you like a glass of milk?" He opened a refrigerator, took out a plastic bottle and poured milk in a glass.

Chubby hands reached out for the glass.

"There, that's better," the cook said. "Pete will see that you get fed all right." He turned to the girl. "Could he belong to someone around here?"

Jane shook her head. "I don't know. I've never seen him before."

"Well, he can stay in the kitchen while you work the shift. I'll watch him."

She nodded, took an apron down from a hook and tied it around her waist. Then she patted the sober-faced youngster on his tousled head and left.

The beefy man studied the boy. "I think I'll put you over there," he said. He lifted him, stool and all, and carried him across the kitchen. "You can watch through that panel. See? That's Jane in there. She'll come back and forth, pass right by here. Is that all right?"

The little one nodded.

"Oh?" Pete raised his eyebrows. "So you *do* know what I'm saying." He watched the child for a few minutes, then turned his attention to the range. The rush hour was on and he soon forgot the little boy on the stool . . .

Whenever possible during the lunch-hour rush, Jane stopped to smile and talk to the child. Once she asked, "Don't you know where your mama and daddy are?"

He just stared at her, unblinking, his big eyes soft and sad-looking.

The girl studied him for a moment, then she picked up a cookie and gave it to him. "Can you tell me your name?" she asked hopefully.

His lips parted. Cookie crumbs fell off his chin and from the corners of his mouth, but he spoke no words.

She sighed, turned, and went out to the clattering throng with laden plates of food.

For a while Jane was so busy she almost forgot the young one. But finally people began to linger more over their food, the clinking of dishes grew quieter and Pete took time for a cup of coffee. His sweating face was haggard. He stared sullenly at the little boy and shook his head.

"Shouldn't be such things as kids," he muttered. "Nothing but a pain in the neck!"

Jane came through the door. "It gets worse all the time," she groaned. She turned to the little boy. "Did you have something to eat?"

"I didn't know what to fix for him," Pete said. "How about some beef stew? Do you think he'd go for that?"

Jane hesitated. "I—I don't know. Try it."

Pete ladled up a bowl of steaming stew. Jane took it and put it on the table. She took a bit on a spoon, blew on it, then held it out. The child opened his mouth. She smiled and slowly fed him the stew.

"How old do you think he is?" Pete asked.

The girl hesitated, opened her mouth, but said nothing.

"About two and a half, I'd guess," Pete answered himself. "Maybe three." Jane nodded and he turned back to cleaning the stove.

"Don't you want some more stew?" Jane asked as she offered the small one another spoonful.

The little mouth didn't open.

"Guess you've had enough," she said, smiling.

Pete glanced up. "Why don't you leave now, Jane. You're going to have to see the Patrol about that kid. I can take care of things here."

She stood thinking for a moment. "Can I use an extra respirator?"

"You can't take him out without one!" Pete replied. He opened a locker and pulled out a transparent facepiece. "I think this'll tighten down enough to fit his face."

She took it and walked over to the youngster. His large eyes had followed all her movements and he drew back slightly as she held out the respirator. "It won't hurt," she coaxed. "You have to wear it. The air outside stings."

The little face remained steady but the eyes were fearful as Jane slid the transparent mask over his head and tightened the elastic. It pulsed slightly with his breathing.

"Better wrap him in this," Pete suggested, pulling a duroplast jacket out of the locker. "Air's tough on skin."

The girl nodded, pulling on her own respirator. She stepped quickly into her duroplast suit and tied it. "Thanks a lot, Pete," she said, her voice slightly muffled. "See you tomorrow."

Pete grunted as he watched her wrap the tiny form in the jacket, lift it gently in her arms, then push through the door.

The girl walked swiftly up the street. It was quieter now, but in a short time the noise and stench and garishness of New Reno would begin rising to another cacophonous climax.

The strange pair reached a wretched metal structure with an askew sign reading, "El Grande Hotel." Jane hurried through the double portals, the swish of air flapping her outer garments as the air conditioning unit fought savagely to keep out the rival atmosphere of the planet.

There was no one at the desk and no one in the lobby. It was a forlorn place, musty and damp. Venus humidity seemed to eat through everything, even metal, leaving it limp, faded, and stinking.

She hesitated, looked at the visiphone, then impulsively pulled a chair over out of the line of sight of the viewing plate and gently set the little boy on it. She pulled the respirator from her face, pressed the button under the blank visiphone disk. The plate lit up and hummed faintly.

"Patrol Office," Jane said.

There was a click and a middle-aged, square-faced man with blue-coated shoulders appeared. "Patrol Office," he repeated.

"This is Jane Grant. I work at the Elite Cafe. Has anyone lost a little boy?"

The patrolman's eyebrows raised slightly. "Little boy? Did you find one?"

"Well—I—I saw one earlier this evening," she faltered. "He was sitting at the edge of the street and I took him into the cafe and fed him."

"Well, there aren't many children in town," he replied. "Let's see." He glanced at a record sheet. "No, none's reported missing. He with you now?"

"Ah—no."

He shook his head again, still looking downward. He said slowly, "His parents must have found him. If he was wandering we'd have picked him up. There is a family that live around there who have a ten-year-old kid who wanders off once in a while. Blond, stutters a little. Was it him?"

"Well, I—" she began. She paused, said firmly, "No."

"Well, we don't have any reports on lost children. Haven't had for some time. If the boy was lost his parents must have found him. Thank you for calling." He broke the connection.

Jane stood staring at the blank plate. No one had reported a little boy missing. In all the maddening confusion that was New Reno, no one had missed a little boy.

She looked at the small bundle, walked over and slipped off his respirator. "I should have told the truth," she murmured to him softly. "But you're so tiny and helpless. Poor little thing!"

He looked up at her, then around the lobby, his brown eyes resting on first one object, then another. His little chin began to quiver.

The girl picked him up and stroked his hair. "Don't cry," she soothed. "Everything's going to be all right."

She walked down a hall, fumbling inside her coveralls for a key. At the end of the hall she stopped, unlocked a door, and carried him inside. As an afterthought she locked the door, still holding the small bundle in her arms. Then she placed him on a bed, removed the jacket and threw it on a chair.

"I don't know why I should go to all this trouble," she said, removing her protective coveralls. "I'll probably get picked up by the Patrol. But *somebody's* got to look after you."

She sat down beside him. "Aren't you even a bit sleepy?"

He smiled a little.

"Maybe now you can tell me your name," she said. "Don't you know your name?"

His expression didn't change.

She pointed to herself. "Jane." Then she hesitated, looked downward for a moment. "Jana, I was called before I came here."

The little face looked up at her. The small mouth opened. "Jana." It was half whisper, half whistle.

"That's right," she replied, stroking his hair. "My, but your throat must be sore. I hope you won't be sick from breathing too much of that awful air."

She regarded him quizzically. "You know, I've never seen many little boys. I don't quite know how to treat one. But I know you should get some sleep."

She smiled and reached over to take off the rags. He pulled away suddenly.

"Don't be afraid," she said reassuringly. "I wouldn't hurt you."

He clutched the little ragged shirt tightly.

"Don't be afraid," she repeated soothingly. "I'll tell you what. You lie down and I'll put this blanket over you," she said, rising. "Will that be all right?"

She laid him down and covered the small form with a blanket. He lay there watching her with his large eyes.

"You don't look very sleepy," she said. "Perhaps I had better turn the light down." She did so, slowly, so as not to alarm him. But he was silent, watchful, never taking his eyes from her.

She smiled and sat down next to him. "Now I'll tell you a story and then you must go to sleep," she said softly.

He smiled—just a little smile—and she was pleased.

"Fine," she cried. "Well—once upon a time there was a beautiful planet, not at all like this one. There were lovely flowers and cool-running streams and it only rained once in a while. You'd like it there for it's a very nice place. But there were people there who liked to travel—to see strange places and new things, and one day they left in a great big ship."

She paused again, frowning in thought. "Well, they traveled a long, long way and saw many things. Then one day something went wrong."

Her voice was low and soft. It had the quality of a dream, the texture of a zephyr, but the little boy was still wide awake.

"Something went very, very wrong and they tried to land so they could fix it. But when they tried to land they found they couldn't—and they fell and just barely managed to save themselves. The big, beautiful ship was all broken. Well, since they couldn't fix the ship at all now, they set out on foot to find out where they were and to see if they could get help. Then they found that they were in a land of great big giants, and the people were very fierce."

The little boy's dark eyes were watching her intently but she went on, hardly noticing.

"So they went back to the broken ship and tried to decide what to do. They couldn't get in touch with their home because the radio part of the ship was all broken up. And the giants were horrible and wanted everything for themselves and were cruel and mean and probably would have hurt the poor ship-wrecked people if they had known they were there.

"So—do you know what they did? They got some things from the ship and they went and built a giant. And they put little motors inside and things to make it run and talk so that the giants wouldn't be able to tell that it wasn't another giant just like themselves."

She paused, straightening slightly.

"And then they made a space inside the giant where somebody could sit and run this big giant and talk and move around—and the giants wouldn't ever know that she was there. They made it a *she*. In fact, she was the only person who could do it because she could learn to talk all sorts of languages—that's what she could do best. So she went out in the giant suit and mingled with the giants and worked just like they did.

"But every once in a while she'd go back to the others, bringing them things they needed. And she would bring back news. That was their only hope—news of a ship which might be looking for them, which might take them home—"

She broke off. "I wonder what the end of the story will be?" she murmured.

For some time she had not been using English. She had been speaking in a soft, fluid language unlike anything ever heard on Venus. But now she had stopped speaking entirely.

After a slight pause—another voice spoke—in the same melodious, alien tongue! It said, "I think I know the end of the story. I think someone has come for you poor people and is going to take you home."

She gasped—for she realized it had not been her voice. Her artificial eyes watched, stunned, as the little boy began peeling off a skin-tight, flexible baby-faced mask, revealing underneath the face of a little man.

THE DOORWAY

by Evelyn E. Smith

A discerning critic once pointed out that Edgar Allen Poe possessed not so much a distinctive style as a distinctive manner. So startlingly original was his approach to the dark castles and haunted woodlands of his own somber creation that he transcended the literary by the sheer magic of his prose. Something of that same magic gleams in the darkly-tapestried little fantasy presented here, beneath Evelyn Smith's eerily enchanted wand.

A man may wish he'd married his first love and not really mean it. But an insincere wish may turn ugly in dimensions unknown.

"IT IS my theory," Professor Falabella said, helping himself to a cookie, "that no one ever really makes a decision. What really happens is that whenever alternative courses of action are called for, the individuality splits up and continues on two or more divergent planes, very much like the parthenogenesis of a unicellular animal . . . Delicious cookies these, Mrs. Hughes."

"Thank you, Professor," Gloria simpered. "I made them myself."

"You must give us the recipe," said one of the ladies—and the others murmured agreement, glad to get their individualities on a plane they could understand.

"Since most decisions are hardly as momentous as the individual imagines," Professor Falabella continued, "and since the imagination of the average individual is very limited, many of these different planes—or, as they are colloquially known, space-time continuums—may exist in close, even tangential relationship."

Gloria rose unobtrusively and took the teapot to the kitchen for a refill. Her husband stood by the sink moodily drinking whiskey out of the bottle so as to avoid having to wash a glass afterward.

"Bill, you're not being polite to our guests. Why don't you go out and listen to Professor Falabella?"

"I can hear him perfectly well from here," Bill muttered—and indeed the professor's mellifluous tones pervaded every nook and cranny of the thin-walled house. "Long-winded cultist! What is he a professor of, I'd like to know."

"Professor Falabella is *not* a cultist!" affirmed Gloria angrily. "He's a great philosopher."

Bill Hughes said something unprintable. "If I'd married Lucy Allison," he continued unkindly, "she'd never have filled the house with long-haired cultists on my so-called day of rest."

Gloria's soft chin trembled, and her blue eyes filled with tears. She was beginning to put on weight, he noticed. "I've been hearing nothing but Lucy Allison, Lucy Allison, Lucy Allison for the past year. Y-you said yourself she looked like a horse."

"Horses," he observed, "have sense."

He was being brutal, but he couldn't help it and didn't want to. Professor Falabella was only the most long-winded of a long series of mystics Gloria was forever dragging into the house. *The trouble with the half-educated,* he thought bitterly, *is that they seek culture in the most peculiar places.*

"I'll bet she would have let me have peace on Sunday," he said. "It just goes to show what happens when you marry a woman solely for her looks." He drained the bottle; then hurled it into the garbage pail with a resounding crash.

Gloria's shoulders shook as she filled the kettle. "I wish I'd decided to be an old maid," she sobbed.

A very unlikely possibility, he thought. Even now, shopworn as she was, Gloria could have a fairly wide range of suitors should something happen to him. She looked sexy, but how deceiving appearances could be!

Professor Falabella was still talking as Bill and Gloria emerged from the kitchen. "I believe that it is possible for an individual who exists on a limited plane of imagination to transpose from one plane to an adjacent one without difficulty . . . Great Heavens, what was that?"

Something had whisked past the archway leading into the foyer.

"Don't pay any attention," Gloria smiled nervously. "The house is haunted."

"My dear," one of the ladies offered, "I know of the most marvelous exterminator—"

"The house," Gloria assured her coldly, "really *is* haunted. We've been seeing things ever since we moved in."

And she really believed it, Bill thought. Believed that the house was haunted, that is. Of course he had seen things too—but he was enlightened enough to know that ghosts don't exist, even if you do see them.

Professor Falabella cleared his throat. "As I was saying, it is possible to send the individual through another—well, dimension, as some popular writers would have it, to one of his other spatial existences on the same temporal plane. It is merely necessary for him to find the Door."

"Nonsense!" Bill interrupted. "Holy, unmitigated nonsense!"

Every head swivelled to look at him. Gloria restrained tears with an effort.

"Brute," someone muttered.

But ridicule apparently only stimulated the professor. He beamed. "You don't believe me. Your imagination cannot extend to the comprehension of the multifariousness of space."

"Nonsense," Bill said again, but less confidently.

"I believe that I have discovered the Doorway," Professor Falabella continued, "and the Way is Open. However, most people fear to penetrate the unknown, even though it is to enter another phase of their own existence. I do admit that the shock of spatial transference, no matter how slight, combined with the concrete awareness of a previous spatial relationship would be perhaps too much for the keenly sensitive individualism . . . "

Bill opened his mouth.

"I know what you're about to say, young man!"

"You don't have to be a mind reader to know that," Bill assured him. His consonants were already a little slurred and he knew Gloria was ashamed of him. It served her right. He'd been ashamed of her for years.

Professor Falabella smiled. His teeth were very sharp and white. "Very well, Mr. Hughes, since you are a skeptic, perhaps you will not object to being the subject of our experiment yourself?"

"What kind of an experiment?" Bill asked suspiciously.

"Merely to go through the Door. Any door can become the Doorway, if it is transposed into the proper spatial dimension. That door, for instance." Professor Falabella waved his hand toward the doorway of what Gloria liked to call "Bill's study."

"You mean you just want me to open the door and go into that room?" Bill asked incredulously. "That's all?"

"That is all. Of course, you go with the awareness that it is the threshold of another plane and that you step voluntarily from this existence to an adjacent one."

"Sure," Bill said. He had just remembered there was a nearly full bottle of Calvert in the bottom drawer of the desk. "Sure. Anything to oblige."

"Very well. Go to the door, and keep remembering that of your own free will you are passing from this plane to the next."

"Look out, everybody!" Bill called raucously, as he pulled open the door. "I'm coming in on the next plane!"

No one laughed.

He stepped over the threshold, shutting the door firmly behind him. A wonderful excuse to get away from those blasted women. He'd climb out of the window as soon as he'd collected the whiskey and give them a nervous moment thinking he'd really passed into another existence. It would serve Gloria right.

For a moment, as he crossed, he had a queer sensation. Maybe there was something in what Professor Falabella said. But no, there he was in the study. All that mumbo jumbo was getting him down, that was all. He was a nervous man—only nobody appreciated the fact.

Taking a cigarette out of the pack in his pocket, he reached for the lighter on his desk. It wasn't there. Time and time again he'd told Gloria not to touch his things, and always she'd disobeyed him. Company was coming and she must tidy up. Cooking and cleaning—that was all she was good for. But this was carrying tidiness too far; she'd even removed the ashtrays.

And where did that glass block paperweight come from? He'd had a penguin in a snowstorm and he'd been happy with it. This was too much. He'd tell Gloria off. Stealing a man's penguin!

He opened the door into the living room and bumped into Lucy Allison. "Don't you think you've been in there long enough, Bill?" she asked acridly. "I'm sure your guests would appreciate catching a glimpse of you."

"Why, hello, Lucy," he said, surprised. "I didn't know Gloria had invited you—"

"Gloria, Gloria, Gloria!" Lucy cut across his sentence. "You've been talking about nothing but that dumb little blonde for months." Because of the people in the room beyond, her voice was pitched low, but her pale eyes glittered unpleasantly behind her spectacles. "I wish you had married her. You'd have made a fine pair."

Gently, caressingly, the short hairs on the back of Bill's neck rose.

"Come back in here," Lucy said, hauling him back into the living room where a number of people who had been enjoying the domestic fracas suddenly broke into loud and animated chatter. "Dr. Hildebrand was telling us all about nuclear fission."

"Can't find an ashtray," Bill muttered, seizing on something tangible. "Can't find an ashtray in the whole darn place."

"We've been over this millions of times, Bill. You know—" she smiled at the guests, a smile that carefully excluded Bill. "—I'm allergic to smoke, but I never can get my husband to remember he isn't to smoke inside the house."

"Now take the neutron, for example," Dr. Hildebrand said through a mouthful of pâté. "What is the neutron? It is only . . . What was that?"

The wraith of Gloria crossed the foyer and disappeared. Bill took a step forward; then stood still.

Lucy smiled self-consciously. "That's nothing at all. The house is merely haunted."

Everyone laughed.

"Forgot something," Bill muttered, and dashed back into the study. He yanked open the bottom drawer of the desk. Sure enough, there was a bottle of Schenley, nearly a third full. "There are some advantages," he thought as he tilted it to his lips, "in having a limited imagination."

SECOND SIGHT

by Basil Wells

Basil Wells, who lives in Pennsylvania, writes that he has been doing research concerning the keelboat age prior to and following the War of 1812 on the "locally famous section of portage-keelboat-rafting stream from Waterford down to Pittsburgh," turning from this to this grimmer future.

Then his hand caught an arm and he exerted his full strength. The entire arm tore away from its shoulder . . . .

HIS FINGERS moved over the modest packet of bills the invisible rockhound had handed to him. He smiled through the eternal night that was his own personal hell. Duggan's Hades.

"Thanks, Pete," he said gratefully. "Here, have a box of Conmos."

His sensitized fingers found the cigars, handed over a box, and he heard the nervous scuff of the other's shoes.

"This eight thousand means I can see again—for a while at least. Take 'em! It's little enough."

"Look, Duggan. I get eight hundred for selling you the ticket on the breakthrough time. Keep the cigars. You need the dough."

Feet pounded, thumping into swift inaudibility along the 10th Level's yielding walkway. His fingers caressed the crisp notes that his lucky guess on the 80th Level's tunnel juncture had won for him, plus the ten dollars, that this meager business could ill afford, it had cost to join the rockhounds' pool . . . .

But now he was free. His own man. He was released from the calculated economies of his wife. Janith knew to within a few dollars what his newsstand on the 10th Level should make. He had never been able to save the necessary thousand dollar deposit, and ten dollars an hour, that a rented super mech cost. And she would never listen to his pleas that he must see again—if only for an hour . . . .

"Waste ten or twenty dollars for nothing," she would storm. "We have all your hospital bills to pay. I need new clothes. Your stock in the stands is too small."

What she left unspoken was the fact that she must secretly have hated his engineering career in the deep levels under Appalachia, and that she was dedicated to preventing his possible return . . . .

After three years of blindness, under his wife's firm dominance, Duggan felt only hate for her. With this sudden fortune he could be independent. He could divorce her. He could rent a super mech—even return to work in the ever-deepening levels of Appalachia City!

332

First of all he must see again.

He closed up the news-and-cigar stand. With his cane's sensitive radar button pulsating beneath his fingers he hurried along the walkway toward the nearest super mech showroom. It was less than three blocks . . . .

*

"Be sure that all the contacts are against the skull and neck," the salesman was saying, his voice muffled by the mentrol hood covering Duggan's head and shoulders.

"Of course." Duggan's impatience made his voice shrill. "I've used mentrols before when inspecting cave-ins and such."

"Very well, sir." The man's voice was relieved. Probably he hated his job as much as Duggan hated his cigars and news.

Duggan tripped the switches and heard the building hum of power. An odd sort of vibration that his mind told him was purely emotional, seemed to be permeating his whole body.

Abruptly the transition was complete. He was no longer lying on the padded bench beneath the mentrol hood. He was standing erect, conscious of the retaining clamps that held him upright.

He gulped a deep draught of air into the artificial lungs that did not need oxygen and his mechanical pulse quickened.

His eyes slitted open, drinking in by degrees the mirrored mentrol booth and the pallid, fat, little man sitting beside his hooded body. He stepped out of the clamps, his sharpened senses aware of softness, and hardness, and scent, and color that human weakness so often blurs.

This super mech that was linked directly with his brain by twin mentrols was tall, chunky and gray of eye and hair. In a general way it was a duplicate of his own body, but there was no facial resemblance.

"How do you like it, sir?" The fat smile was empty, almost apologetic. "We have younger, more handsome models . . . ."

"Well enough." Duggan started donning the clothing that he had removed. "I'll want the mech for five, possibly ten, hours."

"I'll make out the slip for ten hours, sir. We'll refund any balance due you. But after ten hours . . . "

"I know. You must report the mech missing. But with my body here you can't lose."

The salesman smiled enigmatically. "We *have*," he said.

Duggan shrugged. He was impatient to be outside, feasting his starved vision on the stores and parks of the various upper levels. He might even take a lift to the Outside. It had been fifteen years ago, while their youngest son was a baby, that they had taken a weekend motor trip to the great scar that had been Manhattan. He remembered the vastness and the rawness of the uncontrolled atmosphere. It had been beautiful but also a bit terrifying. It was a ten years delayed honeymoon . . . .

And now Merle was in the rocket corps and Janith and he were like strangers.

Duggan zippered shut his gray-checked jacket and left the booth. He walked slowly, savoring every picture of the crowded passenger strips beyond the walkway, and of the fairy spans of moving walkways crossing the travel strips. The soft glow of the level's ceiling, fifty feet above, illuminated the double rows of apartment and store fronts.

It was good to see again.

Every twelfth section of the level was a park. The greenery was fresher and brighter than he remembered; the tree boles and the branches were marvels of grace and strength. He strolled along the paths, impatient to be moving on, but aching with the emerald beauty around him . . . .

He took the lifts to the upper levels. He rode the swiftest walkways and travel strips, his eyes drinking in the long-hidden sights. From an observation dome he looked out over the wooded mountain slopes of Outside, and saw the telltale ridging of rock and earth that marked the scores of hidden vehicular tubes linking Appalachia with its sister cities of Ondack and Smoky.

His five hours stretched into seven, and then, eight. Slowly a determination to keep these eyes, at whatever cost, was building within him. Always before he had agreed when Janith decided. He had been so dependent on her those first terrible weeks. But now, with this money from the breakthrough pool, he could rent a super mech—live as a man should live!

*

Duggan left the employment booth on the 20th Level, a badge on his jacket and a half-grin on his full super mech's lips.

On the records he was now Al Duggan, a second cousin from Montana. He knew that nothing in the world could bring Al further east than Ozarka. Just to be safe, however, he decided to drop Al a line to explain.

As far as his wife was concerned Merle Duggan was gone. Dead and buried. She could get a divorce if she wanted and marry that podgy, pink-skulled boss of hers at the advertising agency . . . .

"Five hundred a month," Duggan told himself. "Two-fifty for the rental, fifty for insurance—maybe fifty or so for spare parts—that leaves about a hundred and fifty for me."

He was starting at the bottom as a rock hog, a mucker, a clean-up man in the newly opened 80th Level. And his wages were the minimum union scale.

He took the lift down to the 79th Level, flashed his new badge at the guards, and took the gritty freight lift to the lowest level of the sprawling metropolis . . . .

"You Gaines Short?" he asked the lanky man bent over the littered desk in the rough plastic bubble that served as an office.

Sharp black eyes studied him—noted the bright new olive badge, and the creased, obviously new, coveralls.

"You're the new rock hog?"

"Yes, sir. Al Duggan."

"Any experience?"

"Montana—mining. Had some engineering. Worked in Ozarka on tunnels."

The lank man nodded, expressionless.

"You'll hog for a while. Later we'll see . . . . Any relation to the Duggan we lost a couple of years back?"

"We're cousins."

"Tough he couldn't see his way clear to try again." Short's lips thinned. "He may snap out of it yet . . . . We could use a few more like him."

"I—I'll talk with him," promised Duggan.

He fought back the words that wanted to pour out. Whether it was a strange sense of loyalty to his wife, or a stubborn sort of pride, he could not bring himself to speak ill of her.

"A super mech is not so bad, Duggan." Short flexed a skinny arm. "I've worn this one since a rock slide crushed my back."

"Yes, sir," Duggan agreed.

Short scribbled on a form, handed it to Duggan.

"Take this down to Ted Rusche, he's the short, dark fellow bossing the rock hogs. He'll see you're issued your tools."

Duggan nodded and turned away.

*

In the super mech hostel, on the 79th Level, Duggan shared a compartment of six sleeping and mentrol plates. All of the others were rockhounds, and three of them worked in his own clean-up gang. His immediate pusher, Ted Rusche, was a legless, dark and hairy man, much like his working super mech. Waide and Myham, the first tall and once-handsome, and the latter, bony and scarred, were both paralytics.

Duggan's share of the attendants' salary amounted to another fifty dollars monthly. He was not growing too wealthy!

"And how do you like it after three weeks, Al?" Rusche demanded from where he balanced on the cushioned sleeping plate.

Duggan stretched cramped limbs and turned his sightless face toward Rusche's voice. "Seems good to be working again, Ted," he said.

"This's your last day with us, Al. Orders from Short. He's transferring you. Office work I guess, or maybe he's making you a foreman."

Rusche's voice was curious.

"He musta found out something about you, Al. S'funny but you look awful familiar to me too. And you know more about tunnels than you let on. How about leveling with a guy?"

"Not now." Duggan was thinking of the other listening men. "After we've cleaned-up and eaten. See you in the park outside the hostel."

"Right."

Duggan's thoughts were muddled. Fingerprints probably; at every super mech hostel all guests were printed and taped, and possibly through his similar name. Short must have been suspicious from the first. And if he had come to the hostel to see Duggan's mentrol-hooded face, while Duggan worked, his identification must have been sure.

Short knew that he was Merle Duggan, and before too long Janith, and all his friends—if he had any left now—would know he had been in hiding here.

He hurried to eat and get ready for another period under the mentrol's hooded probes.

Less than half an hour later he strode out of the hostel, his super mech gleaming and clean and his jacket and shorts newly pressed. He met Rusche in the park and they headed for the lift to the upper level.

En route to the 10th Level he explained.

"I thought you looked like somebody I should know." Rusche scrubbed at his pseudo beard's coarseness. "Accident left you sort of psychoed, huh? So you was scared of the levels? Had to try coming back with a false name?"

Duggan gulped. It made a believable sort of yarn. He hadn't taken time to concoct a story . . . . Why not?

"Something like that. I guess I was badly shook, Ted."

"So now you go back to being engineer at a thousand or so, and I'm still a rock hog." Rusche shrugged. "Less headaches anyhow."

They stepped off the lift at the 10th Level and took the high speed strip toward the business section. Duggan had it in his mind to see Janith and tell her she had failed—that he was his own man again. She would be at the office. He would tell her off, and leave. And then he'd show Rusche some of the high spots of the low-number levels of Appalachia.

The darkness came about them swiftly. To Duggan it was like a return to the nightmare of sightlessness. Under their feet the racing strip faltered and stalled. They were thrown off their feet and sprawled on the fiber-ribbed squares of the checkerboarded way's surface.

"What is it?" demanded Rusche.

He fought back the panic. This was not true blindness.

"Criminals. They set off a few dozen 'midnight' bombs and try to rob banks or stores. We get these attacks quite often."

"Last long?"

"Emergency ventilation will clear it out in a couple of minutes. And the Squads will have them in half an hour. They never get very far."

They sat close together, to wait. From the walkways and stalled strips shrieks and frightened cries sounded. The sounds seemed to increase from behind them.

"This's my first time above the Twentieth Level," Rusche confided. "Thirty-five years and I never saw the Outside. I don't think I like it up this high."

"It will be over in a little while, Ted. Probably just a group of teen-agers looking for thrills." He laughed drily. "They'll end up with blanked memories and new faces like those who tried before them."

"Listen," muttered Rusche.

In the lightlessness, and above the wailing of the terrified people about them, they could hear the scuff of running feet. They were coming closer at a swift pace. In a moment the runners would collide with them!

*

Duggan's years of blindness had given him the ability to judge and gauge distance from sound. At the proper instant he pounced, his hands clamping around a body, and a second body crashed into the leader. They went down in a tangle.

He heard Rusche shouting and fists battering and the tinkle of metal or crystal on metal. He was fighting desperately, his super mech's strength overtaxed. The unseen man's hands tore at his neck and shoulder, ripping away the synthetic flesh and baring the complex framework beneath.

Then his hand caught an arm and he exerted the full strength of his mech power, until now carefully subdued. The entire arm tore away from its shoulder. And yet the wounded man continued to attack.

It was only then that he realized this must be a super mech. The criminals must have stolen one or two super mechs and were using them in this robbery.

He was ruthless, then. He wrenched away the other arm. He battered at the unseen torso. The feet of the desperate mech smashed at his knees and thighs, staggering him. Then he bore the armless torso of the mech backward and fell upon it.

The mech went limp, its mentrols blanked by the distant criminal who controlled it.

Duggan came to his feet, listening for the sound of battle between Rusche and his captive. It came from his right, faintly. About ten feet distant, he judged it. And now the emergency vents were clearing the darkness from the travel strips. Twilight faded and vision replaced it.

Rusche was sitting astride a prone body, and even as Duggan reached his side the struggling criminal's arms and legs went limp. Rusche grunted and started to stand.

"A super mech!" he said. He rubbed thoughtfully at his disarranged nose and cheeks, smoothing them again into their normal contours. "What about yours?"

"The same."

"Here's their loot, anyhow," Rusche said, holding up a small gray plastine bag.

"Drop it, Ted. We better fade out of here before the Squads arrive, too. They might think we're—"

"Not on your life, Al. We should get a reward. Pics on the newswires and tapes."

Duggan shrugged and smoothed at his own neck and face. Four red-uniformed men, their heads hidden by ovoid gas helmets, came hissing toward them along the travel strip. They rode single-wheeled cycles and their rapid-fire expoders were trained on them.

"Careful now, Ted. Let me do the talking. They like to use paralysis needles and question later."

"But—"

"I've lived up here."

The unicycles braked to a halt.

"Step over here, slow," ordered one of the Squadmen.

Duggan obeyed, careful to keep his arms rigid. Of course paralysis needles would cause this mech body no damage, but why make trouble? They *had* more destructive weapons.

"Ran into us," he said mildly. "We figured something wrong—honest men would be standing where they were. We stopped them."

The four members of the Squad were inspecting the damage.

"I guess you did," one of them said, admiringly. "You must be super mechs too?"

"That's right. I'm Duggan, Al—Merle Duggan, and this is my friend, Ted Rusche. We work on the 80th Level—rockhounds."

"Duggan?" The man's voice was suddenly strained. "Maybe you're not so clear as you pretend. A woman got in the way by accident, supposedly, of their getaway from the bank. Her name was Duggan too."

Duggan started forward, remembered the ugly expoder muzzles and backed away.

"Was her name Janith?" he demanded.

"Radio report didn't say. Contact them, Joe," he told one of the other faceless men.

"Couldn't be you hired these two to kill her and pretend the robbery?" he inquired.

"Of course not."

One of the Squad mumbled something. Duggan's interrogator dropped his weapon's muzzle.

"Woman twisted her ankle trying to get out of the way, and fell. Received a cut on her temple and is being taken to the hospital. Accidental all right."

"But her name."

"Janith."

Duggan felt a strange mingling of anger and of tenderness. The anger was directed toward the criminals.

"Could I go to her now? Rusche can fill you in on details."

"It's not—oh, all right. Regulations aren't too strict on these levels. She your sister?"

"Wife." He turned to Rusche.

"See you at the lift in about an hour," he said and headed for the advertising agency where Janith was employed.

*

"We haven't been informed as to her whereabouts yet, Mr. Duggan," the receptionist at Duffey's offices said coldly.

Duggan glared down into the carefully pretty face, the solar-lamp tan and the knife-smoothed wrinkles.

"Now see here, Blanche," he said, and spluttered impotently.

"See here yourself, Merle Duggan," the woman spat back sharply. "After all! You come running back just because she's hurt. Why didn't you come back like this a year ago?"

"I was with her a year ago."

"That wasn't you. You didn't have guts enough to rent a super mech and go back to your old job." The woman laughed. "Janith tried to insult and needle you into being a man again. And you just crawled."

"That's a lie," Duggan cried. "I begged her to let me go back. She wouldn't listen."

"That's what you say now. You don't want to remember. I know. I was here all the time. Many a time Janith has come to the office, crying, and told me how hopeless it seemed."

"You're—you're inventing all this, Blanche," he accused.

"I wish I were. Remember, Merle. Think. Be honest with yourself." Blanche put her nervous, blue-veined hand on his arm. A detached part of his brain noted how bony and brittle her hand was.

"She's loved you all these years, Merle." The tiny hand dug into his jacket sleeve. "To make you well again she risked losing your love—and she lost."

Blanche must be all of fifty, perhaps fifty-five, the analytical portion of his mind noted. Old-maidish in many ways, despite her five ex-husbands; yet so sentimental—

"It's all part of her scheme. Pretend to be the patient, long-suffering wife and then secretly forbid me to go back to the deep levels again! You don't know!"

The woman's tired eyes sparkled green. Her little fist cracked against his chest. She turned half away from him.

"But I do know. I sat up with you many nights, while Janith got a few hours of rest. You were like a baby, slobbering and whimpering in your sleep. The days were worse. You were drunk and shouting and weeping. To you blindness was the end."

Merle gulped. He could remember nothing of the sort. Only the accident and awakening in the hospital to darkness . . . . But there was a strange blankness, a hiatus in his memories, that ended with his hated job in the cigar stand. He could not recall his first day there or—

Could Blanche be telling the truth?

"You—spiteful old hag!" he shouted at her, and rushed out of the offices.

His feet pounded at the yielding softness of the walkway. The hospital was less than two blocks distant—no need to take a travel strip—and he needed the automatic motion of walking to steady his thoughts.

The forgotten months. Four months, or was it five months, ago, he was in the cigar-and-news stand. That was the day when an old acquaintance from the lower levels sold him the chance on the 80th Level's breakthrough.

That night he had begged Janith to let him rent a super mech. And she had scoffed at his wastefulness. Yet, now that he remembered it again, there had been a wistful note of hope in her voice.

Could she have been trying to fan his faint desire for sight into something more powerful and consuming—so he would become again the engineering Duggan he had been?

He had surrendered then, as he did many times afterward. Sullenly, yes, but he had surrendered. Perhaps she knew he was not ready for sight. When he refused to obey her, when he insisted on hiring a super mech—then, perhaps, she would know the cure was complete.

But that was only theory. He remembered her clearly expressed hatred for the mucking, lower-level life of a rockhound. Always his hatred for her grew as she spoke of his work . . . .

She had never expressed herself in that way before the accident. She had gone with him on many exploratory trips into the caverns that the lower levels of Appalachia cut across. And she had enjoyed the experience—he was sure of that.

Remember! Think back. Back before the cigars and papers. Back to the days and months after the accident. It hurt to think. His temples, here on the mentrol-hooded sleeping plate, were pounding irregularly . . . .

Huddling in a bed, knees drawn up and head tucked in, trying to gain somehow the safety that an infant once knew. Janith's voice, soft and understanding, and the acid of panic that set his lips to mumbling meaningless jargon . . . .

Why had Janith not sent him to the medical centers for mental clearing and re-education as was done with all cases of psychoed abnormals? The answer was with him. She loved him as he was, Merle Duggan—not as a new personality in her husband's body.

Artificial amnesia automatically dissolves all marriage partnerships. She had not wanted that. Instead she had three years of hell . . . .

Striking out at emptiness, his fists contacting soft flesh, and the pained cry, swiftly suppressed, of Janith. His voice, cursing and high-pitched, as he fought the straps that now were restraining his sightless body. The bite of a needle and gradual dissolution of feeling . . . .

Memory was coming reluctantly back to Duggan. This was not the self-imagined visionings of an abused helpless man. These memories were true. He had fought against all mental therapy and turned from those who loved him.

Now the hospital entrance was before him. He paused for a moment and then went inside. The automatic hush of the door shutting out the muted street sounds was all too familiar.

"Mrs. Janith Duggan," he told the crisply white woman at the desk.

"Room 212, second floor."

"Thank you."

*

He used the steps in preference to the lift. He needed more time to think—would he ever find enough time?

Undoubtedly, now, Janith's love for him was dead. His desertion of her must have finished the dissolution of their marriage. It had been cowardly—he should have faced her and declared what he was going to do and what she could do.

These past weeks, working with the rock hogs, had been invaluable. They had restored something of his self-esteem.

The second floor. Pastel bare walls and soft voices. The odors. 208 and opposite, 209. A wheelchair, propelled by a timidly smiling white-haired woman. He nodded automatically.

210. What could he say to her? That he was sorry she was hurt and that he was such a fool? And then back to the super mech hostel and the five other cripples who shared the room?

212. The door ajar. A private room. He was glad of that. The headache was more violent now—there was a bitter taste in his mouth as his super mech entered the room.

She was alone, looking tiny and helpless on the high bed. To him, after three years, she was more beautiful than he remembered, even though the pure whiteness of her once-graying hair startled him.

"Janith," he said uncertainly.

She turned her head, curiosity in her expression, and then understanding came. There was no mistaking the warmth and welcome that came into her eyes. She held out her arms.

"Duggy," she commanded, "come here."

And he knew then, without ever being told, that his revolt and flight had all been part of the therapy, and Janith had known all the time where he had been . . . .

LIGHTER THAN YOU THINK

by Nelson Bond

It's possible that you won't agree with us that Pat Pending's latest adventure is a delightful story—possible IF you haven't been used to laughing in recent years. Blue Book printed more than a dozen of these stories by Nelson Bond about the "greatest inventulator of all time".

Sandy's eyes needed only jet propulsion to become flying saucers. Wasn't Pat wonderful? she beamed, at everyone.

SOME JOKER in the dear, dead days now virtually beyond recall won two-bit immortality by declaring that, "What this country needs is a good five-cent cigar."

Which is, of course, Victorian malarkey. What this country *really* needs is a good five-cent nickel. Or perhaps a good cigar-shaped spaceship. There's a fortune waiting somewhere out in space for the man who can go out there and claim it. A fortune! And if you think I'm just talking through my hat, lend an ear . . .

Joyce started the whole thing. Or maybe I did when for the umpteenth time I suggested she should marry me. She smiled in a way that showed she didn't disapprove of my persistence, but loosed a salvo of devastating negatives.

"No deal," she crisped decisively. "Know why? No dough!"

"But, sugar," I pleaded, "two can live as cheaply as one—"

"This is true," replied Joyce, "only of guppies. Understand, Don, I don't mind changing my name from Carter to Mallory. In fact, I'd rather like to. But I have no desire whatever to be known to the neighbors as 'that poor little Mrs. Mallory in last year's coat.'

"I'll marry you," she continued firmly, "when, as and if you get a promotion."

Her answer was by no stretch of the imagination a reason for loud cheers, handsprings and cartwheels. Because I'm a Federal employee. The United States Patent Office is my beat. There's one nice thing to be said about working for the bewhiskered old gentleman in the star-spangled stovepipe and striped britches: it's permanent. Once you get your name inscribed on the list of Civil Service employees it takes an act of Congress to blast it off again. And of course I don't have to remind you how long it takes *that* body of vote-happy windbags to act. Terrapins in treacle are greased lightning by comparison.

But advancement is painfully slow in a department where discharges are unheard of and resignations rare. When I started clerking for this madhouse I was assistant to the assistant Chief Clerk's assistant. Now, ten years later, by dint of mighty effort and a cultivated facility for avoiding Senatorial investigations, I've succeeded in losing only one of those redundant adjectives.

343

Being my secretary, Joyce certainly realized this. But women have a remarkable ability to separate business and pleasure. So:

"A promotion," she insisted. "Or at least a good, substantial raise."

"In case you don't know it," I told her gloomily, "you are displaying a lamentably vulgar interest in one of life's lesser values. Happiness, not money, should be man's chief goal."

"What good is happiness," demanded Joyce, "if you can't buy money with it?"

"Why hoard lucre?" I sniffed. "You can't take it with you."

"In that case," said Joyce flatly, "I'm not going. There's no use arguing, Don. I've made up my mind—"

At this moment our dreary little impasse was ended by a sudden tumult outside my office. There was a squealing shriek, the shuffle of footsteps, the pounding of fists upon my door. And over all the shrill tones of an old, familiar voice high-pitched in triumph.

"Let me in! I've got to see him instantaceously. This time I've got it; I've absolutely *got* it!"

Joyce and I gasped, then broke simultaneously for the door as it flew open to reveal a tableau resembling the Laocoon group *sans* snake and party of the third part. Back to the door and struggling valiantly to defend it stood the receptionist, Miss Thomas. Held briefly but volubly at bay was a red-thatched, buck-toothed individual—and I *do* mean individual!—with a face like the map of Eire, who stopped wrestling as he saw us, and grinned delightedly.

"Hello, Mr. Mallory," he said. "Hi, Miss Joyce."

"Pat!" we both cried at once. "Pat Pending!"

*

Miss Thomas, a relative newcomer to our bailiwick, seemed baffled by the warmth of our greeting. She entered the office with our visitor, and as Joyce and I pumphandled him enthusiastically she asked, "You—you *know* this gentleman, Mr. Mallory?"

"I should say we do!" I chortled. "Pat, you old naughty word! Where on earth have you been hiding lately?"

"Surely you've heard of the great Patrick Pending, Miss Thomas?" asked Joyce.

"Pending?" faltered Miss Thomas. "I seem to have heard the name. Or seen it somewhere—"

Pat beamed upon her companionably. Stepping to my desk, he up-ended the typewriter and pointed to a legend in tiny letters stamped into the frame: *Reg. U.S. Pat. Off.—Pat. Pending.*

"Here, perhaps?" he suggested. "I invented this. And the airplane, and the automobile, and—oh, ever so many things. You'll find my name inscribed on every one.

"I," he announced modestly, "am Pat Pending—the greatest inventulator of all time."

Miss Thomas stared at me goggle-eyed.

"*Is* he?" she demanded. "I mean—*did* he?"

I nodded solemnly.

"Not only those, but a host of other marvels. The bacular clock, the transmatter, the predictograph—"

Miss Thomas turned on Pat a gaze of fawning admiration. "How wonderful!" she breathed.

"Oh, nothing, really," said Pat, wriggling.

"But it is! Most of the things brought here are so absurd. Automatic hat-tippers, self-defrosting galoshes, punching bags that defend themselves—" Disdainfully she indicated the display collection of screwball items we call our Chamber of Horrors. "It's simply marvelous to meet a man who has invented things really worth while."

Honestly, the look in her eyes was sickening. But was Pat nauseated? Not he! The big goon was lapping it up like a famished feline. His simpering smirk stretched from ear to there as he murmured, "Now, Miss Thomas—"

"Sandra, Mr. Pending," she sighed softly. "To you just plain . . . Sandy. Please?"

"Well, Sandy—" Pat gulped.

I said disgustedly, "Look, you two—break it up! Love at first sight is wonderful in books, but in a Federal office I'm pretty sure it's unconstitutional, and it *may* be subversive. Would you mind coming down to earth? Pat, you barged in here squalling about some new invention. Is that correct?"

With an effort Pat wrenched his gaze from his new-found admirer and nodded soberly.

"That's right, Mr. Mallory. And a great one, too. One that will revolutionate the world. Will you give me an applicaceous form, please? I want to file it immediately."

"Not so fast, Pat. You know the routine. What's the nature of this remarkable discovery?"

"You may write it down," said Pat grandiloquently, "as Pat Pending's lightening rod."

I glanced at Joyce, and she at me, then both of us at Pending.

"But, Pat," I exclaimed, "that's ridiculous! Ben Franklin invented the lightning rod two hundred years ago."

"I said *lightening*," retorted my redheaded friend, "not *lightning*. My invention doesn't conduct electricity *to* the ground, but *from* it." He brandished a slim baton which until then I had assumed to be an ordinary walking-stick. "With this," he claimed, "I can make things weigh as much or as little as I please!"

The eyes of Sandy Thomas needed only jet propulsion to become flying saucers.

"Isn't he wonderful, Mr. Mallory?" she gasped.

But her enthusiasm wasn't contagious. I glowered at Pending coldly.

"Oh, come now, Pat!" I scoffed. "You can't really believe that yourself. After all, there *are* such things as basic principles. Weight is not a variable factor. And so far as I know, Congress hasn't repealed the Law of Gravity."

Pat sighed regretfully.

"You're always so hard to convince, Mr. Mallory," he complained. "But—oh, well! Take this."

He handed me the baton. I stared at it curiously. It looked rather like a British swagger stick: slim, dainty, well balanced. But the ornamental gadget at its top was not commonplace. It seemed to be a knob or a dial of some kind, divided into segments scored with vernier markings. I gazed at Pending askance.

"Well, Pat? What now?"

"How much do you weigh, Mr. Mallory?"

"One sixty-five," I answered.

"You're sure of that?"

"I'm not. But my bathroom scales appeared to be. This morning. Why?"

"Do you think Miss Joyce could lift you?"

I said thoughtfully, "Well, that's an idea. But I doubt it. She won't even let me try to support *her*."

"I'm serious, Mr. Mallory. Do you think she could lift you with one hand?"

"Don't be silly! Of course not. Nor could you."

"There's where you're wrong," said Pending firmly. "She can—and will."

He reached forward suddenly and twisted the metal cap on the stick in my hands. As he did so, I loosed a cry of alarm and almost dropped the baton. For instantaneously I experienced a startling, flighty giddiness, a sudden loss of weight that made me feel as if my soles were treading on sponge rubber, my shoulders sprouting wings.

"Hold on to it!" cried Pat. Then to Joyce, "Lift him, Miss Joyce."

Joyce faltered, "How? Like th-this?" and touched a finger to my midriff. Immediately my feet left the floor. I started flailing futilely to trample six inches of ozone back to the solid floorboards. To no avail. With no effort whatever Joyce raised me high above her head until my dazed dome was shedding dandruff on the ceiling!

"Well, Mr. Mallory," said Pat, "do you believe me now?"

"Get me down out of here!" I howled. "You *know* I can't stand high places!"

"You now weigh less than ten pounds—"

"Never mind the statistics. I feel like a circus balloon. How do I get down again?"

"Turn the knob on the cane," advised Pat, "to your normal weight. Careful, now! *Not so fast!*"

His warning came too late. I hit the deck with a resounding thud, and the cane came clattering after. Pat retrieved it hurriedly, inspected it to make sure it was not damaged. I glared at him as I picked myself off the floor.

"You might show some interest in *me*," I grumbled. "I doubt if that stick will need a liniment rubdown tonight. Okay, Pat. You're right and I'm wrong, as you usually are. That modern variation of a witch's broomstick *does* operate. Only—how?"

"That dial at the top governs weight," explained Pat. "When you turn it—"

"Skip that. I know how it is operated. I want to know what makes it work?"

"Well," explained Pat, "I'm not certain I can make it clear, but it's all tied in with the elemental scientific problems of mass, weight, gravity and electric energy. What *is* electricity, for example—"

"I used to know," I frowned. "But I forget."

Joyce shook her head sorrowfully.

"Friends," she intoned, "let us all bow our heads. This is a moment of great tragedy. The only man in the world who ever knew what electricity is—and he has forgotten!"

"That's the whole point," agreed Pending. "No one knows what electricity really is. All we know is how to use it. Einstein has demonstrated that the force of gravity and electrical energy are kindred; perhaps different aspects of a common phenomenon. That was my starting point."

"So this rod, which enables you to defy the law of gravity, is electrical?"

"Electricaceous," corrected Pat. "You see, I have transmogrified the polarifity of certain ingredular cellulations. A series of disentrigulated helicosities, activated by hypermagnetation, set up a disruptular wave motion which results in—counter-gravity!"

And there you are! Ninety-nine percent of the time Pat Pending talks like a normal human being. But ask him to explain the mechanism of one of his inventions and linguistic hell breaks loose. He begins jabbering like a schizophrenic parrot reading a Sanskrit dictionary backward! I sighed and surrendered all hope of ever actually learning *how* his great new discovery worked. I turned my thoughts to more important matters.

"Okay, Pat. We'll dismiss the details as trivial and get down to brass tacks. What is your invention used for?"

"Eh?" said the redhead.

"It's not enough that an idea is practicable," I pointed out. "It must also be practical to be of any value in this frenzied modern era. What good is your invention?"

"What good," demanded Joyce, "is a newborn baby?"

"Don't change the subject," I suggested. "Or come to think of it, maybe you should. At the diaper level, life is just one damp thing after another. But how to turn Pat's brainchild into cold, hard cash—that's the question before the board now.

"Individual flight *a la* Superman? No dice. I can testify from personal experience that once you get up there you're completely out of control. And I can't see any sense in humans trying to fly with jet flames scorching their base of operations.

"Elevators? Derricks? Building cranes? Possible. But lifting a couple hundred pounds is one thing. Lifting a few tons is a horse of a different color.

"No, Pat," I continued, "I don't see just how—"

Sandy Thomas squeaked suddenly and grasped my arm.

"That's it, Mr. Mallory!" she cried. "That's it!"

"Huh? What's what?"

"You wanted to know how Pat could make money from his invention. You've just answered your own question."

"I have?"

"Horses! Horse racing, to be exact. You've heard of handicaps, haven't you?"

"I'm overwhelmed with them," I nodded wearily. "A secretary who repulses my honorable advances, a receptionist who squeals in my ear—"

"Listen, Mr. Mallory, what's the last thing horses do before they go to the post?"

"Check the tote board," I said promptly, "to find out if I've got any money on them. Horses hate me. They've formed an equine conspiracy to prove to me the ancient adage that a fool and his money are soon parted."

"Wait a minute!" chimed in Joyce thoughtfully. "I know what Sandy means. They weigh in. Is that right?"

"Exactly! The more weight a horse is bearing, the slower it runs. That's the purpose of handicapping. But if a horse that was supposed to be carrying more than a hundred pounds was actually only carrying *ten*—Well, you see?"

Sandy paused, breathless. I stared at her with a gathering respect.

"Never underestimate the power of a woman," I said, "when it comes to devising new and ingenious methods of perpetrating petty larceny. There's only one small fly in the ointment, so far as I can see. How do we convince some racehorse owner he should become a party to this gentle felony?"

"Oh, you don't have to," smiled Sandy cheerfully. "I'm already convinced."

"You? You own a horse?"

"Yes. Haven't you ever heard of Tapwater?"

"Oh, sure! That drip's running all the time!"

Joyce tossed me a reproving glance.

"This is a matter of gravity, Donald," she stated, "and you keep treating it with levity. Sandy, do you *really* own Tapwater? He's the colt who won the Monmouth Futurity, isn't he?"

"That's right. And four other starts this season. That's been our big trouble. He shows such promise that the judges have placed him under a terrific weight handicap. To run in next week's Gold Stakes, for instance, he would have to carry 124 pounds. I was hesitant to enter him because of that. But with Pat's new invention—" She turned to Pat, eyes glowing—"he could enter and win!"

Pat said uncertainly, "I don't know. I don't like gambling. And it doesn't seem quite ethical, somehow—"

I asked Sandy, "Suppose he ran carrying 124. What would be the probable odds?"

"High," she replied, "*Very* high. Perhaps as high as forty to one."

"In that case," I decided, "it's not only ethical, it's a moral obligation. If you're opposed to gambling, Pat, what better way can you think of to put the parimutuels out of business?"

"And besides," Sandy pointed out, "this would be a wonderful opportunity to display your new discovery before an audience of thousands. Well, Pat? What do you say?"

Pat hesitated, caught a glimpse of Sandy's pleading eyes, and was lost.

"Very well," he said. "We'll do it. Mr. Mallory, enter Tapwater in the Gold Stakes. We'll put on the most spectaceous exhibition in the history of gambilizing!"

*

Thus it was that approximately one week later our piratical little crew was assembled once again, this time in the paddock at Laurel. In case you're an inland aborigine, let me explain that Laurel race track (from the township of the same name) is where horse fanciers from the District of Columbia go to abandon their Capitol and capital on weekends.

We were briefing our jockey—a scrawny youth with a pair of oversized ears—on the use of Pat's lightening rod. Being short on gray matter as well as on stature, he wasn't getting it at all.

"You mean," he said for the third or thirty-third time, "you don't want I should *hit* the nag with this bat?"

"Heavens, no!" gasped Pat, blanching. "It's much too delicate for that."

"Don't fool yourself, mister. Horses can stand a lot of leather."

"Not the horse, stupid," I said. "The bat. This is the only riding crop of its kind in the world. We don't want it damaged. All you have to do is *carry* it. We'll do the rest."

"How about setting the dial, Don?" asked Joyce.

"Pat will do that just before the horses move onto the track. Now let's get going. It's weigh-in time."

We moved to the scales with our rider. He stepped aboard the platform, complete with silks and saddle, and the spinner leaped to a staggering 102, whereupon the officials started gravely handing him little leather sacks.

"What's this?" I whispered to Sandy. "Prizes for malnutrition? He must have won all the blackjacks east of the Mississippi."

"The handicap," she whispered back. "Lead weights at one pound each."

"If he starts to lose," I ruminated, "they'd make wonderful ammunition—"

"One hundred and twenty-four," announced the chief weigher-inner. "Next entry!"

We returned to Tapwater. The jockey fastened the weights to his gear, saddled up and mounted. From the track came the traditional bugle call. Sandy nodded to Pat.

"All right, Pat. Now!"

Pending twisted the knob on his lightening rod and handed the stick to the jockey. The little horseman gasped, rose three inches in his stirrups, and almost let go of the baton.

"H-hey!" he exclaimed. "I feel funny. I feel—"

"Never mind that," I told him. "Just you hold on to that rod until the race is over. And when you come back, give it to Pat immediately. Understand?"

"Yes. But I feel so—so lightheaded—"

"That's because you're featherbrained," I advised him. "Now, get going. Giddyap, Dobbin!"

I patted Tapwater's flank, and so help me Newton, I think that one gentle tap pushed the colt half way to the starting gate! He pattered across the turf with a curious bouncing gait as if he were running on tiptoe. We hastened to our seats in the grandstand.

"Did you get all the bets down?" asked Joyce.

I nodded and displayed a deck of ducats. "It may not have occurred to you, my sweet," I announced gleefully, "but these pasteboards are transferrable on demand to rice and old shoes, the sweet strains of *Oh, Promise Me!* and the scent of orange blossoms. You insisted I should have a nest egg before you would murmur, 'I do'? Well, after this race these tickets will be worth—" I cast a swift last glance at the tote board's closing odds, quoting Tapwater at 35 to 1—"approximately seventy thousand dollars!"

"Donald!" gasped Joyce. "You didn't bet all your savings?"

"Every cent," I told her cheerfully. "Why not?"

"But if something should go wrong! If Tapwater should lose!"

"He won't. See what I mean?"

For even as we were talking, the bell jangled, the crowd roared, and the horses were off. Eight entries surged from the starting gate. And already one full length out in front pranced the weight-free, lightfoot Tapwater!

At the quarter post our colt had stretched his lead to three lengths, and I shouted in Pending's ear, "How much does that jockey weigh, anyway?"

"About six pounds," said Pat. "I turned the knob to cancel one eighteen."

At the half, all the other horses could glimpse of Tapwater was heels. At the three-quarter post he was so far ahead that the jockey must have been lonely. As he rounded into the stretch I caught a binocular view of his face, and he looked dazed and a little frightened. He wasn't actually *riding* Tapwater. The colt was simply skimming home, and he was holding on for dear life to make sure he didn't blow off the horse's back. The result was a foregone conclusion, of course. Tapwater crossed the finish line nine lengths ahead, setting a new track record.

The crowd went wild. Over the hubbub I clutched Pat's arm and bawled, "I'll go collect our winnings. Hurry down to the track and swap that lightening rod for the real bat we brought along. He'll have to weigh out again, you know. Scoot!"

The others vanished paddockward as I went for the big payoff. It was dreary at the totalizer windows. I was one of a scant handful who had bet on Tapwater, so it took no time at all to scoop into the valise I had brought along the seventy thousand bucks in crisp, green lettuce which an awed teller passed across the counter. Then I hurried back to join the others in the winner's circle, where bedlam was not only reigning but pouring. Flashbulbs were popping all over the place, cameramen were screaming for just one more of the jockey, the owner, the fabulous Tapwater. The officials were vainly striving to quiet the tumult so they could award the prize. I found Pending worming his way out of the heart of the crowd.

"Did you get it?" I demanded.

He nodded, thrust the knobbed baton into my hand.

"You substituted the normal one?"

Again he nodded. Hastily I thrust the lightening rod out of sight into my valise, and we elbowed forward to share the triumphant moment. It was a great experience. I felt giddy with joy; I was walking on little pink clouds of happiness. Security was mine at last. And Joyce, as well.

"Ladies and gentlemen!" cried the chief official. "Your attention, please! Today we have witnessed a truly spectacular feat: the setting of a new track record by a champion racing under a tremendous handicap. I give you a magnificent racehorse—*Tapwater*!"

"That's right, folks!" I bawled, carried away by the excitement. "Give this little horse a great big hand!"

Setting the example, I laid down the bag, started clapping vigorously. From a distance I heard Pat Pending's agonized scream.

"Mr. Mallory—the suitcase! Grab it!"

I glanced down, belatedly aware of the danger of theft. But too late. The bag had disappeared.

"Hey!" I yelled. "Who swiped my bag? Police!"

"Up there, Mr. Mallory!" bawled Pat. "Jump!"

I glanced skyward. Three feet above my head and rising swiftly was the valise in which I had cached not only our winnings but Pat's gravity-defying rod! I leaped—but in vain. I was *still* making feeble, futile efforts to make like the moon-hurdling nursery rhyme cow when quite a while later two strong young men in white jackets came and jabbed me with a sedative . . .

*

Later, when time and barbiturates had dulled the biting edge of my despair, we assembled once again in my office and I made my apologies to my friends.

"It was all my fault," I acknowledged. "I should have realized Pat hadn't readjusted the rod when I placed it in my bag. It felt lighter. But I was so excited—"

"It was *my* fault," mourned Pat, "for not changing it immediately. But I was afraid someone might see me."

"Perhaps if we hired an airplane—?" I suggested.

Pat shook his head.

"No, Mr. Mallory. The rod was set to cancel 118 pounds. The bag weighed less than twenty. It will go miles beyond the reach of any airplane before it settles into an orbit around earth."

"Well, there goes my dreamed-of fortune," I said sadly. "Accompanied by the fading strains of an unplayed wedding march. I'm sorry, Joyce."

"Isn't there one thing you folks are overlooking?" asked Sandy Thomas. "My goodness, you'd think we had lost our last cent just because that little old bag flew away!"

"For your information," I told her, "that is precisely what happened to me. My entire bank account vanished into the wild blue yonder. And some of Pat's money, too."

"But have you forgotten," she insisted, "that we *won* the race? Of course the track officials were a wee bit suspicious when your suitcase took off. But they couldn't prove anything. So they paid me the Gold Stakes prize. If we split it four ways, we all make a nice little profit.

"Or," she added, "if you and Joyce want to make yours a double share, we could split it three ways.

"Or," she continued hopefully, "if Pat wants to, we could make *two* double shares, and split it fifty-fifty?"

From the look in Pat's eyes I knew he was stunned by this possibility. And from the look in hers, I felt she was going to make every effort to take advantage of his bewilderment.

So, as I said before, what this country needs is a good cigar-shaped spaceship. There's a fortune waiting somewhere out in space for the man who can go out there and claim it. Seventy thousand bucks in cold, hard cash.

Indubitatiously!

THE LONG VOYAGE

by Carl Jacobi

When we published Carl Jacobi's last story we had no assurance he would be with us so soon again. For when a uniquely gifted science-fantasy writer becomes radio-active on the entertainment meter and goes voyaging into the unknown, he may be gone from the world we know for as long as yesterday's tomorrow. But Carl Jacobi has not only returned almost with the speed of light—he has brought with him shining new nuggets of wonder and surmise.

The secret lay hidden at the end of nine landings, and Medusa-dark was one man's search for it—in the strangest journey ever made.

A SOFT gentle rain began to fall as we emerged from the dark woods and came out onto the shore. There it was, the sea, stretching as far as the eye could reach, gray and sullen, and flecked with green-white froth. The blue *hensorr* trees, crowding close to the water's edge, were bent backward as if frightened by the bleakness before them. The sand, visible under the clear patches of water, was a bleached white like the exposed surface of a huge bone.

We stood there a moment in silence. Then Mason cleared his throat huskily.

"Well, here goes," he said. "We'll soon see if we have any friends about."

He unslung the packsack from his shoulders, removed its protective outer shield and began to assemble the organic surveyor, an egg-shaped ball of white carponium secured to a segmented forty-foot rod. While Brandt and I raised the rod with the aid of an electric fulcrum, Mason carefully placed his control cabinet on a piece of outcropping rock and made a last adjustment.

The moment had come. Even above the sound of the sea, you could hear the strained breathing of the men. Only Navigator Norris appeared unconcerned. He stood there calmly smoking his pipe, his keen blue eyes squinting against the biting wind.

Mason switched on the speaker. Its high-frequency scream rose deafeningly above us and was torn away in unsteady gusts. He began to turn its center dial, at first a quarter circle, and then all the way to the final backstop of the calibration. All that resulted was a continuation of that mournful ululation like a wail out of eternity.

Mason tried again. With stiff wrists he tuned while perspiration stood out on his forehead, and the rest of us crowded close.

"It's no use," he said. "This pickup failure proves there isn't a vestige of animal life on Stragella—on this hemisphere of the planet, at least."

Navigator Norris took his pipe from his mouth and nodded. His face was expressionless. There was no indication in the man's voice that he had suffered another great disappointment, his sixth in less than a year.

"We'll go back now," he said, "and we'll try again. There must be some planet in this system that's inhabited. But it's going to be hard to tell the women."

Mason let the surveyor rod down with a crash. I could see the anger and resentment that was gathering in his eyes. Mason was the youngest of our party and the leader of the antagonistic group that was slowly but steadily undermining the authority of the Navigator.

This was our seventh exploratory trip after our sixth landing since entering the field of the sun Ponthis. Ponthis with its sixteen equal-sized planets, each with a single satellite. First there had been Coulora; then in swift succession, Jama, Tenethon, Mokrell, and R-9. And now Stragella. Strange names of strange worlds, revolving about a strange star.

It was Navigator Norris who told us the names of these planets and traced their positions on a chart for us. He alone of our group was familiar with astrogation and cosmography. He alone had sailed the spaceways in the days before the automatic pilots were installed and locked and sealed on every ship.

A handsome man in his fortieth year, he stood six feet three with broad shoulders and a powerful frame. His eyes were the eyes of a scholar, dreamy yet alive with depth and penetration. I had never seen him lose his temper, and he governed our company with an iron hand.

He was not perfect, of course. Like all Earthmen, he had his faults. Months before he had joined with that famed Martian scientist, Ganeth-Klae, to invent that all-use material, *Indurate*, the formula for which had been stolen and which therefore had never appeared on the commercial market. Norris would talk about that for hours. If you inadvertently started him on the subject a queer glint would enter his eyes, and he would dig around in his pocket for a chunk of the black substance.

"Did I ever show you a piece of this?" he would say. "Look at it carefully. Notice the smooth grainless texture—hard and yet not brittle. You wouldn't think that it was formed in a gaseous state, then changed to a liquid and finally to a clay-like material that could be worked with ease. A thousand years after your body has returned to dust, that piece of *Indurate* will still exist, unchanged, unworn. Erosion will have little effect upon it. Beside it granite, steel are nothing. If only I had the formula . . . "

But he had only half the formula, the half he himself had developed. The other part was locked in the brain of Ganeth-Klae, and Ganeth-Klae had disappeared. What had become of him was a mystery. Norris perhaps had felt the loss more than any one, and he had offered the major part of his savings as a reward for information leading to the scientist's whereabouts.

Our party—eighteen couples and Navigator Norris—had gathered together and subsequently left Earth in answer to a curious advertisement that had appeared in the Sunday edition of the London *Times*.

WANTED: *A group of married men and women, young, courageous, educated, tired of political and social restrictions, interested in extra-terrestrial colonization. Financial resources no qualification.*

After we had been weeded out, interviewed and rigorously questioned, Norris had taken us into the hangar, waved a hand toward the *Marie Galante* and explained the details.

The *Marie Galante* was a cruiser-type ship, stripped down to essentials to maintain speed, but equipped with the latest of everything. For a short run to Venus, for which it was originally built, it would accommodate a passenger list of ninety.

But Norris wasn't interested in that kind of run. He had knocked out bulkheads, reconverted music room and ballroom into living quarters. He had closed and sealed all observation ports, so that only in the bridge cuddy could one see into space.

"We shall travel beyond the orbit of the sun," he said. "There will be no turning back; for the search for a new world, a new life, is not a task for cowards."

Aside to me, he said: "You're to be the physician of this party, Bagley. So I'm going to tell you what to expect when we take off. We're going to have some mighty sick passengers aboard then."

"What do you mean, sir?" I said.

He pointed with his pipe toward the stern of the vessel. "See that . . . well, call it a booster. Ganeth-Klae designed it just before he disappeared, using the last lot of *Indurate* in existence. It will increase our take-off speed by five times, and it will probably have a bad effect on the passengers."

So we had left Earth, at night from a field out in Essex. Without orders, without clearance papers, without an automatic pilot check. Eighteen couples and one navigator—destination unknown. If the Interstellar Council had known what Norris was up to, it would have been a case for the Space-Time Commission.

Of that long initial lap of our voyage, perhaps the less said the better. As always is the case when monotony begins to wear away the veneer of civilization, character quirks came to the surface, cliques formed among the passengers, and gossip and personalities became matters of pre-eminent importance.

Rising to the foreground out of our thirty-six, came Fielding Mason, tall, taciturn, and handsome, with a keen intellect and a sense of values remarkable in so young a man. Mason was a graduate of Montape, the French outgrowth of St. Cyr. But he had majored in military tactics, psychology and sociology and knew nothing at all about astrogation or even elemental astronomy. He too was a man of good breeding and refinement. Nevertheless conflict began to develop between him and Navigator Norris. That conflict began the day we landed on Coulora.

Norris stepped out of the air lock into the cold thin air, glanced briefly about him and faced the eighteen men assembled.

"We'll divide into three groups," he said. "Each group to carry an organic surveyor and take a different direction. Each group will so regulate its marching as to be back here without fail an hour before darkness sets in. If you find no sign of animal life, then we will take off again immediately on your return."

Mason paused halfway in the act of strapping on his packsack.

"What's that got to do with it?" he demanded. "There's vegetation here. That's all that seems to be necessary."

Norris lit his pipe. "If you find no sign of animal life we will take off immediately on your return," he said as if he hadn't heard.

But the strangeness of Coulora tempered bad feelings then. The blue *hensorr* trees were actually not trees at all but a huge cat-tail-like growth, the stalks of which were quite transparent. In between the stalks grew curious cabbage-like plants that changed from red to yellow as an intruder approached and back to red again after he had passed. Rock outcroppings were everywhere, but all were eroded and in places polished smooth as glass.

There was a strange kind of dust that acted as though endowed with life. It quivered when trod upon, and the outline of our footsteps slowly rose into the air, so that looking back I could see our trail floating behind us in irregular layers.

Above us the star that was this planet's sun shown bright but faintly red as if it were in the first stages of dying. The air though thin was fit to breathe, and we found it unnecessary to wear space suits. We marched down the corridors of *hensorr* trees, until we came to an open spot, a kind of glade. And that was the first time Mason tuned his organic surveyor and received absolutely nothing.

There was no animal life on Coulora!

*

Within an hour we had blasted off again. The forward-impact delivered by the Ganeth-Klae booster was terrific, and nausea and vertigo struck us all simultaneously. But again, with all ports and observation shields sealed shut, Norris held the secret of our destination.

On July twenty-second, the ship gave that sickening lurch and came once again to a standstill.

"Same procedure as before," Norris said, stepping out of the airlock. "Those of you who desire to have their wives accompany you may do so. Mason, you'll make a final correlation on the organic surveyors. If there is no trace of animal life return here before dark."

Once our group was out of sight of the ship, Mason threw down his packsack, sat down on a boulder and lighted a cigarette.

"Bagley," he said to me, "has the Old Man gone loco?"

"I think not," I said, frowning. "He's one of the most evenly balanced persons I know."

"Then he's hiding something," Mason said. "Why else should he be so concerned with finding animal life?"

"You know the answer to that," I said. "We're here to colonize, to start a new life. We can't very well do that on a desert."

"That's poppycock," Mason replied, flinging away his cigarette. "When the Albertson expedition first landed on Mars, there was no animal life on the red planet. Now look at it. Same thing was true when Breslauer first settled Pluto. The colonies there got along. I tell you Norris has got something up his sleeve, and I don't like it."

Later, after Mason had taken his negative surveyor reading, the flame of trouble reached the end of its fuse!

Norris had given orders to return to the *Marie Galante*, and the rest of us were sullenly making ready to start the back trail. Mason, however, deliberately seized his pick and began chopping a hole in the rock surface, preparatory apparently to erecting his plastic tent.

"We'll make temporary camp here," he said calmly. "Brandt, you can go back to the ship and bring back the rest of the women." He turned and smiled sardonically at Navigator Norris.

Norris quietly knocked the ashes from his pipe and placed it in his pocket. He strode forward, took the pick from Mason's hands and flung it away. Then he seized Mason by the coat, whipped him around and drove his fist hard against the younger man's jaw.

"When you signed on for this voyage, you agreed to obey my orders," he said, not raising his voice. "You'll do just that."

Mason picked himself up, and there was an ugly glint in his eyes. He could have smashed Norris to a pulp, and none knew it better than the Navigator. For a brief instant the younger man swayed there on the balls of his feet, fists clenched. Then he let his hands drop, walked over and began to put on his packsack.

But I had seen Mason's face, and I knew he had not given in as easily as it appeared. Meanwhile he began to circulate among the passengers, making no offers, yet subtly enlisting backers for a policy, the significance of which grew on me slowly. It was mutiny he was plotting! And with his personal charm and magnetism he had little trouble in winning over converts. I came upon him arguing before a group of the women one day, among them his own wife, Estelle. He was standing close to her.

"We have clothing and equipment and food concentrate," Mason said. "Enough to last two generations. We have brains and intelligence, and we certainly should be able to establish ourselves without the aid of other vertebrate forms of life.

"Coulora, Jama, Tenethon, Mokrell, R-9, and Stragella. We could have settled on any one of those planets, and apparently we should have, for conditions have grown steadily worse at each landing. But always the answer is no. Why? Because Norris says we must go on until we find animal life."

He cleared his throat and gazed at the feminine faces before him. "Go where? What makes Norris so sure he'll find life on any planet in this system? And incidentally where in the cosmos is this system?"

One of the women, a tall blonde, stirred uneasily. "What do you mean?" she said.

"I mean we don't know if our last landing was on Stragella or Coulora. I mean we don't know where we are or where we're going, and I don't think Norris does either. *We're lost!*"

That was in August. By the last of September we had landed on two more planets, to which Norris gave the simple names of R-12 and R-14. Each had crude forms of vegetable life, represented principally by the blue *hensorr* trees, but in neither case did the organic surveyor reveal the slightest traces of animal life.

There was, however, a considerable difference in physical appearance between R-12 and R-14, and for a time that fact excited Norris tremendously. Up to then, each successive planet, although similar in size, had exhibited signs of greater age than its predecessor. But on R-12 there were definite manifestations of younger geologic development.

Several pieces of shale lay exposed under a fold of igneous rock. Two of those pieces contained fossils of highly developed *ganoids*, similar to those found on Venus. They were perfectly preserved.

It meant that animal life had existed on R-12, even if it didn't now. It meant that R-12, though a much older planet than Earth, was still younger than Stragella or the rest.

For a while Norris was almost beside himself. He cut out rock samples and carried them back to the ship. He personally supervised the tuning of the surveyors. And when he finally gave orders to take off, he was almost friendly to Mason, whereas before his attitude toward him had been one of cold aloofness.

But when we reached R-14, our eighth landing, all that passed. For R-14 was old again, older than any of the others.

And then, on October sixteenth, Mason opened the door of the locked cabin. It happened quite by accident. One of the *arelium-thaxide* conduits broke in the *Marie Galante's* central passageway, and the resulting explosion grounded the central feed line of the instrument equipment. In a trice the passageway was a sheet of flame, rapidly filling with smoke from burning insulation.

Norris, of course, was in the bridge cuddy with locked doors between us and him, and now with the wiring burned through there was no way of signalling him he was wanted for an emergency. In his absence Mason took command.

That passageway ran the full length of the ship. Midway down it was the door leading to the women's lounge. The explosion had jammed that door shut, and smoke was pouring forth from under the sill. All at once one of the women rushed forward to announce hysterically that Mason's wife, Estelle, was in the lounge.

Adjoining the lounge was a small cabin which since the beginning of our voyage had remained locked. Norris had given strict orders that that cabin was not to be disturbed. We all had taken it as a matter of course that it contained various kinds of precision instruments.

Now, however, Mason realized that the only way into the lounge was by way of that locked cabin. If he used a heat blaster on the lounge door there was no telling what would happen to the woman inside.

He ripped the emergency blaster from its wall mounting, pressed it to the magnetic latch of the sealed cabin door and pressed the stud. An instant later he was leading his frightened wife, Estelle, out through the smoke.

The fire was quickly extinguished after that and the wiring spliced. Then when the others had drifted off, Mason called Brandt and me aside.

"We've been wondering for a long time what happened to Ganeth-Klae, the Martian inventor who worked with Norris to invent *Indurate*," he said very quietly. "Well, we don't need to wonder any more. He's in there."

Brandt and I stepped forward over the sill—and drew up short. Ganeth-Klae was there all right, but he would never trouble himself about making a voyage in a locked cabin. His rigid body was encased in a transparent block of amber-colored solidifex, the after-death preservative used by all Martians.

Both of us recognized his still features at once, and in addition his name-tattoo, required by Martian law, was clearly visible on his left forearm.

*

For a brief instant the discovery stunned us. Klae dead? Klae whose IQ had become a measuring guide for the entire system, whose Martian head held more ordinary horse sense, in addition to radical postulations on theoretical physics, than anyone on the planets. It wasn't possible.

And what was the significance of his body on Norris' ship? Why had Norris kept its presence a secret and why had he given out the story of Klae's disappearance?

Mason's face was cold as ice. "Come with me, you two," he said. "We're going to get the answer to this right now."

We went along the passage to the circular staircase. We climbed the steps, passed through the scuttle and came to the door of the bridge cuddy. Mason drew the bar and we passed in. Norris was bent over the chart table. He looked up sharply at the sound of our steps.

"What is the meaning of this intrusion?" he said.

It didn't take Mason long to explain. When he had finished, he stood there, jaw set, eyes smouldering.

Norris paled. Then quickly he got control of himself, and his old bland smile returned.

"I expected you to blunder into Klae's body one of these days," he said. "The explanation is quite simple. Klae had been ill for many months, and he knew his time was up. His one desire in life was to go on this expedition with me, and he made me promise to bury him at the site of our new colony. The pact was between him and me, and I've followed it to the letter, telling no one."

Mason's lips curled in a sneer. "And just what makes you think we're going to believe that story?" he demanded.

Norris lit a cigar. "It's entirely immaterial to me whether you believe it or not."

But the story was believed, especially by the women, to whom the romantic angle appealed and Mason's embryonic mutiny died without being born, and the *Marie Galante*sailed on through uncharted space toward her ninth and last landing.

As the days dragged by and no word came from the bridge cuddy, restlessness began to grow amongst us. Rumor succeeded rumor, each story wilder and more incredible than the rest. Then just as the tension had mounted to fever pitch, there came the sickening lurch and grinding vibration of another landing.

Norris dispensed with his usual talk before marching out from the ship. After testing the atmosphere with the ozonometer, he passed out the heat pistols and distributed the various instruments for computing radioactivity and cosmic radiation.

"This is the planet Nizar," he said shortly. "Largest in the field of the sun Ponthis. You will make your survey as one group this time. I will remain here."

He stood watching us as we marched off down the cliff side. Then the blue *hensorr* trees rose up to swallow him from view. Mason swung along at the head of our column, eyes bright, a figure of aggressive action. We had gone but a hundred yards when it became apparent that, as a planet, Nizar was entirely different from its predecessors. There was considerable top soil, and here grew a tall reed-shaped plant that gave off varying chords of sound when the wind blew.

It was as if we were progressing through the nave of a mighty church with a muted organ in the distance. There was animal life too, a strange lizard-like bird that rose up in flocks ahead of us and flew screaming overhead.

"I don't exactly like it, Bagley," he said. "There's something unwholesome about this planet. The evolution is obviously in an early state of development, but I get the impression that it has gone backward; that the planet is really old and has reverted to its earlier life."

Above us the sky was heavily overcast, and a tenuous white mist rising up from the *hensorr* trees formed curious shapes and designs. In the distance I could hear the swashing of waves on a beach.

Suddenly Mason stopped. "Look!" he said.

Below us stretched the shore of a great sea. But it was the structure rising up from that shore that drew a sharp exclamation from me. Shaped in a rough ellipse, yet mounted high toward a common point, was a large building of multiple hues and colors. The upper portion was eroded to crumbling ruins, the lower part studded with many bas-reliefs and triangular doorways.

"Let's go," Mason said, breaking out into a fast loping run.

The building was farther away than we had thought, but when we finally came up to it, we saw that it was even more of a ruin than it had at first appeared. It was only a shell with but two walls standing, alone and forlorn. Whatever race had lived here, they had come and gone.

We prowled about the ruins for more than an hour. The carvings on the walls were in the form of geometric designs and cabalistic symbols, giving no clue to the city's former occupants' identity.

And then Mason found the stairs leading to the lower crypts. He switched on his ato-flash and led the way down cautiously. Level one . . . level two . . . three . . . we descended lower and lower. Here water from the nearby sea oozed in little rivulets that glittered in the light of the flash.

We emerged at length on a wide underground plaisance, a kind of amphitheater, with tier on tier of seats surrounding it and extending back into the shadows.

"Judging from what we've seen," Mason said, "I would say that the race that built this place had reached approximately a grade C-5 of civilization, according to the Mokart scale. This apparently was their council chamber."

"What are those rectangular stone blocks depending from the ceiling?" I said.

Mason turned the light beam upward. "I don't know," he said. "But my guess is that they are burial vaults. Perhaps the creatures were ornithoid."

Away from the flash the floor of the plaisance appeared to be a great mirror that caught our reflections and distorted them fantastically and horribly. We saw then that it was a form of living mold, composed of millions of tiny plants, each with an eye-like iris at its center. Those eyes seemed to be watching us, and as we strode forward, a great sigh rose up, as if in resentment at our intrusion.

There was a small triangular dais in the center of the chamber, and in the middle of it stood an irregular black object. As we drew nearer, I saw that it had been carved roughly in the shape of this central building and that it was in a perfect state of preservation.

Mason walked around this carving several times, examining it curiously.

"Odd," he said. "It looks to be an object of religious veneration, but I never heard before of a race worshipping a replica of their own living quarters."

Suddenly his voice died off. He bent closer to the black stone, studying it in the light of the powerful ato-flash. He got a small magnifying glass out of his pocket and focused it on one of the miniature bas-reliefs midway toward the top of the stone. Unfastening his geologic hammer from his belt, he managed, with a sharp, swinging blow, to break off a small protruding piece.

He drew in his breath sharply, and I saw his face go pale. I stared at him in alarm.

"What's wrong?" I asked.

He motioned that I follow and led the way silently past the others toward the stair shaft. Climbing to the top level was a heart-pounding task, but Mason almost ran up those steps. At the surface he leaned against a pillar, his lips quivering spasmodically.

"Tell me I'm sane, Bagley," he said huskily. "Or rather, don't say anything until we've seen Norris. Come on. We've got to see Norris."

*

All the way back to the *Marie Galante*, I sought to soothe him, but he was a man possessed. He rushed up the ship's gangway, burst into central quarters and drew up before Navigator Norris like a runner stopping at the tape.

"You damned lying hypocrite!" he yelled.

Norris looked at him in his quiet way. "Take it easy, Mason," he said. "Sit down and explain yourself."

But Mason didn't sit down. He thrust his hand in his pocket, pulled out the piece of black stone he had chipped off the image in the cavern and handed it to Norris.

"Take a look at that!" he demanded.

Norris took the stone, glanced at it and laid it down on his desk. His face was emotionless. "I expected this sooner or later," he said. "Yes, it's *Indurate* all right. Is that what you want me to say?"

There was a dangerous fanatical glint in Mason's eyes now. With a sudden quick motion he pulled out his heat pistol.

"So you tricked us!" he snarled. "Why? I want to know why."

I stepped forward and seized Mason's gun hand. "Don't be a fool," I said. "It can't be that important."

Mason threw back his head and burst into an hysterical peal of laughter. "Important!" he cried. "Tell him how important it is, Norris. *Tell him.*"

Quietly the Navigator filled and lighted his pipe. "I'm afraid Mason is right," he said. "I did trick you. Not purposely, however. And in the beginning I had no intention of telling anything but the truth. Actually we're here because of a dead man's vengeance."

Norris took his pipe from his lips and stared at it absently.

"You'll remember that Ganeth-Klae, the Martian, and I worked together to invent *Indurate*. But whereas I was interested in the commercial aspects of that product, Klae was absorbed only in the experimental angle of it. He had some crazy idea that it should not be given to the general public at once, but rather should be allocated for the first few years to a select group of scientific organizations. You see, *Indurate* was such a departure from all known materials that Ganeth-Klae feared it would be utilized for military purposes.

"I took him for a dreamer and a fool. Actually he was neither. How was I to know that his keen penetrating brain had seen through my motive to get control of all commercial marketing of *Indurate*? I had laid my plans carefully, and I had expected to reap a nice harvest. Klae must have been aware of my innermost thoughts, but Martian-like he said nothing."

Norris paused to wet his lips and lean against the desk. "I didn't kill Ganeth-Klae," he continued, "though I suppose in a court of law I would be judged responsible for his death. The manufacture of *Indurate* required some ticklish work. As you know, we produced our halves of the formula separately. Physical contact with my half over a long period of time would prove fatal, I knew, and I simply neglected to so inform Ganeth-Klae.

"But his ultimate death was a boomerang. With Klae gone, I could find no trace of his half of the formula. I was almost beside myself for a time. Then I thought of something. Klae had once said that the secret of his half of the formula lay in himself. A vague statement, to say the least. But I took the words at their face value and gambled that he meant them literally; that is, that his body itself contained the formula.

"I tried everything: X-ray, chemical analysis of the skin. I even removed the cranial cap and examined the brain microscopically. All without result. Meanwhile the police were beginning to direct their suspicions toward me in the matter of Klae's disappearance.

"You know the rest. It was necessary that I leave Earth at once and go beyond our system, beyond the jurisdiction of the planetary police. So I arranged this voyage with a sufficient complement of passengers to lessen the danger and hardship of a new life on a new world. I was still positive, however, that Klae's secret lay in his dead body. I took that body along, encased in the Martian preservative, solidifex.

"It was my idea that I could continue my examination once we were safe on a strange planet But I had reckoned without Ganeth-Klae."

"What do you mean?" I said slowly.

"I said Klae was no fool. But I didn't know that with Martian stoicism he suspected the worst and took his own ironic means of combating it. He used the last lot of *Indurate* to make that booster, a device which he said would increase our take-off speed. He mounted it on the *Marie Galante*.

"Mason, that device was no booster. It was a time machine, so devised as to catapult the ship not into outer space, but into the space-time continuum. It was a mechanism designed to throw the *Marie Galante* forward into the future."

A cloud of fear began to well over me. "What do you mean?" I said again.

Navigator Norris paced around his desk. "*I mean that the* Marie Galante *has not once left Earth, has not in fact left the spot of its moorings but has merely gone forward in time. I mean that the nine 'landings' we made were not stops on some other planets but halting stages of a journey into the future.*"

Had a bombshell burst over my head the effect could have been no greater. Cold perspiration began to ooze out on my forehead. In a flash I saw the significance of the entire situation. That was why Norris had been so insistent that we always return to the ship before dark. He didn't want us to see the night sky and the constellations there for fear we would guess the truth. That was why he had never permitted any of us in the bridge cuddy and why he had kept all ports and observation shields closed.

"But the names of the planets . . . Coulora, Stragella, and the others and their positions on the chart . . . ?" I objected.

Norris smiled grimly. "All words created out of my imagination. Like the rest of you, I knew nothing of the true action of the booster. It was only gradually that truth dawned on me. But by the time we had made our first 'landing' I had guessed. That was why I demanded we always take organic surveyor readings. I knew we had traveled far into future time, far beyond the life period of man on Earth. But I wasn't sure how far we had gone, and I lived with the hope that Klae's booster might reverse itself and start carrying us backwards down the centuries."

For a long time I stood there in silence, a thousand mad speculations racing through my mind.

"How about that piece of *Indurate?*" I said at length. "It was chipped off an image in the ruins of a great building a mile or so from here."

"An image?" repeated Norris. A faint glow of interest slowly rose in his eyes. Then it died. "I don't know," he said. "It would seem to presuppose that the formula, both parts of it, was known by Klae and that he left it for posterity to discover."

All this time Mason had been standing there, eyes smouldering, lips an ugly line. Now abruptly he took a step forward.

"I've wanted to return this for a long time," he said.

He doubled back his arm and brought his fist smashing onto Norris' jaw. The Navigator's head snapped backward; he gave a low groan and slumped to the floor.

And that is where, by all logic, this tale should end. But, as you may have guessed, there is an anticlimax—what story-tellers call a happy conclusion.

Mason, Brandt, and I worked, and worked alone, on the theory that the secret of the *Indurate* formula would be the answer to our return down the time trail. We removed the body of Ganeth-Klae from its solidifex envelope and treated it with every chemical process we knew. By sheer luck the fortieth trial worked. A paste of carbo-genethon mixed with the crushed seeds of the Martian iron-flower was spread over Klae's chest and abdomen.

And there, in easily decipherable code, was not only the formula, but the working principles of the ship's booster—or rather, time-catapult. After that, it was a simple matter to reverse the principle and throw us backward in the time stream.

We are heading back as I write these lines. If they reach print and you read them, it will mean our escape was successful and that we returned to our proper slot in the epilogue of human events.

There remains, however, one matter to trouble me. Navigator Norris. I like the man. I like him tremendously, in spite of his cold-blooded confession, and past record. He must be punished, of course. But I, for one, would hate to see him given the death penalty. It is a serious problem.

YEAR OF THE BIG THAW

by Marion Zimmer Bradley

In this warm and fanciful story of a Connecticut farmer, Marion Zimmer Bradley has caught some of the glory that is man's love for man—no matter who he is nor whence he's from. By heck, you'll like little Matt.

Mr. Emmett did his duty by the visitor from another world—never doubting the right of it.

YOU SAY that Matthew is your own son, Mr. Emmett?

Yes, Rev'rend Doane, and a better boy never stepped, if I do say it as shouldn't. I've trusted him to drive team for me since he was eleven, and you can't say more than that for a farm boy. Way back when he was a little shaver so high, when the war came on, he was bounden he was going to sail with this Admiral Farragut. You know boys that age—like runaway colts. I couldn't see no good in his being cabin boy on some tarnation Navy ship and I told him so. If he'd wanted to sail out on a whaling ship, I 'low I'd have let him go. But Marthy—that's the boy's Ma—took on so that Matt stayed home. Yes, he's a good boy and a good son.

We'll miss him a powerful lot if he gets this scholarship thing. But I 'low it'll be good for the boy to get some learnin' besides what he gets in the school here. It's right kind of you, Rev'rend, to look over this application thing for me.

Well, if he is your own son, Mr. Emmett, why did you write 'birthplace unknown' on the line here?

Rev'rend Doane, I'm glad you asked me that question. I've been turnin' it over in my mind and I've jest about come to the conclusion it wouldn't be nohow fair to hold it back. I didn't lie when I said Matt was my son, because he's been a good son to me and Marthy. But I'm not his Pa and Marthy ain't his Ma, so could be I stretched the truth jest a mite. Rev'rend Doane, it's a tarnal funny yarn but I'll walk into the meetin' house and swear to it on a stack o'Bibles as thick as a cord of wood.

You know I've been farming the old Corning place these past seven year? It's good flat Connecticut bottom-land, but it isn't like our land up in Hampshire where I was born and raised. My Pa called it the Hampshire Grants and all that was King's land when *his* Pa came in there and started farming at the foot of Scuttock Mountain. That's Injun for fires, folks say, because the Injuns used to build fires up there in the spring for some of their heathen doodads. Anyhow, up there in the mountains we see a tarnal power of quare things.

You call to mind the year we had the big thaw, about twelve years before the war? You mind the blizzard that year? I heard tell it spread down most to York. And at Fort

368

Orange, the place they call Albany now, the Hudson froze right over, so they say. But those York folks do a sight of exaggerating, I'm told.

Anyhow, when the ice went out there was an almighty good thaw all over, and when the snow run off Scuttock mountain there was a good-sized hunk of farmland in our valley went under water. The crick on my farm flowed over the bank and there was a foot of water in the cowshed, and down in the swimmin' hole in the back pasture wasn't nothing but a big gully fifty foot and more across, rushing through the pasture, deep as a lake and brown as the old cow. You know freshet-floods? Full up with sticks and stones and old dead trees and somebody's old shed floatin' down the middle. And I swear to goodness, Parson, that stream was running along so fast I saw four-inch cobblestones floating and bumping along.

I tied the cow and the calf and Kate—she was our white mare; you mind she went lame last year and I had to shoot her, but she was just a young mare then and skittish as all get-out—but she was a good little mare.

Anyhow, I tied the whole kit and caboodle of them in the woodshed up behind the house, where they'd be dry, then I started to get the milkpail. Right then I heard the gosh-awfullest screech I ever heard in my life. Sounded like thunder and a freshet and a forest-fire all at once. I dropped the milkpail as I heard Marthy scream inside the house, and I run outside. Marthy was already there in the yard and she points up in the sky and yelled, "Look up yander!"

We stood looking up at the sky over Shattuck mountain where there was a great big—shoot now, I d'no as I can call its name but it was like a trail of fire in the sky, and it was makin' the dangdest racket you ever heard, Rev'rend. Looked kind of like one of them Fourth-of-July skyrockets, but it was big as a house. Marthy was screaming and she grabbed me and hollered, "Hez! Hez, what in tunket is it?" And when Marthy cusses like that, Rev'rend, she don't know what she's saying, she's so scared.

I was plumb scared myself. I heard Liza—that's our young-un, Liza Grace, that got married to the Taylor boy. I heard her crying on the stoop, and she came flying out with her pinny all black and hollered to Marthy that the pea soup was burning. Marthy let out another screech and ran for the house. That's a woman for you. So I quietened Liza down some and I went in and told Marthy it weren't no more than one of them shooting stars. Then I went and did the milking.

But you know, while we were sitting down to supper there came the most awful grinding, screeching, pounding crash I ever heard. Sounded if it were in the back pasture but the house shook as if somethin' had hit it.

Marthy jumped a mile and I never saw such a look on her face.

"Hez, what was that?" she asked.

"Shoot, now, nothing but the freshet," I told her.

But she kept on about it. "You reckon that shooting star fell in our back pasture, Hez?"

"Well, now, I don't 'low it did nothing like that," I told her. But she was jittery as an old hen and it weren't like her nohow. She said it sounded like trouble and I finally quietened her down by saying I'd saddle Kate up and go have a look. I kind of thought, though I didn't tell Marthy, that somebody's house had floated away in the freshet and run aground in our back pasture.

So I saddled up Kate and told Marthy to get some hot rum ready in case there was some poor soul run aground back there. And I rode Kate back to the back pasture.

It was mostly uphill because the top of the pasture is on high ground, and it sloped down to the crick on the other side of the rise.

Well, I reached the top of the hill and looked down. The crick were a regular river now, rushing along like Niagary. On the other side of it was a stand of timber, then the slope of Shattuck mountain. And I saw right away the long streak where all the timber had been cut out in a big scoop with roots standing up in the air and a big slide of rocks down to the water.

It was still raining a mite and the ground was sloshy and squanchy under foot. Kate scrunched her hooves and got real balky, not likin' it a bit. When we got to the top of the pasture she started to whine and whicker and stamp, and no matter how loud I whoa-ed she kept on a-stamping and I was plumb scared she'd pitch me off in the mud. Then I started to smell a funny smell, like somethin' burning. Now, don't ask me how anything could burn in all that water, because I don't know.

When we came up on the rise I saw the contraption.

Rev'rend, it was the most tarnal crazy contraption I ever saw in my life. It was bigger nor my cowshed and it was long and thin and as shiny as Marthy's old pewter pitcher her Ma brought from England. It had a pair of red rods sticking out behind and a crazy globe fitted up where the top ought to be. It was stuck in the mud, turned halfway over on the little slide of roots and rocks, and I could see what had happened, all right.

The thing must have been—now, Rev'rend, you can say what you like but that thing must have *flew* across Shattuck and landed on the slope in the trees, then turned over and slid down the hill. That must have been the crash we heard. The rods weren't just red, they were *red-hot*. I could hear them sizzle as the rain hit 'em.

In the middle of the infernal contraption there was a door, and it hung all to-other as if every hinge on it had been wrenched halfway off. As I pushed old Kate alongside it I heared somebody hollering alongside the contraption. I didn't nohow get the words but it must have been for help, because I looked down and there was a man a-flopping along in the water.

He was a big fellow and he wasn't swimming, just thrashin' and hollering. So I pulled off my coat and boots and hove in after him. The stream was running fast but he was near the edge and I managed to catch on to an old tree-root and hang on, keeping his head out of the water till I got my feet aground. Then I hauled him onto the bank. Up above me Kate was still whinnying and raising Ned and I shouted at her as I bent over the man.

Wal, Rev'rend, he sure did give me a surprise—weren't no proper man I'd ever seed before. He was wearing some kind of red clothes, real shiny and sort of stretchy and not wet from the water, like you'd expect, but dry and it felt like that silk and India-rubber stuff mixed together. And it was such a bright red that at first I didn't see the blood on it. When I did I knew he were a goner. His chest were all stove in, smashed to pieces. One of the old tree-roots must have jabbed him as the current flung him down. I thought he were dead already, but then he opened up his eyes.

A funny color they were, greeny yellow. And I swear, Rev'rend, when he opened them eyes I *felt* he was readin' my mind. I thought maybe he might be one of them circus fellers in their flying contraptions that hang at the bottom of a balloon.

He spoke to me in English, kind of choky and stiff, not like Joe the Portygee sailor or like those tarnal dumb Frenchies up Canady way, but—well, funny. He said, "My baby—in ship. Get—baby . . . " He tried to say more but his eyes went shut and he moaned hard.

I yelped, "Godamighty!" 'Scuse me, Rev'rend, but I was so blame upset that's just what I did say, "Godamighty, man, you mean there's a baby in that there dingfol contraption?" He just moaned so after spreadin' my coat around the man a little bit I just plunged in that there river again.

Rev'rend, I heard tell once about some tomfool idiot going over Niagary in a barrel, and I tell you it was like that when I tried crossin' that freshet to reach the contraption.

I went under and down, and was whacked by floating sticks and whirled around in the freshet. But somehow, I d'no how except by the pure grace of God, I got across that raging torrent and clumb up to where the crazy dingfol machine was sitting.

Ship, he'd called it. But that were no ship, Rev'rend, it was some flying dragon kind of thing. It was a real scarey lookin' thing but I clumb up to the little door and hauled myself inside it. And, sure enough, there was other people in the cabin, only they was all dead.

There was a lady and a man and some kind of an animal looked like a bobcat only smaller, with a funny-shaped rooster-comb thing on its head. They all—even the cat-thing—was wearing those shiny, stretchy clo'es. And they all was so battered and smashed I didn't even bother to hunt for their heartbeats. I could see by a look they was dead as a doornail.

Then I heard a funny little whimper, like a kitten, and in a funny, rubber-cushioned thing there's a little boy baby, looked about six months old. He was howling lusty enough, and when I lifted him out of the cradle kind of thing, I saw why. That boy baby, he was wet, and his little arm was twisted under him. That there flying contraption must have smashed down awful hard, but that rubber hammock was so soft and cushiony all it did to him was jolt him good.

I looked around but I couldn't find anything to wrap him in. And the baby didn't have a stitch on him except a sort of spongy paper diaper, wet as sin. So I finally lifted up the lady, who had a long cape thing around her, and I took the cape off her real gentle. I knew she was dead and she wouldn't be needin' it, and that boy baby would catch his death if I took him out bare-naked like that. She was probably the baby's Ma; a right pretty woman she was but smashed up something shameful.

So anyhow, to make a long story short, I got that baby boy back across that Niagary falls somehow, and laid him down by his Pa. The man opened his eyes kind, and said in a choky voice, "Take care—baby."

I told him I would, and said I'd try to get him up to the house where Marthy could doctor him. The man told me not to bother. "I dying," he says. "We come from planet—star up there—crash here—" His voice trailed off into a language I couldn't understand, and he looked like he was praying.

I bent over him and held his head on my knees real easy, and I said, "Don't worry, mister, I'll take care of your little fellow until your folks come after him. Before God I will."

So the man closed his eyes and I said, *Our Father which art in Heaven*, and when I got through he was dead.

I got him up on Kate, but he was cruel heavy for all he was such a tall skinny fellow. Then I wrapped that there baby up in the cape thing and took him home and give him to Marthy. And the next day I buried the fellow in the south medder and next meetin' day we had the baby baptized Matthew Daniel Emmett, and brung him up just like our own kids. That's all.

All? Mr. Emmett, didn't you ever find out where that ship really came from?

Why, Rev'rend, he said it come from a star. Dying men don't lie, you know that. I asked the Teacher about them planets he mentioned and she says that on one of the planets—can't rightly remember the name, March or Mark or something like that—she says some big scientist feller with a telescope saw canals on that planet, and they'd hev to be pretty near as big as this-here Erie canal to see them so far off. And if they could build canals on that planet I d'no why they couldn't build a flying machine.

I went back the next day when the water was down a little, to see if I couldn't get the rest of them folks and bury them, but the flying machine had broke up and washed down the crick.

Marthy's still got the cape thing. She's a powerful saving woman. We never did tell Matt, though. Might make him feel funny to think he didn't really b'long to us.

But—but—Mr. Emmett, didn't anybody ask questions about the baby—where you got it?

Well, now, I'll 'low they was curious, because Marthy hadn't been in the family way and they knew it. But up here folks minds their own business pretty well, and I jest let them wonder. I told Liza Grace I'd found her new little brother in the back pasture, and o'course it was the truth. When Liza Grace growed up she thought it was jest one of those yarns old folks tell the little shavers.

And has Matthew ever shown any differences from the other children that you could see?

Well, Rev'rend, not so's you could notice it. He's powerful smart, but his real Pa and Ma must have been right smart too to build a flying contraption that could come so far.

O'course, when he were about twelve years old he started reading folks' minds, which didn't seem exactly right. He'd tell Marthy what I was thinkin' and things like that. He was just at the pesky age. Liza Grace and Minnie were both a-courtin' then, and he'd drive their boy friends crazy telling them what Liza Grace and Minnie were a-thinking and tease the gals by telling them what the boys were thinking about.

There weren't no harm in the boy, though, it was all teasing. But it just weren't decent, somehow. So I tuk him out behind the woodshed and give his britches a good dusting just to remind him that that kind of thing weren't polite nohow. And Rev'rend Doane, he ain't never done it sence.

54096599R00205

Made in the
USA
Lexington, KY